# Playlist

Whethan, MAX, Flux Pavilion - *Savage*

The Chainsmokers, Coldplay - *Something Just Like This*

Halsey - *Hold Me Down*

Axwell & Ingrosso - *On My Way*

Swedish House Mafia, Pharrell Williams - *One (Your Name)*

triste noir, Broderick Jones - *It's Time*

Prismo - *Weakness*

Veorra - *Run*

Zedd, Alessia Cara - *Stay*

Two Feet - *Go F*ck Yourself*

Mickey Valen, Feli Ferraro - *Wildcard*

R3hab, Black Caviar - *Icarus*

Phoebe Ryan - *Dark Side*

Peking Duk, Jackal, Elliphant - *Stranger*

Marshmello, Ookay, Noah Cyrus - *Chasing Colors*

Bebe Rexha - *I Got You*

Years & Years - *King*

System of a Down - *Chop Suey!*

Billy Talent - *Surrender*

Saosin - *You're Not Alone*

Sparta - *While Oceana Sleeps*

Glasvegas - *It's My Own Cheating Heart That Makes Me Cry*

Babyshambles - *Fuck Forever*

# Pet

## ISABELLA STARLING

A DARK MENAGE ROMANCE

Copyright © 2017 by Isabella Starling

Text set in Dante.
Book design by Inkstain Design Studio
All rights reserved. No part of this book may be reproduced or transmitted in any form or by any means whatsoever without express written permission from the author, except for the use of brief quotations in a book review.

*This book is not for you.*
*This book is for me.*

## ISABELLA

Pet

# CHAPTER 1
*Sapphire*

I *was barely legal, eighteen and* a few months. I got a job catering at an art gallery in town. Being shit out of luck, I took it with open arms. My birthday money had run out, and I was struggling to find a job. I was at that point where I didn't want to settle for waitressing just yet.

I'd just graduated from high school the year before, and, to the mortification of my parents, I never enrolled in college. I'd fobbed them off with lies of a gap year, but in reality, I had no idea whether I'd ever go to school again. I was too headstrong, too restless to stick to something for the next few years of my life.

So when my roommate Veronica told me about the job, I listened. It was good pay. One night of work, and I'd leave with a hundred bucks. I was fine with that. My parents were getting tight with money, giving me less and less and probably seeing right through every lie. We'd grown apart in my teenage years.

I used to be Daddy's girl, now I was just a lost lamb.

Veronica and I were standing in a closet in the gallery. She was getting ready to bolt, and I was getting ready to work. My poor body had no idea it would be fucked relentlessly in only an hour or so.

"Wear this," Veronica said, passing me her uniform with an anxious expression. She was my roommate along with another girl, Jessica. We'd never really bonded, but I knew Veronica was grateful I was covering for her. It was her full-time gig, but she had a date with her boyfriend. She'd told me the night before she was hoping he'd pop the question.

I took the clothes she handed me. A black pencil skirt and a white blouse with a black bow-tie – simple enough. I was taller than Veronica, but she was full-figured where I was lanky.

"Do I just tell them I'm Veronica?" I asked, slipping out of my leggings and shirt. "What if they ask questions?"

"Don't worry," Veronica said. "It's not the usual team today, they called in some extra people since it's a big event."

She watched me as I got changed, her eyes grazing my figure and making me self-conscious. My mom had always told me I was a late bloomer. I'd only grown breasts in my final year of high school, and even now, they weren't big. My hips and shoulders were narrow, but my waist was even narrower. As I put on Veronica's clothes, I realized my assumptions about them fitting me were way off. They hung off some parts of my body and clung to others in the most uncomfortable, unflattering way.

"These don't fit well at all." I sighed, giving Veronica a nervous look.

"You look great, Sapphire," Veronica lied with a fake smile. I cringed hearing my name on her lips. I'd always hated that pretentious fucking thing.

"I'm going to head out now," she said, "Please, don't mess this up for me. I know it's a lot to ask of you... But I need this job so badly. Especially if Trevor asks me to marry him and we move in together."

I gave her a reassuring smile and smoothed down the apron I'd just fastened around my midriff. "Seriously, Nic, what could go wrong?" I asked. "It'll be just fine. Go to your dinner, and don't worry. I can't wait to hear all about it later."

She gave me a grin, an actual, genuine grin. Veronica and I weren't close – not by a longshot. But that smile gave me hope that maybe we'd connect over what was happening.

Nic leaned close to me and pressed a quick kiss to my cheek before running off into the night. I was still smiling to myself as I took a deep breath, trying to stop my hands from shaking. Why on earth was I so nervous? My only job was to carry around a tray of canapés and smile like a good girl. Something I was surely capable of, even with my minimal talents.

Another deep breath, and I walked out of the closet and into the lobby. Right away, chaos greeted me. People were running around frantically, setting up for the big night.

"Are you Veronica?" someone asked me anxiously, and I looked down into the brown eyes of a stocky guy with a fervent expression. "Please say you are, otherwise I will lose my fucking marbles."

"Yes," I lied smoothly, an action that came so easily to me lately. "I'm Veronica. Am I late or something?"

"Am I late, she asks," the guy rolled his eyes. "Ten minutes fucking late. Come with me before I call the goddamn company I got you from."

He grabbed my forearm and half-guided, half-dragged me across the room to a group of frazzled-looking people in matching outfits to mine. I caught the eye of a hot guy with dark hair and gray eyes and shot him a sweet smile. He grinned in return and my tummy gave that flutter I love so much.

I wasn't really a femme fatale. I knew that my looks – *extremely long, blonde hair with baby blues and pearly whites to boot* – only merited a cute girl next door. But I knew how to play my best assets. I was the good girl gone bad, just sweet enough to hold their interest, just slutty enough to catch their attention. Too bad none of my exes could do the same for me. I got bored really fast.

"Are you paying attention, Ver-o-ni-ca?"

I looked up to find the guy who'd led me there glaring at me. I motioned for him to go on and he sighed heavily.

"I swear, this is the most incompetent fucking group of..." the guy muttered to himself, before massaging his temples dramatically. "My name is Elliot fucking Richards. I threw this shindig, and you'd better make me proud, or there'll be fucking hell to pay."

He glared right at me.

"And I mean fucking hell. I'll skin you and wear you as a coat if you mess this up," he said, clicking his fingers for emphasis.

We all straightened up and I looked at the floor with burning cheeks. Jesus, this guy was intense. I'd have to bite my tongue and not sass him, or he'd probably crucify me while the rest of the waiters cheered him on.

"So the fucking menu is on the fucking list in front of you. Don't fucking mess it up. Carry the fucking trays. Answer any fucking questions. Do a good fucking job. And make Elliot fucking proud." Elliot flashed an angelic smile. So he was insane *and* bipolar. What a winning combination.

We all milled around the tables for the next hour, setting up the hors d'oeuvres and champagne flutes. As far as I knew, the evening was in honor of a young artist called Helene something or other, who'd gotten a rich benefactor to sponsor her stuff. Veronica told me it was utter shit, and Helene had only gotten as far as she did by banging the right people. I was curious about the actual art, wondering whether it would really be as shit as Nic claimed.

I was too preoccupied with folding napkins and setting trays to wonder, though, and the hour passed in no time. My waist-length hair was getting in the way, so I pinned it up in a chignon as I worked with the rest of the waiters.

Every so often, a tall, light-haired guy would catch my eye, and I played my role perfectly. A shy smile here, an averted gaze there. I was sure he was hooked.

"What's a pretty girl like you doing serving food?"

I turned towards the direction of the voice, pleased to see the man decided to approach me, just like I knew he would.

"Well, I've got to make money somehow, don't I?" I drawled, batting my eyelashes.

He used such a generic line to talk me up, I was almost disappointed. I'd been hoping for something a little more original. A little worthier of my attention.

"That's true," the man said, snapping up a prawn canapé from my platter and taking a bite. "Mm, this is lovely."

Quickly growing bored and disappointed with the way our conversation was moving, I smiled politely, bowed my head and moved out of his path. Once I'd gotten them to talk to me, I seemed to easily get bored. Unfortunately, that meant I didn't get laid nearly as much as I wanted to.

Well… I'd never gotten laid per se. Which wasn't something I liked to admit to anyone, least of all myself.

The man followed me, and when I felt his cold, clammy hand on my elbow, I had this sinking feeling he was going to cause trouble.

"Now don't you run away from me," he said. It was only then that I noticed the slight slur in his words. He was drunk – or at the very least, on a very good path to being drunk.

"I have work to do," I excused myself politely. "You're not the only hungry person around here, sir!"

He scowled at me. "I told you not to leave," he snarled, and his grip on my elbow tightened. My eyes scanned the crowd, noticing several well-to-do people who chose to avert their eyes so they wouldn't have to witness the scene unfolding between us.

"I'm sorry," I said, this time with more determination. "I'm going to have to leave now."

"Says who?" the man demanded.

I moved away from him, forcefully tearing my arm out of his grasp, when I bumped into another man.

Only he wasn't just a man. At the risk of sounding like an absolute twat, he was an absolute god.

Tall. Broad-shouldered. Handsome. Dark. You know the thing, ticking all the boxes to make me go weak at the knees. But there was something else there, and it made my head spin.

He exuded power. My body wanted to obey. I wanted to do whatever this man told me to. I wanted to submit.

Unused to such a strange sensation, I furrowed my brows, and the dishes on my platter rattled as I stared at the mountain of a man before me. I was unnerved by my reaction, and I didn't quite like it. I liked being in control – always. It was the only way I felt safe.

Of course, the man wasn't even looking at me. It seemed as if he hadn't even noticed I'd bumped into him with all my might.

"Excuse me," I muttered, but he stood still, not moving an inch, even though I cleared my throat like six times.

"What's going on, Evans?" he asked in a booming deep voice that made me want to suck on his lips. Jesus fuck, what was happening to me? This man was driving me insane with a few words and his physical stature alone.

He was looking at the man who'd been bothering me, and the guy – Evans, I assumed – returned an angry look.

"Leave me be," he slurred. "Just having a pleasant chat with this waitress."

"Doesn't seem like she's enjoying it," the man said calmly. "Why don't you step away and let me talk to her manager?"

"What?" I asked incredulously, my heart picking up a beat. "You can't do that. I haven't done anything wrong."

The thought of getting into trouble, of fucking things up for Veronica, made me feel sick. I thought I'd retch all over Mr. Trouble's expensive-looking suit, but I managed to keep it in. Instead, I turned my pleading puppy eyes to his, but he didn't even notice.

"Step aside, Evans," he said.

"Fuck off." Evans swayed and, being too focused on Trouble's delicious smirk, I wasn't careful enough and Evans landed right in my platter of canapés, sending it rattling to the floor.

By now, everyone's attention was on us. Of-fucking-course. When I actually needed help, everyone ignored me. Now that I was in trouble? They might as well have shone a fucking spotlight on me.

With my cheeks burning up, I dropped to my knees and quickly started scooping up the food off the floor, gathering the cracked dishes and putting them back on the platter. I heard voices above me, and out of the corner of my eye, I saw Elliot glaring at me and wildly gesticulating for me to get back into the kitchen, probably so he could scream his head off.

I was in big trouble.

As I cleaned up, I noticed Mr. Trouble was wearing a pair of black leather boots, a bit of an unusual choice for a gallery opening, even if I wasn't some kind of fashion guru. And his feet were unmoving, even though Evans had walked away moments prior.

Suddenly, one of the boots nudged my foot gently. I looked up from my kneeling position on the floor, and Trouble was staring down at me, finally acknowledging my existence.

I felt heat rushing to my center. I didn't understand sex very well – apart from the stolen moments I shared with myself while my roommates were sleeping – but I could feel wetness growing between my legs, and I knew it meant fucking trouble.

"Get up," Trouble told me.

"No," I refused blatantly.

He shrugged. "Fine. I like you kneeling, anyway."

As if my cheeks couldn't get any redder, I picked up the platter and glared at him, finally getting up – an act of defiance. "Fuck you."

"What a filthy mouth you have," he told me with disdain, his eyes locking on mine. "A dirty mouth for such a proper, well-behaved little slut."

I was blushing something fierce and my heart was pounding. "I beg your pardon?" I asked. I shook my head to get the thought out, strands of blonde hair leaving my chignon. I propped the tray I was carrying up on one hand, offering it to the man in front of me. "Crab cake?"

"I'm good," he told me darkly. His eyes were on me. All over me. It felt like he was fucking me with his gaze alone, and shit, it was intense. My panties were flooded, a right mess in such a proper place. I felt chastised from his eyes, like he knew exactly what was happening between my legs. The man smirked, an expression full of pity on his face. His expression lingered, just a fraction of a second too long, before someone pulled him aside.

His eyes slid off my face, and I was forgotten. Just like that.

Left standing alone in the middle of the room, I cleared my throat awkwardly and walked off with my fucked-up platter. I was shaking, my legs threatening to give out. I had to hold on to the wall as I made it to the kitchen.

"What the fucking hell are you doing?" Elliot's enraged voice cut through my haze. "You fucking dropped the food, Ver-o-ni-ca. If you don't want me to strangle you right the fuck now, get a new platter and get the fucking hell out of my sight."

I nodded, thankful he hadn't chastised me further. Instead of arguing with him, I grabbed a fresh platter of desserts and headed outside. I needed to clear my mind of Evans and his goddamned rude friend.

I needed to do my job. Fuck knows I needed the hundred bucks badly.

# CHAPTER 2
## *King*

I *could smell the musk of* her pussy from where she was standing, the tray shaking in her hands.

She was pretty, but that wasn't what attracted me to her. The long blonde hair, the blue eyes, her nipped-in waist and long legs didn't hold my attention. I had a woman like her every night, probably with bigger tits too. Hers were small, barely a handful from the looks of her blouse. Not something I usually went for. But she was still beautiful. Stunning, really.

But it didn't matter to me how pretty she was.

No, it was the part of her she kept hidden from everyone else. The submissive side of her that lay under layers of false bravado, snappy remarks and bratty attitude. All of that could be taken away from her, beaten and choked and pinched and fucked until she was nothing but what I wanted her to be.

My pet.

I decided I wanted her the moment I saw her. And I knew she wanted me.

I left her once I'd disposed of Evans and then spent a painfully boring hour with some investors I was trying to impress. I could feel her eyes on me, following me around the room, tracing my every step even though she'd pretended she wasn't interested in me earlier. She was watching me, waiting for me to make a move. But I wasn't going to, and as the minutes passed, the scent of her desperation hit my nostrils, the need she felt for me to notice her, because she was too fucking pretty to be ignored.

Self-righteous little slut.

I excused myself from the investors and went to admire a painting hung on the wall of the gallery. It was pretentious as fuck, some slashes of paint across a blank canvas. What they were meant to represent was unclear, and I didn't give a shit, either.

I felt her presence behind me, and she lingered behind my back for several moments before approaching me with a tray of drinks.

"Another glass, sir?" she asked, but I didn't reply. She shuffled next to me, her motions nervous and unsure. Under that facade of braveness, she was really just a confused little girl. "Excuse me, sir? Would you like another glass of wine?"

"Why not," I finally replied, taking a glass from her tray. I brushed my fingers against her hand deliberately and the glasses rattled as I did so.

"That's a beautiful painting," she said, standing there unnecessarily.

I grunted in response, almost feeling the hotness of her lust. She wanted attention. Spoiled little bitch.

"I don't really have any art to speak of," she added softly. It was all a fucking ploy to get my attention, and she was switching personalities faster than I went through women in my bed. Hard to get, seductive, sweet and innocent. Make up your fucking mind.

"Don't you have a job to do?" I asked her roughly, still without a single glance in her direction.

She shuffled her feet and muttered something under her breath, a curse word I couldn't quite make out. She made a move to leave, but my fingers wrapped smoothly around her wrist. Our eyes connected, hers surprised and mine insistent.

"You have a filthy fucking mouth," I told her.

"That's none of your business," she replied.

"It doesn't suit you," I said.

"Oh, and what would?" she snapped back.

I gave her a once-over. Her neck was long, lily-white and tender. I could imagine the bruises blooming over her skin, could picture my hands cutting off her breath as she thrashed under my hard body.

"A collar," I told her simply, and walked away.

She made a move to go after me, but someone called her back into the kitchen, and she left. I went to discuss something with the gallery owner, nodding and signing a check for him. Then I waited.

I waited until the gallery cleared and I was one of the stragglers left in the room. The staff was diminishing too, but I knew she wouldn't leave without talking to me again. I knew that all too well.

She approached me with a furious expression, her eyes blazing and her hot little body tight with tension.

"You didn't just do that," she spat at me, and I grinned.

"Do what?" I asked her.

"You think you can buy my time like that?" she argued. "You think you can buy me a painting I like and I'll fall at your feet and beg you to fuck me?"

I grasped her tiny forearm between my fingers and pulled her into a corridor where we had more privacy. She gasped when my fingertips connected with her skin, and I felt the vibrations of it right down to my twitching cock.

"Who says," I said, "that I want to fuck you?"

She blushed, opening and closing her mouth like a fish out of water. She was getting angrier, and I knew I only had a few moments before she ripped herself from my grip and told me to go to hell.

"Who says I want you to fall at my fucking feet?" I asked her, coming closer to her pouty lips, my own mouth just an inch away from hers. She parted her lips needily, and the softest of moans escaped her. "Who says I don't want you to fight it? I like girls that struggle."

Her face blanched and I briefly wondered if I'd gone too far, but then the color returned to her cheeks and I knew I had her.

"You'd like that, wouldn't you?" I asked her, and she looked away. Pretty blue eyes on the floor, long black lashes spidery with mascara resting against her cheeks. I reached up to her face and my finger slid across her forehead, pushing back a strand of hair that was out of place. "I'd like to see you cry."

"I haven't cried since I was a child," she said, raising her head and jutting her chin out.

"Proud of that?" I smirked at her. She looked confused and it made me chuckle. "Anyway, I'm about to head out. Enjoy the painting. I'm sure it'll be the centerpiece of your shitty apartment."

I expected her to lash out at me, but instead, she stifled a giggle.

"That painting's fucking hideous," she admitted. "I was only trying to start a conversation."

"I'm glad we agree on something," I told her. I decided I would hang the painting in my apartment once she moved in. Because I knew she would. Then

I could tease her about it relentlessly. "Money well spent, then."

"How can I make it up to you?" she wanted to know, and her flirty attitude was back, all fluttering lashes and luscious, slightly parted lips.

"I'm sure you can think of a way," I said, just as the corridor filled with people. They were getting their coats, the last few visitors leaving. "Don't you have to get back to work?"

"Yeah," she replied, her eyes glued to mine. Her pupils were huge.

"Then go," I said, and she shook her head no. "You'll get in trouble," I added.

She considered my words for a moment, and then finally looked away.

"You must think I'm some..." she started, and I cut her off.

"Come back to my place and cry some pretty black tears for me," I said. Her eyes returned to the floor and she was fidgeting with her fingers. She was biting her bottom lip nervously.

"Got a boyfriend?" I asked, and she shook her head no.

"Parents waiting up?" Another shake of the head.

"Like girls better?" She smiled at that, and shook her head again.

There were still people milling around in the hallway, and someone bumped against her hard, so I pulled her against me. We moved behind a rack of coats and she intertwined her fingers with mine. I gave her a surprised glance, but she still wouldn't look at me. Instead, she lifted the hem of her black pencil skirt and pushed my hand between her legs.

I sought out the wetness of her panties. I didn't comment on what she'd done, just slid my fingers along her soaked pussy lips. She was shaved bare. Smooth. And wet as fuck.

She didn't make a sound, her eyes focused on the floor as she pushed me deeper, past the fabric of her lingerie and inside her cunt. She didn't gasp, or mewl, or beg. She was tight. Unbelievably, impossibly tight. She just pushed me deeper and deeper, until my fingers met with resistance. And then she did gasp.

She was a virgin.

I tried to pull away but she thrust her hips on my fingers, grinding down on them as deep as she could go without breaking her pussy open.

"Please," she begged. "I want it. I really, really want it, sir."

I traced my fingers along her hymen, leaning closer to whisper in the shell of her ear.

"You want me to have this?" I asked her softly, my voice indulgent. She nodded, gasping again when I stretched her unopened pussy around two fingers, her pussy lips open and exposing her sweet clit. "You want my fingers to break you in?"

"Please," she said with a little moan, her body pressing close to mine. "I want that, yes. Please, please."

"No," I told her, pulling my hand away.

She sighed when I put her panties back over her pussy. They stuck to her, wet with her juices and exposing the shape of her pussy. I pulled her skirt back down and she glared at me as I raised my hand to her lips, smearing her own cunt juice all over her mouth.

"Clean them."

Her blushing was adorable, and she turned her head to the side, denying my request. I could've been a gentleman, but then again, when had I ever been a gentleman when it came to fucking?

I pried her lips open with my other hand, holding her mouth stretched wide as I slipped my sodden fingers inside.

"Fucking lick them clean," I hissed, and she did. Her tongue darted between those pretty lips and she licked at my fingers tentatively, tasting herself and letting out a small moan once the sweetness hit her tongue. "Good girl."

She grabbed hold of my wrist then, and I didn't need to hold her mouth open anymore. She sucked my fingers with vigor until they were wet with her spit. I took them out and she gave me a needy look.

"Aren't you gonna ask what my name is?" she asked in a throaty voice, and I grinned at her.

"I don't give a fuck what your name is."

"What's yours?" she asked, her eyes drinking me in.

I let go of her, buttoning up my blazer and bringing my fingers up to my mouth. They smelled of her.

I didn't like virgins. Messy, in every way possible.

She was way too young, probably barely legal, whereas I'd just turned forty. I didn't look it, but around girls her age I sure as hell felt it.

She'd probably be a needy little thing, dependent on me within days. Or maybe even hours.

She looked feisty, like she'd pick a fight for no reason than just to annoy me, or just because she fucking could.

All things I hated. So why the fuck was I considering this?

"King," I told her simply.

"Is that what I should call you?" she batted her lashes at me.

"If you want," I told her. "But eventually, Pet, you're going to call me Master."

# CHAPTER 3
## *Sapphire*

Nothing mattered anymore. Not Veronica, not the hundred bucks, not Elliott probably spitting and hissing fire in the kitchen. All I cared about was King, standing right in front of me, more solid than my reality. I wanted to come with him. I wanted to give him everything.

I knew what I was doing was stupid, I knew I was being foolish, yet I couldn't stop myself. I wanted this, I wanted him.

I followed him out of that coat room with my skirt hiking up on my thighs, my face flushed from the taste of my own juices and my needy pussy clenching. He took my hand firmly and led me out of there without so much as a glance over his shoulder. I didn't get to say goodbye to anyone, or see Elliott's enraged face as we left the gallery. I didn't even get to take my clothes or my damn coat, and I only realized it when we were outside and I shivered in the chill of the night.

"Cold?" he asked, pulling me along the street. He was walking briskly and I had to take long steps to keep up.

"Yes," I nodded, my teeth starting to chatter. "Very cold... sir."

He stopped for a second and slipped off his blazer, placing it over my shoulders. I felt so small when he touched me, like I was a doll he was playing with. I loved the feeling. And I craved more of it.

I looked down as he draped the blazer over me, suddenly too nervous to return his gaze. What was I fucking doing? He was a complete stranger, and I'd let him... touch me. And take me back to his place.

"Are you a murderer?" I asked him out of the blue, and he chuckled.

"No," he replied smoothly. "I'm a man who knows what he wants, Pet."

There was that nickname again. The way he'd discarded my real name like it meant nothing, but it felt oddly liberating instead. My pretentious name had always been the most unique thing about me. Without it, I was just the boring girl next door. But as Pet, I felt anything but boring. As Pet, I felt special.

I wondered briefly if he'd called any other women by that name, but my thoughts dissolved into thin air when a car pulled up to the curb and the driver exited, opening the doors. I realized it was meant for us when King led me inside, his hand firm in mine when he guided me to my seat.

The door closed behind us and we were alone in the darkness, cut off from the driver by a black mirrored partition. The car pulled away and I wondered if the driver could see us. And I wondered again how I could be so stupid to trust a man I didn't know, but my worries turned to dust when his mouth latched onto mine.

I hadn't kissed a lot of guys, let alone men. And I'd never kissed anyone quite like King.

He didn't let me kiss him back. He fucked my mouth with his tongue, pushing it forcefully between my lips and claiming every drop of the wetness that lay behind them. I moaned against his lips and he deepened our kiss, making me tremble against his hard body.

His hand inched its way up to my throat and his fingers wrapped around my neck. He squeezed gently and pulled me back. My breath hitched as he looked at my flushed face, and laughed into it. His thumb rubbed circles into the hollow of my throat, gently cutting off my air supply. I wanted him to take more of it, wanted him to take my breath away.

He made me feel like I was nothing but a set of warm holes for him to pleasure himself with. And he made me fucking like it.

"Open your mouth," he told me, and I obeyed on instinct, my lips parting in a small O. He groaned at the sight, and his free hand went to the bulge in his pants. "Wider!"

I tried, but it wasn't enough. His hand went from the hardness between his legs to my mouth and he forced me open just like he had in the closet.

"Stick your fucking tongue out," he said, and I did. He trapped it between his fingers and held me open like that, like I was some cheap whore. And once again, I loved it.

"So you're a virgin," he grinned at me. I gave him an uncomfortable look, stretched for his pleasure and unable to say a word. "Nod or shake your head when I ask you something. Understood, Pet?"

I nodded.

"Have you sucked a cock before?"

I shook my head. It was dark in the car, the streetlights zipping by just a faint glow through the tinted windows, but I was desperate to see more of him. All I could make out of his cock was a hard outline against his leg. Not that I had anything to compare it to.

"Jacked someone off?"

Again, I shook my head.

"Have you touched yourself before?"

I looked away. He moved his hand from my throat and slapped my cheek hard. I stared at him in shock as my cheek burned with the impact. "Nod or shake your head. Don't be a stupid little bitch."

I nodded, tears burning behind my eyes.

I should've gotten out of the car right then and there, but I was too needy, too fucking wet to make a move.

"Ever made yourself come?"

His voice was low and gravelly, and I shook my head no. It made him chuckle.

"You don't know how to do it, do you?"

I shook my head no.

"This is why I fucking hate virgins," he muttered to himself, and I blushed so fiercely I could feel the heat in my cheeks.

He let go of my tongue and I moaned, my jaw sore from being forced open. King reached for my skirt, pushed it up my thighs, then grabbed my ass and pulled me onto his lap with my legs spread. His cock pressed against my belly, so fucking hard and so big I raised a hand to my lips in surprise. He didn't mention my shock or acknowledge it in any way.

"How old are you?" he asked, his fingers trailing a line down my arm and leaving goosebumps in their wake.

"Eighteen," I replied in a small voice, trying to gather some courage. I didn't know how he'd react to a question, but there was only one way to find out. "How old are you?"

"Forty." He tipped my chin back, grabbing my neck right below it and turned my head sideways like he was fucking inspecting me. "You look younger."

"So do you," I managed to get out, and he laughed again. His cock twitched against my belly and I twisted in his lap, uncomfortable but so damn needy at the same time. "Are you gonna make me come?"

He tangled his fingers in my hair and tugged on it gently, bobbing my head.

"You're gonna make yourself come," he told me. "And then I'll decide if you deserve my cock."

I felt the heat between my legs, my pussy pulsing with the desperate need to be filled for the first time.

"How?" I asked him nervously, and his eyes burned holes into mine.

"However you want," he told me.

"Now?"

"No time like the present."

I glared at him. Why the hell did I have to prove myself to him? He was just some random stranger. Yeah, he was handsome. He looked like a fucking movie star. But was I really going to let him humiliate me just so he could take my virginity?

He rested his palm against my inner thigh and I hissed as his fingers toyed with the hem of my panties.

Yes. Yes, I was going to let him humiliate me. I wanted it.

"Touch me," I begged him, my voice raspy with need. "Touch me there, please."

"Touch your sweet little cunt?" he asked me, his fingers lingering uncomfortably close to my pussy. "You want me to tear those soaked panties off?"

He tapped a finger against the fabric and I hissed again.

"Tell me," he said. "Tell me what you want me to do. In fucking detail, Pet."

I wondered again about the driver. If he couldn't see us, I'm sure he could hear us. My tongue felt so heavy, and the words just wouldn't roll off it.

"Tell me!" he said again.

"Push my panties aside," I managed to get out.

"And?"

"And… feel how wet I am."

"Are you?"

"Y-yeah…"

His palm hit my pussy, fast. I yelped as his fingers lingered over the fabric of my underwear, his thumbs pressing down on my cunt and his fingers digging into my ass.

"You can do better than that, can't you?"

"Fuck you," I bit out, but I stuttered over the words. "Seriously, fuck you."

Carelessly, he yanked the fabric of my panties aside and his thumb was parting my pussy lips, rubbing against my clit. My head fell back and I had to fight the urge to buck my hips against his dirty fucking fingers.

"You will," he promised me. "Eventually. Once I'm convinced you're so fucking cock-starved you'll lick your own pussy juice off the floor if you have to, just to get to feel me pushing inside you."

I mewled as he rubbed my clit, crying out. My head went to his shoulder and I pressed my body close.

"Needy," he told me. "Needy little slut. Keep going. Tell me what you want me to do to that dripping snatch."

"S-stretch it," I whispered into his ear as he toyed with my clit. "Gape it for me, sir."

"Gape it?" he laughed into my hair.

"Yeah," I whined. His fingers dug into my clit and I cried out when he pinched it between his fingers. "Oh God, oh my God. Gape it really wide."

"I'll remember you said that," he said, his voice dripping with sweetness. "You'll be sorry you did."

He put his mouth on my chest and sought out my nipple. He bit it, right through the flimsy lace of my bra and into the sensitive skin. I bucked my hips against him and I saw stars. I rubbed against his crotch with panting breaths and it made him laugh out loud.

"Good girl," he said darkly. "Put your hands behind your back, cross them at the wrists."

I obeyed blindly, my breaths getting heavier and deeper. I awaited my next instruction, but all he did was lean back comfortably against the car seat. I could feel the vibrations of the ride in my pussy, making me want to grind on him more. I wanted to soak his fucking pants, punish him for what he was doing to me, but I had a feeling the dirty jackass would like it.

"Come for me," he said.

I opened my mouth to protest, but thought better of it in the end. I moved my hips tentatively, my head coming to rest on his shoulder. I moaned in his ear as I rode his crotch, his rock hard cock pressing against my belly. I felt his fingers reaching up and he slipped his blazer off me. The blouse was next and I moaned as he pulled it over my head, exposing my body in just lingerie with the pencil skirt wrapped around my waist. My pink cotton panties were soaked, and I was wearing a pretty black lace bra, but they didn't match at all. I didn't have a spare moment to worry about it though, because in one swift movement he'd reached behind my back, undone my bra and it was flung to one side. My hands flew to my chest to shield it from his eyes, but he pried them away from me.

"Behind your back," he reminded me. "And I told you to fucking come for me."

As I clasped my hands behind my back, his hands went to my panties, and when he tore them apart and ripped them away from me I swear I almost came.

My breaths were ragged. My heart racing way too fast. I hated him. I wanted to scratch at his too-handsome-to-exist face. I wanted to humiliate him just like he was doing to me. He tipped my chin back when I tried to lean on his shoulder again, making me look into his eyes.

"Too late to be shy, Pet," he told me with a grin.

He bounced me on his knee and I moaned, my little tits pushing into his face. I felt embarrassed as fuck, embarrassed about how wet I was, about the less than impressive size of my boobs, about the fact that I was so exposed and he was so... in control. Embarrassed about the need deep inside to submit to this man I'd barely just met.

I started grinding on his lap, anything to get that little bit of friction that could set me off in a single fucking minute. My pussy burned as I rubbed it against the expensive fabric of his trousers, ruining them with the wetness that was dripping from my cunt. I forgot to be embarrassed. I just focused on the feeling, on the hardness of his cock on my bare skin, on the way he let a groan slip out here and there as I rode him.

My head was swimming with nerves and unbearable heat, my body shaking with a need I didn't fully understand. Yet I looked into his stony eyes and begged with my pupils dilated and my morals gone.

"What a perfect little slut," he said, his voice strained.

I knotted my fingers together behind my back, riding his lap harder. His cock was twitching against me. I had a feeling the wet spot on his trousers wasn't just from me, and it turned me on so much I cried out.

"Yes!" he said. "Do it! Come for me, slut!"

"Help me," I begged him. "Help me, please..."

"No," he said simply, and I mewled, desperately grinding my cunt on him, bucking my hips at him.

"Please, help me," I begged him. "I don't know how, you won't let me touch..."

"Like this," he groaned, reaching for my hips and placing my bare pussy on top of his twitching cock, the fabric of his trousers the only thing separating us.

"Fuck," I breathed. In the back of my mind, I realized the car had stopped, but I didn't give a shit. "Take it out, please. Put it inside me."

"Soon," he promised. His fingers were digging into my ass and my hips were grinding against him. I couldn't stop myself. My body was acting of its own accord.

"More," I whispered, "I need more."

He pulled me closer by the neck, looking into my eyes as he spoke to me. He was so fucking calm, like this was something he did every day. And maybe he did but I didn't fucking care.

"Keep working that snatch," he told me. "Keep fucking riding my lap, little Pet. And I promise you I will give you anything you want and more."

I thought of all the things I'd worked for in my life. Independence. My own shitty flat. Money, an education. A stable relationship with a guy, and a good one with my parents.

And yet, the only thing I really wanted was his cock.

"Your... cock," I gasped against his lips, and he grinned as he stared me down. "Your cock, deep inside me."

"In every sweet hole," he promised and I yelped as he made me grind harder. I was going fast then, needing to feel the pressure build some more, to what extent, I didn't know.

"Your ass first."

I moaned.

"Your mouth second."

He was so dirty, and I loved it.

"That sweet fucking pussy last, Pet. I want to finish in your pussy once I've split you open."

A shudder ran through me. Sparks flying. My tits. My pussy. Sparks flying everywhere. And I moaned like a whore. "I so want it in my mouth," I whispered.

"Come for me!" he told me again.

"Please let me have it," I begged. "Let me fucking have it."

"Come!"

I wanted to cry out in frustration. It wasn't enough. I'd never done this before. I didn't think I'd ever had a proper orgasm. I wanted it so badly, just so I could please him. Just so he could live up to his word and fuck me, fill me up, break me and make me cry. I felt tears welling in my eyes, and before I could look away, they spilled down my cheeks.

He groaned when a frustrated sob escaped my lips. He reached up to my cheeks and wiped a tear with his fingertip, brought it to his lips and licked it off. I stared at him while more tears fell. He was surely done with me now.

"So pretty when you cry," he said. "I knew you would be."

And then his fingers were in my hair and he was pushing me to my knees. I was on the floor of the unmoving car and he was unbuttoning his trousers and then his dick was in front of me, enormous, bulging, the veins throbbing, the tip so deep red it almost looked purple. I gasped and he used the moment to his advantage, forcing himself into my mouth.

I choked, but he kept going deeper and deeper, driving himself inside me with such force I gagged. His hands went to the back of my head and he held me in place.

I felt him throb in my mouth and I looked up, my eyes connecting with his. It was unfair, he was supposed to give me some time, take it easy, be gentle. He was a fucking prick, he was just using me. And when I looked up at him, he wiped another tear from my eyes with his thumb and grinned at me.

"Take it," he told me roughly. "Come on, Pet. Wider. Open wider."

And I did.

He groaned and I felt it, knew he was going to explode. I sucked my cheeks in and he cursed out loud. He stroked my hair with one hand, but it was when he squeezed my nose shut with the other that I knew I was about to come.

It built and built and built inside me, and then I was moaning on his cock, begging in incoherent sentences, crying like a fucking baby, sucking desperately, trying not to pass out as my fingers found my clit. And it happened, I came with a spluttering cry and a mouthful of cock, and it was all he needed to spill his load inside me.

My teeth grazed his dick because I needed it all. He made me look into his eyes, my vision blurred by tears as he filled up my mouth. There was so much of it, and it was warm. I cried harder when he pulled out.

"Open your dirty fucking mouth," he said, his hand jerking that beautiful cock. "Stick your tongue out, slut."

I did it, and he grabbed my cheeks and made sure it was all gone.

His eyes grew softer and he stroked my hair, still jerking his cock.

"Do you want to stop playing, Pet?"

I shook my head no.

"Then why are you crying?"

"Because you came down my throat," I whispered. "And it was too deep down for me to taste it."

# CHAPTER 4
*King*

I emptied *my balls down her* throat without meaning to. But it was too hard to resist, what with her moaning and begging for it. And her last words, spoken through her tears, had me hard all over again. The little beauty was doing my fucking head in and I wanted more of her crazy mind-fuck.

I didn't wait for her rush to pass. Instead, I draped my blazer back over her shoulders, buttoning it at the front to hide her lithe body underneath. She shivered while I pulled her to her feet, supporting her weight and guiding her out of the car.

She hitched her skirt from her waist and smoothed it down before looking around at her surroundings, the street busy with people, and she was like a deer in the headlights, disoriented and still recovering from her orgasm.

"Take it off," I said.

She gave me a quizzical look before glancing around again.

"Lose the skirt, Pet."

She was trembling, and that made me smile as she undid the skirt and stepped out of it. I nodded to the open car door and she threw the skirt inside.

She looked so sweet in just her heels and my blazer.

We were a block away from my apartment, as per my instructions to the driver. I ushered her ahead of me, down the busy street. She stumbled forward, and I decided to have some mercy on her, wrapping an arm around her waist and walking her down the street like she was a trophy.

"Where are we going?" she asked, her voice weak with nerves.

"To my apartment, Pet."

"How far is it?"

"Not far," I lied, enjoying seeing her blush.

The street was busy with people, and I felt Pet's discomfort with every step we took. She pulled the blazer down over her ass, barely covering her cheeks. While we were walking, I slipped a finger between her thighs discreetly and grinned to myself when I felt her dripping. She moaned and clamped her legs together to shut me out.

"Don't," she warned me in a hiss.

"Keep walking, sweetheart," I told her.

We passed a couple of guys, probably closer to her age than mine. One of them wolf-whistled at her and jealousy cut through me like a knife. I forced myself to press my fingers into her side.

"Show him," I told her roughly, and she gave me a horrified look over her shoulder.

"Show him what?" she asked, her voice shaky.

"Pop the buttons open and flash them," I said calmly.

I didn't think she'd do it, but she reached for the buttons on the blazer with trembling fingers. My cock twitched. The guys were getting closer. Really fucking close. Three of them, not as tall as I was. I could probably take them if they made a move on her.

She unbuttoned the blazer painfully slowly, her fingers slipping over the buttons several times.

"Tick tock," I whispered in her ear, and she moaned out loud. Loud enough to catch their attention. Loud enough to make me want to close that fucking blazer around her tight little body and drag her off into an alley and fuck her brains out.

They were almost next to us now, and time stood still as we both looked at them, with me now walking a step behind her. Slowly, painfully slowly, she opened her blazer and exposed herself to them, pretty tits and a puffy cunt on display for all to see.

I expected a reaction, but their jaws just fell. Someone shouted something lewd, and jealousy bubbled under my surface like a wicked poison. I grabbed her arms and forced them down, closing the jacket for her. I wrapped a hand around her waist and pulled her across the road, a taxi blaring its horn as we made our way to the other side.

She was giggling.

I was fucking furious.

"That was crazy," she said, and my jaw tightened. "Absolutely fucking crazy."

I wanted to slap her. I wanted to slap my-fucking-self.

My Pet. Mine. Fucking mine.

She had to be punished. It was as simple as that. I didn't say a word as I dragged her to my apartment building. She gasped when we got there, the surprise of the magnificent architecture taking her breath away.

"You live here?" she asked, but I couldn't answer, I was too fucking upset. Like a damn jealous teenager.

I dragged her inside the building, nodding a polite hello to the doorman and ushering her into the elevator. I pressed the button for my floor, the top one, and she leaned against the mirror with a smile playing on her lips.

I resisted the urge to slap it off her pretty face.

She didn't say a word, and neither did I. The ride up was short, and I led her out of the elevator and into my apartment.

I was prepared for her amazement, and she didn't disappoint. To be fair, my apartment was nothing short of stunning.

Floor-to-ceiling windows overlooking the city, modern, expensive furniture, and expensive artwork on the walls. I liked my home. I hoped she would like it, too. After all, she'd be spending a lot of time here.

I watched her chatter as I made myself a drink, grabbing a pop from the fridge for her. Fucking too young to drink. What was I getting myself into? She was trouble with a capital fucking T.

I brought the can of soda to her and she asked me if I had a straw.

I got her the fucking straw.

I told her to sit on the couch and wait while I made a call.

I was brisk with it, barking instructions at the person on the other end of the line, vague ones so she wouldn't suspect a thing. Once I was done, I pocketed my cell and turned to face Pet. Her eyes were wide and wanting more, her lips sucking on the cherry-red straw.

She looked so young. I felt like a dirty old man next to her.

The straw fell from her lips and she parted them as she spoke.

"Are you going to fuck me now?"

I didn't answer her, finishing my drink and setting the empty glass down on the coffee table. I undid my tie and the top two buttons of my shirt. It felt good, liberating after a full day in the suit.

"We're gonna play a game," I told her, and her eyes sparkled. "Get up, take the blazer off. Not the heels. Come with me."

I turned my back on her without waiting for a reply, and walked towards my favorite room in the house.

To call it a dungeon would be an insult. The women I played with came willingly, in more ways than one. It wasn't a room out of a lame BDSM movie. The equipment was hidden in plain sight, and the room could look as innocent to an observer as it did dirty to someone who knew their shit.

I heard the clacking of her heels behind me, and I guided her into the room. She stood in the middle of it, fidgeting nervously. I could tell she had no idea what she'd gotten herself into.

I pulled up a chair, a Philippe Starck Ghost Chair that would show off every inch of her beautiful body.

"Sit," I told her, and she did.

I went to work on her ankles first, tying her feet down to the legs of the chair. She didn't protest, in fact, she didn't make a fucking sound. She was staring at me, though, her eyes burning the back of my head as I tied her legs to the chair with silk rope.

I worked on her hands next, tying them behind her back.

Once I was done, I stepped back to admire my handiwork.

Her legs were spread wide. Her pussy was slightly open, her damp thighs shivering under my gaze. Her hair was spilling down her front, covering up those pretty rosy nipples.

"Do you think I'm beautiful?" she asked me, and I moved my eyes from her tight slit to those eyes burning with the need to know my answer.

"You are," I told her, hoping my voice didn't betray my true feelings. I stroked her cheek and she leaned into my hand. "A beautiful little slut."

She seemed pleased with my answer and I wondered just how nervous she was, being here. She was either very brave or very fucking foolish. Probably a bit of both.

"Are you going to fuck me like this?" she wanted to know, but I merely grinned at her.

I walked to my David Collins chest of drawers, a piece I was particularly proud of, and pulled a drawer open, trying to pick the perfect weapon. The tension in the room, the way her breaths were hitching behind my back, made me harder.

I pulled out a vibrator, not a big one, not a particularly fancy one, either. The silver color glinted in the light as I turned around. I watched her eyes spark with fear. For a second, I'm sure she thought I had a knife. And for a second, she was fucking excited.

More fucked up than I thought she would be.

I walked back to her and turned the toy on to the lowest setting. She opened her legs wider when I slipped a hand between them. She was still soaking wet. Her pussy lips were red and puffy, making me give her an indulgent smile she didn't deserve.

I placed the toy at her slit, teasing her pussy lips open with it until it pressed up against her clit. She mewled as I closed her legs.

"Are you gonna keep them closed?" I asked, getting up from the floor.

She nodded obediently as I pulled my belt out of my pants. Her eyes widened. I kneeled back down and slipped the belt around her thighs, pulling them together and buckling it in place. Her legs were bound tightly now, with the vibrator gently working her pussy.

"It's not enough," she whimpered, and I laughed at her.

"Not enough?" I wanted to know.

"To… to make me come." Her eyes were begging me for mercy. "That's not enough to make me come, sir."

My cock twitched at her words. I tipped her chin back, stroking her lips. Her eyes filled with need.

"Quite the expert now, are you?" I teased her, and a nervous giggle escaped her pretty lips.

I moved my hand between her legs and my thumb ghosted over her pussy, coming away wet with her slippery juices. I raised it to her lips and she latched her sweet little mouth onto it eagerly, sucking it like she was still a little girl, with her eyes glued to mine.

I couldn't make her stop, especially when the pathetic vibrations worked their magic and she moaned my name, so softly it felt like a dream.

She looked into my eyes as she sucked my thumb, and I felt a really strong urge to stroke her pretty face. I resisted. She was making me weak.

Her breaths quickened and her sucking got more vigorous. Her eyes didn't move from mine.

I wanted to hate her in that moment, because I knew she would be the fucking end of me.

And then the doorbell rang, and I pulled my thumb out of her mouth with a pop.

"Let's play now, Pet," I said, heading out of the room.

Her soft pleas followed me all the way to the front door.

# CHAPTER 5
## *Sapphire*

I *stared at his retreating back,* not knowing when or if he'd be back. He could just leave me in here, the head of the vibrator trying to work some magic but failing miserably. I was getting worked up, my pussy tingling and desperate to come, but the pathetic vibrations between my legs would never be enough. My heart was pounding with the thought of what might follow next.

I wanted him to fuck me so badly.

I heard conversation in the hallway, two voices laughing like I wasn't tied to a chair in the other room. One of them was his, deep and dark and careless, and the other voice belonged to a woman.

I already hated her, hated the way she laughed, the flirty tone in her perfectly husky voice. I wanted to cry out and let her now I was only a door away. I wanted to tear the ropes away and walk back into the beautiful living room, smack the living hell out of the bitch who now held King's attention.

Jealousy tore through me and I moaned, trying to break free. But he'd buckled the belt against my legs tightly, and my limbs were tied to the chair so firmly I couldn't move an inch. I hated *him*, too. Fucking hated him.

I heard approaching footsteps and I stiffened in the chair. I felt awkward as fuck, nervous and ugly and stupid for getting myself into a situation like this.

The door opened slowly, and he walked back inside. He'd rolled up the sleeves of his shirt, and his arms looked muscular and strong. I longed for him to touch me. He gave me a fleeting look, his eyes admiring the work he'd done with the rope, and briefly lingering on the wetness between my legs. My pussy spasmed when he looked at it, and my clit throbbed. Throbbed for *him*.

"Feeling good, Pet?" he asked me with a grin, and I growled at him like a fucking animal.

"Fuck you," I spat out, and he laughed like it was the funniest thing in the world. "Let me go. I want to leave."

He came towards me, roughly grasping my throat between his fingers and looking into my eyes.

"Say that again," he said, his other hand pushing the vibrator deeper between my legs, right up to the part of me that hadn't been broken yet. I gasped out loud. "Come on, Pet. Say it right now and I'll let you leave. I'll even let you borrow my jacket so you can cover up your sweet ass."

I mewled instead and he laughed in my face, pulling the vibrator back to its spot where it wasn't doing me any good. I tried to rub myself against it but the pressure wasn't enough, and my growl of frustration was pathetic.

"I'd like you to meet my special guest," he told me with a grin, motioning towards the door. My eyes widened in horror as the woman I'd heard strolled inside.

She was wearing a red cocktail dress and heels. Black curls to her shoulders, deep-set brown eyes and a pretty mouth. Her ass was as curvy as her tits. She was beautiful. So much more beautiful than me.

I looked away, struggling against the restraints that held me to the chair. I didn't dare say a word, too scared I'd stutter like a fucking fool.

"This is Angel," King told me simply, and I wondered if he called everyone in his life by pretentious fucking nicknames.

He took the raven-haired beauty's hand and led her to my chair. She smirked at me and I resisted the urge to spit in her ridiculously pretty face.

"I'd like Angel to join in today," King told me with a grin. "Would you like that, Pet?"

"No," I growled, and they both laughed in response like it was the best fucking joke they'd ever heard. "Let me go. I want to go home."

"I don't think you do," King said with a smile. "But we can always remind you of your place, can't we, Angel?"

She nodded and I hated her more. King's hand sneaked around her and he whipped her around, bending her at the waist, his hand coming to rest on the small of her back.

"Isn't she beautiful, Pet?" he asked me, and I was seething with anger, watching him pull her dress up and expose a garter belt with black lacy stockings. "Would you like to watch me fuck her?"

I looked away, feeling the telltale sting of tears in my eyes. I wasn't going to let him see me cry.

I heard the sound of a palm slapping flesh and bit back a pained cry. He'd spanked her butt, and my own sorry ass flinched in response.

"Angel, get us some drinks," he told her simply, and the woman sashayed out of the room, swinging her hips as she did so. I felt King approaching me, kneeling down next to my chair.

His hand came to rest on my knee and I hissed when he rubbed my skin.

"Look at me," he said, and I wanted to resist, but something compelled me to look into his eyes.

He looked strange, almost like he hated the whole ordeal as much as I did. But surely that couldn't be true. Angel was so much more beautiful than I was. Surely he'd prefer her voluptuous curves to my bony body.

"Do you understand why I'm doing this?" he asked, and my bottom lip trembled. "Do you understand why I'm going to fuck Angel?"

"No," I whispered, my voice pathetically soft and needy. He reached for the vibrator between my legs and turned the setting up a notch. I gasped when he placed it back between my legs, suddenly feeling so much more sensitive, so much needier.

"Pets should be trained well," he told me, smoothing a strand of hair from my face and toying with the vibrator, pressing it up against my clit. "If they aren't, what's the point in having them? And I want you to follow every order. I want you to be a good little girl and do as I say. Is that clear?"

I looked into his eyes and fought the urge to ask him why he looked so upset if this was the case. But I didn't. I nodded like a fucking fool.

Angel walked back into the room and again I felt the hotness of tears burning my eyes. She gave King a glass of something fizzy, but he didn't look at her. His eyes were focused on mine.

"Pet," he said roughly. "Will you please ask me to fuck her for you?"

I bit my bottom lip and he pushed the vibrator between my pussy lips, right on my clit. I shivered, feeling the vibrations right at my center, my eyes rolling into the back of my head. He tapped my cheek softly and I focused on the two people in front of me, my heart pounding and my clit throbbing.

"Will you please…" I looked away from him, to Angel, who looked worried for some reason. Her perfect features were marred by concern, and she was looking at King. I looked back at him, his gaze so intense I could barely hold it. "Will you please fuck her while I watch?"

"Yes, Pet," he told me with a small smile. "Of course I will." He got up from the floor and downed the glass of champagne in his hand. He took Angel's too, and placed the glasses on an end table by my chair. Then, he ripped her dress off in an instant.

She was naked underneath, apart from her stockings and the garter belt. Her tits looked so firm and round, the nipples big and brown. And her pussy was shaved. It looked puffy and red. I realized he'd already played with her in the hallway. *Bitch.*

He led her to the chair I was sitting on, making her bend over in front of me and placing her hands on my knees, her full tits hanging so close to me. That's when I noticed her tattoo, a small cartoon angel on her shoulder. I wanted to hate it, wanted to hate it all, but coupled with the vibrator between my legs I was fucking hornier than ever.

"Hold on tight," King told her roughly, and she obeyed without a single complaint, gripping my knees and tensing up. He smacked her ass with his palm and she gasped, her breath hot in my face. "Pet, look at me while I fuck her."

He undid the button on his trousers and I realized this was really happening. The tears threatened to fall again, but I made myself look into his eyes no matter what.

He looked just as intense as earlier, but something was off. It was like the girl gripping my knees with her ass in the air wasn't even there as he pulled his cock out, slipping a condom over his length and slowly, oh so fucking slowly, sliding inside her pussy.

She cried out but I barely noticed it. King's eyes were on mine as he spoke up, slowly thrusting his hips inside the girl.

"She feels so fucking tight, Pet," he told me, his hands going to the girl's ass as he pushed himself inside her. "I bet you'll love watching this."

I blushed and tried to tear my eyes away, but I couldn't bring myself to do it. I focused on his eyes, the dilated pupils, his gaze relentless as he looked at me.

"Do you think she likes having a big cock up her cunt?" he asked and fucked her hard.

Angel mewled, flooding my chest with her hot breath as her head dipped. Sparks flew from my clit to my tits. My nipples tightened so nicely. I held my chest proud and he kept on fucking her but his eyes betrayed him.

He wanted me. He wanted my pussy, not hers. She was just a ploy.

"I hate you," I whispered as she moaned his name against my skin over and over again. "I hate you, I hate you, I hate you."

"I know, Pet," he told me gently. "I know you do, sweetheart."

He kept on fucking her, taking his fucking time. Her moans grew louder and so did her wet pussy, squelching and slurping, and soon, she was riding him, thrusting her hips back, her tits swinging as she begged for his cock to split her open. I knew she was close to coming, her gasps getting huskier and her *oh-God-pleases* bringing her closer to the orgasm she so badly wanted.

King reached over her body and took the vibrator in his hands, putting it on the highest setting. I mewled in anticipation as he slid it back in place, and adjusted my hips against it greedily.

"You're gonna come for me, Pet," he told me, pushing deep inside the girl. "And when you do, I'm gonna fucking explode."

I wanted to cry at the thought of him doing that, but the gasps and moans took over my body and I knew I wouldn't be able to last long. I hated the thought of him coming inside her, but I knew my own orgasm was inevitable.

"That's a good girl," he told me, thrusting hard with a groan. "Fuck, she feels amazing, Pet."

Angel shifted position, put her arms around my waist, held herself in place. Her mouth was dangerously close to my tits. I could feel her hot exhales on my nipples and it was almost too much.

"Let go," King told me in a whisper. "Just let the fuck go, Pet."

So I did. I let the orgasm take over my body, and hot tears of humiliation ran down my cheeks when I moaned my release. King groaned, pushing inside her for the last time. I knew he was coming and I hated him, hated what he'd done to me.

Angel was gasping his name but I kept my eyes locked with his, disregarding her completely. He did the same, and it felt like we were alone in the room. Just the two of us. And it was beautiful.

# CHAPTER 6
*King*

I escorted Angel out of the room, my palm resting on the small of her back. She hugged me close at the front door and I smacked her butt on her way out. She whispered something in my ear and I gave her a smile before I sent her on her way. I took a moment for myself after she'd left, leaning against the doorframe and hating myself for what I'd done. But I'd had to.

Slowly, I made my way back to the room. My eyes drank in Pet's features from the doorway and my dick got hard again at the sight of her. She looked so fucking beautiful with tears streaming down her face, her mascara ruined, her bottom lip jutting out and trembling.

I approached her without saying a word, and stroked her cheek gently. She whipped her head away from me, and more hot tears ran down her cheeks. I fucking hated myself in that moment, because as much as I knew we'd both enjoyed what I'd done with Angel, she was hurting now, and that wasn't the purpose of the exercise.

I kneeled next to her and took my time undoing the ropes around her feet. I didn't remove the vibrator from between her legs, my fingers trailing a line up her thighs as I moved to work on her wrists. Slowly, I undid her bindings, and as soon as her hands were free, she grabbed the vibrator and threw it across the room. I would've laughed if she hadn't launched herself at me next, her hot, tight little body glistening with sweat as she pounded her little fists against my chest.

"Fucking prick," she hissed. "Why would you do that? Why the hell would you do that to me? Why would you?"

I let her hit me, my hands resting by my sides. She tired herself out pretty fast and collapsed in a helpless little heap on the floor by my feet. I kneeled down next to her, my hands smoothing back her light hair, my other hand tipping her chin up. She looked like a wild animal, feral and scared and so vulnerable.

"It's ok," I told her gently. "I know you're angry, Pet. It's going to be okay, I promise. I do everything for a reason. Don't worry."

She sobbed as I pulled her against my chest and I wondered how overwhelming this must've been for her. She felt so small in my arms.

"Let's get you cleaned up," I said, and she didn't object when I pulled her to her feet. But her knees buckled, and I knew she wouldn't be able to keep herself up.

I gathered her in my arms, and she cuddled closer to me, her head going to the crook of my arm, her arms around my neck. She held onto me as if I was her lifeline, and I liked the feeling. I liked being responsible for this one, caring for her. I knew right then and there I was going to hurt her very badly when our time together came to an end. But because I was a selfish damn prick, I couldn't bring myself to keep my hands off her.

I carried her out of the room and into the bathroom. I hesitated between using the bath but finally decided to go for the shower instead. I set her down inside the glass walk-in shower, and she got down on her knees, crawling into a corner of it and hugging her knees to her chest. A pang of guilt and regret went through my body. I was such a fucking jackass.

I turned on the water above us, and it sprayed us with hot steam. I didn't give a shit about my shirt and the pants I'd zipped over my cock. I couldn't stand the sight of her like that, hugging herself in the corner, like she wasn't even in the same room with me. She was staring into space when I sat down next to her, my clothes fucking soaked from the spray of the water above us. She shrank away from my touch when I reached for her.

"Come on, Pet," I said gently. "Let me clean you up."

Fresh tears spilled from her eyes as I reached for a bottle, squeezing body wash into my palm. She didn't say a word as I pulled her flush against me, my shirt sticking to her naked body. The water beat down on us as I worked a lather into her skin, cleansing her of the sweat and the worry and the sadness.

She shivered in my arms even though the water was hot.

"It smells like lemon," she said in a soft voice. "Smells nice."

"It does," I murmured against her wet hair. She smelled so fucking good it made me want to smash something, knowing how our story would end. I worked some shampoo into her hair and washed her clean. Halfway through, she started humming something, the melody of a song I didn't recognize. I felt guilty. Really fucking guilty.

I washed the suds off her and pulled her up. She struggled to stay on her feet and leaned against me as I washed her body. I knew I'd hurt her by fucking someone else like that, that was the point. But there was something else there, something hiding behind those distant eyes of hers. But she'd locked me out of her thoughts, and even though my hands were exploring the silky soft skin of her naked body, it felt like she wasn't even there with me.

I made sure she was okay before stripping my clothes off. She stared at me when I did so, her eyes drinking in my cock hungrily. It twitched for her and I had to resist every urge in my body from lifting her up, parting that pretty little cunt and popping that cherry she so desperately wanted rid of.

I washed myself and she pressed herself against me, surprising me with her need for my touch. My fingers trailed down her back as she held me, hot water beating our backs. I could've screamed at the world then, cursed at the unfairness of it all.

I led her out of the shower and wrapped her in a thick, fluffy white towel. She looked so small in it, and it hurt.

I dried myself off and did her next, rubbing her skin with the soft Egyptian cotton until she felt supple and soft to the touch. I wrapped her in my own robe, the size of it overwhelming her small frame. I wrapped a towel around my hips and held open the door for her. All this without saying a word.

I led her back to the living room and she sat down on the couch, looking really lost.

"Do you want to go home?" I asked her, and she stared at me in response. "You can stay the night, if you'd like. I'll get you a ride to wherever you want tomorrow morning."

"Okay," she nodded. "I'll stay."

It wasn't going according to plan at all. If it had, I would've been balls deep inside her cunt by now, listening to the sweet little sounds she was bound to make when a man bottomed out inside her for the very first time. But I couldn't bring myself to do it.

"I'll set up a room for you," I told her, and she shook her head no, making me raise my eyebrows. "No? You want to go home?"

"I'm not going to sleep by myself like some fucking servant," she hissed, and it nearly made me laugh out loud. "I'm sleeping with you."

I liked the little bit of personality that shone through her submissiveness. It was cute.

"Okay, you can sleep with me," I said. "But you're gonna be naked for me."

She got up from the couch and slipped my robe off, exposing her playground of a body. She seemed oddly comfortable with it for a girl with no experience, and I liked it.

"Where to?" she asked me, and I showed her the way to my bedroom.

If she was impressed by the big, sparsely decorated room, she didn't say a word. But she did walk up to the floor-to-ceiling windows and look outside at the view. Sparkling lights and cars as tiny as ants on the roads below us. I wanted to fuck her against the window. It was unbearably hot that she just stood there with her tits exposed and her naked ass on display, wet hair falling down her arched back.

I walked to the bed and pulled back the covers, and she looked at me over her shoulder.

"Come to bed," I told her as I got in myself. Slowly, she made her way to the bed and crawled under the sheets with me.

She'd made a big deal of sleeping with me, but she scooted to the very edge so she wouldn't have to touch me.

I knew full well it wasn't how the night should've gone. I'd never let a pet sleep in my bed before. Every one of them had the same room. I'd never fucked another woman in front of a pet, either. She was the one I'd changed all my rules for.

"Come here," I ordered her, but she turned her back on me instead, nearly toppling over the edge of the bed with her efforts to stay as far away from me as possible. "Pet. Come sleep in my arms, you silly fucking thing."

She glared at me over her shoulder and I rolled her over and into my arms. She still smelled like lemons, like the body wash.

She didn't fight me when I held her, but she was rigid and frozen against my body. So was my cock.

"Aren't you going to fuck me?" she asked in a small voice, and I smoothed her hair back.

What was I supposed to tell her?

That I was so desperate to break her I had to bite my tongue before I ordered her to impale her pussy on my cock? That if I moved my hands an inch lower from her back to her ass, I wouldn't be able to control myself, and I'd fuck her sweet little ass too?

"Not yet," I told her simply. "Go to sleep."

"Am I going to see you again?" she wanted to know.

"If you want to," I replied.

"Are you going to fuck me, then?"

I looked into her eyes and nodded.

"How?" she asked, and I grinned at her.

"Mean," I told her. "Really fucking mean. You'll beg before I fuck you."

She rolled her eyes and tried to move away from me, but I wouldn't let her. I was being too lenient with her, too fucking indulgent.

I slipped a hand between her legs and she gasped as I pried her thighs apart. My fingers went to her pussy, and she was already soaked. My cock twitched against her belly.

She moaned against my cheek as I pinched her pussy lips between my fingertips. She bit her lip with her eyes closed, and I knew without a doubt she would've begged right then and there if her pride had let her.

I slipped my finger from her pussy to the tender skin between her cunt and her ass, and she shifted uncomfortably. I restrained her movements and her eyes flew open, a silent plea in them as my finger sought out the ring of her asshole. A small, pathetic little sound escaped her lips when I pressed down on it.

"No," she begged me. "Not there, please."

"Why not?" I asked her softly, and she wriggled under me. "I'm going to take everything from you, Pet. I'm going to break you so slowly you'll beg for mercy. And then I'm going to put you back together into the perfect little pet for your master. So if I want to fuck your asshole…"

I pushed inside, barely opening her up, and she cried out.

"You better fucking offer it to me," I groaned into her hair, my finger sliding inside her tight little hole. Tears welled in her eyes and I knew I was hurting her as I pushed it all the way in, but I couldn't fucking resist. There was something about her crying, something so damn primal I couldn't control myself when she did it. And she didn't tell me to fucking stop, even though I knew it must've hurt like hell.

I leaned down and licked her tears off her cheeks while she mewled helplessly. Her lithe body was shaking against mine, setting off every fiber in my body. I forced my fingers away from her asshole and grabbed her cheeks instead, pulling her against me until my cock was flush against her cunt.

She looked up at me through wet black lashes, her eyes big and needy. She was mine already.

Pet didn't say a word, and I realized she was waiting for instructions. I took her hand in mine and guided it to my crotch. She gasped when I wrapped her fingers around my cock and held on to it like it was her favorite toy. She licked her lips, her eyes never leaving mine. I realized her whole body was shivering.

I stroked her hair and her cheeks so softly as I spoke to her.

"Thank you for the tears," I said. "I love it when you cry."

# CHAPTER 7
## *Sapphire*

I *woke up with his fingers* caressing my naked hips. My eyes opened slowly and I looked at his hand on me, his fingers trailing along my hipbones and pressing down on my skin. He'd pulled down the covers around me, exposing my naked body to the morning sun that was pouring through the window. It felt warm on my skin.

"Good morning," I said, my voice husky.

He didn't look at me. He kept touching me, though, gentle, sweet little caresses that felt nothing like him.

"You need to go home," he told me, and I seethed at his words.

"Then get me some clothes so I can leave," I said, and he looked into my eyes, his fingers rubbing my hip.

"Might send you home naked," he said. "Just make you walk down to the car with your ass bare and your tits out."

I pushed him off me and giggled, but he grabbed me by the waist and pulled me against him. He was still naked and his cock pressed against my ass as he held me in place.

"Let me go," I said, and he laughed into my hair.

"In a second."

He reached for his cock and guided it between my legs, the tip pressing against my pussy. My breath hitched but I didn't want to give him the satisfaction of knowing the effect he had on me. He eased my thighs open and pressed himself between my pussy lips. I could feel the bead of precum he was smearing all over my cunt. And I did my best not to react even though I wanted to, badly.

I wondered if he was just going to fuck me like this.

"I want to," he said, and I wondered if he could read my mind. "I want to just take it from you now."

It felt like he was talking to himself, but I wanted him to do it nonetheless. I didn't care how it happened, I just wanted it to be with him. After everything that had already gone down, it was almost impossible to believe I was still a virgin.

"Do it," I whispered. My fingers dipped between my legs and I touched the tip of his cock, earning a hiss. "Just do it right now…"

He hesitated, toying with his cock and pushing it as far between my pussy lips as it would go. I gasped, and my heart pounded in my chest. Would he really do it?

He groaned and pushed deeper. I could feel his cock against my hymen and it made me wiggle my ass against his hips desperately.

"Please," I begged. "Just do it now."

His free hand caged me in as he wrapped it around my middle, pinching my nipple between his fingers. He tweaked it into a point and I swallowed hard, wanting so much more. But I didn't say a word.

"You drive me fucking crazy," he whispered in the shell of my ear. "Insane, Pet, really fucking insane. You make me want to hurt you so bad."

"Please," I choked out. "Please, hurt me."

My pussy spasmed on top of his cock and he cursed out loud. I could feel his dick throbbing against me, and his arms were so tight around me I thought he would break me. I wanted him to.

Everything stood still as I waited for him to do it. Waited for him to break my pussy open around his cock and make me a woman. It felt like I was dying and it was beautiful.

"Just tell me what you want," I managed to get out. "Anything, I'll do anything for you... Whatever you want."

He groaned, his fingers finding my throat and squeezing it shut. "Why? Why the fuck would you do that, stupid little girl?"

"Because..." I swallowed hard, my heart racing. What the hell was I supposed to tell him? "Because I'm addicted to you already... Because I want you, and I need you, and I'm falling for you..."

He pulled away from me with a groan and my heart nearly exploded. Stupid stupid stupid, so fucking stupid.

"Let me call you a cab," he said, getting up from the bed and picking up his cellphone from the nightstand.

I allowed myself one second of curling up into a little ball, alone with my fears and the sadness he'd invoked when he'd disregarded my words. I knew it was moronic. This was a man I'd known for less than a day. But how else could I explain what happened to me when he was around, when he so much as looked at me?

I picked myself up, carried all the broken pieces to the other end of the room, as far away from him as possible, and hoped he got a good look at my body before he kicked me out.

"Can you give me some clothes?" I asked in a harsh voice, and he nodded.

He opened a closet, filled with expensive suits and carefully pressed shirts, and pulled out a striped blue and white shirt. He passed it over to me and when my hand brushed his, I felt sparks flying. I took it from him and slipped it on, buttoning it up over my nakedness. It was way too big, covering my ass.

I walked over to where he'd discarded his clothes last night and stole his belt, putting it around my waist to make the shirt look like a dress.

"Ready," I told him with a big, bright smile. Fake as fuck.

He stared at me as he called a cab and my heart broke all over again because I was sure I'd never see him again. He ended the call and ushered me out of his bedroom and into the living room.

I put my heels on in there, feeling so ridiculous in my getup, it made me giggle out loud. He didn't acknowledge it and I stood there like an idiot, unsure if he'd walk me downstairs or what. It was awkward as fuck. I walked to the front door and he followed behind me.

"I'll be going then," I told him, and he nodded, running a hand through his hair. There were a few gray ones at his temples. He looked so hot. "Well, bye."

"Goodbye, Pet," he said, and opened the front door for me.

I was so angry I could've just burst into flames on the spot.

I stormed out of his apartment and looked over my shoulder in time to see him closing the door. That pissed me off even more and I ran back, jamming my body between the door and the frame and glaring at him.

"Seriously?" I asked him. "Fucking seriously?"

"Seriously what?" he asked, his face blank. He was so fucking painfully handsome.

"You won't even ask for my damn number?"

"Why?" He looked confused. I wanted to cry.

"You don't even know my name," I spat out.

"Your name isn't important for what I want," he said simply.

That was when I slapped his face.

Or tried to.

He grabbed my wrist and I yelped with pain as he pried it away.

"My name is Sapphire," I told him. "Sapphire Rose Faye, and I'm a person. And you're fucking hurting me."

He leaned in against me and grinned in my face.

"You look pretty when you're hurting," he said. "I fucking like it."

I tore myself from his grip so fast I nearly toppled over.

"Fuck you," I told him. "Fuck you so hard."

"But you didn't," he reminded me.

"And I won't," I said, and he laughed. "I'm fucking serious!"

"I think that's up to me, not you," he said, and the bastard closed the door.

⚜

"*What. The fuck. Have you done?*"

Veronica was furious, her eyes blazing when I came home. She nearly jumped out of her skin when she saw my outfit, my mussed hair and my ruined makeup.

"Are you fucking serious right now?"

"What?" I asked innocently, setting down my stuff on the kitchen counter. "I'm home."

"I got a fucking call from the company!" she shouted. "I'm fucking fired!"

"Shit." I bit my bottom lip. "I'm so sorry, Veronica, I…"

"You didn't fucking think," she spat out. "You just left with some fucking guy! You didn't even think about me! And what in fucking hell's name is that monstrosity?"

She pointed to a huge canvas leaned against the wall and I nearly cried with laughter when I realized it was the painting from the previous night, the one he'd bought for me. A giggle escaped me and she roared with anger.

"I'm fucking done here, Sapphire," she told me. "Done. I was going to do this later, but might as well get it over with now."

She crossed her arms in front of her body and the ring on her finger glinted. It was a shitty, tiny stone.

"You got engaged?" I asked her, hoping to distract her. I really was a bad friend.

"Yes," she replied sharply. "And he's moving in. So I was going to give you a week to leave, but you know what? Fuck that, Sapphire. Get the fuck out of here."

My mouth dropped open and I stared at her incredulously. "Are you being serious?"

"Yes!" she screamed, the rage coming off her like steam. "I am, you got me fucking fired. All for some guy... You know, Sapph, I really thought we could be friends. But I do not associate with sluts."

I just stood there awkwardly, thinking about the previous night. I really was a slut.

"Fine," I replied in a small voice. "I'll go pack up my shit."

"Good," she said, watching me leave.

I got to my tiny, cramped room and slammed the door closed behind me. I looked at the space I called mine and wanted to fucking cry. But there'd been enough tears today. I went to the creaking closet and started pulling my shit out. How I'd get it out of here, I didn't know. I didn't even own a fucking suitcase.

I spent the next few hours packing up my room. I put everything in piles, deciding whether I should swallow my pride and ask Veronica to lend me a hand with the heavier stuff. Or maybe I needed to call my parents. Mom and Dad hadn't even called me the past few weeks. No one gave a shit anymore.

I swallowed back a sob and sat on the bed. How had my week gone from so fucking amazing to a complete fucking nightmare in a matter of hours?

There was a knock on the door, and I called for Veronica to come in.

She stood in the doorway, her arms crossed – probably to show off that stupid fucking ring – and glared at me.

"Who was the man you left with last night?" she asked, and I glared at her.

"I don't see how that's any of your business," I snapped, and she smirked.

"He got me my job back," she informed me. "At least I think it was him. And a pay raise. Good for you, Sapph, at least you know how to whore it out with the right people."

I got up from my bed and walked up to her until our faces were inches apart. She had lipstick on her teeth.

"Don't fucking talk to me like that," I told her. "You don't know shit."

"I do," she smirked, tilting her head. "I know you gave up your fucking cherry for the first guy that found your bony ass hot. You probably screamed like a pig when he fucked you."

"Veronica," I told her sweetly. "When I *give up my cherry*, you'll be the first to know. And I'll fucking think about your pathetic, ugly face when I'm done coming, because that shitty ring on your hand? It's as good as your life is ever going to get."

"Get the fuck out," she hissed, and I laughed in her face.

"Gladly."

I pushed past her, not bothering with any of my shit. I didn't care, I just needed to get away from her.

"By the way, you're welcome, about the pay raise. And tell Craig I said hi." I grinned at her sweetly. "Oh, he's fucking Jessica, by the way."

Her face blanched when she heard that. I'd known about her boyfriend fucking our other roommate for weeks now.

"Too bad he couldn't have me," I finished. "He did try, you know. Told me my pussy would be so much sweeter than yours."

I remembered the night he got drunk as fuck, making a move on me in the kitchen. Fucking prick. They deserved each other.

"Get the fuck OUT!" Veronica screamed at me.

"Bye, honey," I smiled wide. "Hope you like tasting your best friend's cunt on your boyfriend's cock!"

# CHAPTER 8
## *King*

I *didn't want to think about* her. Didn't want to spend a single minute worrying about getting her back, because I knew I would, eventually.

But the girl had a way of sneaking up on me when I was least expecting it. My thoughts were all of her, my mouth alive with her lingering flavor. It had only been a few hours, but I wanted her back. Back in my apartment, back in my life. Legs spread, mouth open, begging for more. I knew my resolve was weakening, and I knew the clock was ticking.

I made some calls to find out more about her. They said her name was Veronica, which definitely sounded more mundane than the name she had given me. I made sure she got her job back, knowing I'd fucked up back there. And then I went about my day. Work shit took up hours at a time, and when my driver took me back home that night, I was fucking exhausted.

My phone rang as I walked through the door, and my heart lurched when I saw *unknown number* flashing across the screen. I picked up on the second ring.

"Yeah?" I barked into the phone.

"Is this... Mr. King?"

The voice wasn't hers, but it was a woman. A sugary-sweet woman who was already annoying the shit out of me without doing much of anything.

"Yes," I said. "Who am I speaking to?"

"My name is Veronica Campbell," she purred. "I think there's been a bit of a confusion at my workplace."

I raised my eyebrows as I poured myself a drink. "What makes you say that, Miss Campbell?"

"Well..." She sighed dramatically. "I trusted a friend of mine to work my shift last night, and it appears she took advantage of that in the worst possible way. I just wanted to call and thank you for getting me my job back."

I waited for more, sensing her getting more and more uncomfortable on the other end of the line. Finally, she spoke up again.

"I was hoping I could thank you in person?" she asked sweetly.

I could practically smell her desperation through my phone.

"And why would I want that, Miss Campbell?" I asked her and she giggled nervously.

"Well, I'm sure I could think of plenty of reasons..." Her voice was flirty.

"Where is she?" I interrupted her.

"Where's who?"

"Sapphire." It felt weird saying her name. "Is she with you right now?"

"No," she replied in a clipped tone. "I made her leave. I can't have people like that around me."

"You made her leave?" I slammed my glass on the bar. "Where did she go?"

"How should I know?" she said, now obviously irritated I wasn't giving her the attention she so badly wanted. "I told her to leave. She left all her shit here, too."

"You need to tell me where you think she went," I told her.

"What's in it for me?"

Stupid calculating bitch.

"Miss Campbell," I replied as nicely as I could. "Tell me where you think your friend has gone, or I will make certain you're unemployable in this entire state."

She went quiet, but finally spoke up, her voice trembling.

"She might be in her favorite coffee place, Beans. But I don't know."

"Any other places you can think of?"

"Maybe the library… I… I don't know."

"Thanks for your help, Miss Campbell."

"Wait!"

"What?" She was really getting on my nerves now.

"You're not going to get me in trouble at work, are you?"

"Let's wait and see," I said, and ended the call.

I poured myself another drink and downed it in a single gulp. The blazer went back on and I found the directions to Beans on my phone. Closed. The library too, probably. So where the hell could she be?

I drove my own car that night, and instinctively ended up at the gallery where I'd met her. Something told me she'd be waiting, and she was.

A small, vulnerable little shape was curled up on the sidewalk. She was wearing a hoodie and cut-off denim shorts, curled up so tight it was like she was trying to disappear. Her blonde hair was spilling out from her hood.

I pulled over and left the car running as I got out of it. Three steps and I'd reached her. Two heartbeats and she looked up.

"No," she said, her voice shaky and sweet.

"Yes," I said, and offered her my hand.

She stared at me with contempt, and then picked herself up without taking my hand. She wasn't wearing makeup and her too-pretty-for-her-own-good face looked even younger this way. Her lashes were light, thick and long. Her lips looked better with no lipstick. Her skin was perfect.

"I hate you," she said.

"So?" I asked. "That doesn't change a fucking thing. You're still coming with me, aren't you?"

"Do I have a choice?" she asked bitterly.

I moved closer and stroked her hair. She turned her head to the side when I did it and I hated myself for hurting her so many times already.

"You always have a choice, Pet," I told her simply.

The rain came down then, heavy and cleansing at the same time. She looked up at me as I tugged on her strands of her hair. It was naturally a little wavy. I stared at her and she blushed, looking away.

"You really don't think you're beautiful, do you?" I asked her.

She didn't answer.

"Confidence is the best thing a girl can wear, Pet," I told her.

"Good thing you have enough for both of us," she said.

I laughed. "Don't be snarky."

"Don't be patronizing."

"Don't be a brat."

"Fuck off."

She tried to get away, but I pulled her back by her hair. She mewled when I did it, but didn't make a move to get away. I held her tightly against my chest, and she let me, giving me piece by piece by piece. I was greedy. I wanted all of her, and I wanted it then and there. She was like a fucking puzzle I was trying to put together, but I kept missing the most important pieces.

"Will you let me take you home?" I asked her, and she nodded against my chest. "Good girl," I said.

I took her hand and guided her to my car. I opened the door for her, made sure she put her seatbelt on and we took off into the night. Moments after we started driving, she pressed a hand to her mouth.

"Okay?" I asked.

"Feel sick," she gasped. "You drive like a fucking crazy person."

I laughed and slowed down. "Motion sickness. Cute."

"Don't ever call me cute again," she bit out. So feisty.

"Why not?"

"It's the worst adjective in the English language," she said. "I want to be sexy or hot instead."

"Fishing for compliments?" I teased.

She didn't say a word, sulking in her seat instead.

I drove back home in silence, careful with every turn we took. She placed her hand on her thigh after a few blocks and it made me feel better. This weird fucking need to protect her, to make sure she was okay, rose inside me, and I didn't know what the hell to do with it. She wasn't my responsibility. She wasn't even supposed to be my pet.

After what happened, I'd promised myself I wouldn't have another one.

And yet, here we were.

I parked in the garage below my apartment building and opened the door for her. The whole night felt like a dream, buzzing with tension and wet with the rain, making for a fucking terrible, combustible combination. She stalked out of the car without so much as looking at me, but when I led her to the elevator, her small hand pressed against mine.

I gave her a sideways glance as we rode up. She was looking at the floor, her fingers holding onto my hand desperately.

She was a fucking girl. She wasn't even a woman yet.

And I was going to make her into one, whatever the hell it took.

We got off on my floor and she still wouldn't look at me. I led her into my apartment, and she followed closely, her fingers intertwined with mine. I had a feeling she wanted to let go, but fucking couldn't. Her fingernails were digging into my palm desperately.

"Do you have any of your stuff?" I asked her, and she shook her head. "Do you need anything?"

She gave me a blank stare.

"Like a toothbrush… some pajamas? Do you take any medications, do you need contact solution, anything?"

She kept staring.

"Pet," I said. "You need to work with me here."

"What am I doing here?" she asked me. "Why would you come get me? Haven't you fucked me up enough?"

"You're here because you want to be here," I said.

"I don't!" she screeched.

"Did I drag you here?" I asked her. "Did I fucking do something to you that you didn't beg for?"

"Fuck you," she spat out. Her favorite phrase, apparently.

"I don't do non-consent, Pet," I said. "And I'll never take something from you that you wouldn't want me to have. Okay?"

"You fucked another girl," she accused me in the softest of voices. "You just fucked her to… punish me."

"That's not why I did it," I said.

"Then why?" She was tearing up. "Are you fucking blind? I like you so much…"

I kneeled in front of her and took her shaky hands in mine.

"You need to trust me," I told her.

"No. Why would I?" She was seething with anger, but she wouldn't pull those hands away.

"Because you want to," I reminded her. "Because you need this as fucking badly as I do."

"You don't need me," she sobbed. "You just want a pussy to fuck. A mouth to push your cock inside. An ass to rip apart."

She.

Just.

Didn't.

Get it.

And there was nothing I could have done.

"It's okay," I told her. "You can be angry."

"Okay," she said defeatedly, her shoulders falling. "Okay."

"I'll make you feel better, though."

"Why?" She gave me a sad look. "Just so you can fuck with my head some more?"

"That too," I smiled.

I resisted the urge to rip her clothes off. I wasn't a sadist. But she made me want to hurt her so badly, because she loved it so much.

"Do you have another place to go?" I asked, and she shook her head no.

"Not really."

"Do you want me to call your parents? Maybe a friend?"

"No," she replied.

"Do you want to stay here with me, Pet?" My heart pounded. I wanted her to say yes as badly as I wanted her to storm out the door.

She looked up at me, those pretty blue eyes as picture-perfect as her beautiful face. "Can I?"

"Yes," I said without hesitation. It was bound to happen eventually. "For as long as you want, okay?"

"Why?"

Because I can't.

Fucking.

Let.

Go.

"Because you don't have a place to stay," I said. "And I want to take care of you for some weird reason."

"You're an old pervert," she said and a nervous giggle escaped her.

"Probably. You're a fucked-up teenager."

"Probably."

We stared at each other.

"Take your clothes off," I said.

Her hand finally left mine. She stared at me as she pulled off that hoodie. She wasn't wearing anything under it, and her little tits bounced when she tossed it aside. Her shorts followed next, and she slipped them off over her long, toned legs. I was mesmerized, unable to look away for a single second. She was a beautiful fucking sight.

She stood there in a tiny black thong and I took her in as if she was my last fucking meal. How fitting.

"I can't just stay with you," she told me, and I grinned at her.

"But you're going to."

"I don't know you," she objected.

"You like it better this way."

"Will you tell me your first name?"

"Will it make a difference?" She was amusing me.

"To me it will," she said in a small voice.

"Okay," I replied. "My name is Hayden."

She giggled. "And your middle name, please."

"Pushing it," I warned her. "My initials are HSK."

"And what does the S stand for?"

She came closer to me, her hand sliding down my chest. She was even more beautiful up close and my heart panged painfully with the thought of losing her forever.

"Seth," I murmured, and she smiled at me.

"Thanks for telling me," she said softly. "Master."

My cock swelled so much it felt like it doubled in size. I had to physically restrain myself from reaching out for her. But she was doing my job for me, touching me here and there, her dainty fingers wrapping around my hand. She toyed with the ring on my finger.

"You weren't wearing this last time," she said.

I glanced down at my hand where a heavy signet ring was resting.

"My mother got it for me," I told her.

She inspected it closely, raising my hand up to see.

"Your initials," she said.

"In our family crest," I said.

"It's beautiful."

Her fingertips stroked across the initials, and it felt like she was memorizing every single line on that ring of mine.

"Almost looks like a brand."

Her voice was soft, but my cock jerked at her words.

A brand.

And just like that, the seed was planted.

"Are you going to fuck me tonight?" she asked.

"No," I told her. "I don't think so."

I expected her to pout and fight me, but she nodded instead.

"I think we need some rules if you're going to stay with me," I said. "Nothing terrible, don't worry. But as long as you're staying here, I want you to follow my rules. Is that clear, Pet?"

I could see the internal battle inside her. She wanted to say no, but she couldn't. She wanted to submit so badly, even though her mind was telling her not to break.

"What rules?" she wanted to know.

"Do you have a job?" I asked her, and she shook her head, looking embarrassed. "Good. I don't want you to have one. I want you to be here as much as possible, okay?"

She nodded.

"Make sure you're home before 9 p.m. if you go somewhere. And I always need to know where you are. You'll give me your phone number, and I want to make sure you keep your phone on. I'll need to know who you're with, too."

"You sound like a parent," she smirked.

"No," I corrected her. "I sound like someone who gives a shit about your safety, Pet."

She toyed with my tie and I fought the urge to slap the firm globes of her ass.

"Do you want to stay in my room or have your own?"

The question slipped out without me meaning to let it. But I wanted to know.

She looked up at me, big, beautiful eyes with huge dilated pupils.

"With you," she told me. "Don't make me sleep by myself."

"I won't," I told her gently. "You can sleep in my room."

She grinned and I wondered if she noticed I didn't tell her she could sleep in my bed. My room, sure, but she'd have to earn the privilege of sleeping beside me. Not the first night, though. The first night was about making her feel safe, and good.

"Do you want me to send someone to your old place to pick up your stuff?" I asked her, and she gave me a shy nod. I made a mental note to arrange that the next day. But I also wanted to take her shopping. I wanted to see her in the clothes I picked out for her, not these teenager-y leftovers she probably had from high school.

"Is that it?" she asked me, and I grinned at her.

"No, that's not it. But I guess it's enough for one night. Would you like to go to bed?"

"Yeah," she said, and yawned the next second. "I'd like that, please, sir."

She was switching between names so fast it was confusing me. It felt like each one was there for one of her personalities. King when she was bratty. Sir when she was horny. Master when she really fucking wanted to please me.

I was going to have a really hard time that night, keeping my hands off her.

She solidified this thought when she turned to walk towards my bedroom, her ass sashaying out of the room without a care in the world, because she knew how good she looked. Or maybe she didn't, she was just too young and too stupid to care.

I had the feeling that this pet was going to be really good for me.

# CHAPTER 9
## *Sapphire*

I'd been awake for hours.

King was fast asleep, his eyes closed and his lips slightly parted as he took breath after breath. I wanted to touch him, but I didn't want to wake him. So I just looked at him and tried my best to understand him.

He was an enigma. I was almost certain he cared about me. Fuck the age difference, fuck the fact we'd only known each other for two days. Fuck it all; he cared.

And yet he seemed intent on hurting me. As if he was trying to push me away. I swore to myself he'd never succeed.

"Stop staring, Pet," he muttered with his eyes still closed.

"I'm not," I lied.

He reached for me and pulled me against him, but I only struggled a little.

He held me against his chest and I took it gladly, familiarizing myself with the contours of his body.

"Liar," he whispered into my hair. His eyes opened and he licked my cheek. "Filthy little liar."

My ass jerked against his groin and he groaned.

"Don't do that."

"I can't help it," I said, and my ass grinded on him more.

His arms tightened across my middle and he held onto me, not moving at all. His grip was hard and so was his cock.

"You're going to get yourself in trouble," he said.

I looked at him over my shoulder. The sun was rising outside, the sky colored in pretty pinks and blues. It was so quiet. So still.

"You need to fuck me," I told him softly.

"I don't need to do anything, Pet."

"I'll beg."

"Begging won't help you."

"Then I'll just have to take what I want."

I slipped the covers from my body until I was completely exposed. The room was cool and my nipples tightened into tight little points as he stared at me. His hand slid down my chest, over my tummy, and stopped on my left inner thigh. He was wearing boxers, but I could see how stiff he was, the outline of his cock against the fabric almost painfully hard.

"No more waiting," I said, and he groaned.

"Don't fucking tempt me, Pet."

I laughed. "I wouldn't do such a thing, *sir*."

He stared at me as my legs opened for him, his fingers digging into my thigh but not moving a single inch, that small distance that would've changed everything for me. I threw my head back in frustration but didn't make a fucking sound. I pushed my tits up, arching my back, and his nails dug deeper.

"You want this?" he said.

I didn't reply, I just looked at him. It was obvious what I wanted, and he was being an idiot not taking advantage of me when I was practically begging him for it.

My lips parted slightly and I moaned so softly he might not even have heard it. So softly he'd have to press his ear against my mouth to hear.

And he did.

I moaned again, and he grabbed my waist with his free hand, slamming me into the mattress.

"Stop," he told me, his mouth hot against mine.

"I can't," I said, and my hips bucked against him. "I can't, I'm so sorry, I just can't."

He groaned. Both his hands wrapped around my waist and he held me in place as if preventing me from moving would change a single thing between us. His hands were so big his fingers touched in the middle of my tiny waist. He held on so tightly it hurt.

"Shut the fuck up, Pet," he said and I breathed his warm breath.

I moaned into his mouth, so low and sensual.

He shook his head like he was trying to tell us both to stop.

But I kept going.

Moaning.

Whispering.

Soft little pleas for him to fuck me.

He was shaking now. His grip was intense and his touch was electric. I couldn't think about anything else other than having him inside me. Right then and there.

"Don't do it," I said, and my legs parted for him.

He looked confused for a second, but I went on.

"Promise you won't fuck me," I said, my voice shaky. "Promise you won't do it."

"Why, Pet?" His voice was gentle. "Why did you change your mind?"

"You're going to hurt me," I realized out loud. "This is going to end badly for me."

My legs trembled. I was sure he could feel my heart pounding. He didn't say a thing. He just stared at me, his grip on my waist so hard I knew I'd have bruises in a few hours.

"Ask again," he grunted.

"Don't fuck me, Master," I whispered. "Please, fucking please, don't ever fuck me."

My legs wrapped around his waist, my naked pussy pressing against his boxers. I could feel the tip of his cock through the fabric, pressing against my hotness.

"Keep asking," he said. "Keep fucking asking and I'll punish you for every time you beg me not to do it."

"Promise you won't."

He pinned my hands above my head and my chest heaved under his watchful eyes.

"I don't want you touching me."

He licked me from my bellybutton to my collarbone and I cried out.

"I'll do anything if you just let me go right now."

He bit my neck, hard and I cried out again.

"Don't... don't do this to me."

His teeth dug into my skin. His nails dragged painful lines along my stomach.

"Please don't. Please promise you won't."

He exhaled against my mouth and took it for himself, tasting me, claiming every inch of it with his tongue. One hand left my waist and went to his boxers. He pulled his cock out. I started to cry.

"Don't," I begged.

"I won't," he said and pushed his cock between my pussy lips.

I whimpered. A tear ran down my cheek. I hated him so much.

"No?" he asked me, and I shook my head.

"No, don't, please."

Words. Just fucking words. Words that didn't mean a thing when my pussy was dripping all over him, when my body was begging for him to use it. He could feel it. The trembling, the shivers, the sparks. It was all there in my mess of a body.

His hands held mine above my head. I fought against him, desperate to touch him, desperate to wrap my arms around his neck, desperate to touch every inch of his skin. But he wouldn't let me.

"Please," I yelped in frustration. "Please, let go!"

He pushed his cock in a little way. So tight. The pain. I could feel it ripping.

"No?" he asked again.

I looked into his eyes, and my heart broke for the first time.

"No," I begged, and he pushed inside me, slowly, firmly, breaking me all the way in. It felt so fucking good, and it hurt even better.

I cried out pathetically, and it made him groan so loud. His lips met my ear and he exhaled against it, his cock buried hard and deep. I could feel him holding back. I could also feel how close he was to letting go.

"I'm so sorry, Pet," he said gently.

"It's okay," I promised, and then I couldn't stop repeating it as he started to fuck me.

"It's okay."

His apologies, soft murmurs in my ear as he broke down every bit of me.

"It's okay."

The warm trickle of blood down my thigh as he really started fucking me.

"It's okay."

His painful exhale as he pounded inside me without mercy, ignoring my sobbing.

"It's okay."

The pain. The fucking blinding, white-hot pain that built and built and built and then exploded until I saw black.

"Please," I cried out. "Please, oh my God, please!"

"Come for me," he ordered, and I did, and it hurt better than anything he'd ever done to me. "Fuck, good girl…"

I could only whimper. I felt him getting bigger, so big it felt like he was ripping me apart.

"Pull out," I begged him. "Pull out, don't come."

"No," he growled, his voice so angry it scared me.

"I'm not protected," I said, whimpering again.

He fucked me harder, punctuating every thrust with a word.

"I. Don't. Give. A. Fuck. *Pet!*"

He broke me with a searing kiss, and I screamed my release into his mouth. He was fucking insane. And maybe so was I.

He hitched my hips, pushed a pillow under my ass and it made him go in deeper. It was strangely cathartic.

No more words, no more thoughts, no more feelings.

No way to express what he was doing to me.

No chance for me to go back from this.

"Pet," he hissed, his balls slapping off my ass. "Spread your whore legs."

I did.

"Beg for it," he grunted.

"Please." My voice was so soft, even though I wanted to scream. "Please, oh God, please."

It turned into a mantra, please and oh please, and oh God please, over and over again until it was the soundtrack to that moment, forever in my mind.

His hand left my ass and wrapped around my throat. He looked into my eyes as he fucked my needy cunt.

"What are you?" he asked.

"Yours." It was so simple.

"My what?" His fingers tightened. His cock throbbed.

"Yours!" I cried out, but he wouldn't let me look away. His eyes. His fucking eyes were on fire.

"My fucking what?" He squeezed again. It hurt. Hurt so bad. So close to passing out. So close to letting go.

"Pet," I whispered, and he squeezed tighter, and fucked harder, and stared deeper.

One final thrust and he stopped moving. I sobbed and he stayed still, so still it felt like time had frozen, so burning deep I thought he'd broken something else inside me. And then I felt him coming, so slowly, so painfully slowly, and then all at once, his cock spasming inside me. I clenched my pussy and his cum oozed into me and I just stared at him with my eyes wide, and my mouth open. And he held me in place like a fucking toy and waited until his balls were empty.

"Say thank you," he said, without moving an inch.

"Th-thank you."

My pussy swelled with him inside me. So tight I was sure he wouldn't even be able to pull out. But he didn't even try to.

He held me by the throat and watched my eyes roll back as he took my breath away. And when I was close to passing out, he kissed me.

Sweet.

Gentle.

Firm.

With so much love in that single kiss, I'd never be able to believe him when he told me he didn't care about me.

I closed my eyes and accepted the darkness.

ONE WEEK LATER

# CHAPTER 10
*King*

She was settling in well.
And every day made it worse. The feelings I promised myself I wouldn't have were getting stronger and stronger until it felt like I'd lose my damn mind if I didn't make her submit fully.

I didn't push her those first few days. I let her do her own thing, settle into my home at her own pace. I spent most of the time in my office, and was sparse with my questions when I came back home. She seemed timid and brave at the same time, quickly laying claim to my place.

Pet was messy, really fucking messy. She'd leave clothes everywhere, strewn across the floor along with her shoes. I'd had her stuff delivered the day after she moved in, and the amount of shit she owned was fucking appalling. Clothes and shoes and bags and makeup, perfume and teddy bears and notebooks, books upon books upon books. So many fucking books.

She was always reading, always carrying a book around with her. Stuff I didn't know, stuff I recognized from bestseller charts, classics. She read everything. I'd caught her reading the back of a shampoo bottle once, intently. The girl was born to be a reader. Her books were everywhere. She didn't dogear or leave coffee rings on them, she just let them litter every-fucking-thing. It was driving me insane.

I'd told her several times she wasn't supposed to do it. She needed to clean her shit up because it was driving me mental having to walk through the mazes of crap.

She did it half-assedly here and there. I told her that day she needed to sort her stuff out, and she seemed especially petulant about it.

I knew why that was.

I hadn't fucked her, hadn't so much as fucking touched her in a whole week.

And she was desperate for it.

I was pretty sure she was asking for it, and when I opened the door to my apartment that night, my suspicions were confirmed by the ridiculous sight that greeted me.

The brat had cleared everything up, but she'd stacked her huge collection of books in piles and had built a fort around the couch with them. A fucking fort.

The little slut was sitting on the couch, feet kicked up, wearing a scrap of fabric she called panties. She had socks on, cute pink ones with white ruffles. Her hair was down and wild and covering her naked tits. And she was wearing her glasses, the ones she usually pretended didn't exist.

She giggled when I walked in, and my blood boiled.

"Did I not tell you to clean up?" I asked as I set my briefcase and blazer down.

"I did," she pouted. "I cleaned up really well."

She pushed her glasses up her nose and put the book she was reading aside, carefully closing it around the bookmark and placing it on one of the stacks. She lay there with her legs splayed and her pussy dripping, pushing aside the fabric of her panties and teasing me. I didn't know how she did it, but every time I saw her naked, she was smooth as can be. It was driving me fucking insane.

"You built a fort," I accused her, and she rolled her eyes. Her tits jiggled when she sprang from the couch.

"I was just having some fun," she said, walking up to me.

"Not my idea of fun," I said.

She stopped in front of me, nearly naked and beautiful and so frustrated because she wanted me to touch her.

I reached out and pushed her glasses higher up the bridge of her nose. She grabbed my wrist and held it to her mouth, sucking on my fingers one by one. I watched her do it.

"You need to put those books away," I told her, and she shook her head no, her mouth latched onto three fingers at once. "I'm serious, Pet, they're annoying the fuck out of me."

She popped my fingers out of her mouth with a loud sucking sound.

"Make me?" It was a request, not a dare.

She made me so weak.

I grasped her wrists and pulled her towards me. Her hot little body was excited, her ass bumping against my cock and making me want to choke that disobedience out of her.

But no, we weren't playing that game tonight. I had something else in mind for my special little Pet.

My fingers traveled down her back, pressing down on her spine. I reached her ass, the thong she was wearing so miniscule it made me angry. I wrapped my forearm around her throat and she gasped when I caged her in.

"Panties off," I told her.

Her hands shook as she pulled them down. Her ass trembled against my groin and had to remind myself she was new to this, she couldn't take too much, she couldn't take it too hard.

"Please," she said in that raspy voice of hers, and I put my hand over her pussy, shielding her from myself. "Oh God, please, sir."

"Shut the fuck up," I groaned, and she did.

Her breath hitched and I could almost feel her holding back. Trying to stop herself from making a single sound.

"Breathe in," I whispered in her ear.

She wheezed when she did it, her body shaking.

"Good girl, now breathe out. Nice and deep, okay?"

She nodded and breathed for me. It didn't calm her down. She hyped herself up more until her body was a shaky fucking mess in my hands.

I whipped her around to look at her, my hand still between her legs.

"You know I'm not trying to hurt you?" I asked her roughly, and she nodded over and over again. "You know I'm just trying to teach you some manners?"

"Yeah," she whispered, and I smacked her cheek with my free hand. She gasped in shock when I did it, holding her cheek and giving me a searing gaze.

"Why?" she wanted to know.

"Is that how you answer me?" I asked her, and she shook her head. No. No, it wasn't. Damn right it wasn't. "So tell me fucking properly."

"Yes, Master," she said.

"Yes, Master what?"

"Yes, I understand you're not trying to hurt me." She swallowed thickly. "Master."

"Are you going to like this?" I asked her, my hand taking her throat. "Promise me you will, Pet."

"I will," she whispered. Her eyes were so trusting it was killing me. "I promise I will love it, Master."

I bent her over the kitchen table and she gasped when her tits hit the cold surface. She parted her legs on instinct but the rest of her body was frozen. I made her stay down, one hand on her head, one on the small of her back. Like a good little girl, she crossed her arms at the wrists on her back. It made my cock twitch in my pants.

I unzipped and the sound made her go feral, her body bucking and her pretty little mouth begging for me. She moaned when I pressed the tip of my cock against her pussy. She was dripping down her thighs and it didn't even make her flinch anymore.

"You want this, don't you?" I asked, and she nodded, looking at me over her shoulder. "Tell me how bad."

She stared at me with her eyes wide open, but she didn't say a word.

I dragged the tip of my cock over her pussy lips and she moaned softly.

"Please, I need it," she whispered.

"You *need* to give me more than that," I told her, wetting my dick with her juices and sliding it across her pert ass.

"Please, Master, I'll do anything, I need it so much." She licked her juicy little lips as she begged. "You've left me waiting for too long, please…"

"So you've been playing games with me, Pet?" I asked, and she looked away. "Come on, answer me."

"You wouldn't touch me," she tried to defend herself. "You would barely look at me."

I let my fingers slide over her lips, my cock pressing against the skin between her pussy and her tight ass.

"I'm looking at you now," I reminded her. "I'm touching you now…"

"But I need more," she mewled, and I grinned at her.

I made an impulse decision. I could fuck her pussy for hours, make her come so many times she wouldn't be able to hold herself up anymore. But I wanted something else.

With a groan, I spat down, and time stood still before she realized what I'd done. When she felt it running down the crack of her ass, she flinched. She knew what was coming.

"Are you going to…" she whispered, and I smoothed my hands over her ass before smacking it, hard. She yelped. "Please, I…"

"Shut up, Pet," I warned her, and she retreated into a place inside her, her body shaking. She didn't object and she didn't move away. I pressed my cock at her entrance and she kept so fucking still I thought she'd passed out.

"Ask for it," I told her gently, my hands smoothing circles into her ass.

She wouldn't.

"Fuck, Pet," I growled. "Don't make me go hard on your ass."

I pressed my thumb to her tight hole, rubbed my spit in.

But she didn't move. She didn't say a word.

My cock was throbbing, and I stroked it in long, jerking motions as her body waited beneath mine. I could've done anything to her in that moment and yet there was something missing. Something was wrong.

She was frozen to the spot. Paralyzed by something I didn't understand.

"Hold yourself open for me," I told her, and she let out a single sob, so desperate it made me want to force her to tell me what this was doing to her.

I zipped my cock back in my pants, even though it was throbbing. She didn't move an inch from that table. She was so fucking still.

I had no idea what had changed for her; what this was doing to her. But I needed to understand.

"Come off the table, Pet," I told her. "Let's go sit down."

Nothing. Not a word. Not the slightest of movements. She wasn't even there anymore.

I pulled her up by her hair and she didn't even react to the pain. When I stood her up, she crumpled, and I had to catch her in my arms so she wouldn't crash to the floor. My heart was pounding. I could only imagine how she felt. Something was so very fucking wrong.

She wouldn't move, so I made her.

She wouldn't walk, so I took her in my arms.

She wouldn't make a sound, so I filled the silence for her, talking about nonsensical things that had never mattered less.

I carried her into the bedroom and arranged the covers around her on the bed. I lay down next to her and she was on me in a second, holding me so close it was like she needed my body to live.

"Tell me," I said, and she shook her head no. "You have to."

"I won't," she whispered, and I pulled her hair and made her look at me.

"You will," I told her. "Fucking shit, Pet, tell me right the fuck now."

Her bottom lip was trembling and she tried to get the words out one by fucking one.

"I..."

I wanted to shake her. I wanted to make her explain so I could get rid of the problem. So I could punish her like she deserved and give her the aftercare she so badly needed. It was eye-opening. She was a girl. A fucking little girl in my bed, with my bruises on her, with my marks all over her skin. I hated myself.

"Say it," I said, and she shook her head.

I felt rage boiling inside me, not for Pet, but for whatever the fuck she was hiding from me. Because it must be really, really bad.

I pulled her on my lap and she clutched me tightly.

"Pet," I said, and I hated the gentleness of my own voice. "You need to tell me what that did to you. I need to understand where you went. I can't help you if you don't tell me."

"You don't need to help me," she said softly against my chest.

"Fuck that," I growled, holding her dainty little wrists in my hands, and jerking her up so she was forced to look at me. "Tell me, Pet."

"It's all over now," she said, and my blood boiled some more.

"What's over? Stop talking in fucking riddles, you're driving me fucking insane," I said. "Tell me why you spaced out, or I'll beat the shit out of everyone you know until I find out what happened to you."

She straddled my lap. She looked so small.

"There was a man," she said. "I won't tell you who."

"Okay," I got out through gritted teeth.

"When I was younger," she went on, toying with a stray strand of her hair, twirling and twirling it in loops around her finger. "He found me when I was really young, I didn't really know what I was doing."

"Do you know what you're doing now?" I asked.

"I was rubbing on the carpet," she said. "I didn't know… I didn't know you weren't supposed to do that. I was too young."

"Okay," I said. "And did he tell you that you weren't supposed to?"

"He…" She swallowed. Her eyes were darting here and there without really looking at anything. "He did."

"And did you stop?" I asked.

"Yeah," she nodded. Her eyes were filled with tears that she wouldn't let out. "I… He made me."

"How?" My hands were in fists and my stomach was in knots.

"He said he was going to teach me a lesson," she whispered. "That he was going to punish me. That he was going to teach me some manners."

My own words echoed back at me and I hated myself like never before.

"He made me pull my butt open," she went on, her voice calm now, like she wasn't even talking about herself. "He didn't spit on me. He went in dry, and he held my mouth so I wouldn't make a sound."

I stared at her. Name. I needed a fucking name.

"He said he'd have to keep doing it," she said. "Or I'd go bad again. That he had to remind me."

"How many times?" I interrupted her.

She pulled on a lock of pretty blonde hair.

"Seventeen," she said, reaching for my fingers. She brought my hand back, placing it on her neck. She moved her hair out of the way and pressed my fingertips to her skin. "Right there."

I felt the ridges in her skin. Tiny, deep little cuts. I didn't need to count them to know how many there were.

"Did you hurt yourself?" I asked her. It was hard to keep my shit together.

She nodded.

"Only on your neck?"

A shake of her head.

"But only those matter," she said. "The rest were for my parents and my teachers and my friends. These were just for me. So I wouldn't forget."

I took up her body and slammed it down on the mattress. Her chest was heaving and she wouldn't look at me. She wasn't crying. She wasn't even there with me, not really.

"How old were you?"

Her eyes zeroed in on mine and my heart beat a single time.

"I was five," she said. "And six. And seven. He stopped after that. He said I was…"

She choked back a sob and I stared at her, a fucking broken mess of a girl that I wanted to avenge.

"He said after that, I was too bad," she went on. "And he couldn't help me anymore. I was too dirty."

I lay on top of her and she sighed with relief when she felt my weight sink against her. She kissed my collarbone and I screamed against her skin because I was so fucking angry. She licked at my flesh with her little tongue and I cursed into her mouth.

"I'm going to fucking kill him," I told her.

"I know," she said. "That's why I'm not telling you who it was."

"But I… I fingered your ass." I remembered the sweet sounds she made, the way she resisted but loved it at the same time. I didn't know. I didn't fucking know.

"I know," she whispered. "I liked it…"

"What happened today?" I asked her. "Please, tell me."

"You…" Our eyes connected and she whispered her answer against my lips. "You were trying to punish me…"

Like him. She didn't need to say it.

I got up from the bed and slammed my fist into the wall. My knuckles opened up and blood spilled down my hand. She was next to me in a second. She was still naked, and my blood left gruesome marks all over her lithe body as she guided me to the bathroom.

She patched me up and I sat there like a fucking moron, plotting how I was going to kill this guy, whoever the fuck he was.

I could tell she needed it, needed to feel like she was helping someone after what she'd told me. But when she was done bandaging me up, I grasped her hand and pulled her between my legs.

"I'm so sorry," I told her. "I'll never do that again, Sapphire."

Her face paled and she evaded my eyes.

"Please, look at me."

"Don't call me that," she said, and her hands slid around my neck.

"Why not?"

"It's not who I am anymore," she whispered against my throat, licking a line up to my Adam's apple. "I'm Pet…"

# CHAPTER 11
## *Pet*

The apartment was a safe place. A good place. A home.

I didn't like leaving it anymore, unless it was with him. He took me out after that conversation, bought me tons upon tons of clothes, shoes, and makeup. I didn't protest. It felt good to be pampered, and from what I'd seen he had more than enough money to splurge on me. I let him pick out everything, too, mostly because I was curious to see what he'd want me dressed in.

He didn't like trousers, or God forbid, jeans. He didn't buy me a single thing without a skirt. Some of it tight, some of it nipped in at the waist and going out into a flowing shape. Always showing off something – my legs, my cleavage, my arms, or my back. Sometimes more than one thing. The shoes were all heels. Tall, in a rainbow of colors. Always with a strap around the ankle. Always tall enough so I could reach his lips in them. And the lingerie. Bras, thongs, stockings, garter belts. So much lingerie I couldn't have worn it all in a single lifetime. He liked that the most, I think.

He touched me carefully now. Soft caresses that made it obvious how hard he was holding back, his fingers rigid as they slid along my skin. I let him be gentle, because we both needed it. But I knew he would break eventually, and I couldn't wait for the moment he'd finally fuck me again.

He never touched my asshole. It had been two weeks and he hadn't done it. My pussy, my mouth, my hands, my tits. Never my ass. It was for the better, I guess. I wasn't sure it was helping anyone though.

With a full closet of new clothes, he took me to the hairdresser. He actually came with me and practically threatened the girl cutting it, telling her to keep it long. I giggled at the memory, how fucking intense he was being about an inch of hair. He didn't let them color it, either. Just cut it a little and make it glossy and pin-straight. And then came my nails, and my toes, and the Brazilian wax he insisted on even though he knew I shaved every day.

"It's not about that," he'd told me.

"What is it about, then?" I asked him, feeling angry. "You just want to control everything, old man."

"Of course I do," he smiled at me, and left the room.

The wax fucking hurt, and I made him aware of that as he made love to me that night, his fingers trailing lines down my smooth, waxed pussy. I scratched his back until it made me scream in frustration because he only laughed when my nails broke his skin.

He pampered and groomed me until he thought I was perfect. He primed and probed and coiffed and glossed me over until I looked like an elevated version of myself. But he still wasn't satisfied.

He circled me in his bedroom, and I felt exposed even though I was wearing lingerie and heels. A low growl escaped his lips as he stalked around the room.

"You're being weird," I said. "I look fucking amazing."

"That's not it," he said. "It's you... it's your attitude."

"What's wrong with my attitude?" I put a hand on my hip and glared at him, and he laughed at me.

"That. Just that, Pet."

He smoothed my now perfectly glossy hair and my cherry-red lips parted for him.

"You're disobedient," he said, and I giggled. "You fucking are. And I let you do it."

"Why?"

He wouldn't answer, just turned around and took something out of that chest of drawers he liked so much. Truth be told, I thought it was the ugliest fucking thing in the house.

He came back and my eyes zeroed in on what was in his hands. Just a phone. He put it in his pocket and tipped my chin back, making me look at him.

"Do you remember Angel?" he asked me, and I nearly spat in his face.

Bitch.

Bitch.

Fucking *bitch*.

"Yes," I hissed, and he laughed at me.

"I want her to come over tonight."

"No," I said.

"Who asked you?"

"Don't," I said, and hated the way my bottom lip trembled. "Don't bring her here. We don't need her."

"I'll do whatever the fuck I want," he said, and I hated him more than ever.

"And you'll be a good girl and take it, and do what I fucking tell you to do. Isn't that right, Pet?"

I looked away, my face burning.

"She'll be here in twenty minutes. Do you want to have some fun before she arrives?"

"No," I snapped.

"I think you're lying," he said, his hands running down my cheeks. "I really think you are, Pet."

I jerked against his touch and he smiled at me as he ran his fingers along my jaw, down my neck and over my tits.

"Why won't you trust me?" he asked.

Because you've fucked her before.

Because you want to hurt me.

Because you *will* fuck her again.

I didn't answer, instead I just looked away, and he sighed in response.

I heard the sound of his belt being undone, and my eyes found his. He stared at me as he took his belt off and moved behind me. I didn't know why, but I let him take my hands and wrap the belt around my wrists, tying them firmly in place. My chest heaved as he came to my front and made me look at him, not by moving my head, but by staring at me until I returned his gaze.

"You need to trust me, Pet," he said, his voice almost gentle. "I do everything for a reason."

Those fucking words again. Stupid fucking words.

He tugged on the belt and walked me over to the room we hadn't spent that much time in, the room where he made me watch him fuck Angel. I hated going there and I hated the memories it brought on. He didn't give me a choice.

As soon as we walked in, my eyes darted to the chair he'd had me sit on the last time. If he did that again, I swore to myself I'd fucking bite him.

But he led me to the bed instead, and bent me over unceremoniously with my ass up and my hands twitching helplessly behind my back. He placed the phone he'd gotten earlier in front of my face. I saw the camera recording.

I heard him getting naked, his clothes falling to the floor. Next thing I knew, he ripped the expensive lingerie off me, but I only regretted the loss of it for a second before his cock was pushing its way inside me.

"P-please," I managed to get out, my hands struggling against the belt. "Please, don't fuck me in here."

"No?" he teased, his cock sliding all the way inside. A single thrust was enough to make me moan out loud, and within the next few, I was whimpering his name. King. My King.

He fucked me slowly, but his thrusts were powerful. It was a terrible combination. I would've hated him if my pussy wasn't throbbing with the need to make him go just a little bit faster.

"Changed your mind?" he asked, and I begged so pathetically I knew I'd feel ashamed of myself in the morning.

He did that for so long it felt like days. Painfully deep, painfully slow thrusts that made my head spin. The sounds I made were making him groan out loud, and he gathered my mane of hair in both hands as he fucked me. I didn't understand how he was staying so calm, how he didn't just take advantage of the situation.

"You don't like me," I whispered through the moans. "You don't even like me."

"Why wouldn't I?" His voice was low and guttural.

"You… You're holding back," I whimpered. He slammed inside me and I cried out. "Fuck… You wouldn't be able to hold back like that if you liked me better…"

He leaned against me, my hair still in his hand and his cock twitching so deep inside me I thought I would soon come from it.

"You're never going to break me, Pet," he promised me. "I don't fuck for hours, I fuck for nights. And you, I'm going to fuck for a lifetime."

The doorbell rang and he pulled out of me, making me cry out so pathetically tears sprang from my eyes.

"Be a good girl and wait for your master," he said, put on a robe, and left the room.

I knew she was going to be with him when he came back and I hated them both for it.

I didn't hear a single sound this time. No conversation or laughter, nothing.

They walked back into the room. She didn't look as good as last time and it gave me a weird burst of energy.

She was wearing a T-shirt and shorts, simple sneakers on her feet. She looked dazed. Like she was on something. I had to do a double take to make sure it was the same girl.

King made her sit down on the bed with her eyes on me. I seethed but I didn't make a move. The phone was blinking at me.

"Angel is feeling upset today, Pet," he told me as he took off his robe. I heard her little gasp when she saw him and I fucking hated the bitch for it.

"I don't care," I told them both.

"I do," he said, his hands sliding down my ass. "So we're going to make her feel better, okay?"

"No," I hissed.

"Yes."

I heard him jerking his cock and then he pushed it inside me. So fast this time, no teasing, no foreplay, just all the way in until his balls slapped against me. Despite wanting to resist it, I heard myself cry out for him.

"Look at her," he said, and my eyes focused on the bitch.

She looked younger now. Still older than me, but more vulnerable than the last time she was here. No makeup, her face blotchy from crying. She was very pretty. But she didn't have him. I did.

She looked frail and broken. Good. She deserved it.

King started fucking me as if she wasn't there. It only took moments to make my eyes roll back and the first orgasm to rip through my body, leaving me helpless in its wake. He made me keep looking at her. She looked so upset and horny at the same time. I didn't really care what had happened to her, it felt too good to have taken her place. But the tears that leaked from her eyes, and the helpless little moans that left her mouth, made me feel a little bad.

We looked at each other as he fucked me. I couldn't look away anymore, and she seemed fixated on the little sounds I made when King fucked me. The moans, the whispers, the pleas, she lived for them, she absorbed them the second they left my lips.

She looked so sad, it made me think he'd want to fuck her just because of that. My fingers cramped behind my back and I came again with a frustrated cry. I didn't get it. Why was he doing this? What was the point?

He felt unbelievable inside me, filling me, stretching me. He grunted and put on a show for the bitch, for Angel. And I just lay there and took it, my eyes begging for an answer from her.

My body tired out too quickly after the first few orgasms. But I kept my eyes open, kept looking at her. And she lived for every move I made, for every sound that left my lips, and every twitch of my muscles.

"You're hurting her," I whispered, and King slammed himself inside me with a groan.

"Angel asked for this," he said, his cock pumping inside me so fast it felt like he was a machine. "She asked for all of this, Pet."

He was playing some fucked-up game again and I didn't even care. All I cared about was milking his cock with my pussy while Angel watched. Revenge. Sweet fucking revenge.

"Faster," I begged him, and Angel whimpered. "Faster, sir, please."

He grunted and his hands came down against my ass as he lost control.

Hard thrusts stretched me around him as he held me firmly in place. My hands were twitching under the belt and my eyes were so ready to roll back and let the darkness take over.

Angel stared at me with her lips parted and I smiled at her. Not in a selfish way. In a way I hoped would tell her it would all be okay.

She smiled back weakly and tears ran down her face. She really was pretty.

"Pet, clench your fucking pussy," he told me through gritted teeth, and I did. It made me come in an instant, and he was close behind, his cock jerking so deep inside me it felt like he was in my womb.

The pain was unbearable, and he slammed deeper for good measure. I screamed my release to the other girl in the room and she fucking sobbed for some reason I didn't understand.

I felt his cum dripping down my thighs as he pulled out. His hand smoothed my back and he leaned down to whisper in my ear. "Good girl," he said, "I'm proud of you, Pet."

And then he took the phone from the bed, the phone I'd completely forgotten about. He stopped the recording and I whimpered as he handed it over to Angel.

"There you go," he told her. "Just like I promised."

"Thank you, sir," she whispered, and I hated her again for this weird fucking intimacy she shared with him, even though he didn't even touch her. "When will I see you again, sir?"

His hands ran down my spine and I shivered.

"When my Pet wants you to," he told her with a smile, and she nodded. Fucking *never*.

She turned on her heel and walked out of the room on very shaky legs. He didn't go after her. Instead, he undid the belt around my wrists and prevented me from falling to the floor. He pulled me up on the bed and gathered me in his arms. His cum was still oozing from my pussy, but he didn't seem to care I was getting it everywhere. He held me painfully close.

"Why was she here?" I asked him, and he kissed the top of my head.

"You'll understand in time," he promised.

"I want to understand now."

"Such a fucking impatient Pet…" his fingers reached for my still hard nipples and he toyed with them, making me moan. "Just like she used to be."

I twitched in his arms but he wouldn't let me move.

"You're not the first one," he said against my hair. "You know that, obviously."

"Fuck you, fuck you, fuck you," I choked out.

"I'm not eighteen, Pet," he grinned against my hair. "I'm not some fucking teenager from your school. Of course there have been others."

"But you didn't fuck her this time," I said. "Why didn't you fuck her?"

He pulled on my hair gently.

"Because you didn't want me to," he said. "Because I didn't want to."

Relief flooded me.

"Why was she here, then?" I wanted to know.

"She was in a bad place," he said. "She… she thought last time meant something. It was a fuck-up on my part."

Hearing him admit that felt terrible, because it was for all the wrong reasons.

"So you thought it would make her feel better to make her watch you fuck another girl?" I asked. "Questionable logic that."

He laughed. "I know what I'm doing, Pet. If you stopped questioning me for just a fucking minute, you'd see why I do things the way I do."

"Sure." My voice was dripping with sarcasm, but I settled my body against his nonetheless.

"I think you and Angel are going to be good friends," he told me with a grin, and I bit his neck with all the strength I could muster. Of course, it only made him laugh.

TWO WEEK LATER

# CHAPTER 12
## *King*

**S**he was at her most beautiful when she let go. Of course, she never did that willingly. This pet held onto her pride like it was a fucking saving grace. We both knew the moment was coming when she'd break completely, but neither of us cared to acknowledge it. I let her be a little brat, indulged in her tantrums and her needy personality. But I was being too lenient with her; I knew it was only building up to the punishment of a lifetime. And when it happened, she'd be mine to break and own completely.

"I'm leaving," I told her that morning.

"Okay, I'll see you this evening." She was flipping through a magazine, barely looking up at me as she spoke.

"Pet, look at me," I told her, and she did so with a dramatic sigh. "I'm leaving for four days. I'll be back on Sunday."

"What?"

She was up on her feet in seconds, crowding my personal space like a yappy little puppy. She was obviously upset, and her bottom lip trembled as she glared at me.

"Why are you leaving me?" she asked, and I smoothed her hair down.

"I'm not," I promised her. "I'm just going on a business trip I've been putting off for way too long."

She looked so upset I wanted to pack her shit up and take her with me, but I knew from experience this distance was going to be good for us.

"Don't go," she begged, her hands finding their way around my neck. She looked sinful in one of my dress-shirts and a pair of panties, her hair messy and her lipstick smeared from sucking on my cock. "Please, don't go, King."

"Staying is not an option," I told her, and she sulked in my arms. "It's only four days, Pet."

"Yeah, but…" She let the words hang in the air, and we both knew what she was thinking about. "You're going to fuck someone else, aren't you?"

I unwrapped her arms from my neck and pinned them above her, pushing her against the wall. She let out a soft sound and I ran my free hand under the shirt she was wearing, making her shiver.

"I'm not," I told her firmly. "Listen to me, Pet. I'm never going to fuck anyone else while I'm with you."

"But Angel…" she protested, and I put my hand over her mouth to shut her up. Her eyes were needy.

"When I fucked Angel," I said. "You weren't my pet yet. You didn't live here. And I did it for a fucking reason."

I knew she hated me for not giving her specifics, but I didn't have time to deal with that.

"I won't fuck or sleep with or touch anyone else," I told her firmly.

"Do you promise and swear and promise again?" she asked sulkily, and I nodded.

"I want you to keep your phone on," I told her. I'd gotten her a new one a week or so ago. "At all fucking times. Don't go out if you don't have to, and answer my calls."

She clung to me for another second, muttering something I didn't understand against my chest. My hand circled her back.

"Come on, I need to go."

She let go of me and retreated to the couch like a good girl.

"I'll see you on Sunday, little Pet," I told her, and she just glared at me as I got my stuff and left. The image of her on that couch, with her knees held against her chest, would be burned in my mind until I came back in four days' time, hornier for her than ever.

What Pet didn't know was that I'd lied to her.

Not about the sleeping with someone else part. I wouldn't have been able to do that even if I wanted to. But I wasn't really going on a business trip either.

My driver took me to a hotel in the city, one where I had a suite reserved at all times. I left my shit in the room and fought the urge to call her an hour after I'd left. Too fucking needy.

Instead, I opened up my computer and found her. Sapphire Rose Faye, the girl she used to be. The girl I'd erased from her mind when I made her into Pet.

I found her social media shit, it wasn't hard at all. A different girl stared at me from those pictures.

She'd had her Facebook profile up for years, and I scrolled through hundreds of pictures looking for clues.

She looked so much different when she was younger. So… broken. Her eyes were empty, her posture defensive. She looked scared in even the most candid of pictures. Even the ones she took herself. Like she was constantly awaiting punishment. My hands tightened into fists when I remembered her confession.

I made a list of the people she interacted with most on social media, and dug up their information.

Then, I started calling them.

Friends, classmates, family. I called them all.

I pretended to be her long-lost family friend. I dug for information and wrote down everything I found out.

"Is she okay?" from one of her schoolmates. "I haven't seen her in months. I've been worried."

"She's fine," I promised. "I just spoke to her today, she's just been busy."

"I'm glad she found something," the girl said. "She always seemed a little lost to me."

I found out she cut off contact with everyone six months ago when she decided to take a gap year. All her friends from school were kept in the dark as she disappeared on them. They were more than willing to talk about her, tell me about her, and I drank up the information hungrily.

I even called her old roommate. Not the bitchy one, the one that whored around.

She wasn't as nice. It quickly became apparent her roommates didn't give a shit about her.

Very carefully, she had cut off anyone and everyone she meant something to. She'd removed herself from the equation until the only people left around her were those who didn't give a shit. And I had no fucking idea why. No idea what had happened after she graduated high school and left everyone that cared about her. But I was going to find out.

I wanted to get to the bottom of it badly. But I also realized three hours had gone by, and I couldn't fucking stand not hearing her voice a moment longer.

I called her on video and she picked up on the second ring.

Her hair was up in a towel, she wasn't wearing makeup anymore. She was wearing a nightie now, a cute silk and lace slip.

"Lonely?" I asked her, and she rolled her eyes. She moved on the bed and her movement gave me a glimpse of skin. It almost made me shiver.

"Bored," she replied. "What are you up to?"

Missing you.

Wanting you in my arms, where you fucking belong.

"Boring work shit," I told her.

She held the phone close so the only thing I could see were her full, plump lips.

"I want you in my pussy," she told me, and I groaned. "I want you fucking me right now. I guess I'll have to do it myself since you're not here."

The phone went between her legs and I glared at her as she slid a finger inside her wetness, moaning softly.

"Pet," I growled. "Hands off your fucking self, right now."

"You can't stop me," she giggled, but the sound was interrupted by a long, sensual moan. "I'm gonna do whatever the hell I want."

I gritted my teeth, contemplating ending the call. But I didn't.

"You'll regret that," I told her.

"I don't care."

"You will soon enough." I angled the phone towards my pants where my dick was straining against the fabric and she mewled. "Miss me?"

"Yes," she whispered. "So much."

"You want to act like a little porn star?" I asked her, and she laughed. "Fine, Pet. I'll give you what you want."

Her phone only showed a glimpse of her face, and it was twisted in a moan. I wanted to choke her for disobeying.

"What… what will you give me?" she gasped.

"I'm leaving now," I told her simply. "You're allowed to come only if you film it for me. I'll be waiting for the video in my inbox."

"You can't fucking-"

I disconnected the call.

And then I sat on that hotel bed like a fucking moron for what felt like ages, with my dick throbbing in my fist and my thoughts full of her. She was messing with my head and I was letting her.

My phone pinged with a message what felt like hours later.

The grab I made for it was so desperate I would've felt embarrassed about it if she were there with me.

I opened her message. Something was waiting for me.

It was her pretty face, contorted in pure ecstasy, the moment she came. Her hair hung around her shoulders, wet from the shower. Her eyes were rolled back, her cheeks red, and her mouth slightly parted. I memorized every detail of that fucking picture for later.

It wasn't a fucking video, though.

But it still made me spill my load all over my fucking fingers. I hadn't even noticed I'd started stroking myself until my cock was already pulsating with the need to explode.

She was going to pay for that, the little slut.

I ignored the picture, not bothering to tell her what she'd done to me. Better to leave her wondering.

Instead, I pulled up some more information on my laptop and filed through every single fact about Sapphire Rose Faye I could get my hands on.

Birthday, place of birth, astrological sign, parents' names.

A search for her parents revealed pictures of a boring looking couple. She definitely didn't inherit her beauty from either of them.

Her father worked in an office, a boring marketing job. Her mother worked in a library. I wondered if she was the one Pet had inherited her love of books from, and it made me smile.

My phone pinged with a message, and I glanced at it. It was her. Another picture. Even though my cock twitched at the thought, I refused to look at it. Served her right for disobeying.

I filed through websites and Facebook posts and tweets and even a blog post on some website Pet had since abandoned but I'd managed to find via an old email of hers.

It was nothing like the girl I knew.

My Pet was beautiful, confident and cheeky.

Sapphire Rose Faye was shy, sweet and broken. Really fucking broken. Her eyes screamed it from every picture and her words trembled with her need to be understood.

What had changed? What happened six months ago when she up and left her life?

My phone pinged again, and this time, I picked it up.

The first picture she'd sent was followed by a picture of her licking her fingers. Those big baby blues fixed on the camera, her manicured talons all the way inside her mouth. Dirty girl.

And the last one was confusing. I could barely make out what was in it.

I peered closer, making out the shape of her legs. She was kneeling on my bed, our bed. One of her hands was on her thigh and the other one held the phone up. She'd spilled something on the bed.

*Look what I did for the first time!* her caption read.

I stared at the fucking picture and my blood boiled.

She.

Fucking.

Squirted.

Without me.

I resisted the urge to call her and tell her off. I set my phone aside after turning it off so the temptation wouldn't be so fucking great. I went back to my laptop, back to Pet's life before she met me, and I buried myself in the sorry facts of her past while my mind fought off images of her fucking her own pussy so hard she'd gushed all over our bed.

Little fucking bitch.

She was going to pay for that.

She was going to regret taking that moment from me.

Once I got home, I'd really fucking break her. And it was about fucking time.

⋘⋙

*I kept my phone off* for the next three days, resorting to using my business cell, which didn't have Pet's number, and which she didn't know about. I didn't check the email she had; I didn't acknowledge her in any fucking way. Apart from the constant turmoil in my head, and apart from the digging I was doing.

At the end of my trip, I wasn't much closer to unlocking Pet's secrets. I didn't understand why she'd upped and left her bright future. I wasn't a single step closer to finding out who abused her when she was a little girl. But I understood her better. I knew she was troubled. I knew she pushed people away, hoping they'd prove how much they needed her, and I knew they'd always let her down. But I wasn't going to.

I also used the time away from her to take care of some other shit that needed sorting, and I was pleased with the results.

I packed up my stuff on Sunday and grunted a hello at my driver who picked me up from the hotel. He didn't comment on the fact I hadn't left my hotel room in days. Just as well.

On the ride home, which took about an hour, I finally pulled out my phone and turned it on.

I kind of expected silence. I thought maybe she would've sulked after not getting a reply from me, gone quiet and ignored me to try and punish me for not calling her back.

But no.

My phone pinged once.

Twice.

Three times.

And then I stopped counting and started looking.

There were pictures, videos, texts. There were voicemails. There were threats, there were random thoughts, there were tears. She gave me everything on a silver platter.

I scrolled through the pictures first.

Sexy.

Sweet.

Some were fucking unbelievably hot. Close-ups of her dripping wet pussy.

Then the voicemails.

A lot of crying, a lot of begging.

Messages filled with empty threats.

And the videos, the fucking videos.

So many of her pussy. So many of her disobeying. So many of her fucking herself. One of her actually squirting onto the sheets, her buckling legs and agonized mewl enough to make me fucking hard.

I was getting worried for her, because after all of that, I was really going to fucking hurt her.

I went through it all when my phone pinged again – another video. I opened it and wished I hadn't.

She was in a club.

She was drunk.

She stuck her tongue out at the camera and a guy behind her laughed as she winked at me.

"Not gonna be home tonight," she told the camera with a grin. "Don't wait up."

I smashed the phone against the window of the car until it was nothing but garbage.

I ordered my driver to hit up the club I thought I recognized from that fucking video.

I told myself to stay calm and not overreact, and with every excruciatingly slow minute that passed, I knew it would be impossible.

It was time for Pet's first real punishment.

# CHAPTER 13
## *Pet*

"*Come here, princess.*"

"Fuck off."

I pushed the guy off me and wobbled away in my too-high heels. The alcohol was clouding my judgement, and I realized I might not have chosen the best night to have my first drink.

And second.

And third…

I managed to get into the club with a bunch of guys I met outside, but they wouldn't leave me alone anymore, and I just wanted to go home. But my pride wouldn't let me. I'd sent King that video; I needed to stick it out.

I knew he was going to punish me. But at that point, anything would've been better than the cold shoulder he'd been giving me for the past four days, no matter how hard I tried to get his attention.

The weekend had passed slowly, with a lot of self-doubt and worrying. I hated being ignored. I hated the way he seemed to just forget I existed.

My mind was constantly plagued with thoughts of him with someone else. What kind of business trip could he have taken over the weekend? Surely, he was lying to me.

I stumbled to the bar and sat down on a stool, but the guy still wouldn't leave me alone. He came after me, his hands on my back and so close to my ass it was making me feel really uncomfortable.

"Would you please leave me alone?" I asked him, but he just laughed.

"Little bitch," he said. "You think you can use me to get your teenage ass in here and not even let me touch you?"

My face blanched as he sat down next to me.

"I fucking own this club, princess," he said with a sly smile.

"You don't," I objected.

"I do." His smile was so self-righteous. The face I thought was handsome only a few hours ago was now almost ugly. I wanted King. I wanted to go home. "And I'm going to show you how much fun it can be."

"I'd like to go home," I said in a small voice. "Could you call me a cab please?"

The guy leaned in closer and grinned against my ear.

"And why the fuck would I do that, princess? We've only just started having some fucking fun, haven't we?"

He grabbed my wrist and forced me up. I mewled in pain but no one heard me over the loud music. He walked me across to a raised VIP area and made me sit down in a booth with him. We had a good view of everything below us and this just didn't feel right at all.

I sank into the red cushiony seat as the guy ordered drinks. I'd long since forgotten his name, and my body was starting to give in to the situation at hand. I felt so fucking dizzy from the drinks I'd downed at the bar.

I pulled my phone out of my purse and the guy glared at me.

"You're gonna check your phone while you're with me?"

I tried to ignore him, but he snatched the phone from my hand and made me look up at him.

"Please," I begged him. "I need to let… someone know I'm okay."

"Someone?" he laughed in my face. "Got a boyfriend, princess?"

I bit my bottom lip. "It's… complicated."

"Not anymore," he grinned at me. "When you're with me, you don't have one."

He smashed my phone on the floor and crushed it beneath his foot.

I was up in a second, panicking.

"You fucking jackass!" I screamed at him. All he did was laugh. "You're going to get me in so much trouble!"

"You want trouble?" he said. "You scream trouble from those gorgeous blowjob lips to your pretty fucking heels, princess."

I whimpered as he pressed me against the wall of the booth.

"You messed with the wrong guy," he said against my ear. "Now you gotta pay, little girl."

"Let me go!" I struggled against him, a surge of adrenaline pulsing through my body. I pushed him off and the guy stumbled back, giving me a vicious glare.

I tried to make a run for it, but a bouncer blocked my path. I looked up at him with my eyes fearful, but he didn't even acknowledge me. The guy's long fingers wrapped around my forearm.

"Not so fast," he told me. "We're not done until I say we're fucking done."

I caught a glimpse of King in the crowd below us and my heart leapt. "You shouldn't mess with me," I told the guy. "I know some people who…"

The guy glanced to where I'd looked, but it wasn't King at all. I must have imagined it. Shit.

"Sure," he laughed, looking back to me. "I know everyone, princess. No one you know is a threat to me. Now get the fuck over here and sit on my lap before I drag you over by your hair."

And then there was a fist in his face.

And blood splattered his expensive shirt.

He stumbled to the floor and the bouncer who was helping him moments earlier just stared.

"I am so sorry, sir," he said in a shaky voice. A man of his stature looked ridiculous apologizing like that. "We had no idea she was with you…"

"You're fucking done," a familiar voice barked at him. "And this joke. Get him out of my face before you leave or I'll beat you both into a fucking pulp."

The bouncer picked up the club owner and half-carried him out of the booth. A hand gripped my forearm and I cried out from the pain… and the relief. He pulled me flush against his body, and my ass pressed against his crotch.

"Big mistake, Pet," he muttered. "Big fucking mistake."

We stood there, frozen, for what felt like hours. I couldn't even hear the music or the sounds of the club. All that mattered was him, and that he'd found me, come back for me, saved me.

"Take me home," I begged as his fingers ran down my spine. It felt like I was naked in my tiny dress and the stupid heels.

He didn't say a word. Just kept standing behind me until my whole body was shivering, begging for release, just from feeling his breath on my neck.

"Walk over to the bar," he whispered into my ear, his hands circling my waist. My body would have responded even if I hadn't wanted to.

I forced myself to rip my hips out of his arms. I didn't look back over my shoulder as I walked to the bar, but I felt him follow me slowly.

His voice was soft in my ear.

"Place your hands on the bar," he said. "Palms down."

I hesitated and it made him growl in my ear.

"Fucking right now."

My hands flew up and I placed them on the bar. It was cold and sticky from spilled drinks. It felt like everyone was staring at me, so I focused my eyes on the bar and pretended I wasn't dying of embarrassment.

King came up behind me. Really close, his crotch touching my ass.

"Bend over," he told me, and I obeyed with my mind reeling. "Order a drink for me."

I tried to get the bartender's attention when I felt King's hands on my ass. He tugged on the hem of my too-short dress and pulled it up unceremoniously. I gasped so loud I was sure everyone could hear it over the thumping music. He pulled my dress above my ass, his body hiding it from other people's sight. His hands slid over my ass, long, sweet stroking motions that made me swallow my gasp.

"What did you want, miss?"

I could barely look at the bartender as King's fingers slipped between my legs, outlining the wet lips of my pussy.

"I…" I just stared at him.

"Go on," King whispered in my ear. "Order me a drink, Pet."

"An Old Fashioned," I gasped.

The guy nodded and King fucked my pussy with three fingers. I clenched around him and he pressed his groin closer, hiding what he was doing.

"Don't you dare fucking come," he growled in my ear. "If you do, you'll only make things worse for yourself."

"Please," I whispered. "Just take me home. Please, I just want to go home, I want to be with you…"

"Sure didn't seem that way to me, *slut*," he grinned against my skin, his fingers fucking me deeper and making me mewl out loud. Thank God for the music. Thank God for the noise.

He finger-fucked me almost maliciously and I gripped the bar for dear life. The bartender returned what felt like hours later and gave me a look. I guess from where he was standing, King just looked like another customer at the already full bar. He probably had no idea what he was doing to me.

"Here you go, sweetheart," he said with a big smile. "Little young to be here, aren't you?"

"I…" I swallowed again, grabbing the drink. "It's not for me."

King's fingers curled up inside me and my legs nearly gave out.

"Whose is it?" the guy asked and I nearly shouted at him to fuck off.

King took the drink from the bar and grinned at the guy, taking a sip. His fingers went so deep my knees buckled, and he held me up by my waist.

"Mine," he said simply, and I rolled my eyes back as he pulled his fingers out and put my dress back in place.

He finished his drink and I stood there shaking. Then, he gripped my forearm and led me out of the bar. His fingers held on tightly enough for me to know he was going to leave a mark.

He led me to his car and made me sit. His hands left me and I sat there feeling utterly alone as the driver took us back to King's apartment.

When we arrived, I nearly toppled over on my way to the elevator. The drunkenness was starting to fade, but I felt terrified.

We arrived in the apartment, and as soon as the front door closed, he slipped his jacket off and rubbed his wrists. He wouldn't look at me, but my heart was pounding needily, because it had been four days and I wanted him so fucking badly, despite what he might do to me.

"Strip," he told me.

I'd never done anything faster. Dress, lingerie, jewelry, until all I had left on were my heels.

"Those too," he growled.

I hesitated.

"Did I fucking stutter?"

The heels followed. Usually he liked it when I kept them on.

He didn't look at me as he sat down on the couch. I stood frozen to the spot.

"Lie down on the floor."

I did, with my heart pounding.

"Spread your legs."

They were spasming hard from my nerves, but I did it, my eyes on his.

"Wider."

Wider.

"Fucking wider."

Even wider.

"Hold your pussy open," he told me, and I did. "One hand only. With your other hand, slap your clit."

I made a move to do it, but he stopped me by holding up a hand.

"Not like you're fucking playing. I want to hear the slap. I want it to fucking hurt."

"S-so you do it," I whispered, and he stared at me.

"You think I feel like touching you?" he asked me. "After all the shit you've done?"

Tears sprang from my eyes and my palm shook above my pussy. Despite everything I was fucking soaked. I'd never wanted him more.

"Seven slaps," he told me. "As I count you down. You better make them hurt if you want to make it up to me."

I whimpered and waited for the first number. He was torturing me to the point I craved those slaps, craved any sort of contact with my needy clit.

"Seven," he said.

My hand shook as I slammed it down. Too gently. It barely hurt.

He kneeled down next to me, his fingers grasping my throat so softly I cried out, because I needed so much more.

"Do you understand this is a punishment?" he whispered against my lips, and I couldn't stop nodding. "Why aren't you treating it like one, then?"

I trembled.

"Six."

His fingers didn't move from my throat as I slapped myself harder. This time, it made me cry out.

"Five."

The slap echoed around the room and my body twitched.

"Four."

I bit my lip so hard I felt blood trickle down my jaw. That one really hurt.

"Three."

I arched my back off the floor and howled like an animal.

"Two. Pet?"

My eyes found his through the haze.

"You're going to come with the last one, Pet. Yes?"

I nodded. My clit was on fire.

"Do it!" he said and my breath hitched as I slammed my palm down again, and my clit begged for more.

But he waited.

He waited for ages, until my whole body was shaking, trembling, eager for the last number, eager for him to just. Let. Me. Fucking. Come.

"One," he said. His voice was gentle, but his grip tightened around my throat.

I watched him as I brought my palm down against my pussy, hitting myself so hard I screamed.

He put his mouth on mine and tasted my tears and my blood and my screams, and I came crashing down with only one thing on my mind.

*Please don't let this be the end for us.*

I'd never had an orgasm that long. It wouldn't stop.

He caged my body under his and pinned me down. He licked the traces of my tears from my cheeks and pinned my hands above my head when they sought him out.

"You're fucking killing me," he groaned against my throat. "You're making me… so fucking weak."

I mewled and his free hand found my ass, lifting me up until my pussy was pressed against the bulge in his pants.

My clit was pulsing from those slaps, I needed him so badly I could beg for hours, if only for one taste.

"I should let you go," he muttered against my chest, and my nipples tightened at his breath.

"Don't," I begged, feeling delirious. "Please, don't, I'll do anything. I'm so sorry. I'm so fucking sorry…"

His hips started grinding against me and I cried harder. We were so fucked up. This whole… relationship, or arrangement, or whatever the fuck it was, was going to destroy us.

I was never going to leave, though.

"You should go," he said. His voice was rough.

"I won't. I'm never going to leave."

His fingers found the zipper of his pants and he pulled out his cock. I almost cried with relief.

"You need to go," he said again, and I grabbed onto his hair as he pushed inside me.

"I'll never leave," I said. "I'm never fucking going."

He looked into my eyes, his cock throbbing inside me.

"I wasn't supposed to fuck you," he groaned. "Or touch you. You're being a fucking brat…"

"I'll do anything," I said again. "I thought you were leaving, I thought you were done."

He groaned and started fucking me, and my eyes rolled back and my pussy took all of him in and clenched around his length.

"I'll never be fucking done," he growled. "Don't you fucking see that?"

I fought the orgasm that was building inside me and clawed at his back.

"You…" I swallowed. "You need to punish me…"

He grabbed my jaw and fucked me until I cried.

"I. Fucking. Can't," he groaned and my heart pounded. "I fucking can't!"

# CHAPTER 14
## *King*

**W**e *didn't talk about it again.*

And she got better, she did. I could tell she was consciously trying not to upset me. But it also meant she was walking around me on eggshells, twitching at every sign of trouble and biting her lip nervously at any sign of conflict. It was making me angry. She acted almost as if she was afraid of me, and I didn't fucking like it.

We'd fucked. Every day. The sex was insane. Intense, crazy. She'd end up in tears or passing out and I'd dig the hole I was in just a little deeper with every touch I shared with my Pet.

It was the weekend, and I had special plans for Pet. Of course, she had no idea yet, so when I came home that Saturday and gave her a big cardboard box, she gave me a quizzical, but excited look.

"What's this?" she asked me, and I grinned.

"Open it."

Her hands shook as she took off the lid and sifted through the tissue paper. She pulled out the garment, a pretty black dress I thought would go well with her complexion. Her eyes widened as she looked it over, draping it over her arm. The dress was modest for my taste, but still sexy enough. It was short, with long sheer sleeves and bejeweled cuffs. It would look beautiful on my Pet.

"Thank you, it's gorgeous," she said softly as I shrugged my jacket off. "What's the occasion? Are we going somewhere?"

"Dinner," I told her, and she perked up. I hadn't really taken her out anywhere. We'd been cooped up in the apartment for weeks.

She grinned at that. "Where to?"

"La Maison. I got a table for four in an hour, so you might want to get ready now, Pet."

"A table for four? Who are we going with?" she asked, and I walked over to her, smoothing her hair away from her face.

"Your parents." I grinned, and she swallowed, hard.

"My parents?"

"Yes," I confirmed. "I spoke to your father a few days ago."

"And you didn't think to tell me?" She was getting feisty, and I gave her a warning look. She backed down right away, and I almost regretted it. "One hour?"

"Yes, an hour, so be a good Pet and get ready now."

She nodded meekly and made a move for the bathroom. I grabbed her wrist and pulled her towards me.

"It'll be fine," I told her. Her eyes were dancing over my face, trying to understand why I was doing this. "We'll have fun. I won't be a dick, promise."

"Okay," she nodded. "I wasn't worried about... that."

"What then?" I rubbed my thumb along the inside of her wrist and she moaned softly.

"I didn't think… you'd want to meet my parents. I guess it's a bit of a surprise."

"I want to know everything about you, Pet," I told her simply. "And don't worry. I'll call you Sapphire in front of them."

I expected her to giggle, but she frowned instead.

"What should I call you?" she asked softly.

"Whatever you want to," I told her, and let her go.

She took her time getting ready, but once she walked out into the living room again, I was left speechless. She looked fucking stunning. That mass of hair, tumbling down her back in pretty waves. Her heels were high and her dress was much too short. Perfect. She'd painted her lips a cherry-red I wanted to ruin. I made a promise to myself to do just that. Preferably in the restaurant.

"Shall we go, Pet?" I asked her, and she nodded.

I took her hand and led her downstairs to the car. As always, my driver was sitting in the front and the partition was up. She got into the backseat and I followed behind. For the whole ride, Pet fidgeted with the hem of her dress and would barely look at me.

"Why are you nervous?" I finally asked her.

She gave me a fleeting look, but no answer.

"Pet." My voice held a warning tone. "No fucking secrets."

"I haven't seen them," she admitted, looking out of the window at the moving city outside. "My parents. I haven't seen them in a while."

Six fucking months, I wanted to remind her.

Six months of them being worried fucking sick.

Her father nearly crying with relief when he talked to me on the phone.

Why, Pet?

Why?

I didn't say a word. Instead, I pulled her into my lap and held her close, her head resting in the crook of my arm while we drove towards the restaurant.

She nearly stumbled when she stepped outside, but I caught her hand and helped her into the building. I felt so many pairs of eyes on us as we walked inside. And why shouldn't they look? We were a good-looking couple. Let them fucking stare.

I led Pet to my usual table. Her parents were already there, fidgeting in their seats. Their faces brightened as soon as they saw her, though her dad's expression was a little shocked when he noticed the transformation of his beautiful daughter.

*Mea culpa.*

I smiled at them and shook their hands.

They were both kind people. Simple, but kind.

The theory of either of her parents abusing her, or even knowing about it, disappeared from my thoughts as soon as we sat down. Pet sat between her mother and me, and the woman, Sylvie, placed a hand on hers and stared at her adoringly.

"Sweetheart, we've missed you so much," she told her. "You have no idea how worried–"

"Have you ordered?" I cut in smoothly.

"Err," Pet's father looked embarrassed. "The menu's in French, I believe. We're not really fluent."

"Would you like me to recommend my favorite?" I asked.

"That would be fantastic," Pet's father, Robert, said.

I ordered for the whole table, though Pet cut in and changed her order from the duck to the chicken. I was pretty sure it was only so she could prove to her parents she was still somewhat in charge. I knew she hated chicken, called it dry every time we had it. But I let her do it, and even gave her a smile.

The conversation was stilted at first. Her parents seemed desperate to find out what had happened, and Pet kept steering the chat away from that. Sensing the discomfort at the table, I finally took matters into my own hands.

"Your daughter is absolutely lovely," I told Sylvie, and she beamed with pride. "I haven't met a young woman as talented, beautiful or… stubborn as she is."

Pet rolled her eyes and my hand sneaked under the table, squeezing her thigh. She nearly jumped in her chair.

"We always knew Sapphire would be successful," Robert told me with a grin. "She always had that special something."

"Well, you must know," I said, "I have every intention of pushing her to her limits."

Pet shifted uncomfortably but her parents nodded obliviously.

"I'll make sure she's used to her full potential," I added, almost feeling her discomfort.

"We truly appreciate it, Mr. King," Sylvie gave a solemn nod.

"Please," I said, "call me Hayden."

I fucking hated that name.

"Hayden," she smiled.

"I must ask," Robert said. "What exactly is your… relationship with our daughter?"

I stroked Pet's thigh. Her skin was hot to the touch. Almost scalding. But I smiled smoothly as if the question didn't bother me at all.

"I would say we've gotten very close in a relatively short time," I said. "I can safely say your daughter means a lot to me, and I think the world of her. I only hope she thinks the same of me."

They ate up my words, though Pet glared at me through the rest of dinner.

Her parents ate their food with gusto, relaxing with each glass of wine the maître d' poured for them. Just as well.

I peppered the conversation with the questions I needed answers to.

What was she like as a child?

Did she have any friends that left, maybe moved away?

Big family?

Religious?

I felt her eyes on me. Felt her getting angrier and angrier as the dinner went on. When I asked about her moods when she was younger, she pushed my hand off her lap and pushed her plate away.

I didn't give a shit. I needed to know. I needed to know every fucking brain cell in that head of hers if I wanted to make her mine, really mine. And I didn't give a fuck if she liked it or not.

Her parents remained oblivious, and answered every question in detail. Not that it helped, or brought me any closer to the truth.

We said our goodbyes two hours later, with Sylvie and Robert tipsy, and Pet furious.

"Sapphire, you have to promise to stay in touch," her mother begged. The wine she'd had added a tone of desperation to her voice as she clung to her daughter's hand.

"I will," Pet said noncommittally.

"Are you safe?" her dad asked. "Where are you staying?"

Pet looked away uncomfortably.

"She's perfectly safe, Robert," I promised her father. "She's staying with me."

He seemed both surprised and relieved by that information.

"And here," I added, pulling out a business card and scribbling on it. "Pet's…"

Fuck.

"Sapphire's number."

I smiled them a charming smile, and it seemed as if they hadn't noticed. Pet was glaring at me, though, but I pretended not to feel the intensity of her gaze.

"Thank you so much," Sylvie gushed. "Sapphire, I'll call you next week."

"Okay," Pet said softly.

She seemed surprised when her parents hugged her, unsure of how to react to the contact. She relaxed after a few seconds, and it pleased me to see it.

I shook her father's hand, but her mother surprised me by giving me an extremely uncomfortable hug.

"Thank you for everything, Hayden," she said, and I cringed hearing my name.

"You're most welcome. And we will see you soon," I promised them.

I made sure they got a cab back home and tipped a valet handsomely to drive their car back to their home.

And then I led Pet into our own car, fully expecting her to lay it on me as soon as the doors closed.

"What the fuck was that all about?" she hissed.

No surprise there. "What?" I asked her. "I wanted to meet your parents, Pet."

"The fucking twenty-one questions," she spat out. "Why are you digging?"

"Why shouldn't I be?" I asked her. "I like to know my pets very well."

My fingers cupped her chin and she groaned, looking away.

"You make me feel so fucking worthless," she muttered, and it made me laugh.

"Yeah, I can see that," I told her. "Treating you to a new dress, and a nice dinner with your estranged parents. Fuck, I really am a jackass, aren't I?"

Her eyes shot daggers at me, and on an impulse, she climbed on my lap and straddled me almost forcibly.

"You think you pull all the strings, don't you?" she hissed against my lips.

I took her wrists in my hands and pinned them behind her. Stroked her pretty neck and made her moan like a needy little kitten. The tough girl act was gone in seconds.

"I want to take care of you," I told her simply. "So you better fucking let me, Pet."

"So stop making me feel inferior," she said, a sad tinge to her voice. "Stop talking about… the others."

I tugged on her arms in warning.

"I'm being honest here, Pet."

*Which is more than I could say for you*, I wanted to add, but bit my tongue.

"Your honesty is hurtful," she complained, and I laughed against her lips.

"No," I told her. "This is."

I bit into her shoulder roughly and her hips bucked against mine. She responded to pain like she fucking craved it. I wasn't sure whether it excited me or made me fucking upset. But the way her body reacted… It was like a chemical reaction. Like she couldn't fucking help it. Like she needed it.

I bruised her throat with my mouth and she melted in my hands.

"I'm going to find out everything," I muttered against the hollow of her throat. "Every single fucking thing that defines you, Pet."

"No," she protested weakly.

"Yes," I promised her. "And by the time I'm done with you…"

I pressed my thumb down on her throat and she gasped, her breathing ragged.

"You're going to scream your secrets at me."

"No," she mewled.

"Yes." I was determined about that. "And once I know them all…"

I could feel the heat of her pussy against my crotch.

"I'm going to make it all better," I said, my voice gentle. Her breath hitched at that, and I caressed her neck softly. "I'll make it all okay, Pet. I fucking promise."

## CHAPTER 15
*Pet*

The walls in that apartment were closing in on me.

I felt caged. I felt trapped.

King was obsessed with my past.

If I didn't know before, after the dinner with my parents, it was painfully obvious how badly he wanted to find out what happened to me. And there was no way in fucking hell I was going to tell him. It would ruin everything between us.

Instead of picking fights with him like I usually would, I just avoided any kind of conversation. We'd never fucked as much as we had during those next few weeks. My pussy was permanently swollen and my ass always bruised, and I didn't care. I loved it. Every moment I spent with him made me fall for him more, not that I would ever admit it to him – though it was probably pretty obvious.

I was getting claustrophobic, though. Apart from some shopping trips and the dinner with my parents, we hadn't really gone anywhere. And while I liked it in his apartment, it was always just the two of us, and it was almost too intense to handle.

I told him I had to take a day off that morning.

"A day off?" he asked me with a grin. "To do fucking what, exactly?"

I fidgeted on the spot. What on earth was I supposed to tell him? That it was getting harder and harder not to beg him to keep me with each day that passed? I was pretty close to breaking already.

"I'm going out," I told him. "Maybe the library, maybe the coffee shop, I don't know."

He gave me a contemplative look as he put his tie on.

"You know I'm not keeping you here," he reminded me, and I nodded.

He wasn't. But I was so desperate to please him I just didn't leave, in case he needed me.

"Be back by the evening," he said. "6 p.m., okay? I want to make us dinner."

"Okay," I nodded. He was a good cook. I liked it when he fed me.

He came up to me and left a fleeting kiss on my cheek. I felt myself blushing as he took his stuff and headed out of the door.

And then I was all alone, and the freedom was terrifying.

I couldn't even leave for hours. I paced the apartment and spent hours choosing an outfit before settling on a simple summer dress and the Converse sneakers I'd brought with me from my old apartment. If King had seen me in those, he'd be fucking pissed. He hated flat shoes. It made me smile.

I left the apartment a few hours later, and wandered around the neighborhood aimlessly. I ended up at the train station, unsure of how and why I got there. King always told me to just get a cab and pay with a card he'd given me, but I didn't feel like it. I didn't want everything I did to be influenced by him.

I got on the train and traveled for hours. Aimlessly. Through towns and landscapes that I didn't know. I changed trains, I changed seats. I stared out of the window not knowing where I was, and it felt good to get lost, if only for a little while.

I ended up in a small town only an hour or so away from the suburbs where my parents lived. On an impulse, I decided to pay them a visit.

The ride was too short, and in a mere forty-five minutes, I ended up on the doorstep of my parents' home. It was afternoon by then, so I knew they'd be home from their jobs.

I knocked on the door, a knock so soft I almost prayed they wouldn't hear it, and my visit could go unnoticed.

But no such luck – the door opened a second later, and my mother's face lit up when she saw me.

"Hey, Mom," I muttered, and she pulled me into a tight hug.

I usually hated being touched like that, but this time around, it felt good. I let her hold me, lead me into the house, and make a fuss about me coming over. She called Dad downstairs and he seemed just as delighted to see me there. They sat me down in the living room, in the overly stuffed armchair I'd always hated. Mom made some tea and brought cookies to go with it. I crumbled them in my hands, sipped the hot drink, and pretended my head was in the same place as my body.

It didn't take them long to start asking questions about me, about King, about us.

"He's a real gentleman," Mom said, nodding vigorously. "We were so glad to meet him, Sapphire. He seems like a wonderful man."

"He is," I agreed softly. "He's helped me a lot."

"Of course we can't help but wonder…" Mom and Dad shared an

uncomfortable look, and Dad cleared his throat before going on. "We were wondering what exactly your relationship is, with… Hayden?"

"I…" I looked at the teacup in my hands, my fingers gliding along the porcelain. I knew this cup. I knew every chip and dent and pattern in it. I knew this house. Once upon a time, it used to be a home. "We are together."

Mom clapped her hands with excitement, saying, "Together? As in, dating?"

"I guess you could say that," I laughed nervously. What the fuck else was I supposed to tell them?

"Oh, you young people and your no labels," Dad grinned. "Honestly, Sapphire, I'm so glad you met someone like him. He seems like an amazing person, and a great businessman to boot."

I gave him a blank look. I didn't really know much about King's job apart from the fact that he owned a building in the city. I'd never been to his office, and I'd never asked for details. It seemed like a minor, unimportant detail that had nothing to do with the two of us.

"He's very successful," Dad went on. "Owns several buildings in the city. I checked him out, on the internet."

I almost cringed at his words. My parents were so painfully suburban it hurt, and it was very obvious they hadn't grown up in the city.

"He's a good man," I said. "He's taking care of me."

"I'm so glad," Mom smiled and patted my leg. I winced, and she gave me a worried look. "What is it, honey?"

"Nothing," I smiled brightly.

"Well, you'll have to bring him over sometime soon," Dad said. "We would love to introduce him to everyone."

"Sure," I lied. No way in fucking hell was I doing that.

I got up from the armchair, and my napkin fluttered to the floor. I bent down to get it, and when I did, my mom gasped. I got back up and gave her a weird look. She was staring.

"What?" I asked.

She was looking at my legs, "You're hurt," she said, the worry obvious in her voice and I winced at her words.

I didn't even know which part of me she meant. Of course I was hurt.

"What do you mean?" I asked her, and she got up from the sofa, came over to me, and lifted my skirt over my ass.

"Mom!" I cried out, but she ignored me, looking at my exposed butt.

"Your... behind." She gasped again, a hand flying to her mouth. "I saw when you bent over... Your skin, Sapphire! What on earth happened?"

I tried to remember.

I'd been spanked a few days earlier. He didn't want to, even though I'd misbehaved on purpose. So I'd begged and begged and cried and cried until he'd turned my ass black and blue.

"Oh, Mom." I gave her a big smile and pulled my dress down. "It's nothing, I promise."

Dad was staring at me and Mom burst into tears.

"What the hell, Sapphire?" he said, his voice shaky. I tried to ignore the fact my dad had seen my butt. "Did that man hurt you?"

"Of course not," I said. "He did nothing I didn't ask for, Dad." God, I was burning up here.

"What on earth..." Mom cried harder.

"Calm down!" I giggled nervously, realizing I was only making things worse. "Mom, Dad, seriously. I deserved it."

"What?" Dad glared at me. "Are you kidding me? You let that man hurt you?"

"It's not like that at all," I stuttered. I really was getting us both in trouble now. "I… You just wouldn't understand, I'm sorry."

"Understand what?" Mom wheezed through the tears. "That the man you're seeing is beating you?"

"He's not," I insisted. "I asked for this! I swear, he never meant to hurt me."

Dad came up to me and gripped my forearm tightly between his fingers.

"You've fallen down a rabbit hole," he said. "The one your therapist talked about, remember, Sapphire?"

"Don't talk about that," I hissed.

"I have to!" Dad insisted. "We were told this would happen again. We knew it would! We've been worried sick!"

"I'm fine," I said, but my voice was shaky, and I felt tears pricking my eyes. "I swear, Dad, I'm totally fine."

"You're not," Mom said. "You're bruised. I'm going to report him."

I reached her in two steps, grabbing her hand. She gave me a hurt look.

"Don't," I told her pointedly. "Don't tell anyone. King hasn't done anything wrong."

"I thought he was a good man," Mom whispered, and I fought the urge to roll my eyes.

"I'm going to call the police," Dad spoke up. "He's abusing you."

"Please don't," I begged. "You don't understand at all, please. Let me explain."

"There's nothing *to* explain," Dad said darkly, and Mom nodded.

"I agree," she said. She made me look at her. My bottom lip was quivering. "It's okay, Sapphire. We always knew you were broken."

"What?" I choked out, staring at her.

"It's okay," she repeated. "We'll get you the help you need. We'll get that man away from you."

"You can't," I hissed. "King's the only one who's helped me. The only one I feel close to!"

"Close enough to call him by his last name," Dad scoffed.

"Close enough to let him treat you like a piece of meat!" Mom howled. "That's it, Sapphire. You're moving back home, and cutting off all contact with that man."

"I will do no such thing," I told her coldly. "No fucking way."

"It's not your choice," Dad argued, "and mind your language!"

"We'll get you the help you need," Mom said. "We'll get you back to your therapist. We'll make sure you're okay. You should've never stopped going."

"Don't," I whispered. "I'm not doing this. I'm leaving."

I ripped my arm out of hers and took my purse, nearly stumbling on my way to the door.

"You're not leaving, Sapphire!" Dad called out after me. "Get back here!"

Mom was on my tail, desperately grabbing at me to stop me from leaving.

"Let me go!" I screamed. "I don't want to be here."

"You won't let me help you!" she sobbed. "I want to help you!"

Too.

Fucking.

Late.

"You're not really going to choose that man over your family," Dad got out through gritted teeth. "Are you, Sapphire?"

I hesitated and he laughed.

"Brilliant," he said. "Some loyalty, Sapphire!"

"I always knew this would happen," Mom muttered. "Always knew you'd get in trouble! Since you were a kid, Sapphire."

"Stop," I begged her. She was hurting me. "Please, don't talk about it."

"It's true," she hissed, giving me a hurt look. "You were trouble since you were a child."

I felt tears pricking my eyes. "Mom, please. You're making me feel terrible."

"How do you think we felt?" Dad argued. "We lost you for half a year, Sapphire! You're barely eighteen!"

"I know what I'm doing," I said. "I promise. This is the best thing I can do for myself right now. And I need to go."

"If you walk through that door," my father bellowed. "You are done with this family. You didn't accept our help, Sapphire! You walk out of here, you are done!"

Mom sobbed harder. I took a good, long look at the two of them.

And I left.

I left my old life behind, finally.

I chose him.

---

*"Where the fuck have you been?"*

He advanced on me the moment I came into the apartment. My hands were shaking and I dropped the key, tried to bend down to pick it up, but King smacked my hand away.

"I've been fucking calling you!" he said. "And you're two hours late, Pet."

"I'm sorry," I muttered.

"Not fucking good enough," he said. "Not good enough!"

"I… I had to get away," I said.

"From me?" He was really upset.

"No," I muttered. "Not from you."

From me.

From myself.

"I don't believe you." He rubbed his temples. "I fucking don't! You want to get away so badly, don't you?"

I shook my head no and he paced the room. He didn't say a word.

"Maybe I'll leave for a while longer," I said, feeling numb. "Go... somewhere, I don't know."

"Please." He never said that word. When I looked into his eyes, I could see how hurt he was. "Don't go."

"I have to," I said. "I have to, I can't be here right now."

I wanted him to stop me.

So.

Fucking.

Badly.

But he didn't.

I walked out of that door, and as soon as it closed behind me, I collapsed in the hallway, pulling my knees to my chest and holding back the sobs.

And then I picked myself up, and walked out of there.

I knew how to pretend everything was okay by now, and do it well.

After all, I'd had a lot of practice.

# CHAPTER 16
## *King*

Life without Pet wasn't worth living.

Of course, I'd known that for a while. Ever since she stumbled into my life and showed me her everything.

It had only been two days and I was going stir-fucking-crazy. She'd left a gaping hole behind, but I kept my distance. I knew it was important for her to come back by herself. This time, I had no plans of dragging her back home. She needed to realize where she was supposed to be.

I blew off work, and spent the time alone digging. I needed to fucking know, and I was no closer to finding out who had abused her.

But then, on a rainy afternoon, I finally made some progress.

I had gotten Pet's school records a few hours prior, and had been putting off going through them. I'd pulled on so many strings to get those files, but now that I finally had them, the prospect of what could be inside terrified me.

Finally, I poured myself a Scotch and sat down with my glass in hand, opening the heavy file.

Her name stared at me from the paper, offensive and inappropriate. She'd only ever been Pet to me.

I read through her file. Her grades had been average, though several tests she'd taken indicated a higher level of intelligence. There was nothing special in terms of disobedience, she'd been written down for being late here and there, but that was it.

Until I hit the jackpot.

A file from the school counselor, who had arrived at her school a year before Pet graduated.

It was brief, to the point, and eye-opening.

The notes the counselor had made on her were clear, words scribbled in tilted handwriting. They felt like bullets to my chest.

*Impulsive.*

*Reckless.*

*Emotional.*

*Self-harm.*

*Anxiety.*

*Boredom.*

*Emptiness.*

*Unstable.*

My Pet, in those barely legible scribbles that devaluated her from a person into a textbook case.

I got so angry I nearly tore the file into pieces. Instead, I set it down, and dug up some dirt on the school counselor on my phone.

Mr. Davies. Ezra Davies.

He was a middle-aged man. Handsome enough, according to my image search, not balding, either. Not that I should've given a shit, but Pet being in the company of a man like that, him analyzing her, trying to understand how her pretty mind worked… it set me right the fuck off.

I found his phone number and called without a second thought.

He was working as a therapist now. I got through to his secretary and faked my way into a meeting with Mr. Davies. I name-dropped my own name and she got me an appointment in the next hour. I got off the phone and grabbed my shit before heading to his office.

I tried not to think about my Pet, and where she could be, but fucking failed.

I made a quick call to someone I trusted to make sure she was fine, and headed out the door.

❈

"*Let's be honest with each* other," Ezra Davies said with a smooth smile.

I shifted on his uncomfortable couch, wondering how he expected anyone to talk to him openly while sat on such a shitty piece of furniture.

"I'm an open book, Mr. Davies," I told him, and he gave me a doubtful smile.

He'd let himself go since those pictures I'd seen were taken. He had a gut now, though he was still reasonably handsome. His shirt had pit stains on it, even though the AC was on in his office. He looked like he'd given up.

"I assume this isn't really about supporting my small business," he told me with a sly grin. "So why don't you start by telling me exactly what you're doing here, Mr. King."

I hated the bastard. He was slimy.

"Well, I have a... personal interest in one of your former patients," I said with a smile, and the man chuckled.

"I'm sure you know, Mr. King," he said. "I am not at liberty to discuss my patients."

"It was before you started working here," I told him. "When you worked at Pine Hill High School."

"Oh?" His brows shot up. We both knew exactly who I was talking about, yet he feigned ignorance. "And who might you be interested in, Mr. King?"

"Sapphire Rose Faye," I said through gritted teeth. "She was a senior. Graduated half a year ago."

"I remember her," he said, and I wanted to punch his teeth out.

I bet you fucking do, prick. Bet you still jack off to her tight little ass every night.

I focused my gaze on the wedding ring on his hand, and he rubbed his fingers when he felt me staring.

"What would you like to know about Miss Faye?" he asked. "Of course, I am not willing to say too much, you understand."

I glared at him, pulled a couple of hundreds from my pocket and laid them plainly on his desk.

"How about now?" I asked.

He made a semi-desperate grab for them. So business wasn't going that well, then.

"Sapphire Rose Faye was a very troubled girl," he said with a sigh, pocketing the cash. "Very pretty. Very aware of it. A very, very troubled girl she was."

"Elaborate," I said.

"She was a poster child for Borderline," he said. "Of course, I wasn't allowed to prescribe her medication, but I did my best to help with her situation."

"Situation?" I asked, and my heart pounded painfully in my chest. Surely, she hadn't told this monkey what had happened to her?

"She was a very dramatic girl," he said. "Very… prone to lying."

"That's news to me," I said.

"You better believe it," he said, his tone almost patronizing. "She lied to me so often, Sapphire did. To the point where I didn't believe a word she was saying."

I wondered if we were even talking about the same girl.

"And how did you attempt to help her?" I asked him.

He sighed and stretched on his chair.

"In my expert opinion," he started. "Sapphire was extremely troubled, and would not accept help."

"What do you mean?" I stared him down.

"She refused to take my advice," he said. "Refused to do what I said."

"So?" I asked. "Doesn't every teenager rebel?"

"Perhaps," he said. "But she refused to get better. She refused to admit to her own mistakes. The fact that she was mentally older than her age suggested."

"What's that got to do with anything?" I asked.

"She was seventeen at the time I met her," he said. "Yet she didn't act like a girl. She fought me on everything. It was like she was a combination of a petulant child and a know-it-all adult."

"Your point?" My tone was cold.

"My point," he continued, "I deemed her unfit to attend college."

"You what?" I practically jumped out of my seat.

"I suggested to Sapphire, as well as her teachers, that she take a gap year," he said. "She was unfit to be in school."

"Did you ask her what she wanted?" I asked.

"She had some dreams of an Art History major," he waved a hand dismissively. "Not realistic, given her situation."

"So you fucking buried her academic career," I sneered. "Did she apply to colleges?"

"She did," he said simply, looking irritated. "It was my decision to deny those applications, in Sapphire's best interests, of course. I explained all this to her."

I was ready to knock him out, but I had more questions.

"You told her to take a year off," I said, and he nodded. "What did her parents say to that?"

"They were not aware of my conclusion," he said. "Sapphire dealt with it herself."

So he fucking made her deal with his executive fucking decision. Way to be a fucking adult. Way to fucking help a seventeen-year-old with fucking Borderline.

"One last question," I sneered, getting up from my seat. "I want to know why you keep talking about her in the past tense."

He sighed and rubbed his temples, and I fantasized about dislocating his jaw.

"When Sapphire walked out of here," he said. "She told me she would kill herself."

"What?" I was left speechless.

"Of course, it was all part of her dramatic personality," Davies said. "I knew it was an empty threat. However, the girl did disappear. He parents contacted me after, told me she was gone. All her friends, the school, everyone lost touch with her."

"And you…" I just stared at him. "What the fuck did you do about that?"

"What could I have done?" he asked. "I'd done anything and everything I could have. She was an adult – on her own. My job was done."

I walked around the bastard's desk, pulled him from his seat, grabbed him by the throat and slammed him against the wall.

"You ruined an innocent girl's life," I spat in his face. "You convinced her she was overreacting."

"Let go," he wheezed.

"You told her she was being dramatic when she was looking for fucking help. Begging for it. You told a girl who'd been abused as a small child she was unfit to continue with her life."

"I..." The fucker was turning purple.

"You ruined her fucking life," I hissed. "Tell me one thing, Davies. Did you make a fucking move on her?"

The fear in his eyes told me everything. I fought every urge in my body so I wouldn't snap his slimy neck.

"She acted older," he choked out. "She was a fucking tease!"

I slammed him against the wall again before letting go. He doubled over, choking on his own breaths.

"She was a manipulator," he got out. "The little bitch led me on."

"You're done," I told him. "In this career, this city, this fucking country. Your life as you know it is fucking over."

"Please," he laughed. "You can't touch me."

"Watch me," I spat out.

"Is she dead?" he asked, smoothing down his shirt and giving me a big grin. "Is this some kind of fucking vengeance thing? Little bitch finally offed herself like she threatened she would?"

I counted to three, stepped right up to him, and broke his arm in a single motion. His scream was ear-piercing, and he cried like a fucking pussy.

I twisted his arm uncomfortably and looked him in the eye.

"I want you to know," I told him smoothly. "What's going to happen to you is your own fault. And you fucking deserve it."

I left him bawling on the floor of his office, and walked right past his hysterical secretary, and away from the emergency sirens pulling up on the curb.

It was a nine-block walk back home, and I practically ran the whole way.

It all made fucking sense. The way she'd isolated herself, cut off everyone who meant something to her. The dead-end jobs she worked, the non-existent friendships.

She was getting ready to end her life, gathering the courage to do it. She'd been planning to kill herself. That's why she dropped off the face of the earth.

I dialed the same number I'd called before and barked into the phone.

"You found her yet? You fucking need to. Right now."

I listed some locations off the top of my head, fighting the urge to smash my fist into a streetlamp.

"Fucking find her! NOW!"

# CHAPTER 17
*Pet*

Running away was proving to be difficult since I didn't have anywhere to go.

I wandered around town aimlessly, pissed off with myself for not taking my phone or anything else when I left. Not that I had any money to speak off.

I ended up at the library, the only place I felt safe enough in. I hid between the bookshelves and picked out some of my favorite classics.

*The Little Princess, The Secret Garden, Rebecca.*

Enough to distract me for a few hours.

I curled up on an uncomfortable chair in the emptiest part of the library, pulled my legs up and ignored people's stares as I opened Rebecca and started reading. It only took me a few moments to fall into the world I'd found solace in so many times before, and I accepted the distraction gratefully.

Daphne du Maurier's words pulled me in and I forgot about my surroundings for a blissful hour, until my stomach reminded me it was time to eat.

When I looked up from my book, I realized I wasn't alone. And when I saw who was standing in front of me, blinding rage ripped through my body.

"How long have you been standing there?" I asked, my voice shaky.

"Long enough to see you're not going anywhere." She gave me a playful smile, and I wanted to smack it off her once-again-pretty face.

I got up and stacked my books, trying to get past her, but she grabbed my arm and wouldn't let go.

"I'm here to help," she said.

"Like fuck you are," I sneered. "Get your filthy hands off me."

"You're jealous for no reason," she told me. "It's been a long time since… since I was King's pet."

I nearly spat in her face.

"Oh, I'm sorry," I snapped. "I guess you're his Angel now."

"You don't know anything," she said.

"I know enough. Let the fuck go!"

Someone shushed us and gave us a mean look. Angel just rolled her eyes and half-dragged me out of the library. She took my books and placed them on a random shelf and I seethed with anger, not wanting to make a scene. We left the library and she didn't stop dragging me along until we were in the street. Then, I finally ripped my arm out of her grip and glared at her.

"You're literally the last person I want to see," I told her.

"I know." She gave me an apologetic smile. "But I'm here to help. Even if you don't understand, Sapphire."

It felt odd hearing my name from her lips. The lips that had been begging for King's cock the last time I heard her talk.

"My only purpose in your relationship is to help," she said. "I know you don't get it, but trust me. I'm not here to steal your man."

"As if you could," I rolled my eyes, but my bravado was false.

She really was beautiful, and so much sexier than me. Even I could tell that. Fuck, a lamppost could tell.

"You need to go back home to him," she said, and I shook my head.

"I can't deal with it right now," I said. "And I don't like you meddling."

"He sent me," she protested.

"Fucking great," I muttered. "Got someone else to do his bidding, once again. What, am I not worthy of him getting me back by himself?"

"You're one angry girl," Angel laughed.

She looked at me with a bemused expression, then extended a hand. I stared at her with contempt.

"My name is Maria," she said. "I thought you should know, since I know yours."

I glared at her as she pulled my hand towards her and shook it. Her laughter was melodic, and she linked her arm with mine.

"Come on," she smiled. "I'm buying you a drink, and then we can get you home."

I had the feeling I wouldn't get anywhere if I objected.

---

*She took me to a* cafe. Not even a fucking bar.

I kept glaring at her as we ordered our drinks, two Cokes with ice and lemon.

"I don't like you," I told her.

"Yeah?" she licked her straw. "I think you're a fucking peach."

"King thinks so," I grinned.

"He has awful taste." She sucked her drink through the straw. "Ever since he dumped me."

Knowing that he'd dumped her gave my heart palpitations. Good. Bitch fucking deserved it.

"I think we could really be friends, you know," she said and I burst out laughing. After a moment, she joined in, and we giggled for what felt like ages.

"You're not going to touch him again?" I asked her.

"I do what he tells me to," she said. "And what we did was for your own good."

"Sure." Another eye-roll. "You don't have feelings for him anymore?"

She toyed with her straw and I wanted to stab her in one of her pretty brown eyes.

Kind of.

Not really.

"Why did you agree to come get me?" I asked.

"He asked me to," she shrugged.

"That wasn't my question."

She let go of her glass and glared at me.

"When King asks you to do something," she said. "You say yes."

Well, she had a point there.

"I'd really prefer it if you stayed out of my life," I said, and she gave me a long look.

"I think you could use a friend," she said.

"Yeah? And you think you'd fill that role well?"

"I'm saying it wouldn't hurt to give it a try. I know all of this is new to you, I'm just trying to help. So, if you let me…" She reached for my hand and laid her palm on top of it gently. It felt all kinds of weird. "I think we'd make a great team."

"I'll think about it," I muttered.

There was something about her that I liked, now that I saw her as Maria, not Angel. She seemed almost… sweet. Caring. Of course, my judgement wasn't always spot-on with these things.

"Let's take you home," she suggested, and I shook my head.

"A little while longer." My voice was soft and shaky, so she just nodded and ordered us another round of Cokes.

Somehow, she managed to involve me in a conversation that had absolutely nothing to do with King.

We talked about anything and everything from our favorite movies to the best skincare brands we liked to use. And finally, we touched on the subject of school, and it made me curious.

"You're a student?" I asked her, and she shook her head.

"I finished two years ago," she said.

"What's your degree in?"

"Drama," she grinned. "I've always wanted to be an actress."

I looked her over. On second thoughts, she might have what it takes. There was something about her – she was beautiful, yes, but a bit unusual with that wild hair. Her skin was a sharp contrast to her dark hair and eyes, pale and almost creamy. She really was beautiful, but there was more to it than that. Almost like a charisma, something I would never have. I assumed that's what attracted King to her in the first place.

"I can see you as an actress," I told her, and she beamed. "Have you done much work?"

"A few ads," she said. "And I have a spot on a TV soap opera."

"Which one?" I asked. My mom used to be obsessed with them. I bet she would've freaked if I told her I met an actress from one of her favorite shows.

I tried not to think about the fact that we weren't even really talking at that point.

"Pembroke Pines," she said, and I giggled.

"That's like, the cheesiest one of them all."

She stuck her tongue out at me. "It's a solid show!"

"I'll bet," I teased her. "So, what's your role?"

She looked at me with a wicked sparkle in her eyes, then leaned over and told me over our drinks, her voice hushed.

"I play Debra McMillan's long lost daughter," she told me, and I nodded. Debra was one of the older members of the show. She must've been on TV for decades. "I come back to her in her dreams and then she starts seeing me in real life, too."

"Exciting," I raised my eyebrows bemusedly.

"BUT!" Maria grinned. "What she doesn't know... is that I'm a ghost!"

I gasped and faked a fainting, and we both giggled.

"I'm really excited about it," she said. "They're talking about giving me a permanent spot on the show as well."

"Yeah?" I gave her a doubtful look. "They're giving a ghost a permanent spot on the show?"

She laughed. "Stranger things have happened."

"True," I nodded.

Like this friendship.

"Hey," I said in a small voice, toying with the lemon slice in my empty glass with the straw. I couldn't really look at Maria, but I could feel her eyes on me. She probably knew what I was going to say before I even opened my mouth. "I kind of want to go home now."

I thought she'd make a big deal out of it, with 'I told you so' and meaningful looks, but she merely nodded, took her wallet out of her bag and pulled out some money. She left it on the table, winked at the bartender who'd been in awe of her since we'd walked in, and offered me a hand to help me up.

I stared at her for a second. This gorgeous, selfless Amazon that was willing to help me, even though I was with the man she presumably still had feelings for. What a strange creature.

I took her hand and got up. She linked her arm with mine and we walked out of that bar, feeling everyone's eyes on us as we sauntered through the door.

# CHAPTER 18
## *King*

When the doorbell rang, I practically fell over myself to get to the door.

Before I opened it, I tried to regain some composure. I couldn't let her see me weak.

I cracked my knuckles and pulled the door open, a neutral expression on my face.

My Pet stood in front of Angel, with her hands demurely clasped in front of her body. She couldn't quite look at me, her eyes trained on the floor and her cheeks blushed a red so deep it could've been scarlet.

I couldn't even look at Angel, even though I owed her as much. I could only stare at Pet and battle with the desire to shake her. Make her tell me all her secrets.

"Thank you, Angel," I said without looking at her. "You can leave now."

She didn't say a word, merely turned around and walked out of there on her fuck-me heels. Not before she gave Pet a gentle nudge in my direction, though.

Pet stumbled into the apartment and I stepped aside so she wouldn't have to touch me. She was shivering.

I closed the front door and locked it, then walked to the sofa in the living room. She just stood in the middle of the room, looking like a lost little lamb. It was making my cock all kinds of hard.

"Pet," I called out. My voice was so fucking rough, strained and tired like I'd been up for days. "Come here."

She looked up at me and her bottom lip trembled. She didn't move, just wrung her hands in front of her. Her eyes were terrified and it made me scared. I wasn't scared very often.

"Come on." My voice was gentler now. Sweet. Caring. Nothing like me, but everything she needed in that moment. "Come sit on my lap, Pet."

She made a half-hearted attempt to move, but it felt like she was glued to the spot. Her eyes danced over my features and the room felt oppressively hot.

I tilted my head to the side and stared back. I patted my knee and motioned for her to come with my finger. It made her moan out loud.

"I'm not going to ask again," I said gently.

She dragged herself over to me and practically collapsed on my lap. I pulled her on my knee and ran a hand down her back, making her fucking shudder. She wouldn't look at me, covering her face with those dainty little hands instead. Fuck, she was making this even harder. All I wanted to do was bend her over my lap and punish her tight ass for making me wait. But, like always, I didn't have a fucking clue how I was supposed to punish someone so damn broken.

"I'm sorry," she whispered, and I stroked her back some more. I couldn't say a word. Made myself shut up. I knew if I did speak, I'd tell her off, tell her how much she fucking meant to me already. And I couldn't have her knowing that.

"I had to get away," she said, and I peeled her dress off her shoulders. Her skin erupted in goosebumps under my fingers and it was so hot my fingers shook with the need to bruise her.

"It's okay," I lied. "I understand." I didn't. "I'm glad you're back now, Pet."

"Why didn't you…" She finally looked up at me, those big blue eyes watering and making me ache for her. "Why didn't you come find me yourself?"

"You didn't want to see me," I told her. "I thought someone with no ties to the situation would be better."

"Yeah, but… her?" She laughed bitterly, and my hand moved from her back to her hair. I smoothed over her messy waves. She was really heart-stoppingly beautiful like this. So much better than when I got her all dressed up, primped and primed to perfection. This was the real her, and the rawness of it made my balls swell painfully.

"You don't like her?" I asked her, teasing a little.

"She's ok." She shrugged.

"You should give her a chance," I told her. "She's a great girl."

Suddenly, Pet threw her arms around my neck and straddled me. I pretended it didn't make me want to push her panties aside on the spot, and held her waist instead.

"I hate that you think that," she muttered against my ear, and my grip tightened. "I want you to only want me, not her."

"I do only want you," I said.

"You fucked her," she whispered.

"Because you weren't ready for me," I said. "And neither was I."

I'd never be fucking ready for her, either, but she didn't need to know that.

"You need a friend, Pet," I told her. "I think she'd make a good one. And you know I won't touch her anymore."

"How would I know that?" she asked, moving away and staring at me with hurt eyes. "I don't believe that for a second."

"No?"

I pulled her dress down in one motion and ripped her bra off. She didn't make a sound, but her whole body shivered as I ran my hands down her front, between her tits and down to her stomach.

"You should," I told her roughly. "She's not you. And all I want is you."

"Prove it," she begged, and I groaned.

"Gladly," I told her. "But you will give her a chance. I want you to have a friend."

She glared at me and I grinned, my fingers tugging on her nipple. Her eyes rolled back and she arched her back, pushing her little breasts into my face.

"Say you'll give her a chance," I told her.

"Fine," she gritted out, and I squeezed her nipple harder.

"Say the whole thing," I said.

She glared at me, but not for long. I pulled her nipple towards me and her hips bucked against my lap.

"Please…" she muttered.

"Say it."

"I'll give her a chance," she got out.

"Good girl." I twisted her nipple between my fingers and she twitched on my lap. It probably hurt. Good. "Tell me what you want me to do to you now."

"Anything." This time, she was quick to answer. "Anything you want, please…"

"Tell me what you want," I repeated. "Right now."

Her glazed-over eyes focused on mine and she tore at my hair, leaning closer and giggling in my ear.

"I want you to make me cry," she whispered. "I want you to make my makeup run and show me what happens when I misbehave."

"How?" I groaned.

Her nails dug into my back and she moaned in my ear. Her whole body was begging to be fucked, writhing on my lap.

"I want you to fuck my ass," she whispered, so softly I could barely hear her.

It made me really fucking hard.

I practically growled as I pulled her up. My hands went into her hair and she breathed with relief when I dragged her to the bedroom by that pretty blonde mane.

I let her go and she crumpled to the floor in front of the bed. On her knees in a second, hands behind her back in the next. Eyes on me, mouth slightly open.

"Like this?" she asked me.

"No," I growled. "On your back. On the bed. Right the fuck now."

"Why?" she asked, and I gave her a single look that made her scramble to her feet and lie down like a good girl. I tore at the rest of her clothes, her panties ruined in seconds. She lay back shaking and I stared at her for so long she started to sob.

"Please," she begged. "Don't just look at me, I can't take it. Do it… do something!"

I took off my clothes as slowly as I could. Blazer, tie, shirt, pants. My boxers last. My cock sprang free and she writhed at the sight of it.

"Master, please," she whispered, and I shook my head.

"No," I told her. "None of that shit today."

I climbed on top of her and she cried harder. Her tears were streaming down those pretty cheeks, and she looked too fucking young to be in that kind of situation. I felt like an old fucking pervert.

My cock pressed against her pussy and she howled. Really fucking howled, like an animal. I could've torn her apart in that second, and it took every cell in my body to hold back before I attacked her like a savage.

I pushed inside her so slowly it felt like a punishment, and I fucked her with measured thrusts, slow and steady, making her go crazy. She didn't even say a word, it was all those primal little sounds she couldn't hold back anymore. She felt unbelievable like that.

Her red-rimmed eyes found mine and I stared at her as I fucked her. She opened and closed those full lips as I did it, and the sounds leaving her lips made me want to, fuck, I didn't even know, they made me want to go insane. Let it all go, just for her. Change the rules, change my life, change it all, just so she could fit in the hole inside me.

"F-fuck my ass," she whispered, and I fucked her even slower.

"No," I told her. "Not doing that as punishment, never again."

"Please!" She was so fucking desperate, more tears ran down her cheeks. "Please, you can't do this to me!"

"Watch me," I growled into her ear and went even slower. Barely pushing in, just feeling my cock throb inside that tight little pussy, and it was fucking enough.

"I hate you," she said weakly. Her hands reached up to my chest but she couldn't even scratch me. She was so weak, completely at my mercy. I could've done anything to her in that moment.

"No, you don't." I grasped her chin with my fingers and made her look into my eyes. "Tell me how you really feel."

"I…" She bit back a cry and I stopped moving completely. She squirmed under me, but I pinned her down hard, not letting her move an inch. Just letting her feel my cock inside her, her walls pulsating so needily against my length I could feel her milking me.

"I don't want to," she said, and I tightened my grip.

"Say it," I ordered her. My own voice was shaky. I could barely hold back. It would've been fucking embarrassing if it wasn't so damn hot.

"Will…" Her eyes were so desperate. "Will you say it back?"

I leaned down against her and kissed those desperate lips, pushing my tongue into her mouth and making her arch her back against me. It only made my cock throb more.

"I don't need to," I said into her mouth. "You know how I fucking feel."

She mewled but didn't say a word. It made me really, really angry.

"No?" I asked her, and she shook her head, her pupils so wide with fear it felt like she'd pass out under me. "Okay."

I put my hand over her mouth and her eyes rolled back as I started to really fuck her. Not like ever before. I let it all go inside her. I fucked her with everything I had and she bit my fingers with her sharp little teeth.

I could feel her opening her mouth, licking at my skin, her eyes begging me to let her speak as I hit her cervix.

"Jesus," I groaned, and she whimpered.

The words she got out were muffled but we both knew what she was saying. I clamped my hand down on her mouth harder so she couldn't get a word out, and she struggled so violently she almost overpowered me because I wasn't prepared. Her body was thrashing under mine and I had to come so badly I couldn't let her. My hands left her mouth and gripped her waist, and I fucked her like she meant everything to me, which she did.

The moment my hands were off she screamed it, desperate and covered in her own tears.

"I love you, I love you, I love you!"

Over and over again, so loud, so angry.

I couldn't take it. I felt her pussy tightening, felt her desperation to get every drop out of me, and I stopped fucking fighting it. I lost, for the first time in my life, and I did it willingly.

I pumped her pussy full of cum and she sobbed with relief, still staring at me, still saying those three words, even though they were barely a whisper anymore, barely a sound.

She took it all.

Until there was nothing left to give.

And then she just lay back and stared at me with those doe eyes, and I couldn't even fucking move, or take my cock out of her. I lay on top of her, crushing her with my weight, and stared at her because there was nothing else to do anymore.

I'd never say those words to her.

"You don't have to," she whispered.

She looked so pale. Completely exhausted. I heard myself trying to catch my breath, my cock still hard inside her. She was so tight it hurt to be inside.

I had to bite my tongue so I wouldn't say it. Bite it so hard I felt blood in my mouth, and it tasted like metal.

I couldn't do that to her. I couldn't ruin her life with those three words.

She arched her back and her eyes closed, while mine kept staring at her desperately.

I was so close to breaking the rules for her. The rules I'd written especially for her, that were there to benefit her. She made me so fucking crazy I would've hurt her just to tell her how I really felt.

There was a serene smile on her face as she came down from her high, and her eyes stayed closed.

"You don't have to say it," she repeated. "I fucking know."

I wished like a fucking madman she'd open her eyes and let me say it, but she wouldn't. And I kept my mouth shut and swallowed the blood, and knew I was going to ruin her life.

# CHAPTER 19
## *Pet*

I *should have hated myself for* saying it, and I should have hated him more for not saying it back. But I couldn't. It felt too good, too natural. It felt right.

Since the night I'd told him I loved him, King had been even stricter with me.

Everything I did was under his control. Every meal I had, every orgasm he let me have, every piece of clothing I wore.

And I loved it.

It was like I finally discovered what had been missing in my life. This... *need* to have someone so in control over me. It was so sexy. I would've submitted to everything he said, but I loved pushing him, too. If nothing else, just for those punishments he doled out with a stern hand. And I still hoped one day I'd misbehave so fucking badly he'd just finally fuck my ass.

The day hadn't come yet, but I was pushing for it with everything I fucking had.

He'd started giving me tasks as his work took over most of his time.

Sometimes it was simple things, like making him his favorite dinner. I'd learned how to cook a little, though I still wasn't great at it, but he seemed to enjoy my efforts.

Other times, he'd make me wait for him at the door on my knees. He'd give me a vague time of when he'd be home and I had to kneel in front of the door until he finally showed up, seething with anger and my pussy dripping on the floor. He'd laugh and stroke my hair and make me lick my own juices off the floor, and I lived for those moments. Anything to please him.

Other tasks included taking pictures for him. After our failed experiment, I'd gotten better at it, mostly because I wasn't disobeying him as much.

Pictures, videos, sound clips, either sent to his phone while he was at work, or waiting for him when he got home to see what I'd been up to when he'd been gone.

Sometimes I misbehaved on purpose and sent them to his work phone, the one he checked all day long. And he punished me accordingly when he came home.

It was all worth it.

The last idea I had was one I'd come up with together with Maria.

The friendship that had bloomed between us was unlikely, but for some odd reason it seemed to work.

We talked almost every day, either on the phone or through texts. She even video called me a few times, and showed me around the set of her soap opera. Once, King made me talk to her on video while he was balls deep inside my pussy. He held the phone up for me so she wouldn't see a thing but my face, and made me fucking sweat as she chatted about her day innocently.

He was so bad, and it felt so good.

Maria told me he'd punished her often, and it made me angry. He'd been really lenient with me, she said, but instead of that making me feel special, it just pissed me off. I wanted him to punish me. Hurt me. Show me how much I meant to him by disciplining me. But it seemed as if he'd been avoiding doing that on purpose.

"I have an idea," she whispered to me over the phone the previous day.

King was at work, and I'd just finished his task of the day, the proof of my ruined panties waiting for a reply on his phone.

"What is it?" I asked her, taking a bite out of my apple. "It better be fucking good. I'm getting desperate here."

"How about…" Her voice was devious and I liked it. "You do something you know he would hate."

"Like what?" I asked her.

"I don't know!" I could almost see her rolling her eyes. "You know him better than I do, Sapphire."

That made me smile really wide, and I stared at my apple before taking another bite.

"He hates my scars," I said softly. "I mean… I think he likes them, but he hates that they're there."

"So, he hates marks on your body," she said.

"I guess."

"Well, maybe you could get a piercing," she giggled. "Get your nipple pierced or something. I bet that would drive him insane."

"You're crazy," I told her. "He would kill me."

"How about a tattoo then?" she suggested.

I thought of her angel tattoo. The image of King fucking her while I stared at it helplessly, that fucking tattoo forever ingrained in my memory. For some reason, it didn't even upset me anymore. In fact, it made me a little wet.

I ignored the sensation and finished off my apple.

"I'm really scared of needles," I admitted.

"Pussy," she laughed, and I rolled my eyes. "Well… what then?"

"Maybe," I said. "Maybe I could fake getting one."

"How?" She sounded doubtful.

"You drew the design for yours, right?" I asked her.

I could tell she was getting excited.

"Yeah."

"Can you come over now?"

It felt kind of awkward to have her over at the apartment after everything that had happened, but I couldn't help it. It made me giggle with excitement.

"You're so bad," she laughed. "I'm on my way."

I couldn't help grinning, not even when she rang the doorbell twenty minutes later. She looked even giddier than me when she sat down on the couch and told me to take my clothes off.

It didn't even feel awkward, but when I felt her eyes on me, it was a little weird. I never thought she liked girls that much, but the way she stared at me made me twitch a little.

She took out some ink pens from her bag and gave me a devilish grin.

"They don't smudge that much," she explained, and I nodded. My heart was pounding.

She made me walk up to her, standing in front of the couch. She took out her pens and went to work on my skin. I held my hands over my nipples, her pen tickling my sensitive skin.

"What are you gonna draw?" I asked her.

"Something pretty," she grinned. "Something that's gonna make him go fucking crazy."

The drawing took over an hour, and she wouldn't let me look down until she was finished. By that point, my legs were cramping up and I was fidgeting on the spot.

"Okay, you can look," she said with a big smile, and I ran over to the mirror in the hallway. When I saw what she had done, I gasped.

"He's going to kill me," I giggled.

"Oh well," Maria shrugged, putting her stuff back in her bag. "Been nice knowing you, you had to go sometime."

"Bitch," I giggled.

She stood up and took my phone, and I covered my nipples again, sticking my tongue out at the camera. She snapped a picture and grinned as she looked at the screen.

"Sent," she exclaimed with a big smile and I giggled nervously.

She kissed my cheek on her way out, and her hand lingered on my hip. I forgot I was naked down to my waist, and only wearing a thong underneath, and her touch made me feel all kinds of weird. Her eyes lingered on mine before she winked, blew me a kiss, and told me to have fun. I closed the door behind her.

It only took a few seconds after she left for my phone to start going off.

Calls, texts, messages. King was fucking pissed. All I could do was laugh.

I admired Maria's handiwork in the mirror one more time.

Intricate patterns decorated my body, starting at my collarbone and going down between my tits and around my waist. They looked like pretty chains, and my nipples stood out from the black design like sharp pink points.

I almost felt him coming home, but even if I hadn't, I would've been alerted to his presence when he nearly tore down the front door.

I turned around, only wearing a little thong, my full body on display. His mouth gaped.

"What. The fuck. Have you done?" he growled, and I giggled as he came at me.

He grabbed me by the throat and turned me to the side, looking at the drawing on my body.

"You fucking didn't," he growled. "You didn't get a tattoo."

"You don't like it?" I pouted. "I got it just for you."

"You fucking…" His eyes were all pupils as he pulled his cock out from his pants and stroked it, almost violently. "You fucking little slut."

He held me at arm's length by my throat and I giggled as his eyes drank in the whole design hungrily.

"I think it's pretty," I told him innocently, and he growled.

"You'll pay for this," he told me, his hand going crazy against his cock.

"Doubt it," I said. "You never punish me, anyway."

"That's about to change," he told me, and pushed me to my knees. "Present your tits to your fucking master, Pet."

My hands shook as I cupped my tits and pushed them up and he groaned.

"You fucking ruined your pretty skin," he said. "So I'm going to ruin you now."

"Okay," I whispered, and opened my mouth, sticking my tongue out.

He cursed out loud, his hand working his cock faster than ever.

"You don't get to taste it," he told me. "Not now, not even for fucking weeks."

"Not fair," I mewled. I got upset at that, it wasn't good.

"Shut the fuck up," he groaned, holding my throat so tightly I could barely draw a breath. "Put your hands behind your back and push your tits out for me."

I did it, my legs quivering under me. The friction of that thong against my pussy almost making me come.

"Look at me," he barked, and I did.

He looked so angry. So pissed, and so turned on, it made me giggle. I thought I'd get a slap for that, but he just kept fisting his cock, so hard now I could hear how close he was.

"Say you're fucking sorry," he said in a pained voice, and I fluttered my lashes.

"I'm sorry, Master," I said, and he let go of his cock suddenly, his hands rushing against me, pulling on my hair and making me look up at him. He didn't even need to guide his dick to my chest, he was so hard. He came all over my tits without even touching himself and I stared at him, loving the feel of his warm cum on my skin.

He grunted and his hand went down to my torso, slapping my tits so hard I yelped, smearing his cum all over my chest.

"What the fuck?" he said, and I forced myself to look away from him, feeling almost delirious. I looked down and saw the design, all smudged from his cum, his thumb circling the drawings frantically and smearing ink all over my sticky skin. "What the fucking hell, Pet?"

"Surprise," I giggled.

"You…" He kneeled down next to me, one hand pulling my head back so far I gagged, and the other spooning his cum into my mouth.

"You're fucking unbelievable," he told me, his fingers shaking as I sucked them clean. "What the fuck am I going to do with you?"

"Something fun," I whispered. "And terrible."

He groaned and kissed me, not caring that I had his cum in my mouth. He kissed me differently this time, sweeter. Until he bit down on my bottom lip and dragged it between his teeth, making me cry out loud.

"Now I really have to punish you," he said against my lips.

"I can't wait," I said, feeling the last of his cum running down my throat. "Make it good."

"I don't think so," he grinned. "You'd like that too much, my little whore. But I have the perfect task in mind for you…"

# CHAPTER 20
*King*

She looked *so fucking smug*. Not for long.

"What's the task?" she asked, licking her sinful lips.

I stroked her cheek with my thumb. She was a fucking mess.

I helped her to her feet and led her into the bathroom. She didn't say a word as I pulled off her soaked thong and pushed her inside the shower. Pet placed her palms on the wall, her back facing me. She looked over her shoulder and smiled at me.

I turned on the water, took off the rest of my clothes, and joined her in the shower. My right hand caressed her ass and my left one went to her tits, washing away the black ink and what was left of my cum. She melted against my touch, her back arching firmly against my chest and her head thrown back so she could look me in the eyes while I cleaned her.

I should've made it as clinical as possible, but with her standing like that and soft little moans leaving her lips, it was fucking impossible. I washed her tits clean with some body wash, the lemon one she liked so much, and watched black ink run down the drain. Once the fake tattoo got in touch with water, it left her skin in seconds. A shame, because it was fucking hot, and a relief at the same time. If she'd really done that to herself, I would've had her ass. It was only a matter of days now before I took that from her. She didn't know that yet, though. And she was really going to hate me after this next task.

I washed her hair next, soaping it up with shampoo. She moaned with pleasure as I rinsed it out, the remains of her makeup, too. Everything, until she was a blank canvas for me to use.

Her knees were weak as I helped her out of the shower, and she had to lean against the wall as I toweled her off. Her skin was raw from being scrubbed, raw and red.

She looked at me with so much longing it only reinforced what I had to do.

I hated it, much more than she ever would. But I knew it had to be done.

I dried her hair next, and she stared at our reflection in the mirror as I wielded the hairdryer clumsily. It made her giggle, and I laughed back. She pressed her ass against my groin and I held her in place with one hand, drying her hair with the other. Pet closed her eyes and nearly purred with pleasure as I did it.

Once I was done with her hair, I blasted the dryer against her skin, and she gasped with pleasure as the hot air blew against her. Neck, chest, down her belly, between her legs. Almost close enough to burn her. And then right next to her skin, enough to make her yelp and smack my hand away.

"You're crazy," she told me, and I grinned at her. Her eyes drank me in hungrily. I was still naked, apart from the ring I always wore, and her eyes lingered on it like they had a thousand times before. But it wasn't time yet, I had to remind myself.

"I want you to get dressed up," I told her, and her eyes sparkled. "Something you feel really fucking hot in. Really fuckable."

"Okay," she said in a small voice. "Are you going to play with me some more?"

I didn't answer, just touched her skin lightly. She wanted so much more.

"Something really hot," I told her again. "Something you wouldn't mind others seeing you in."

Her eyes were mischievous as she walked past me.

"I'll be back soon," she promised, and I stared at her retreating back, pretending the jealousy wasn't there.

She took fucking ages. So fucking long I'd had three drinks to calm my nerves, and was feeling a little shaky by the time she called out my name.

"I'll come out now, okay?" she asked.

I turned around on the barstool and stared at the hallway. "Okay, Pet."

She walked out.

I tried to assess the situation objectively.

Legs for fucking days, her favorite stockings decorating her skin. The ones I'd gotten her from Agent Provocateur. White, with a black top, a line down the backs of her legs and words scribbled alongside it.

*Whip me.*

*Bite me.*

*Eat me.*

*Tease me.*

An intricate garter belt held her stockings up, with a caged design around her stomach.

A tiny pair of black panties that were completely see-through.

The bra she was wearing didn't even cover her tits. One of those things that went under them, pushing her nipples up so high she could probably lick them herself.

And heels, the tallest she owned. The red sole winked at me as she spun on her heel.

"Jesus," I grunted, and finally looked at her face.

Her hair was curled to perfection, every wave in place on her shoulders. Her makeup was flawless. A lot of eyeliner. And pink lips. Her cheeks were pink, too. Not from the makeup, at least it didn't look that way.

"Fuck. Come here."

She walked over to me, the perfect mix of shyness and absolute, blinding confidence. She stepped between my legs and I ran my hands down her back.

"You know someone's gonna see you like that," I told her gently.

"Yeah," she answered. "Are we gonna take some pictures?"

Poor little Pet.

"I'll let you borrow my jacket again," I told her, and her eyes sparkled with excitement.

"Are we going somewhere?" she asked.

"I have to go back to work," I said, and her expression fell. "I did fucking rush out of there without an explanation, because someone fucking teased me into coming home."

She gave me a weak little laugh, still looking nervous.

"So where am I going?" she asked me, and I tugged on her curls very gently, so they wouldn't fall out.

Any man who'd see her like this would want her. Crave her. Need her.

She was beautiful, of-fucking-course. Irresistible. And yet I wanted to strip it all off her, reduce her to a shaky mess again, and taste her tears. I'd have to resist it this time around, though.

"Are you ready for your task?" I asked her, and her shoulders hunched in defeat. "Stand up straight, Pet, I want to see your pretty tits."

She obeyed, but she was shaking pretty badly.

"Answer me," I reminded her gently, and she swallowed, hard.

"Yes," she said in the softest of voices.

"Come on, Pet," I said. "Tell me."

"Yes, Master, I'm ready," she got out, and I stroked her hair, pressing her against my chest.

"Good girl."

She snuggled against my chest and I let it happen for a few moments before I pulled away.

"Pet," I said. "You'll do anything I tell you, right?"

She nodded, her bottom lip trembling. I could tell she knew she wouldn't like this.

"And you won't complain," I went on. "You'll like it, yes?"

Another weak nod.

"And most of all," I made her look at me. "You'll know I'm doing it for you, yeah?"

"Yes," she said. Her legs were trembling and I caged them between mine so she wouldn't fall over.

"I want you to go outside," I told her gently, brushing my fingertips over her skin. "You can take my jacket, but you have to look exactly like this otherwise."

She stared at me.

"You're going to find someone on the street," I told her in the gentlest of voices. "Someone you like. Or someone that likes you. Preferably both. A stranger."

I could practically hear her heartbeat.

"You'll bring him home," I went on. "A man you don't know. And you're going to beg him to fuck you in the playroom."

I could see the tears brimming in her eyes, so I tipped her chin back before they fell.

"Don't cry, Pet," I said softly. "Don't ruin your pretty makeup now, it'll be harder to find someone to fuck you if your pretty face is stained with tears."

She stared and stared and stared.

"I'll be back in a few hours," I promised. "You can get rid of him by then, or you can make him wait for me."

I didn't mention that if she let him stay, I'd probably knock the guy's teeth out.

Her chest heaved. She didn't want it. Not yet, at least.

"I don't care how," I told her.

She gasped as I slid a finger over her pussy, her little panties already drenched.

"But I want you to make him come."

I got up from the stool and walked over to the couch. She stared and stared and stared some more.

I brought my blazer to her, the one she'd worn when I made her flash those guys on our first night together.

"Put this on," I told her, and she slipped it over her shoulders almost robotically. "Good girl."

I smoothed down the fabric and buttoned the jacket up for her, covering up her half-naked body. It was too short to cover up everything, and you could still see a hint of her garter belt, those stockings, and her sexy heels. She looked like a treat. A fucking sex kitten. I was so painfully jealous I felt bile rising in my throat.

"Now." I looked at my watch, then into her fucking terrified eyes. "Are you going to do as I asked you, Pet?"

Her lips parted and the word leaving her lips excited me as much as it crushed me.

"Yes."

"Good girl," I bit out, kissing her on the cheek. She tried to kiss my lips instead, but I moved away before she could do it. She looked so fucking small in that oversized room, with my jacket too big for her shoulders, and her confidence suddenly in a tiny ball at her feet, trampled all over.

I walked towards the door and gave her a final look over my shoulder.

"You look like trouble," I told her. "You'll get it done in no time."

"Yes," she answered automatically, and I gave her a big, fake-as-fuck smile. "I will."

"Good fucking girl," I said.

I left her standing there with my heart in her hand, and closed the front door firmly.

As soon as she was out of my sight, I lost it.

I barely managed to walk over to the elevator before I slammed my fist into the wall, opening up the cuts I'd made only a few weeks ago when she told me she'd been abused.

It was becoming a nasty little habit.

Leaving had never been harder.

And neither had my cock.

# CHAPTER 21
## *Pet*

I *was furious. The moment he* left the apartment, I wished I'd scratched his eyes out. Fucking prick.

As soon as I thought we had something, as soon as he lured me into this fucking false sense of safety, he knocked my confidence over again. And I fell like a line of dominoes. I hated him for it.

I couldn't even move for what felt like hours. I stood in the living room, glued to the fucking spot with my knees weak and my legs shaky.

My phone buzzed with a message and I looked down in a daze. It was from Maria, asking me how it went. My little prank seemed so far away, and so insignificant.

I felt anger then, blinding, white-hot anger, surge through my body. And I let it, because I was going to fucking need it if I was going to do this.

I attempted to walk to the door but nearly toppled over. The heels I was wearing were too high, and I was too fucking nervous. I badly wanted a drink, but at the same time I knew it would only make things worse.

It wasn't even dark outside, and the sunlight streaming through the floor-to-ceiling windows just made me feel more nervous and awkward.

But I had to do it.

If King thought he could push me around like that, I'd have to prove him wrong.

I was pretty sure he thought I wouldn't go through with it. That he'd only done it so he could come home that night with every intent of punishing me for my disobedience.

But I'd be damned if I'd let him.

I took a deep breath, feeling nauseous. And then I walked out of that apartment, locked it behind me, and rode the elevator to the bottom floor. I stared at the numbers in the elevator, going down down down. My heart felt heavy, but my pussy was really fucking wet. I hated myself for it.

I ignored the doorman, or maybe he ignored me. Neither of us said a word as I walked past him in that ridiculous get-up, my heels clacking on the marble floor.

It was sunny outside, but clouds littered the sky and it was a small consolation, fuck knows why.

I stood on the street with my eyes trained on the floor. All I had with me were the keys to the apartment. I'd never felt more naked in my life.

I knew I was in an upscale part of town. There weren't going to be any sketchy characters around these parts, which could be either good or bad.

At least no one would wolf-whistle or try to hurt me.

But it also meant it would be much, much harder finding someone on the street when it was filled with businessmen in expensive suits and yummy mommies with buggies that cost more than the rent at my old apartment.

I raised my eyes.

There were a few people walking down the block and none of them seemed to notice me. Not yet, anyway.

I scoped out everyone.

A woman with her hair pinned up intricately, and a briefcase in her hand. Her pencil skirt was too tight for her curvy body and her blouse strained against her generous chest. She looked at me distractedly, and her eyes widened. I stared her down, because I didn't have a choice. If I backed down now, I would go back to the apartment with my tail between my legs.

She stared and I stared back for what felt like ages. I stood in front of King's apartment building and she walked down the street, her eyes on mine. Finally, she bowed her head and kept walking as if she hadn't seen a fucking thing. I wasn't sure how I felt about that.

I looked around some more.

There were a few businessmen on the corner, three of them, engaged in an intense conversation. All of them handsome and older. One stood out. His hair was graying, his jaw chiseled. He was very handsome.

I started walking, reminding myself silently how to do it. One foot before the other, careful, careful. Heels clacking on the floor, the jacket just short enough to show off my belt.

I felt their eyes on me, all of them. But I focused my gaze on the guy I liked until I was nearly next to him.

He was still talking, but seemed to notice his friends had stopped paying attention. He finally stopped mid-sentence and looked in my direction, and his jaw fell.

He stared at me. Not at my body, not my legs, or my cleavage or my heels. He just stared at my face, and I stared back.

I was almost next to him. I could've reached out and touched the lapel of his blazer. Time felt like it had frozen.

They were all staring. Their eyes hot, their dicks probably twitching.

I stared at the man and he stared at me. He reached up for his tie and tugged at it like it was suffocating him.

I felt my pussy dripping down my legs, and I didn't give a fuck if anyone noticed.

I was almost next to him. Almost close enough to touch him. So close I could smell his cologne. It reminded me of something my counselor wore in high school.

I walked past him.

I felt almost sick as I passed their group, none of the men saying a fucking word as I kept walking like nothing had happened. I felt their eyes on me. Stripping me.

For a second I thought I would really just bend over and throw up the apple I'd had earlier.

But I made myself keep walking.

I crossed the street and kept walking. Always walking.

Just a little bit longer.

My breathing was so labored I didn't know how I didn't pass out.

People kept walking past me. Women, men. Pretty girls, overweight women. Drivers in uniforms, men in a rush. Nannies with screaming children, guys in suits so expensive I'd be afraid to brush my fingers against the fabric.

All of them stared at me. I could feel their eyes drinking me in. The women, the men, the children. Almost stunned when they saw me. Some of them stopping in their tracks, others blushing and pretending they hadn't seen a thing. I just kept on walking, because I knew if I stopped, I'd never be able to keep going. I'd just collapse on the spot and have to wait for someone to help me.

My heart pounded as I reached another block.

Someone's hand wrapped around my forearm and I looked up, startled.

A man.

Uniform.

Driver.

I swallowed hard.

He had gray eyes and blonde hair. There was a small nick on his jaw from when he'd cut himself shaving.

"You okay there, miss?" he asked me. His voice was heavy with lust.

I shook my head no and his hand moved down my arm. I could feel the butterflies; in my pussy this time.

"Jenner, let's get fucking going."

"In a second, sir," he replied and kept staring at me.

I parted my lips and gave him a needy look and he groaned, reaching up to my face.

I tore myself out of his arms and ran down the block.

I stopped in a side alley.

Not even that was trashy, not in this part of town.

I felt like I was going to pass out. My palms touched the brick wall of the building behind me and I slid down until my ass was resting on my ridiculous heels.

My heart pounded with a rhythm of some song I used to know. I stared at the floor and tried to get to my senses.

I must've been out for ages. I didn't have a watch, but it felt like hours. I'd walked around aimlessly for so long. But I'd been walking in circles. I was nearly back to King's apartment building.

The sky was a darker shade of gray now.

My time was running out.

I didn't want him to win.

I couldn't let him do that.

*Tick tock, tick tock, tick tock.*

I picked myself up again, not knowing how when I felt so broken. My legs barely worked, but they managed to carry me back to the main street. I kept my eyes down. On the pavement. On my shoes.

Step after step after step I headed back to the apartment building. I still felt their eyes on me. Still felt them looking.

I needed a fucking miracle.

I needed to cross the street.

I looked up and crossed it.

Someone blew their horn at me and I stopped in my tracks, right in the middle of the road. I felt like a deer in headlights, frozen, completely frozen.

Curses, screams. Someone pulling me out of the way, screaming their head off at me.

I'd never felt more terrified.

A couple. The woman was frantic, screaming at the man to make sure I was okay. She was holding a baby in her arms.

I looked at the guy. He was holding my arm, but he seemed mesmerized despite his woman screaming at him to do something, to make sure I was okay.

He stared into my eyes and I breathed in short, panicked breaths.

"She's fine," he told the woman. His voice was heavily accented and deep.

I could fuck him.

I would fuck him.

I had to.

"You…" I whispered, and his pupils dilated even more.

The woman kept chattering and he stared at me like I was a fucking Happy Meal.

"I…"

"Do you need help?" he asked me, and I swallowed so hard it hurt my throat. His eyes zeroed in on my neck and he watched me swallow again. His free hand was in a fist.

"Jason, I need to feed her," the woman said, cradling the screaming baby. But her man didn't move an inch. She gave us an incredulous look and smacked his shoulder. "Are you fucking kidding me?"

I giggled.

And then I laughed.

And then I left.

This was too fucking hard. I would never be able to find someone, fucking never.

I walked the short distance to the other side of the road, my eyes dancing over the people on the street.

I had to do it, I fucking had to.

In the end, it was so simple.

I looked over to the townhouses on the other side of the street. Pretty brick houses with well-groomed plants lining the steps that led up to the front doors.

He was sitting on the steps. He looked as out of place as I felt.

It wasn't that warm, not really.

Not warm enough for the sleeveless shirt he was wearing. His arms were bulging with muscles. Tattooed muscles.

The jeans he had on were ripped to shreds. His wore black leather boots and his hair was messy and a few inches too long. Dark brown, like his eyes. He wasn't shaved. His beard was almost at the point where it looked unruly, but still groomed enough to make me think he had it on purpose.

He rubbed his palms together, looking across the street. His eyebrows were knitted together. It looked like he was waiting for someone.

He was closer to my age than King's.

There was something weird about him, something off. He looked like a ticking time bomb.

*Tick tock, tick tock, tick tock.*

He looked across the street again, his motions frantic and fast.

He saw me, and he didn't look at my face for long.

His eyes drank me in, from the shoes, to the stockings, up my legs, lingering between them. Over my jacket, licking his lips as he stared at my chest. Over my neck, up, up and up and to my lips, to my flushing cheeks, to my needy eyes.

He didn't stare for long, it seemed like he made a decision in seconds. Impulsive.

He got up, well, jumped up from the steps really. He looked angry. Still frowning. He didn't look at me again. Just crossed the road and reached me in what felt like a heartbeat.

Once he came up to me, he still wouldn't look at me. He stood next to me, his hands in the pockets of his jeans. Our hips touched so very slightly I could have imagined it if it wasn't for the bolt of electricity that shot up my spine.

He still wouldn't look at me as he pulled a pack of cigarettes from his pocket, put one in his mouth and lit it.

He took a long drag. His fingers twitched when he put the packet back in his pocket, took the cigarette out of his mouth and sighed.

I knew I was staring but I couldn't fucking help it.

He tapped the cigarette and offered it to me without giving me a single look.

My fingers shook as I took it from his and took a drag. It was fucking disgusting, and I had to fight myself from choking.

I gave it back to him, and he finally looked at me. Tits first, and then my eyes.

"Hey," he said. His voice was rough as hell, probably from the smoking. Rough and deep.

I looked up at him. He was frowning still, not touching me. I knew he would be, though, in just a few minutes.

"Hey, stranger," I whispered and he licked his lips.

# CHAPTER 22
## *Stranger*

"You look like trouble."

She was very small.

"I… I'm really not."

I wondered if her tits would fit into my hands as perfectly as I imagined they would.

"A little liar too."

She looked even better when she blushed.

I reached out, grabbing her face between my fingers roughly. Her eyes widened and her breath hitched so loudly I thought she'd pass out right there.

"Calm the fuck down," I told her. "I'm just looking at that pretty face, little girl."

"You… Can't just…"

She stared at me incredulously as I turned her face from side to side. Oh yes, she was really fucking stunning.

"Can't just what?" I asked. When she didn't reply I yanked her against me, really hard, her body smashing against mine with so much force it would've knocked anyone else over. But not me.

"Do you…" Her eyes were begging, even though she wasn't. Yet. "Do you want to fuck me?" she said, her voice shaky.

"I don't fuck little girls," I told her. "I fuck little whores, though. What's your name?"

She licked her lips. "I… My name is Pet," she said.

"The fuck kind of name is that?" I ran my thumb over her jaw. Over her lips. I could tell she wanted to suck on it. "Are you a little whore, Pet?"

She just stared at me, and finally nodded.

"Oh yeah?" I moved my hand to her throat and rubbed my thumb against that hollow spot roughly. "Do you swallow?"

A siren blasted in the distance and I looked in the direction of the sound. Then back at her. Her outfit was definitely slutty, but under all that makeup and expensive fucking clothes she looked like a girl. A little girl.

"Yes, I swallow," she breathed.

"Show me," I ordered her.

She stared at me as she swallowed her own moan. I felt it through her throat, and laughed when she was done.

"Fun," I told her. "Come on, let's go."

Sirens again. I looked away for a second.

"J-just like that?" she stuttered, and I looked back at her.

"Yeah," I grinned at her. "And don't pretend that's not why you're parading down the street at 6 p.m. dressed like a high-class fucking hooker."

She fumbled with something in her pocket and I stared down her jacket.

"Jesus," I groaned. "Are you even wearing anything under that?"

She looked up, a set of keys dangling from her fingers.

"Come see," she told me, and walked towards the building we were standing in front of. I looked around, and followed her.

Fancy fucking place. All marble and high ceilings. A chandelier. It sparkled. Not as pretty as her eyes, though.

The doorman stared at us and I flipped him off before we got in the elevator.

"Can you not do that?" she hissed at me, and I leaned against the mirror as the elevator started moving. "I live here, you know."

I stared at her with my hands in my pockets. She looked pretty furious. It was a cute look on her. "You mad at me or yourself?" I asked her.

"Why on earth would I be mad at myself?" she rolled her eyes.

I motioned for her to come closer and she did, because obviously that's what she was made to do. Follow orders.

She stopped a few inches away from me.

"Take your jacket off," I said, and she looked away. And then back at me in the next second. Needy little eyes. Needy little girl. "Do it."

She unbuttoned the thing with shaky fingers and slid it off her shoulders.

I stared at her face as she exposed her sweet little body to me. And then down, when she couldn't hold my gaze anymore.

Pretty fucking tits, pink nipples, really small. Smaller than I thought they'd be.

She was wearing a full-on whore get-up. Her legs were quivering under the weight of my gaze. That tiny patch of fabric between her legs had to go.

"You always dress up like that?" I asked her, and she made an attempt to close the jacket.

I moved towards her, and took it off for her. She let me. I folded her jacket over my arm and motioned for her to turn around.

She did.

Tiny ass, too. Really perky. Legs up to her neck. Nice long neck.

She tried to turn back around, but I came up behind her, twisting her arms behind her back. She gasped.

"You should be mad at yourself," I said into her ear. "Because you're a very fucking naive little bitch. Who told you to trust strangers?"

She arched her back against me just as the elevator doors dinged open.

Her breath caught in her throat.

There was a couple standing in front of the elevator. When they saw us, their jaws dropped.

"Wanna join in?" I asked with a smile, and they just stared at us.

I pinched her nipple. Really hard. She made a pretty noise, and the doors closed. And up we went.

"You... I..." She was shaking pretty badly.

"Shut the fuck up, little slut," I told her. The doors opened again, top floor. "This us?"

She nodded and I marched her down the hallway, tits out and all. There was only one door on the floor, and I let go of her so she could open it.

I didn't look at the apartment because I didn't really give a shit what it looked like. Whether she lived with her loaded parents or a sugar daddy didn't really matter to me. As long as they weren't there so I could bury my cock inside her and fuck her naïve brains out.

I threw her jacket on the sofa and looked around. Paintings. Modern shit that could either be functional or a piece of shit decoration. Weird place.

"It's... can you come with me?" she asked, and I followed her into a dimly lit room. Floor-to-ceiling windows like in the rest of the apartment. A big bed.

A whole lot of kinky fucking shit.

She made a move to close the blinds on those windows, but I stopped her, stood in front of her.

"Don't," I said.

"I... Someone could see," she argued.

"Good."

I pulled her against me, and her body trembled as I peeled her clothes off her. All of it, even the pretentious fucking stockings. I wanted her totally naked. And shivering.

She stood so close to me I couldn't get a good look at her, and I knew she was really scared. It made me excited. Made me fucking hard.

"Hey," I said against her cheek. "Why are you so fucking terrified?"

All I could see were those ridiculous lashes against her cheeks.

"Because I... I want this," she admitted.

"No shit," I said. "Come on, little girl. Tits against the window, legs spread."

She did as she was told, pressed her tits against the glass and spread those slender pins for me. Someone had trained her well.

"Look outside," I told her. She did.

I took my clothes off, littered the floor with them.

My head was empty.

For once, my fucking head was empty.

No background noise, no annoying fucking voices, no damn distractions.

Only her.

Her reflection stared at me from the window. I stared back.

"So, listen," I said, running a hand down her back. She mewled and my cock twitched for her. "I really want to fuck you."

"Do it," she whispered.

"Yeah, I will," I muttered against the nape of her neck. She was gasping again. Loud. Almost out of control. Almost on the verge of panic. "I'm not gonna use a condom, though."

"P-please," she whimpered. "You have to, I'll get in trouble."

"Nah," I said. I tasted her skin and her legs nearly gave out. "I don't have to do anything, little slut."

I thought she would cry, but she surprised me by biting the tears back.

"But hey," I said, my fingers wrapping around her throat, the other hand guiding my cock between her legs. She cried out. "I'll fuck your ass, okay? So you don't get in trouble with your guy."

She cried out then, finally, her little body resisting. It was too late, though.

I pressed my tip against her little hole and she went fucking wild. I held her in place when I spat on the crack of her ass. She didn't say a word as I slicked her hole with my thumb. Not begging me to stop, or to go on. So fuck being the good guy.

I pushed my thumb in and she hissed.

"Ready?" I asked but she only bit back a sob.

Fuck it. I pulled my thumb away, replaced it with my tip and pushed in, just past the tight muscle.

She howled with pain and I groaned with pleasure as her ass gripped me.

I had never in my life been inside an ass that tight.

"Fuck," I breathed, just feeling my cock pulse inside her. She went rigid and motionless in my arms. "Have you had anything up your ass before, little girl?"

She nodded. Her eyes found mine in the window and I stared at her. I felt a little bad. But not bad enough to stop. Especially when she reached behind her and felt around, touching my cock. She gasped when she realized I wasn't even fully inside her.

"Please," she whispered. "I... I'm really scared."

"Do you want me to stop?" I stroked her hair. Pretty curls. Pretty little blonde. Very hard to resist. "I'll try to if you ask nicely."

I still hadn't started fucking her. Being inside her felt too good, and I wanted to relish the moment for a little while longer.

"I..." She stared at me in the window. Her eyes were really fucking wild. For a second I thought she was on something.

"Time's up," I told her with a grin. "Don't worry, little girl, I'll make sure you like it."

I wrapped one hand around her waist and pulled on her hair with the other one. She let me, just like I knew she would.

I started fucking her little ass nice and slow. She felt unbelievably good.

She felt frozen in my arms, though. Her skin was really fucking cold and her eyes were glassy. Something was off.

"Jesus," I groaned against her skin. "You need to... You need to meet me halfway here, little one."

"I-I'm... okay," she got out.

I licked her neck. Bit it. Sucked her skin. She melted slowly. First, her fingers stopped cramping behind her back. Then, she threw her head back a little, looking at me over her shoulder. And then she moaned for the first time. A hot fucking moan.

"Just like that," I told her gently. I fucked her ass harder. She was so fucking... innocent, yet slutty. It was driving me insane. I needed her to want this as much as I did.

"It h-hurts," she said, and I thrust a little less.

"No," she cried out. "More like that, please don't stop."

I didn't stop.

I used her sweet little asshole to pleasure myself and with every thrust of my hips, she let me have more of her. Submitted more, gave me another piece of her puzzle.

The silence in my head was deafening. Just her. It was only her that mattered, and it was the first time I had ever felt that way. Like I'd stumbled on a good place, a happy place, where I could tune out everything and everyone, and just make her mine. Because that was all that mattered in that moment.

I could've come a few times but I needed her to do it first. From a cock up her ass. Nothing touching her pussy. Nothing touching her tits. Just a hard cock up her asshole and a hand around her throat.

I gripped her neck tightly and fucked her ass so roughly she dug her nails into my skin.

"Oh my God," she whispered. "You're fucking crazy. You're insane. This… it's so wrong. He's going to kill me."

"Probably," I grunted against her skin. "You need to come for me, little slut."

"No," she whispered. "Not from that, I… I can't come from that."

I took it as a fucking challenge.

I knew I was going to burst if I kept going at that pace. I could already feel my cock dripping precum inside her ass, mixing with my spit from before.

"You will tonight," I told her, and she went so slack I had to hold her up so I could keep fucking her. "Oh, little one. You like being fucked like that? Like a fucking ragdoll?"

She couldn't stop her next moan. It was long and delicious, and she didn't want me to hear it, because she blushed all over when it left her lips.

"That's right," I said. "Moan just like that, and you'll get your ass filled up just the way you want to."

She struggled half-heartedly, more for show than anything else. I was really close. Too fucking close to worry about her own orgasm.

"Fuck," I muttered against her shoulder, my cock making a really loud noise when it left her ass. She cried out.

"Put it back," she begged. "Please fucking please, put it back inside me. All the way."

"I thought you couldn't come like that," I grunted, rubbing my tip all over her wet little pussy. She was a mess. Such a loud little mess. "Did you lie again?"

"I..." She sobbed, just once, but no tears came. "I don't know, just put it back, please."

I did. All the way. I rammed into her so hard and when my balls hit her clit she came apart at the seams from one... Fucking. Thrust.

"Jesus," I groaned as her body writhed on my cock. I'd never seen a girl come like that. Like a fucking storm. She screamed too, really screamed her heart out. And I held her little body with my hand and pumped inside her one last time, until I felt myself spilling everything inside that tight little ass. There was so much it ran down the sides of my cock and the girl cried when she felt it leaking out. Fucking cried.

"Don't pull out," she begged. "Don't, please don't pull out."

She was hysterical. I could barely breathe.

"I have to," I groaned. "I want to see your ass gape, little girl."

She howled and I forced my dick out of her with the loudest, nastiest sound. For a second, I looked at her little stretched asshole, the cum leaking out of her while she cried so hard she made herself come. Without anyone touching her. Just squeezing my cum out of her own body, her hands still held behind her back. She just came like that. Fucking crazy.

"Fuck, baby," I said. "Fuck."

"You need to leave," she gasped. "You need to fucking go, now."

I looked at the door. I'd heard him walk in a while ago. I could feel the anger radiating off him.

"I think it's a little too late for that, baby," I said.

# CHAPTER 23
## *King*

**I** *could tell the guy saw* me walk in, and he didn't give a shit. I had to restrain myself from dragging him off her, out of her, and smashing his skull against the wall until his brains splattered red over the whiteness. My blood was fucking boiling and my fists ached for the hit I wouldn't let myself take.

I watched him fuck her. My little Pet's ass. And she fucking let him. I watched her break, and I watched him make it all better, and hated myself for not being the one to do that for her.

But I forced myself to think it was okay. She needed this, and I wasn't able to give it to her. She deserved to get better, and if I wasn't up for the task, I had to find someone else to replace me.

I didn't really realize I was touching my throbbing dick through my pants until I felt myself leaking precum all over the front of them. I moved my hand away and leaned against the door because I felt really fucking lightheaded. And I watched him finish in her ass, and wished I could get away with snapping his neck on the spot.

I watched my Pet, *my* fucking girl, come from having a stranger's cock up her ass, and then come again just from having his cum leak out of her stretched hole. I fisted my cock through my pants and waited for her to stop screaming. It felt like she never would.

When he said it was too late, I waited for her reaction. She had to calm down first. Deep, labored breaths while the two of us just fucking stared at her bare body coming down from its high. And then she turned around, slowly.

Her eyes were fucking wild. Her hair was a mess, and she had black smudges around her eyes from crying too much. Her lipstick was somehow still in place, and the ring of pink on her face looked stark against the rest of her ruined makeup.

She didn't look at him. She looked right at me. And her lips parted in a silent moan.

Pet came rushing towards me, crashing into my arms. I had to hold her up, my hands wrapping around her tiny waist and my lips going to hers. She opened her mouth and sobbed for me. For me, not for him.

"I didn't want to," she whispered into my mouth. I fought the urge to kiss her hard. I stroked her hair, down her back, over her naked ass. Fuck, I was going to kill him.

"I know," I said against her hair. "I know you didn't, it's okay."

Her sobs were so fucking pathetic and so damn hot I could barely resist.

"It felt so good," she whispered against my lips. "It felt so good. So good."

"I know," I repeated. "It's okay, I know it did. That's okay, Pet."

I could see the guy staring at us, his cock still hard as hell. His hands were stroking it absentmindedly, and his eyes were on Pet. He wanted more. If he so much as fucking touched her I'd tear his fucking heart out through his ass.

"Fuck," he grunted, and Pet shivered harder in my arms. Jesus fucking Christ, what had I done?

"You need to leave," I told him, excluding the part about me knocking him the hell out if he didn't. "Now. You need to leave now."

"Yeah," he said. His eyes were delirious as he looked at her. "Fuck, man. I can't. I can't leave now."

I didn't want to let go of her. She clung to me so desperately.

"Please," she sobbed against my chest. Her fists went up to me and I held them up for her, kissing her knuckles. "Please, I can't."

"Go," I told him again.

"Don't," he groaned. "I'm not fucking leaving, not now. Is she fucking okay?"

"No," I hissed. "She's not, you fucking moron. Are you fucking blind?"

"I'm fine," Pet whispered against my chest. "I'm fine."

"You're not fucking fine," I reminded her. God, I wanted to punch him. I played it out in my head, knocking out his teeth, slitting his fucking throat until blood gushed down his fucking tattooed chest.

"I want her again," he said. His cock was in his fist. His eyes were on my Pet. "Fuck, I want her again, please. I'll do anything."

I let go of her and she tumbled to the floor. I stepped closer to him, and he didn't back down. He just stared at me like an addict, like he couldn't give up this fucking fix.

"You need to get the fuck out of here," I told him.

We were about the same height, same weight. He was my complete opposite though. And it pained me to know it might've been exactly what Pet needed.

"I'm coming back," he said, reaching for his clothes. He pulled on his boxers, his eyes never leaving Pet on the floor. "I have to."

"If I ever see your fucking face again," I said. "I'm going to kill you. I'm going to slit your fucking throat, and I'm going to enjoy watching you bleed out like the pig you are, you bastard."

He stared at me, his eyes wild and crazed.

"She needed that," he said. "She fucking needed that, and we both know it."

"Get. The fuck. OUT!" I glared at him and he backed away towards the door. His eyes danced between me and Pet and I took a furious breath. I knew I'd regret not killing him on the spot for the rest of my life.

"I'm coming back," he grunted, and I slammed the door of the playroom in his face.

I was back with her in a second. She sat in a crumpled ball on the floor, hugging her knees to her chest. I couldn't believe the guy had done that. Couldn't believe she didn't stand up to him. And that I didn't.

I wanted to fucking wash him off her. Every trace of that filthy cunt, every drop of his cum, every lick of his tongue across her skin. I reached for her and she shied away from my touch, and it fucking killed me to see that.

"Pet," I whispered. "Please, come here. Come to me, please, you know I'll take care of you."

She shook her head no over and over again. Rocked on her heels. Let out a small cry.

"Let me help you," I begged her. "I'll make it okay, I promise. I'm so fucking sorry."

"It's okay," she said softly. "It's really okay."

"Sapphire." I nearly choked on her name. Her eyes looked at mine, so desperate.

"Yes," she said. "Yes?"

"I... just..." I stared at her. What had I done? *What had I fucking done?*

I felt like a selfish fucking bastard. I was one, there was no doubt about that.

"Tell me you love me," I said, and she parted her lips as the words slipped out, like it was the most natural thing in the world.

"I love you," she said, and I knew she wasn't lying. It was as true as it had been the first time she said it, when she shouted it against the palm of my hand.

"Will you let me make it better?" I asked her. "Please, Sapphire."

"Okay."

I picked her up. She weighed next to nothing and it made me worry. Had she been eating? Such a fucking ridiculous concern after everything that had just happened. I walked towards the shower but she whimpered in my arms.

"No," she begged. "Bed, please. Our bed, I want us both in our bed."

I did as she asked, even though I wanted to scrub her fucking clean.

Carrying her over to the bedroom, I pulled back the sheets and she crawled under them until the only thing I could see were her eyes and her hair like a halo on the pillow. I lay down next to her, her body naked and mine still in the suit I'd worn to work. Work that I'd actually missed, because I sat in the fucking car and felt sorry for myself while she found a guy to fuck her. Fuck her damn ass. I should've killed him. I was going to, next chance I got.

She crawled into my arms and looked up at me as I stroked her back. Long, soothing motions of my fingers, sweet little words whispered in her ear. She sighed contentedly after a while and I reminded myself she was still mine. She'd always be mine. I wanted her so badly. I craved every bit of her. I would fucking hate having to share her like this. And that fucking guy… He wasn't the right choice. No matter how good it felt for her in the heat of the moment. She was done with him.

She was drifting off, her breaths getting slower. She sighed here and there, and let out a very soft cry every once in a while. Sometimes her eyes would flutter open just to make sure I was still there.

"I won't go," I promised her. "I won't go anywhere, go to sleep."

"Okay," she whispered, her head resting on my chest. "Thank you."

"It's okay," I said. "I'll always be here, Sapphire."

The lie felt ominous, but she believed it. She needed to believe it for her own fucking sake.

"I know," she said sleepily, her eyes heavy as she looked up at me. "Thank you."

"For what?" I asked roughly.

"For… everything," she said. "For trusting me. For giving me that task. For making it all better."

I would kill him. I fucking had to.

"Of course, Pet," I told her, kissing her forehead. "You know I do it all for you."

"I know," she whispered, and drifted off to sleep.

And I just lay there and held her in my arms, knowing it was the beginning of the end.

# CHAPTER 24
*Pet*

I*t felt like I slept* for days after that evening. And I probably did. I didn't even remember leaving the bed, or eating, or any other things I was surely doing during the following week. I just remembered the bed, and King's hands on me. Always touching me, always stroking, and pinching, and caressing me where I needed it the most. He didn't fuck me for a few days, not until I begged so much he couldn't resist anymore. And when he finally did, it felt like a relief for both of us.

We didn't speak about his task once. I could tell he was angry, but I wasn't sure who it was directed at. Maybe me, maybe himself, but mostly *Stranger*.

I tried not to think about him, and failed miserably every single day.

I couldn't fucking stop myself. He kept creeping into my thoughts, demanding to be acknowledged.

I couldn't forget the way he'd felt inside me. The way he'd spoken to me, the way he'd treated me. It almost felt like a dream, or maybe a nightmare. I couldn't decide which. But the truth was, I wanted him again. I wanted him again so badly it hurt.

King stayed home from work for a week. It almost felt like he was guarding me, as if he was afraid Stranger would come back and try to steal me. I didn't argue with him. I craved his closeness, and begged him to stay at home. He spent most of the day taking care of me, and most of the night holding me so tightly I could barely breathe.

There was no doubt in my mind that I loved this man. I did. From the moment I met him, I knew he was the love of my life. This pull he had on me, it was incredible.

But the way he'd thrown another man at me, the way he'd tested my limits once again, might have backfired.

Because I kept thinking about Stranger.

Not alone.

Never alone with me.

Always with King there as well.

He'd left to take a shower that morning and I lay in bed with the sunshine streaming through the windows and caressing my naked skin. I stretched on the bed, feeling the sheets rub against my bareness.

I thought about him again. The way he'd fucked my ass, not giving a damn about it hurting or about whether or not I wanted it. He just took what he wanted, and for some reason, my body responded.

My hand slipped between my legs and I touched my pussy. King had shaved it for me the day before, and it felt smooth and wet to the touch.

I parted my pussy lips and thought about it. The most forbidden fantasy out there, the craziest one, because it was never going to fucking happen.

Both of them, at the same time. My King, and my Stranger.

I mewled as I slipped a finger inside me, thankful for the spray of the shower in the bathroom which meant he wouldn't hear what I was doing.

We'd had sex a few hours ago, but not like this. Not with my mind on them both. When King was fucking me, all I could think about was him. My love, my everything.

When I was alone, I could think about the two of them, together.

I bit my bottom lip as I played with myself. I'd never gotten a good look at Stranger's cock but I sure as hell knew what it had felt like inside me. The way it had filled me up until I was almost impossibly full; the way his grunts sounded against my skin.

And I coupled that with King. The way he held back, his whole body shaking when he fought the urge to hurt me. The way he laid claim to my body and my mind from the moment he met me.

I gasped. So fucking close. Another finger inside me, that would do it. Not in my pussy, though.

My eyes flew open and I listened to the sound of the shower for a second. I'd never played with my ass before. Never. But now I wanted to.

I raised my hand to my lips and licked my fingers tentatively. Back between my legs then, and tried to press the tip inside. I yelped in pain. It wouldn't fucking go in.

My fingers went to my mouth again and I really sucked at them. Really made them as wet as possible before letting my hand wander back between my legs.

A finger in my pussy. And, with all the force I could muster, another one in my ass.

My eyes widened at the sensation. I clamped my free hand over my mouth and stared at the ceiling, at the stars dancing before my eyes. I wasn't even moving my fingers and it felt insane. Like nothing I'd ever felt before.

My fingers twitched involuntarily and I moaned against my own palm. Fuck. I wanted them. Stranger and King, just like that. Each in one hole. I needed it. I'd beg for it, if I had to.

I arched my back as I started to fuck myself. Slowly. But deeply.

It didn't take long for my back to arch so painfully it felt like my body was barely touching the mattress. I moaned against my hand. Fuck, I needed this. My own fingers would never be enough, not now that the idea was firmly planted in my head.

I rode my fingers to an orgasm, as slowly and as quietly as I possibly could for fear of King hearing me. He still hadn't fucked my ass. I doubted he ever would at that point.

I was so close, so painfully close. But I knew that if I kept going, I wouldn't be able to keep it down, and he would hear. I resisted it for as long as I could.

And then it was too late. My finger curled up inside my pussy and the other one fucked my ass and I had to bite my palm to stop myself from screaming King's name, begging him to come out of the shower. Except I couldn't. It was too much.

I bit my own palm too hard and screamed in agony the moment I came. His name on my lips, two cocks fucking me in my mind.

"King, please!"

I heard the water turn off in seconds and I couldn't fucking stop. There was no way I'd be able to stop myself before he came into the room. So I forced my eyes to open and stared at the doorway until his figure appeared in it, his hair dripping wet and his body glistening. I just gave him my most desperate look as I came, really quietly, barely making a sound.

He stared at me. My fingers working both of my holes, my mouth begging for him to take me.

"Pet," he groaned, and his cock twitched at his own words. "Jesus, what the fuck are you doing?"

I kept playing and he came closer. My free hand was tangled in the sheets.

"Suck on your fingers," he told me roughly. "I want all three of your holes filled. Right the fuck now."

I did it, and it made me mewl against my knuckles because there wasn't much else I could do.

"Come for me," he ordered me. "Now, Pet."

I did, and he watched, stroking his cock in painfully slow motions. My whole body shivered as he watched me, and I pulled out my fingers. It made me moan even louder.

"Good girl," he grunted.

I rolled over to my stomach and hid my face in my hands as he lay down next to me. His body was wet next to mine. I wanted to lick the droplets of water off his skin.

His fingers stroked my back, down my spine. He tugged on my hair.

"Pet," he muttered against my neck.

I prepared myself for a lecture, or questions I didn't want to hear. But they never came. Instead, he tugged on my hair some more.

"What?" I finally asked. "What is it?"

"I think you need an upgrade," he told me.

"What?"

I rolled to my side and he pulled me against him, grinning at me.

"You're not really the same girl you were when I met you," he told me. "I want… something different."

"What do you mean?" I asked, my dirty thoughts momentarily forgotten.

He grinned as he stared at me, toying with long strands of my hair.

My hand pulled on it self-consciously.

"My hair?" I asked him, and he nodded. "But I thought you liked my hair."

"You like turning heads, don't you?" he asked me and I nodded. "Good. That's what I want you to do."

<hr>

*"Do you like it?"*

I stared at my reflection in the mirror.

"Do you?" I asked back, and Maria gave it another thoughtful look.

"Yeah," she finally said. "It's a little crazy. But I like it on you."

I toyed with my hair. It was the same length. Blown out to perfection.

Except now it wasn't blonde anymore. It was pastel. Somewhere between gray and lavender.

"It's weird," I giggled, and she agreed.

I paid the hairdresser who was so excited she could barely shut up. She kept telling me how great I looked, but I felt self-conscious as fuck. I'd never really done anything that drastic with my appearance, and it felt awkward. It didn't feel like me. But what King wanted, King got.

I couldn't wait for him to see it, but I was really nervous that he wouldn't like it.

"Makes your eyes pop," Maria said encouragingly, and I twisted my mouth into a frown.

"I don't know," I muttered.

"You're really hung up on your hair right now?" she asked me, and I give her an I-feel-so-sorry-for-myself look. She sighed. "Listen, you just let go of the last part of you before him. Before King. Now you're really his. Only his."

I liked that, I liked it a lot.

She walked me to the apartment building and kissed my cheek before getting into a cab.

"Say hi for me," she said, and I rolled my eyes. "Give him a kiss from me."

"You wish," I said, and she laughed as the taxi took off.

The doorman stared at me just like he always did, but I wondered if he was really even surprised anymore with all the scenarios he'd seen me in. I took the elevator upstairs.

My heart pounded painfully as I got off on our floor, and knocked on the door, like King had told me to do.

He didn't go to the salon with me that time. Told me to surprise him. The only instructions he gave me was that there needed to be a change.

He opened the door, towering over me. I looked at the floor while his eyes drank me in. His fingers went to my tresses and he tugged on the conditioned locks.

"Well, fuck," he said, and pulled me inside the apartment.

I sat down on the couch self-consciously, unable to meet his eyes.

"I…" I stared at the floor. "I wasn't sure you'd like it. It's not very… classy."

"Since when do I like classy?" he asked, and I finally looked up at him.

His eyes were sparkling.

"We'll look really weird together now," I giggled. "The businessman and the girl with the purple hair."

"I like purple," he grinned.

"I know."

He made me get up and held me close. I looked into his eyes and stifled my laughter. It felt like he was doing the same thing.

"I like it a lot," he said, and I nodded. "It looks like… I don't know, it just looks like you. Special."

I stared at him. He was never like this. Never this sweet, or this open. I had to take the chance and run with it.

"I wanted to ask you something," I said. So softly he tipped my chin back and stared into my eyes.

"Louder, Pet," he told me, and I blushed at his words.

"I... I don't want you to get mad," I whispered.

His fingers tightened on my chin and I looked at him desperately. From the hardness in his eyes I knew he was aware of what my question was going to be.

"You want to fuck him again," he said, matter-of-factly.

"Stranger," I said. "Yes, I do."

He glared at me. He was really fucking angry, I could tell.

"Do you think you could find him?" My heart was beating so fast. So painfully fast.

"Probably," he got out through gritted teeth. "You really want it?"

"Yes," I nodded.

"Fine," he bit out. "Whatever you want, Pet."

He made a move to get away, but I held on to his hand and he let me pull him back.

"I want you both," I whispered. My cheeks bloomed with color as he stared at me.

"Both?" King repeated. "At the same time?"

"Y-yes," I answered.

He was quiet for a while. His fingers were rigid in my hand.

"We'll see," he grunted.

"I..." I looked up at him. Desperate. "I want you both to fuck me. Not watch as the other one does it."

"Yeah," he hissed. "I fucking got that, Pet."

"Under one condition," I added, and he stared at me.

"A condition?" he said. "You want me to fucking share you, and you have a condition?"

"Yes." I smiled softly. "I want you to fuck my ass. Because it's about fucking time."

# CHAPTER 25
## *Stranger*

I'd never really been hung up on a girl before.

Especially not one like her.

I'd beaten off to the thought of her so many times it felt like I'd fucked her every day since the day I met her. The feeling of being inside her tight ass was imprinted on me, and I couldn't get through a single fucking day without touching myself just for her.

Not that I had anything fucking else to do, anyway.

The job I was supposed to do, the one I was in her neighborhood for, fell through. Even though I bailed, I later found out the guy I was supposed to meet there never even fucking showed up. Figures.

The next two weeks of my life were kind of fucking terrible.

After a few days, I realized I had to fuck someone else to make myself forget.

It was obvious I'd never get to see her again. Not after those murderous looks from her man, or whoever the hell he was. I was lucky I'd gotten out of there alive. Not that I couldn't have taken him, but I assumed a guy like that, in such a powerful financial position could have easily ruined me – or worse.

I went out to a bar. Several nights in a row.

I had girls hit on me, girls dance with me, girls grind on me.

But nothing fucking worked.

Not one of them got me off, not one of them got me hard. It was fucking excruciating. The only way for me to come was picturing the girl, with her tight little ass, and her ridiculous get-up. Her pretty face with tears streaming down her cheeks, and her palms leaving prints on those windows.

I was fucking whipped, and it made me fucking furious.

I tried to find out more about her. I knew all about him. It was the first thing I did when I got home that night, look up the bastard who'd stolen her from me. Because after what I'd done to her, I should've been the one to put her back together. Not her sorry-ass piece of shit boyfriend.

I didn't know what their story was, and I didn't really care either. All that mattered was that in the end, the girl would choose me. Just like they always did.

Finding out who he was proved to be easy enough. Not that it helped, because he kept his affairs private.

Hayden Seth King. Pictures of him showed a beautiful woman on his arm, a different one every single time. Galas, events, gallery openings, business shit. A different chick each fucking time. All of them fucking stunning, all of them younger, but none as young as the one he had now.

I envied the guy. Really fucking envied him. He wasn't like me. He was a self-made man, a man who made his own fortune. And I'd squandered mine away.

Over the course of the next week, I became slightly obsessed with this

King character.

He was fucking impressive. Owned half of town, and all three holes I wanted for myself. His apartment was worth millions. His company was worth several times that. I wondered if the girl knew about that.

I briefly considered showing up on their doorstep. I even lingered in the neighborhood a few times. I looked up at the sky-high building and wondered whether I should just go the fuck up there and tell the guy I wanted her, and he'd just have to fucking deal with it.

I even tried to do it once. But the piece of shit doorman I'd flipped off the last time I was there took great pleasure in throwing me out on my ass.

I lingered some more. Neither of them ever left the building. So either they were away, or holed up in that damn apartment. I couldn't get to her that way. So I'd have to make her come to me.

There was no trace of the girl in his social media, no trace in the gossip websites that wrote about him. She was a nobody. And since I didn't even know her name, I couldn't really track her down.

By the time the second week had passed, I was really antsy. I wanted her. I wanted to get over this obsession for a silly little girl that wasn't supposed to mean shit to me. Even though I woke up every night, the sound of her sobbing so fresh in my mind I could almost feel her body convulsing under mine.

And then my phone finally fucking rang.

Unknown number, and somehow, I just knew.

I picked up and didn't say a word. I could practically feel his anger through the line.

"You remember?" he barked.

"Yes," I replied. I grinned to myself as I lit a cigarette. "Hard to fucking forget."

"Shut the fuck up," he said. "You need to come back."

"For her?" I took a long drag of the cigarette. Fuck. Yes. "I'd be happy to do that. Are you going to watch again?"

If he was into some cuckolding shit, I'd let him watch, just because I wanted her so badly. Though it would make me want to fucking kill him, knowing he was the one that got to take her to bed at night, and I was just there because of my dick and what it did to her tight little ass.

"No," he hissed. "She wants us both."

"Both?" I grimaced. "I'm not fucking into that, man."

"And you think I am?" he asked, and I chuckled.

"Well, fuck," I replied. "You want to do it?"

"No," he said. "I fucking don't. But I don't really have a fucking choice."

"Tough luck." I stubbed out my cigarette, running a hand through my hair. "When?"

"Tomorrow. Midnight. Same place." His voice was strained and I felt more than a little smug knowing he had to call me, had to ask me to come fuck his girl again.

"What's her name?" What a stupid fucking question. There were so many other things I had to know. Like if I'd get to fuck her ass again. If he'd make me wear a damn rubber. If I'd get to fuck her alone anytime soon.

"Pet," he bit out, and I rolled my eyes.

"Yeah," I said. "I don't know about you but I refer to women by their actual fucking names unless I'm fucking them."

"Then it shouldn't matter," he told me. "Since you'll only be fucking her."

I seethed with anger. "I want to know her name."

He didn't respond for a while, but when he did, his voice sounded defeated.

"It's Sapphire."

"She a fucking porn star?" I asked, laughing.

"Shut your fucking mouth," he snapped. "Tomorrow. Midnight. And if you don't do as I say, I'm cutting your balls off and feeding them to you."

He cut the line and I laughed at my phone.

Twenty-four hours. A day until I'd be inside her again. Only one day until my head would feel blissfully empty, just like last time.

---

*I felt like a moron* going into the building again.

If the doorman said a single thing to me this time around, I'd punch him. I hyped myself up to do it, until I was so angry my fingers shook.

But when I came into the lobby, a different guy sat there. He gave me a look, but nodded in greeting, and I felt pissed I didn't get to take my anger out on anyone.

I took the elevator to the top floor and enjoyed the sensation of déja-vu.

Standing in front of their door was awkward. But not as awkward as ringing the bell and having him open the door.

We glared at each other. I wished she'd opened the door for me.

It was like a fucking competition with this guy. And I was desperate to beat him.

He was wearing a shirt, pressed and ironed to perfection. And slacks. And dress shoes.

I was wearing a band shirt and my oldest pair of jeans. And Converse.

"Where is she?" I asked him.

He stepped aside, even though I could tell every cell in his body was shouting at him not to do it. I followed him inside.

No fucking sign of her. My cock ached to be inside her.

"Do you want a drink?" King asked me, and I glared at him.

"Do I look like I need a drink?" I asked him.

"I don't really give a shit," he said. "But I'm having one, so if you want one too, feel free."

He poured himself a glass of whiskey, leaving the bottle on the table.

He stood next to the windows facing the street and stared down.

"How old are you?" he asked.

"Thirty-two," I replied, walking to his bar and rummaging through the bottles just to fucking piss him off. "This all you got?"

"You're thirty-two?" he asked, giving me a doubtful look. "You dress like a teenager."

"You dress like a fucking old geezer," I told him. "Appropriate, I guess. You're what, fifty?"

He stared and I laughed to relieve the tension.

"Calm down, jackass," I told him. "Can I have this?"

I raised a bottle of rum at him, and he shrugged. "Whatever. Glasses are in the–"

He stared at me incredulously as I drank from the bottle.

"Are you fucking serious?" he asked me, and I grinned at him.

"Get off your high horse, old man," I told him.

"You're eight years younger than me," he said. "She's fourteen years younger than you."

"She's eighteen?" I stared at him, taking another swig from the bottle. "Jesus fucking Christ."

We didn't look at each other as we drank. Not enough to get me hammered, just enough to loosen up the nerves I never knew I had.

"I need to see her," I said, and he bit back something he was gonna say.

"Yeah," he said, setting his glass down. "Come with me."

I put the bottle of rum on the bar and followed him. Playroom again. I wondered where she slept when he wasn't using her in there. If they shared a bedroom, or if he made her sleep alone. He seemed like a possessive fucker, so I was pretty sure he wouldn't let her out of his sight.

He reached for a key in his pocket and slid it in the lock.

"You had to lock her inside?" I asked him with my eyebrows raised. "She that eager to see me?"

He left the key in the lock and grabbed my shirt, pulling me close. I stared him down.

"You're here because she wants you here," he hissed. "Not me. Never me. And if you do one thing that pisses me off… One thing to upset Pet."

"Sapphire," I said, and he nearly growled in my face.

"Don't fucking push it, boy. You wouldn't like me when I'm angry."

I swallowed any Hulk remarks that came to mind and gave him an angelic smile.

"If you don't get your hands off me," I said. "I'm gonna find it hard to believe you didn't want me here."

He let go of me disgustedly and I laughed as he opened the door. My heart was fucking pounding as we walked inside.

The room was dark, but he switched the light on, illuminating the space in a soft glow. Almost like candlelight.

The girl, Sapphire, was sitting on the bed.

Her ankles were tied together, and so were her wrists. She was wearing a blindfold. A black lacy one.

When she heard us walk in she whimpered so loudly I could feel it in my balls.

"Fuck," I muttered to myself.

She was naked, except for the scrap of lace across her eyes.

Her hair.

Her hair was somehow purple.

She looked like a fairy or some shit. Really tiny on that bed, with that long hair falling over her tits. She didn't have heels on this time. Her feet were bare, and her toenails were painted a pastel pink color. It was oddly endearing.

I took a step towards her, but King intercepted me, a heavy hand on my forearm.

"You remember one fucking thing, kid," he said with a grim expression. "She's fucking mine."

I stared back at him.

"Let's let Sapphire decide who she belongs to," I said, and she gasped in response.

# CHAPTER 26
## *King*

I *kept my eyes on her,* because I knew if I looked at him I'd do something I would regret.

Her breathing was labored and her chest rose and fell so fast I thought she was having a panic attack.

The guy looked at me. His eyes were dark with lust, probably the same as mine. We didn't say a word. I guess he figured out why she was wearing a blindfold.

We both took our clothes off. In seconds. I tried not to look at him as we walked over to the bed in unspoken agreement.

He reached for her, and his hands were shaking. The moment his fingers met her skin she gasped. I let the jealousy burn me, so painfully slowly it felt like a fire in the pit of my stomach.

Stranger flipped her over with ease. On her knees on the bed, with her head down against the mattress. She crawled to the center of the bed and I stared at her dripping pussy. This was really happening.

I moved closer to her. Behind her, placing a palm on her ass gently. It made her twitch and she looked around the room, even though she couldn't see a thing.

Stranger walked to the other side of the bed and sat down next to her. She whimpered when she felt his weight sink the mattress, and I stroked her ass, hating myself for what I wanted to do to her.

I looked at the guy, but he didn't even seem to realize I was in the same room. His cock was in his fist, hard and dripping with precum already. He reached for her, his rough fingers caressing her face.

"Oh God," she whispered.

She thrust her ass out at me and leaned into his touch. I had no idea if she knew which one of us was where. It didn't really fucking matter.

I rubbed her pussy with two fingers while he took hold of her throat. The noises she made with his fingers so tight around her neck sounded like she was drowning.

I groaned and parted her pussy lips with my cock and she thrashed under me. He squeezed her neck harder and she calmed down enough to stop resisting.

"Please," she said. Her voice was so raspy it sounded painful when she spoke. "Please, talk to me."

I looked over at him, my cock poised at her entrance. The jackass grinned at me and put a finger to his lips, his other hand on her mouth next, slipping a thumb between her lips. She sucked on it greedily.

I wanted to prolong the moment but I fucking couldn't. I rammed my cock inside her and Pet bit down on Stranger's finger so hard he was gritting his teeth and holding back a curse.

"You have to talk to me," she begged with her mouth full. "I can't see, please, talk to me."

I couldn't. I fucked her instead. Deep, angry thrusts of my hips against hers, enough to make her cry out. I looked up, even though I didn't want to.

He was stroking her hair, softly, gently, his fingers lingering on her jaw every time they reached it. He looked at her like she was his, and it pissed me off.

I made my thrusts harder and fucked her like I was punishing her. She was holding back. I could tell by the way her body tensed up impossibly, so desperate for one of us to tell her to just let the fuck go.

Her pussy made wet sounds as I bottomed out inside her. She gripped the bedsheets so tightly her knuckles cramped around the fabric.

"I want to come," she whispered. "Please let me. Tell me I'm allowed to, please. I have to hear you, please."

I bit my fucking tongue, but that bastard pulled on her hair and groaned so loudly she cried out.

"More," she said. "Please, more. I need to hear you."

He leaned closer to her and her lips parted for him. She was fucking desperate.

He kissed her. My fucking Pet. The sweetest of kisses, his tongue sliding into her mouth and teasing her, making her moan my name against his lips.

She thought it was me.

She thought he was fucking her pussy and that's why she was fucking holding back. So she wouldn't upset me.

I grunted and pulled out of her. She cried at the loss desperately, and I forced her on her back. I didn't need to tell the guy what to do. He ripped the blindfold from her eyes himself.

For a second, we both just stared at her. Her eyes were dilated as fuck. I could tell she was so close, just from the situation we were in. And it wasn't fucking working.

"Hold her the fuck still," I growled at him, and he grabbed her waist and held her down. His breaths were ragged. His cock was inches away from her lips and she opened her mouth to lick him, but he was too far away.

Her eyes went to me and she begged silently.

"Pet," I said. "This was a bad fucking idea."

"Yeah," Stranger groaned. "Really fucking bad."

"Very b-bad," she stuttered.

I smacked her thighs apart, "So now," I said. "You're going to pay for making me do this."

She nodded vigorously. "Yes, please, I want to. Let me."

I looked at her for a long time, knowing how nervous the waiting was making her. Then, I beckoned Stranger to me, and he joined me in front of our little toy.

"I want her ass," I told him in a growl, and Pet whimpered, whether in anticipation or fear, I wasn't sure.

But for once, I was sure of what I wanted. I was going to have that tight little butt of hers, and she didn't have a say in it. I'd kept myself away from her for too long, and I'd forced myself to not even think about it. But then to think he'd had it before me… It drove me fucking insane. I couldn't let him inside her again.

Stranger joined her on the bed, and I watched in absolute seething jealousy as she settled on top of him. She was about to feel him inside her pussy for the first time, and it drove me insane with red-hot rage, but I knew it had to be done. Everything there that night was going to happen for a reason, and I couldn't disrupt the order of things.

I stared at his hands going to her ass as she positioned herself over his crotch. His cock was so hard it looked painful as it throbbed beneath her. Pet moaned so loudly as she sunk her cunt onto it I could feel it reverberating in my veins, and then she looked at me over her shoulder.

Those big baby blues, so wide and so very scared. She had tears in her eyes, but they never fell. She just looked at me, and in that moment, I saw inside her, every bit of her she'd kept hidden from me, from her family, and from herself. And in that moment, she was finally completely, and utterly mine.

She smiled then, a big smile with her pearly whites on display and her eyes rolling back in pure ecstasy as she rocked a little on Stranger's cock. She moaned so sensually my dick throbbed, and she turned back to face him as she rode herself to an orgasm so fast I wanted to punish her for it.

I was up behind her, and I couldn't keep away any longer. Not with his dirty hands all over my girl and her cheeks splitting open every time she slammed down on his cock. I needed to be inside her. I needed to show Pet who she belonged to.

I opened her ass cheeks and her tight ring of flesh stared at me, puckered and so tight. I had no idea how anyone had ever fit inside her. She whimpered when I spat on her, right on that sweet little spot that opened up so invitingly when I stretched her.

"Are you ready for me, Pet?" I groaned in her ear, and she mewled when my hot breath hit her long, pale neck. I grabbed her hips, trying to ignore how angry having my hands on Stranger's hands made me, and I thrust inside her. All the way, no mercy, just rammed my cock inside that hungry little ass and she screamed for more.

And fuck, did she scream. And it was for me, not for the man claiming her pussy, and all three of us knew it. She said my name, over and over again as we fucked her, a whisper on her lips, then a scream at the top of her lungs. Over and over again, *King, please King, more King, my King*. I sure as hell hoped it was pissing Stranger off, though by the looks of it, the sick bastard was actually enjoying it, riding my pretty girl's pussy for all she had and groaning like she was the tightest, sweetest ride he'd ever experienced.

I let myself feel the inside of her, tight and impossibly smooth, something I'd never felt before, never this sweet, never this special. Never like this. I let my cock reach a new depth inside her and she clawed at Stranger's chest as I kissed her neck, her shoulders, all over that perfect creamy skin that only belonged to me.

I stared at her skin as we fucked her, stared and stared until it blurred in front of me in milky white perfection. My fingers gripped her tightly, and I stared at the marks I left on her. Scratches from my nails, red marks from my fingers, and the imprint of my heirloom ring. I stared at that one the most, and the idea sprang up on me so fast, until I couldn't fucking stop it. Until I could think of absolutely nothing fucking else but my mark on Pet's perfect, unmarred skin.

I pulled out of her and she cried when my cock left her ass, and stopped bouncing on Stranger's cock.

"King!" she cried out. "Don't stop, please, I want to feel you while he fucks me."

Her words made my blood boil, but I had other things on my mind, more important things.

I took my ring off and stared at it for a long time, and Pet climbed off Stranger's cock and joined me in the middle of the room.

"Please," she whispered. "Please, play with me… I don't want to stop now."

I stared at the ring, at my initials in the silver, and then I grabbed her by the throat and pushed her against the wall. She struggled feebly against me, but I could fucking smell how wet she was, her own juices dripping down her legs.

"Are you mine?" I asked her, the question a low growl against her lips. "Are you my Pet?"

"Yes," she said breathlessly as I raised her above the ground, her feet barely touching the floor. "Please, King! You know I am, I'm only yours…"

"Do you want to make that official?" I asked her. My fingers twitched I was so angry. I wanted to punish her, and my mind screamed at me to stop this madness. This wasn't how it was supposed to happen, but I couldn't fucking stop myself now, not anymore.

"Yes," she whispered. "Please, I want to."

I showed her the ring, and she gave me a confused look, but then her eyes started sparkling.

Wicked girl.

Naughty girl.

Bad, bad girl.

"You know what I'm gonna do to you, don't you, Pet?" I asked her, feeling Stranger joining us. I could feel his presence and it pissed me the fuck off, because this should've been between the two of us only. But in a weird way, it felt right that he was there with us. I wanted Stranger to see, I wanted him to watch her become mine completely.

"I do," she said, her voice shaky and full of anticipation. "Oh, I do, King, please…"

# CHAPTER 27
*Pet*

King *disappeared from the room* after pinning me against the wall, and being alone with Stranger suddenly felt so intimate it made me blush. I turned my naked body away from him, finally out of the ropes that bound me before. I could feel him moving behind me, the clanging of his metal belt buckle as he pulled his jeans back on. And then he approached me. I felt his breath on the back of my neck and a shiver ran through me, making my skin erupt in goosebumps. And he just stood behind me, breathing against my skin, never touching me once or saying a single word.

I looked at the window in front of us, seeing our reflections in the glass. He was shirtless, just in a pair of torn-up jeans, and I was still completely naked with my arms protectively folded in front of me. I felt so vulnerable like that; he was standing so close to me. But I didn't want him to move away. I wanted him to come closer.

I could hear King talking on the phone outside, and it made my heart pound. I wasn't sure what he was trying to do, but I remembered that ring of his, remembered the promise I'd just made, and a part of me — a big part of me — already knew what was coming next.

"You smell like fucking sin."

Stranger's words felt even hotter against my skin, and my back arched, trying desperately to make contact with him. I couldn't understand what it was about that man that made my body react so instantly, almost as if it was a chemical reaction binding me to him. I didn't want to understand, either. It scared me too much.

"Are you going to leave?" I asked him, my voice soft and shaky.

"I…" I could feel his mouth moving against my shoulder blades, moving up until he breathed heavy, labored breaths in my mane of hair. "I don't think I can… Pet."

King walked back in moments later, and we sprang apart guiltily even though we weren't doing anything wrong. King's eyes lingered on the space Stranger had occupied a moment ago, but he didn't say a word. He just moved to stand by me, his hand wrapping possessively around my waist. He was wearing pants now as well, but his chest was bare, just like Stranger's.

"She'll be here in twenty minutes," he told me, loud enough for Stranger to hear.

My heart pounded louder. I wondered what would happen next. Would he kick the other man out and pretend none of this had ever happened? I could feel the resentment he felt for Stranger. It was so obvious in every word he said and every move he made.

"I want you to stay," King told him.

I finally looked over my shoulder, not wanting to miss this exchange.

"Me?" Stranger asked bitterly. "Seems like you changed your fucking mind about having me around pretty fucking fast, old man."

"Don't try me," King spat out. "I said I want you here. If you want to stay for the girl, you will. You sure as fuck won't do it for yourself."

Stranger walked up to us, and just like always, my body tensed when he was around. I wanted his fingertips on my skin. I wanted him to feel what he was doing to me. Of course, I could never admit that out loud, especially not with King in the same room.

"Do I get another turn?" Stranger asked, the hint of a laugh in his voice so obvious it made me cringe for him. Surely King wouldn't let him get away with that tone.

"You will," King replied smoothly, and my body shook with anticipation.

They both held on to me, as if they were afraid I'd just topple over. King's arm wrapped around my waist, pulling me close against his taut and toned body, and Stranger's fingers squeezing my forearm like he owned me.

"Then I'll stay," Stranger said with a smile, looking into my eyes. Somehow I managed to hold his gaze, even though it felt burning hot. "For the girl."

King pulled me against him, and I could feel his erection through his pants as he held me close. Stranger looked out of the window, his breath leaving marks on the cool glass.

King led me to the couch and sat me down on the cushions. Somehow, I didn't feel naked at all. I felt like I belonged right there, in that room, with those two men having a plain view of my body. I couldn't even think of what had happened earlier. Having two cocks inside me, fucking me with so much recklessness… It would make me lose my mind all over again, and I needed to stay focused.

"Do you know what's going to happen, Pet?" King asked me.

My eyes finally left Stranger at the window, and lingered on my master's concerned expression.

"I-I think so," I whispered.

He took the ring off his finger and laid my palm out flatly between us. He placed the ring in my palm and clasped my fingers around it.

"I want you to wear my mark, Sapphire," King said softly. "I want you to wear it forever."

"Yes, I want–" I started, but he cut me off, placing a finger over my parted lips.

"You have to understand this means forever," he said again. "No matter what happens, that brand stays there. It's not like a tattoo, Pet. You can't have it removed, maybe covered up, but it will always be there, underneath whatever you put over it."

"You're going to fucking brand her?" Stranger's voice was incredulous as he moved away from the window, his eyebrows shooting up as he looked at us on the couch. "She's not fucking cattle, you jackass."

"I... I want it," I said, my voice not nearly as frightened as I really felt. But I knew I wasn't lying. I wanted this. I'd wanted it since I'd first seen his ring, those initials curving and intertwining together to make a beautiful pattern. I wanted to wear it on my skin, and if he would let me, I would keep it forever. I wanted to.

"Good girl," King muttered, ignoring Stranger completely. He got up to his feet, leaving his ring in my palm.

Stranger laughed and shook his head, looking from one of us to the other.

"You two are both batshit fucking crazy," he said, and I let a small smile break out on my lips as I stuck my tongue out at him. He stared at me for a long moment before running his hand through his hair and groaning. "I must be just as fucking crazy."

The doorbell rang, and I exchanged a look with King, hoping it didn't show

how panicked I was really feeling.

"She's early," he muttered to himself, and got up to answer the door. Once again, I was left waiting alone with Stranger, and having him in the same room made me nervous as hell. Thankfully, the door to the playroom opened again, and in walked King, with someone all too familiar following behind.

"Maria," I said, and she gave me a nervous smile before looking away.

"Angel," King corrected me, striding into the room in front of my new friend. "Don't call her by her name in here, Pet."

My bottom lip trembled as he guided me to my feet. I could only stare as my friend laid out a sheet on the floor. She put on a white robe over her clothes, and her hair was pinned up in a hairstyle that didn't show off her pretty curls. I felt so nervous it almost made me sick, and I could barely look at any of them.

Stranger was standing to the side of the room, as if he was pretending he wasn't playing a role in this. King hovered over Angel as she prepared everything, and I almost felt like I was a part of a medical experiment. It made me shake so badly King came over and cradled me in his arms. I could see Stranger shaking his head with an incredulous laugh over his shoulder. But he still didn't leave. None of us could, not now.

"Pet, I need you to lie down," Angel told me with a smile. I didn't know whether she was jealous or felt sorry for me, and I didn't know which one I'd prefer, either.

I let them both help me to the floor, lying down on my back. My eyes went to Stranger for some reason, and my gaze begged him to help me. He muttered something under his breath as he came to stand closer to me. He kneeled down next to King, and the two men shared a grudging look of acceptance, each taking one of my hands.

"Everything is sterilized," Angel told me in her calm, soothing voice. But it wasn't doing much to calm my nerves, not this time around. "You don't have to worry about anything. The pain will be intense but it will dull into an ache you will be able to withstand."

I stared at her with my breath catching, and for the first time, I wondered if King had done this to all of his pets. Jealousy wracked my body so intensely I thought I would retch, and my eyes begged my master to tell me the truth.

"It will be okay," he said softly.

"I…" I swallowed thickly, my head swimming with thoughts I couldn't put into order. "Am I the first one to get this?"

He stared at me for a long time, and I tried to predict his answer, but I had no idea what it would be.

"Yeah," he said finally. "You're the only one, Pet."

His eyes lingered on mine until Angel cleared her throat.

"Could I have the ring?" she asked softly, and I finally unclenched my fingers. My palm was covered in half-moon imprints from where I'd dug my fingernails into the skin. She took the ring from my hand, and we all watched, mesmerized, as she sterilized the metal.

I knew I could have stopped the whole thing if I wanted to. But somehow, I wanted to see this through to the end.

I watched Angel clean the ring and raise a small metal rod to it. I didn't know what it was until she turned it on, and fire bloomed on the end of it. She heated up the ring, holding it up with something that looked like large metal tweezers.

"Jesus fucking shit," Stranger muttered next to me as the metal glowed red.

That was when my body started to resist. Fear took over in its most primal form, and my back arched off the floor, gasping for air and crying out so pathetically I felt sorry for myself and what King would do to punish me.

"Pet," he said softly. "Please, do you still want to do this?"

"Y-yes," I cried out while my body begged for it not to happen. "Please, just hurry, do it now, hurry the hell up, please…"

My voice broke into sobs and they all just stared at me, Angel poised over my body with the brand ready.

"Part your legs," she said softly, and my heart pounded louder. Where was she going to put it? Where on earth was she going to put that thing? I wailed in horror.

"Please," King begged me. I could hear the panic in his voice, and it mimicked mine. "Please, Pet, if you don't want it, we'll stop now."

"You have to do it," I begged him. "Please, you have to…"

"For fuck's sake," Stranger muttered under his breath. In one swift move, he was between my legs, and he parted them as wide as he could. My thighs trembled until he pinned them under his hands, so fucking tightly I couldn't move a single inch. I cried out in pure terror.

King's weight sank against my chest and they both stared at me as the brand made contact with my tender skin, burning a mark that would forever label me as King's property.

I'd never screamed so loud.

Before that moment, I hadn't even known it was fucking possible.

My scream echoed in the room, and when I passed out, either from the shock or the pain, it echoed in my mind as well.

Over and over again.

# CHAPTER 28
*King*

**A**fter a week, Angel deemed Pet's branding was healed enough to be touched. I'd kept my hands off her for the seven days and it had been excruciating. But what I hadn't expected was to enjoy spending time with her as a companion, as if we were in a real relationship not dominated by my sexual preference.

I held her close and watched movie after movie she picked, cringing hard through most of them and getting swatted by her when she caught me. I fed her ice cream and popcorn and held an ice pack to the inside of her thigh when her brand hurt. For the first time since Pet came into my life, I felt fucking normal, but only until I realized it was all an illusion. Only until she asked the question I'd been dreading to hear.

"Is he coming back?"

My fingers stopped toying with her hair and I wanted to tug on the strands of her lavender mane, but I fucking restrained myself. This was the plan, right? This was what I was working towards, and I couldn't punish her for the idea I'd planted in her head.

"Yeah," I told her, my voice strained even though I tried to hide my anguish. "If you want to, he can come back."

Pet gave me a shy smile and settled into the crook of my arm.

"I just meant, because we didn't really finish what we started last time…"

Because I was scared I'd fucking kill the guy, I wanted to tell her, but I bit the words back. I gave her a tight-lipped smile instead and promised her I'd get him back there. That was when I got the idea… The perfect idea to get back at my little Pet, even though she wasn't really doing anything wrong.

I made a quick phone call and returned to my impatient little girl after spending a few minutes in the study.

"He's busy for a while," I told her, and she deflated visibly.

"Oh," she said lamely. "Let's hope he'll have time again soon."

"Let's hope so," I growled.

She seemed to sense my bad mood, and her legs parted as she gave me a cheeky little smile. My brand winked from between her legs, right on her left inner thigh. Hidden to everyone but those fucking her, and ensuring that everyone would remember sweet little Pet was mine and mine alone.

"Did you forget about something?" she purred, running her long fingernails along her inner thighs. "I'm all yours now, Master, and I have the mark to prove it."

I couldn't help pulling her in my arms and nuzzling her neck, biting into her shoulder to mark her again.

But my head was fucking swimming.

After weeks, almost months, of not digging up any new dirt, I'd finally come a bit closer to finding out what had happened when she was younger. I hadn't forgotten about the abuse she suffered at the hands of a man she refused to name, and I still had plans to act on it. I'd gotten distracted with all the plans I had for Pet, but I sure as hell hadn't forgotten. I was going to get that revenge for her, any way I fucking could.

I let her crawl onto my lap. I even let her get my dick hard for her even though I knew I had way too much shit to do to spend time with her like she deserved. I let her work me through my pants until she moaned so sweetly it nearly drove me insane, and then I pushed her off my lap while she protested with soft whimpers and groans.

"I have work to do, little thing," I told her with a grin. "But I promise I'll make it up to you tomorrow."

"Okay," she said grumpily, settling back in front of the TV with her half-empty bowl of popcorn and a shitty movie. "I'm sleeping next to you tonight, right? You won't spend all night working again?"

I'd done it the previous three days, just buried myself in fucking research, trying to find more dirt on who I now believed was the man who had abused her. Of course, I couldn't have told her that, so I fobbed her off with lies of an important deadline coming up at work. And she ate it all up, even though she spent several hours a day sulking because of it.

"I'll come sleep with you," I promised her, kissing the top of her pretty purple hair. "But don't wait up for me, Pet."

She blew me a kiss as I left, and I spent the next few hours buried in something I really shouldn't have in my possession.

I'd sent someone to Pet's parents place when they were out. I made sure they'd never even notice the break-in. There was only one thing I wanted, and it was the old computer in her childhood bedroom.

I'd spent the last few days digging through so many old messages, history and files, I felt myself going insane from the absolute overload of information. It felt like I was getting to know a different girl, definitely not my sweet Pet.

This girl was her complete opposite. She was nasty at times, almost a mean girl. Other times she was painfully insecure, sweet and needy at the same time. And all of those emotions seemed to rely so very heavily on a single person I'd managed to track down through her computer.

She used a messaging program that had since gone out of style, but the records of her conversations were all still there on her computer. I read through all of them – well, I'd tried to. I'd gotten pretty far, but sleep had gotten the better of me, and I still couldn't let my girl know exactly what I was doing. So I lied smoothly and spent every free moment I had reading that shit.

She was talking to someone who went to the same school as her almost every night. Apparently, they were both part of a forum her high school set up, and Pet – who was quiet on the boards and barely posted – found this guy's email and started messaging him back and forth without having any idea who he really was.

I found the whole story weird as fuck. She messaged him out of the blue replying to a joke he'd made on the forums, and over the course of weeks and then months, they'd developed a strong friendship with an obvious crush from Pet's side. She flirted clumsily, and the guy poked fun at her for it. It was obvious her friend was a man from the way he spoke. He sent her pictures, but none of himself, and over time, the secret of who he was seemed to cause a bit of a rift between them.

I knew as much as she did – he was older. I realized he must've gone to school a few years before her, not at the same time, sooner than Pet did. But that didn't make sense with the timeline she'd given me.

She'd said the guy raped her when she was just a kid, so he must've been older than her. I couldn't make sense of things.

At first, I dismissed the messages as unimportant. Until I realized she'd recognized the guy at some point and completely severed any contact with him.

I looked at her emails after that, and found him messaging her there. Over and over again. And that's when I realized what the bastard had done to her.

*Sapphire, I'm sorry. I didn't want to tell you – I was worried you still remembered. Please talk to me.*

*SR! I'm so sorry. I'm not like that anymore, I swear. We were kids when it happened. Why are you so hung up about it?*

*Sapph, you need to talk to me. Don't be a nasty little bitch about this.*

*Bitch, you think you can blow me off like that?*

The messages got nastier and nastier as time passed and it made me worry. There was a single email to his address from Pet's, and it was asking him to leave her alone. Of course, he never did, and before she could block him and sever contact, the threats started coming. Nastier and nastier with each message.

*Do you think your mother would like knowing what her little girl's ass felt like? You didn't even fight it, Sapph…*

*I'm going to tell everyone how you begged for more while I fucked your asshole.*

*Never thought about me taking pictures? I could have a dozen or more Sapphire, and you'll never know… What would everyone think of that?*

*You were a little whore when I met you. I remember you rubbing your little cunt on your parents' carpet like a slut. You were only five, Sapphire, how big of a whore are you now?*

That's when I knew. I remembered her telling me about the guy, in tears, so scared she still couldn't confess what exactly had happened. And I realized this guy had come back to haunt her, even when she was just a teenager. So not just the fucking therapist, this damn prick as well… I was going to kill him when I finally found out who he was.

His email didn't offer a single clue. The emails kept coming over and over again, to an email address Pet didn't seem to use anymore. She hadn't even seen the last few, which he must've sent over the last year when she'd all but disappeared.

I saw several unopened ones, and my blood boiled when I read them. The guy had gone from empty threats to real fucking dangerous ones, ones I'd rip his throat out for. He threatened everyone from Pet to her parents and her old friends from school. I wanted to kill him for it.

I spent hours trying to figure out who he was, getting more and more enraged with each minute I spent without the prick's name, without his still beating heart in my fucking fist. He was insane. Fucking insane, and I was going to punish him for what he'd done to my girl.

And finally, there it was. A simple clue, hidden in plain sight. It had been there the whole time, and I'd missed it.

He'd sent Pet these pictures, these gifs, all from the same website. And I realized it was a sort of blog of really fucking disturbing stills from porn, moving images with no sound which made them even creepier. Finally, I realized he must've been the owner of the blog. And once I figured that out, finding the sonofabitch was easy.

I knew I would have to break my promise to Pet; I wouldn't be sleeping in our bed that night.

I was going to avenge her innocence, and I was going to kill a man for the very first time that night.

*I found her sleeping on* the couch, covered up with a blanket. She barely stirred when I picked her up and carried her into our bedroom, bundling her under the blankets. Her hands reached for me before I left, and I wished I could've stayed with her. Feel the warmth of her skin against mine, feel her heart beat for me. But she closed her eyes before I could change my mind, and snored peacefully.

I grinned at her sleeping frame, so small in our bed, and I left.

Not before changing and getting ready, though.

I was almost at a point where I didn't give a shit if I got caught. I wanted the prick dead, and if someone found out I'd done it, I'd go to jail for it, fucking gladly. He'd hurt her too much for one lifetime though, and I wouldn't let him have that final victory. I had to be careful.

I took a taxi to his neighborhood. It wasn't far away from where her parents lived. A nice upper middleclass neighborhood a guy like him shouldn't be living in. I walked the short distance from the store the taxi had dropped me off in front of to his house.

A suburban, nice-sized place in a cul-de-sac. There was only one light on in the house. I rang the front doorbell.

My heart pounded as I waited for someone to answer. I had no idea what to fucking expect. What would Pet's abuser look like in person? I wanted him to be ugly, mean-looking. It would make it easier to hurt him.

But the man who opened the front door to the picture-perfect family house was far from that.

He was handsome, in a classic way. Chiseled jaw, not unlike mine, and a full head of light hair. He was a few pounds overweight, but it didn't take away from his looks.

But my punch would.

I slammed my fist into his face before he had a chance to speak, and he howled in pain.

"What the fuck, you jackass?" he screamed, and lunged at me.

I was ready to take him, and we nearly tumbled to the ground when a little voice called out behind him.

"Daddy?"

I looked over his shoulder to see a little boy standing there, holding a toy car.

I wanted to kill him then, really kill him, in the most gruesome way possible. How could this bastard have a child? Had he hurt him as well, or was his taste for little girls only? I wanted him dead. If the kid wasn't standing on his doorstep I would have finished him. I would wear his blood on my hands with pride.

"You know what that was for," I snarled at the man. "And you better sleep with one eye fucking open."

He picked himself up and glared at my back as I stalked down his driveway. He didn't speak up until I'd reached the street.

"She's not worth it," he yelled after me. "That fucking girl isn't worth jack shit, man."

I looked over my shoulder at his damn smug face, and I knew I was going to kill him.

And soon.

# CHAPTER 29
## *Pet*

Things *finally felt like they* were falling into place.

I was happy for the first time in so long I could barely remember how much time it had been.

King was perfect, unless he wasn't. And that was good too, because I loved him, his temper, his inexplicable jealousy, and his erratic mood swings. I finally admitted it to myself – the feelings, the quickened heartbeat, the weak knees, they meant I was totally, head over heels in love. And that was okay, even if he never said it back.

I was hoping he'd let me see Stranger soon. The memories of them both haunted me, and I wanted more. I'd never realized what a powerful feeling it was to be craved by two men at the same time, and I wanted so much more.

King had a busy week at work, and I was spending more time with Maria than usual. I'd gotten so close to her over time, and I was lucky to call her a friend. She was amazing, and it made me happy that King seemed to approve of our friendship as well. At first, I was nervous when they saw each other, but they acted like there was no history between them at all, and I kind of liked it. Still, I preferred to meet Maria outside, not in our apartment, and she never objected to that.

But that day, I invited her over to watch some silly TV show we both liked, and when King got home, we were sprawled on the couch, eating cookie dough ice cream and laughing at the silly antics of the couple on TV.

On instinct, we both took our legs off the coffee table when he walked in, and he smirked at me when I smoothed down my hair.

"Hello, Pet," he said in his rough, dark voice. It gave me shivers.

He looked at Maria and smiled politely, saying a hello to her as well. He never called her Angel anymore, the last time was when she gave me my brand. I wasn't even sure if they kept in touch anymore. He didn't call her Maria either, just avoiding her name altogether. I wondered how that made her feel. It made me feel pretty smug.

"I'll be going," Maria said in a rush, and we both got up.

"You don't have to," I told her hurriedly, but she gave me a pointed look and we both giggled. "Okay then. Will I see you soon?"

"Maybe tomorrow, if you have time?" she asked, putting on her jacket. "I was going to go shopping, I need a new dress for this dinner I'm going to."

"I'd love that," I answered honestly, shooting King a quick look. He nodded and I smiled broadly at Maria. "I'll call you later."

"See you, babe." She kissed my cheek and then she was gone in a cloud of Dior's Poison and fleeting touches.

I went back to the living room and sat down with King after he'd poured himself a drink. He put a hand on my knee and I resisted the urge to climb on his lap.

"I missed you," I told him, and he gave me a smile, but it was a little tense. "Are you okay?"

"Yes, Pet," he told me. "Perfectly okay. What have you and Maria been up to?"

"Just watching that show you hate," I giggled.

"Oh God," he groaned. "Spare me the details."

But I didn't, and I told him all about the drama on the new season. By the time I was onto the third story's couple, we were both laughing, and King was begging me to stop.

"Fine," I pouted. "But now you have to tell me about your day!"

Immediately, I saw his shoulders tense. I didn't mention it when he shrugged it off and told me it was just another boring day in the office. Sometimes it bothered me that he barely spoke about his work, but I never brought it up. Maybe I was still too nervous to really question anything, but I promised myself that would change in the near future.

We spent the rest of the evening curled up on the sofa. By the time it got late, I was getting sleepy, and I curled up closer to him, my legs on his lap and my head in the crook of his shoulder. King held me close as I drifted off to sleep very slowly, even though it was still early. It just felt so good to be near him like that.

"So you're seeing her again tomorrow?" he muttered against my hair, and I stirred in my half-state.

"Maria?" I asked with a yawn. "Yeah, I guess so. Why?"

He toyed with my hair, and I stared at the lavender strands in his strong, long fingers.

"It doesn't bother you?" he asked me, his voice careful. "Our history."

I got up and glared at him.

"Not unless you talk about it," I said grumpily, and he laughed, tickling my feet. I giggled when he pulled my ass onto his lap. "Stop it, you big oaf."

"Never," he promised, and nuzzled my neck. "You know, I do think it's kind of hot seeing the two of you together."

I fought the urge to smack him and gave him an incredulous look instead.

"You're weird," I told him. I looked away so he wouldn't see how much I was blushing, and he made me turn back around.

"I knew it," he said with a shit-eating grin. "You like her. Little slut."

"I don't!" I cried out. "She's a girl."

"So?" King laughed in my face. "This may be a playground, but we're not five years old, Pet."

I looked at my palms while he pulled me in close, made me straddle his lap.

"Have you thought about her?" he whispered in my ear. "Thought about kissing her?"

"No," I said weakly, and he tugged on my shirt.

"I think you're lying," he told me. "I think you've thought about it a lot…"

"I haven't…" But now I was.

Thinking about her dark curly hair. Remembering her naked body, so much different than mine. I wondered what she tasted like. I wondered what her skin felt like, at the spot where she had her small tattoo. I may not have thought about it much before, but now King had filled my head with the idea of her.

"Why don't I make it easy for you, little Pet?" he asked me, biting down on my shoulder and making me moan out loud. "I'm gonna give you a task. You'll like it, I promise."

"I'm not sure," I muttered. "What if she doesn't like it? What if she doesn't want to do it?"

I couldn't imagine anything more humiliating.

"She will," he grinned at me, barely holding back a laugh, and I wondered briefly if he knew something I didn't.

"So, my sweet little Pet, here's what I want you to do…"

---

*The next day, before Maria* came over, I was nervous as hell.

King hadn't told me if he'd let her in on what we were supposed to do. Probably not.

He chose my outfit. Nothing too out there, but definitely provocative. I pulled on the mini dress that barely covered my ass.

No panties, no bra. King had banned underwear.

I felt silly with no shoes on, but I painted my toes a color that matched my hair.

I felt pretty. I felt stupid. I felt excited.

She arrived ten minutes early, and when I opened the front door, I knew he hadn't told her, just to make this more excruciatingly embarrassing.

"Hey," she said, eyeing me up and down and whistling. "Wow, we going somewhere?"

"Um," I said awkwardly. "Not exactly. Come in."

I took her jacket and hung it up, and we went into the living room.

"Do you want something to drink?" I asked her, and she gave me another weird look.

"Trying to get me drunk?" she asked, and I laughed in such a high-pitched tone it only made things weirder. "Sure, what you having?"

"I'm eighteen, remember?" I giggled, and she rolled her eyes.

"God, that man of yours is old-fashioned as hell," she told me. "He'll fuck you sideways but won't let you have a damn drink with me. Fine, bring me some wine."

I brought out a bottle. Maria declined a glass and drank from the bottle in a way that made me squirm on the couch as I drank my water with lemon. I felt like a kid, a stupid, silly little girl.

"I know you're up to something."

I looked up at Maria with my eyes wide, and she grinned at me. She really was beautiful. So different than I was.

"I..." I started, swallowing uncomfortably. "Maybe."

"He put you up to something?" she asked.

"He always does," I muttered, and she laughed, sitting closer to me. She pulled her legs up, her dress riding up.

I stared at her like that, her panties clearly visible between her legs. They were black, lacy.

"So what is it then?" she asked me. "Spit it out, I want to know."

"He wants..." I swallowed again. God, why had I agreed to do this? It was awkward as hell. "He wants pictures."

"Of us?" Maria asked, and I nodded. My throat and mouth felt like sandpaper. "Doing what, exactly?"

"Looking at the camera," I replied in my smallest voice. She gave me a meaningful look and I cleared my throat. "Kissing. Touching. You know."

"I don't, actually."

She was taunting me and I stared at my own knees, feeling her eyes on mine.

"Sapph. Come on, look at me."

I forced my eyes up, even though I wanted to do everything but.

She was sitting even closer. Her hand was dangerously close to my thigh. My heart was pounding.

My phone was on the coffee table and I glanced at it before looking back at her.

"You want to do it?" I asked her, and she giggled.

"Yeah, I've had worse," she winked at me, and I slapped her thigh.

"Slut!"

"Don't say it till you know it."

She took my phone from the coffee table and turned on the camera, taking a selfie with her lips pouted and handing me the phone.

"Tell him I'm here," she said. "Is he at work?"

"Yeah." I sent off the text and we sat there in silence until I got a reply.

*Why is your tongue not down her throat?*

I gasped at his words, and Maria took the phone from my hand, laughing when she read the reply.

"Well?" she asked me, looking cross. "You better please your master, little Pet."

It felt fucking weird. Really weird, sitting there with her and knowing what was about to happen.

I'd never really been turned on by a girl. It was the scenario, knowing how much King would like it. It made me wet just thinking about it, and I shifted my weight on the couch uncomfortably, hoping Maria hadn't noticed.

I looked up at her, and her eyes were on me. She made a grab for me, her fingers wrapping in my hair. My heart pounded so loudly. Was I really going through with this?

In the end, she didn't leave me a choice.

She pulled me close, tipped my head back just like King had done so many times before her.

And then she was kissing me, her mouth cold and her tongue tasting of wine.

I gasped against her and she took the chance to kiss me deeper. A part of me wanted to push her off. Another part wanted her to make me come so I'd really have something to show King.

As she deepened our kiss, that desire grew.

I mewled against her mouth and I felt her grin.

"Smile, pretty Pet," she said against my lips, and snapped another picture.

She moved away for long enough to send it, and then she was back, her body hot against mine. Her dress had slipped off her shoulder and I touched her skin tentatively. She felt hot to the touch. Her skin was smooth, not peppered with goosebumps like mine.

I let her get on top of me. I couldn't make sense of anything, of the sudden charge she'd taken over me. She reminded me of King as she took what she wanted, and her hand slipped between my legs.

"Maria!" I protested, and she grabbed my throat with her free hand. Just like King.

"Shut the fuck up, Pet," she grinned at me. "Give him something to be jealous about."

I tried to get away half-heartedly, but I couldn't. I was too horny, too needy to feel something inside me.

"Lie back," she told me, and I did.

She moved away and took a picture of me like that, sprawled with my legs open and my wet pussy exposed. She sent it and I heard the phone going off a second later.

"Bet you he'll be home in ten minutes," she winked at me. "You can thank me later."

"I..." I whispered. "I'm not sure I want to."

"We can either have some fun while we wait," she told me, taking a sip of her wine from the bottle. "Or we can wait and watch TV. Up to you, little Pet."

I stared at her hard, hating her for making me decide.

"Fuck you," I muttered.

"I'd love to."

She moved back and caged my body under hers. She wasn't much bigger than me yet she took control so easily. But I knew she had submitted to King so easily. I couldn't make sense of that either.

In seconds, her fingers were inside me and I cried out.

"Please," I begged her. "I can't, this is too weird!"

"It won't be weird when you get fucked because of it," she told me slyly. "Won't be weird when he comes home and drags you to the playroom to fuck your pretty brains out."

My pussy clenched around her, I could feel it, and so could she.

"Nasty little Pet," she told me. "I knew he'd make you do this."

"H-he told you?" I stammered, crying out when she curled her fingers inside me.

"No," she confessed. "I just knew it. He always liked a bit of girl on girl action."

I growled in anger. I didn't want that to be true, and I especially didn't want her knowing things I didn't know.

I got up, her hand slipping out as I straddled her.

"Fuck you, Maria," I told her. "He's mine."

"He used to be mine," she snarled at me, and I smacked her across the face. Just like that.

She held her cheek and stared at me in shock. And I giggled.

"That felt good, you bitch," I told her, and she let out a shocked little moan. "He's mine now, and don't you forget it."

"Fine," she said. "Fine, just stop hitting me!"

I tugged on her hair and felt my pussy leaking on top of hers.

"Jesus," she panted. "You really are a horny little thing."

I responded by moaning out loud and rubbing myself all over her, and she pulled me down into a heap on the couch. She felt different when we kissed that time. Sweeter.

I didn't even hear the door opening. Didn't even know we weren't alone until someone pulled me off the couch by my hair and I shrieked.

King made me get up and I cried out in protest, looking at Maria in her messy state on the couch.

"Get the fuck out," he told her. "Thanks for helping."

She scampered to her feet, giving me a wink and blowing a kiss before she pulled her dress down.

"Call me," she giggled, and then she was gone, and he was still holding me up by my hair, my toes barely touching the ground.

"Slutty Pet," he told me, his fingers tangling in his tie. "Did you like that? Did you like kissing a girl for your master?"

"No," I told him. "I don't like girls."

He pulled me closer, his free hand going between my legs while I helplessly tried to move out of his reach.

"I can see that," he told me mockingly. "That's why you're fucking soaked, then?"

"Let me go," I mewled, and he threw his tie over his shoulder.

"No fucking way," he growled. "Tonight, my little Pet is getting fucked like the whore she is, I promise you that."

And he kept his promise, all night long.

# CHAPTER 30
## *Stranger*

She was on my mind. Always, all the fucking time.

Pretty, pretty girl. I remembered the last time I saw her. She looked like a different girl with that fucking hair. But she was still innocent, sweet. Still so fucking small.

I wanted to hurt her until she screamed with pleasure. All I could picture was her pretty face all twisted up when I fucked her holes, while she begged me to do so much more to her. Pretty little girl. Pretty little girl in tears that I put on that face. God, I wanted her.

She was a distraction. It drove me fucking crazy . I couldn't do jack shit with Pet on my mind.

I hated that nickname. Like she was a damn animal. She had a name, didn't she? Except neither of them seemed to use it.

That guy of hers annoyed me as well. Jackass. Trying to hog her for himself any chance he got, even though we could both tell she wanted me. It was in her sighs, in those breathy little moans, in the way her fingers cramped around me when I touched her. Yeah, she fucking wanted me, even if she didn't want to admit it. Pretty little thing. I wanted her for myself. Not to share with the suited-up fuckhead. He reminded me of shit I didn't care to think about.

Maybe it was harder because I didn't have her number. I couldn't just text her or talk to her when I wanted. I had his digits, and I sure as hell wasn't about to call and ask for hers.

So my mind, my fucking sick mind, was left wandering in circles around the girl.

Pretty pretty so fucking pretty.

The purple hair was almost too much. Didn't really suit her, I didn't think so. She was made for those blonde locks she used to have, pretty and almost white, all natural. Big blue eyes, long black lashes. Lots of thick black liner for me to mess up. That was my favorite memory of her, pinning her against the window and fucking her like she really did belong to me.

I wanted her.

It was going to mess every-fucking-thing up.

I moved away from the wall, my back sore from standing there for too long. It was a cold night, and my hands felt frozen when I shoved them into the pockets of my torn-up jeans. There was no sign of her, but I saw him leave hours earlier, probably to work. He had a driver, the whole shebang. I wanted to just barge up there and see her by myself, but I was chicken shit, like a teenage fucking moron with a crush.

A girl came by later, and I knew she was her friend. I'd seen them together before, it was the one who gave her that fucking brand.

Another thing that drove me crazy.

The thought of that jackass' mark on her, right between her legs. I couldn't lie, it had been hot as sin when she got it done. Holding her down like that, seeing her beg for his mark on her skin... That was something fucking else. Almost like she craved the pain, but not as much as she was afraid of it. And she wanted his name on her thigh. Like she really was his property.

Maybe I'd misjudged her. But it sure as hell felt like she wanted me. I saw it in her eyes, in the way her body responded to mine like every touch of my fingertips was a shock to her lithe body.

I knew I'd get to fuck her again. But I didn't want the guy there with her.

It couldn't have been more than half an hour later that his car pulled up in front of the building, and the jerk got out.

I stared at him almost racing into the building, and then watched the dark-haired girl exit a while after. She looked fucking messy, her dress all rumpled and her hair a wild halo around her head.

I shouldn't have done it, but I couldn't fucking stop myself.

When she crossed the street, I followed her. She didn't hear me, she had earphones in. Probably thought she was in a nice enough neighborhood to walk around like that, silly bitch.

I made a grab for her just as we were passing an empty alley. She didn't even get a chance to squeak when my palm covered her mouth and I pulled her into the alley by her waist.

"Shut the fuck up," I growled at her as she tried to get away. "I'm not going to hurt you. This isn't about you."

She wouldn't stop struggling, and the girl had some fight in her. I lowered my mouth to her ear and nearly fucking lost it.

She had my girl's smell all over her, and it drove me fucking nuts.

She got to touch her, and I didn't, and it wasn't fucking fair.

"This isn't about you," I repeated, my words loud in her ear. "It's about her. Pet, whatever the fuck you call her."

She stopped struggling, and I let her go, knowing I risked her running off and telling the guy when I did so.

The moment I let her go, she turned around and slapped me hard. I didn't even fucking flinch, just laughed in her little red face.

"Feisty," I told her. "Admirable."

"What the fuck?" she snarled at me, digging in her purse.

"Don't bother with the pepper spray," I told her. "No fucking point, cause I don't want your shit, and I'm not planning on fucking you."

I gave her a onceover. I hadn't noticed the last time, but she was quite the looker. Any other time, any other place, and I probably would have been fucking tempted.

"Don't even think about it," she warned, her words breathy.

"I won't if you don't," I tossed back, and she rolled her eyes and crossed her arms in front of her body. "I want to ask you some stuff."

"Like what?" she asked. "And why would I tell you anything?"

"Because…" I stared at her. "I think that guy… King. He isn't good for her."

She shifted her weight uncomfortably. "What do you mean?"

"I think he's being weird," I told her. "Like, hurting her."

"So?" she laughed in my face. "It's what she likes, dumbass."

"Not in that way," I snarled. "Like, emotionally. Mental damage and all that shit."

"Big fucking theory you have there," she told me. "Why would you say that? I remember you, you know."

"Of course you fucking do." I grinned at her and she rolled her eyes again. "I knew you liked me. Now, are you gonna talk?"

"At least buy me a damn drink first," she said.

"Well, if you insist. And stop trying to get in my pants," I said.

"As if!" Her voice was shocked, but we both knew she had the fucking hots for me.

She pulled her dress down self-consciously, and I smacked her ass as I walked her out of the alley.

"Why'd you pull me in here anyway?" she asked, glaring at me. "You could just come up to me to talk like a normal person."

"Because I knew you'd like it," I told her with a shrug.

The girl looked away guiltily, and we walked to a bar in silence, just her heels clattering on the pavement.

---

*"He fucked me so good.* No one will ever fuck me like that. No one." She stirred her drink miserably.

While I would have loved proving her wrong, I had other things on my mind. Mostly the girl. Pretty Pet.

"I want to see her again," I said. "Any way I can do that without going through her jackass of a man?"

"I doubt it," she told me. "He knows everything she does. Even when she's out with me, she texts and he calls. He's controlling, always has been."

"Sounds like a fucking nutjob to me," I growled, and she laughed, the sound bitter. "So, can I come with you next time you see her?"

"You?" She stared at me over the rim of her glass. "That's a bad idea. If he knows you're sneaking around behind his back, you'll never get to see her again on his terms."

"Fine." I downed my drink and got up to leave.

"Not even going to pay for my drink?" she asked indignantly.

"You ain't been much help," I said, and she rolled her eyes.

"Fine," she shrugged. "Leave me here, then. Bye."

I was going to, but she looked so fucking miserable sitting there I sat back down, even though I should've known better.

"What is it about this guy, then?" I asked her. "Why are you both so damn hung up on him?"

"King?" she asked me, and I merely rolled my eyes in response. Such a pretentious fucking name for a rich, spoiled asshole.

"Whatever the fuck he calls himself," I muttered.

"He's..." She sighed, trying to find the words. "He's different. He isn't the first dominant guy I've been with, but he is the most intense."

"What makes him so special?" I asked.

"Have you seen him?" she giggled. "He's hot as sin."

"If you like that kind of thing," I shrugged.

"What, movie-star looks, expensive suit, dick so big you can barely swallow it?" she raised her eyebrows. "Yeah, you could say I'm into that."

"What the fuck ever. Think she'd ever leave him?" I wanted to know.

"Sapphire?"

Her name. So pretty.

"No, I doubt it," she admitted. "I wouldn't have either."

"So why are you not with him?" I asked.

"He let me go," she whispered.

Again, like they were both fucking animals. How this guy had gotten these two women this hung up, I'd never know. Sure, he was a rich fuck, he was a bit kinky, and he liked to give orders... But I was ten times the man he was, and I sure as fuck intended on proving it to sweet little Pet.

Only after having an inner monologue did I notice how hung the girl, Maria, really looked.

"Hey," I said roughly, nudging her forearm. "You alright?"

"I guess," she muttered. "Doesn't really matter."

"You can't still like him," I said, shaking my head. "How long has it been?"

"Just about a year," she admitted.

"You need to move on," I told her.

"He has a way of doing this," she said. "I was almost over it. Almost. But he keeps pulling me the hell back. And I can't leave, not with him calling and asking for shit…"

"Then cut him off," I said. "Simple as fucking that."

"But what about her?" she asked. "What about Sapphire? I'd hurt her. I actually like the girl. Like, a lot."

She blushed saying that, and I wondered whether there was more to the story. I wanted to find out, but it wasn't the time to ask.

"You need to move on," I told her again. "Cut him off. Screw him. I can let you know what's going on with her, if you'd like."

"Oh, so I'm no longer the one who's in the clique," she laughed. "Suddenly I need your help?"

"You might just," I winked at her, scribbling my number on a paper napkin. "Call me if you need me, sweetheart."

I threw some money on the table and she stared as I waved her off.

The girl was stupid. Every man in that bar only had eyes for her, and she was hung up on that old piece of shit.

I still didn't get how he did what he did, but I had to admit, even I admired him a little. That didn't change my plan, though.

King, I'm taking you down.

And Pet, you're *my* fucking slut, not his.

# CHAPTER 31
## *Pet*

It had been two weeks since I'd mentioned seeing him again.

Two weeks of radio silence from King when it came to the subject of Stranger.

Until he finally came home one Friday night and gave me the news.

"He'll be here in two hours. Get ready, Pet."

He was seething with anger, and it was so obvious he hated the thought of Stranger coming over again. I had no idea why he kept doing it if he hated it that much, but I wasn't about to object. I loved having both of them to play with. I wanted them both inside me… I wanted what had been cut short the last time we'd been together.

King picked out an outfit for me; a pastel pink under-bust basque that pushed my tits up, and a sheer pink thong to match. White stockings and a garter belt to hold them up, and my heels were pink as well. He told me to do my makeup pretty, not sexy. Even though I was wearing an outfit fit for seduction, I felt like an innocent little girl with all that pink stuff on my body.

The doorbell rang ten minutes early, and I shot up like a spring, looking away guiltily when King caught me. I'd been doing my makeup, and my hand lingered over my face, still holding a rosy lipstick over my mouth.

"Wait in the playroom," he growled at me, and I scampered away like my heels were on fire.

He closed the door of the playroom behind me and I stood shivering and scared as fuck. But I only had to wait a few minutes this time.

King opened the door, and they came in. Their clothes were already flying off, both of them trying to get naked as fast as fucking possible. I gasped in surprise, not ready at all for the speed they came at me.

Rough hands lifted me up. Another pair felt my body, my exposed tits, my already soaked thong. Long, skilled fingers all over me. Two mouths on my lips, inside my mouth, fucking it already. Too fast, so fast, happening all at once and all of a sudden, taking me, not letting me have a choice in what was happening to my body.

"Wait," I cried out. "Please, too fast, wait…"

One of them clamped a palm over my mouth to shut me up and I struggled, but only a little. They lifted me up, carried me to the bed. I was on my back in seconds, and they both lingered above me.

"It seems like you've been playing us both," King told me roughly. "Thinking you're the one running the game, Pet."

"Not anymore," Stranger said, and I shivered when I heard his voice again. "This is our game now, little Sapphire."

I thought King would smack him when he said my name, but nothing happened. They stared at me and I shivered under their glaring eyes, wanting so much more.

"Okay," I whispered. "Please… That's okay."

"Who said you have a choice?" Stranger asked me.

"Please," I repeated, as if it was the only word I knew.

"Please what?" King asked me roughly. "Tell us exactly what you want, Pet."

"I want you everywhere." My voice was soft. "I want you in all my holes. I want to be filled up completely, please, just take me…"

Stranger groaned when King forced my head back.

"I want you to show him what a good little cocksucker you are," he told me sweetly. "You want to, Pet, don't you? You want to make me proud?"

"Yes!" My voice was husky as hell and I nodded when he caressed my cheek. "Please, I want to."

"You want him in your pretty mouth?" He was practically snarling at me.

"Yes," I begged. "Let me, master. Please, I want to."

"Get on your fucking knees," he told me, and I nearly fell off the bed in my efforts. I didn't kneel, I stood on my knees and waited eagerly for him to let me have more.

King was still in his pants, but Stranger had stripped down to everything but boxers. I tried not to stare at either of them, focusing my eyes on King's and silently begging for more.

He forced his fingers between my lips.

"Open that pretty little mouth," he said, and I did. Wide as I possibly could. "Good girl."

Stranger walked up behind him, and King moved out of the way, but he didn't stop telling me what to do, and it made me so very wet I felt my juices drip down my thighs. I ignored it, too horny to be embarrassed.

"Pull his boxers down," King told me.

His own pants went down, and so did his underwear. I couldn't help but stare at him as he stripped. I loved his body, and I wanted him, too.

"Stop fucking staring, just do it," he said, and I looked up at Stranger instead.

"That's a good girl," King said. "Keep looking into his eyes, the whole time. Don't fucking forget, Pet. Now his boxers. I want them off."

I reached for the hem, my hands shaking so very badly I felt ashamed. Stranger's hands reached for mine, and he helped me, his eyes burning dark as he watched me wanting him. We pulled his boxers down together, and when his cock sprang free, King groaned and I let out the softest of gasps.

I reached for him on instinct, but Stranger slapped me away.

"No fucking hands, Pet."

King came to stand behind me, grabbing my hands and holding them behind my back firmly. He held my head with his free hand and I looked at him for a long second before going back to Stranger.

"Just your mouth, pretty girl," King said gently. "I only want you to use your mouth when you suck his dick."

I tried to reply, but it was too late. Stranger's cock was between my lips, so fucking hard the tip was throbbing already, leaking drop after drop of precum down my throat. I gagged right away, and King pulled on my hair sharply. I could feel him jerking his cock while the other hand held my hair back so I wouldn't suck too eagerly.

"Bad girl," he told me. "You don't usually gag like that. Take it all, Pet. I want his whole cock inside your wet little hole."

Stranger forced himself deeper inside me until I felt his whole cock throb in my mouth. It was too much, way too much. The way it stretched me would make me gag any other time, but I was so eager to have him inside me, so needy for his cock in my mouth, I fought against the gag reflex and just let him fuck me like that. He gripped my hair in his hands and fucked my mouth like I was just a toy for him to play with, and I kept my eyes focused on his because that's what I'd been told to do. I looked at him, trying to swirl my tongue over his cock, needing so much more of him.

"Good fucking girl, Pet," King told me, his fingers touching Stranger's at the back of my head. "You're doing so well. Show him how you suck my cock when I let you. Show him what a good girl you are."

My eyes watered when he fucked me deeper, and I heard them both groan. I heard the fast motions of King jerking his cock behind me, and I felt Stranger throb so deep down in my mouth I knew if he came then and there, it would run right down to my stomach.

I started sucking as best as I could, and I felt him tense as my tongue and mouth worked his cock, heard King's motions getting wetter when his cock leaked precum, watching us.

"Tease him, Pet," he told me. "Suck him harder, I want you to take all of him, I want you to drive him fucking insane."

I did my best, and nearly lost my mind in the process. It felt too good to finally have him inside my mouth, to suck his cock like that's what I was made to do. I couldn't stop, I just worked him with my hands trembling behind my back. With nobody holding them now, it was getting really hard not to reach forward.

I swirled my tongue over him, not the tip because that was too deep down, and he groaned, pulling on my hair so roughly my head jerked forward.

"See how fucking crazy you make him?" King's voice was a rasp in my ear. "Look at him, Pet, look at what you're doing to him."

I looked up at Stranger's dark eyes, and I moaned around his cock. I thought he was going to come then. His cock jerked inside my mouth, and I could feel every vein throb inside me, feel the cum running down the length of him, and I wanted so much fucking more.

He pulled out of my mouth so suddenly I cried out at the loss of having my hole filled, and he ran a hand through his hair as I stared at him needily.

"I need to fuck her." The words were meant for King, not me, and Stranger stared at him with so much hate it didn't even look like he was asking for permission. "I need to fuck her right now."

"We both will," King responded darkly, and my skin prickled at the thought. I wanted them to, wanted them both inside me so very badly. "Get the fuck down, Pet, on the bed."

I had to practically crawl to the bed again, and then their hands were on me again, using my body. Someone ripped the soaked little thong off me, just ripped it off and threw it on the ground. I felt fingers I knew, King's fingers, all over my pussy, spreading my wetness up to my ass, and I cried out, already scared of what they were going to do to me.

"Which hole do you want?" he asked Stranger, and my pussy leaked at the question while my body shook. I didn't dare say a word.

"I want her filthy cunt," Stranger growled, and he got on the bed beside me, pulling me on top of him. I felt his dripping cock find my pussy and I gushed when I felt him break inside me.

And I didn't even dare to look back as they grunted and groaned, getting their cocks ready to be inside me and fuck me senseless.

I'd never wanted anything more, and that moment, with the anticipation building up to the second they'd both be inside me, drove me so crazy I could've come right then and there.

"Cry pretty for us, Pet," King ordered, and I felt the tears pricking my eyes already as he spat down on my hole, lubing his cock up with his own spit, and then slowly pushing inside my tight little hole.

I wanted to cry then, but it was nothing compared to the next moment when I felt Stranger fully inside me. His cock filled me in a different way than King, and I liked that, I felt so fucking full.

But it wasn't everything they were going to give me, and King reached forward while Stranger reached up both of their fingers forcing their way into my mouth until I was filled so completely I couldn't make a sound. I still cried out around their hands, covering them both in spit as my tears leaked down my cheeks and they finally, finally started to fuck me.

I started coming in seconds, and I stopped counting in minutes. Long minutes of having all my holes filled, of getting my ass and pussy pounded with no barrier between the two of their cocks and my holes. It was almost too much, being filled up like that, having my whole body full of them. I could've screamed, but their fingers wouldn't have let me, so I just took it. Two big, throbbing cocks stuffing me full, two big, skilled fingers filling my mouth while I gagged around them.

I'd never come like that, and I suspected I never would again. I wanted to look at them, but having my eyes open proved to be too much. I couldn't even bring myself to stare at Stranger right below me. If I would look, I'd want to see both of them.

I closed my eyes and took it, took both of them, took it all. And it felt so beautiful, like everything was finally right in my world, and that was exactly where I belonged. Between two men who could never see eye-to-eye on fucking anything, unless they were both buried balls-deep inside me. And it felt amazing, it felt like I was, for once in my life, finally in the right place at the very, very right time.

I didn't want it to end, and when I felt King leaking, I knew he didn't either, but he couldn't stop himself.

"Fill her up," he told Stranger. "I want to see her ass and her pussy leak cum at the same time."

Stranger grunted in agreement and it only took moments for them to have their fill, to fuck me until both their cocks exploded inside me and filled me to the brim. I could barely feel it, so far gone in my own world I couldn't even move as they pulled out, couldn't even protest.

I stayed on my knees when Stranger got up from under me, standing beside King and jerking his still hard cock. I could feel their eyes on me, hear their groans as they watched my holes leak all over the bed. And I pushed their cum out of me so they could watch, and felt like the dirtiest girl on the planet. But it felt so fucking good, and I wouldn't have changed it for the world.

I felt their hands on me then, caressing me, fingers touching my tits, tugging on my nipples, palms smoothing down my hair.

"Good girl," they said in unison, and I really fucking felt like one too.

# CHAPTER 32
## *King*

I *had to force my mind* off the guy whose house I'd showed up at several times per day.

There was no way I could let him get away that easy. The only thing I'd done was hit him, but I wanted to hurt him much, much more.

Pet's past finally revealed how bad I felt inside. What a wicked, jealous and sick fuck I'd really become. And she wasn't to blame, but the need to avenge her innocence felt like it was taking over my life.

She seemed pleased lately, reveling in the memories of both me and Stranger inside her. I knew she'd loved fucking us both, and we'd done it several times since that. I hated every single time that prick came over, although I couldn't really deny it felt hot as sin to feel him throb in her other hole. It got me off as well, the only thing I really hated was him developing feelings for my girl so fast.

I had to keep reminding myself not to let it get it to me. This was what I'd wanted. All of it had been my idea.

But looking at Pet in our home, happily cooking or flicking through channels, or flashing me her pretty pussy, didn't fill me with the ease I was hoping to feel. Instead, it made me fucking anxious.

I needed to know she was safe, once and for all.

I caught myself driving more than I ever used to, and every single time, I ended up in the same neighborhood. The one where her abuser lived with his new family.

The need to feel his blood on my hands grew. I wanted to kill him. I wanted him to pay. And I wanted him gone, with no chance of ever coming back.

Through several drives up to his place, I found out more about the guy, and what I found fucking sickened me.

His name was Aaron James and he was a teacher.

He'd taught at Pet's school and posed as a teenager on the forum she and almost every student had joined. I wondered how many other girls he'd hurt. I wondered how many children had lost their innocence because of the disgusting prick. It was the only thing on my mind unless I was fucking my girl. She was the only person who could make me forget, which was ironic, since my revenge was to be in her name.

I learned and learned about Aaron James. I studied him.

He taught Math. He was a calculating, evil sonofabitch. His wife was his own age, but she looked much older. Harrowed, tired and thin as a rail. Every time I saw her outside their home, she looked scared, her eyes dancing across her field of vision as if she was expecting a blow any second. I had no doubt that he'd hit her plenty of times. I'd even heard them fighting from outside, her wails pathetic compared to his dominant screams.

And his children… A little boy about five years old, and a girl who must've been eleven or twelve. I watched them too.

They didn't spend much time outside. The boy seemed relatively normal, but I never saw much of the girl. She seemed to prefer staying inside, and while I found out the boy did several after-school activities by following them around, she didn't seem to have many interests. My spot in the street looked into her bedroom, though, and I saw her reading a lot of the time. It was a painful reminder of Pet. I hoped her father hadn't hurt her.

I knew what I was doing was insane.

I was following a man around without any proof of what he'd done.

I was trying to hurt him without knowing if he truly was the real culprit.

But all of that was about to change.

I'd tracked him for long enough to find out he'd be home alone that night. As he pulled into his driveway, I wondered whether his wife had finally packed up the kids and left like she should've done a long time ago. Maybe I'd never get the question to my answer.

I didn't knock this time. I went around the back once it was past eleven, and I sneaked through the door that led into the backyard. The moron had left it open. Must be hard to feel afraid of monsters when you're one yourself.

I found him on the couch with his sorry excuse for a dick out and porn on the screen. He tried to scream when he saw me, but I knocked the fucker unconscious before he could.

---

*"Wake up."*

I poured a glass of water over his head, and the man came to with a yell of shock and surprise.

"And shut the fuck up while you're at it," I said calmly. "I don't want to hear a fucking word from you."

Of course, he ignored me completely, panicking when he realized he was tied to the chair in his office.

"Who the fuck are you? What the fuck do you want?"

I stared at him, the once handsome face, the body he'd let go of. I wondered if he really was stupid enough not to know.

"I'm here because of Sapphire Rose," I told him. "That name ring a bell?"

He blanched and cleared his throat. "She was a girl in my class. You have the wrong man."

"Oh, but Aaron," I told him, leaning over. "I haven't even told you what happened to her."

His face reddened as I stared him down.

"She was asking for it," he told me. "She was always asking for it."

"Even when she was a kid? When she was only a few years old?" I snarled at him, and he looked away, shutting his eyes. "Was she asking for it then, Aaron?"

"How do you know about that?" There was real panic in his voice this time, and I enjoyed it way too much. "She wasn't supposed to be telling people. Still as stupid as ever…"

I hit him then. I think the impact broke his nose and blood dribbled down his face, over his chin and onto his shirt. He cried like a little bitch.

"I only have one question," I told him simply. "And you better fucking answer me honestly, otherwise I'll tear this place apart until I find out the truth. I know you're alone tonight, you nasty fuck."

He stared at me and breathed heavily, and I leaned in and asked the only question on my mind.

"Have you hurt anyone else besides her?"

He didn't answer at first, staring at me with his eyes fearful. He was afraid of me. Good.

"There..." he started, swallowing the blood that was still trickling from his nose. "There have been a few."

I swept his laptop off the desk in rage, and it clattered to the floor, breaking.

I realized that might have been a stupid move, and I cursed out loud, moving away from the jackass in front of me.

"Who?" I asked him simply. "Who have you hurt?"

"Not hurt," he objected, and I didn't fight him. I wanted to know the truth. "A student... Maybe a few. At her school. It wasn't bad... They were all older than she was. They knew what they wanted."

"Fifteen-year-old girls?" I asked him, and he looked away, gulping.

"Yes, most of them," he said. "Maybe some were a little younger."

I stared at him because I didn't know what the fuck to say. This sadistic, disgusting bastard had been abusing young girls for years, and no one had done shit about it. Not his wife, not the authorities, not the schools he worked at. I did find out he was fired from the job at Pet's school, but it was all swept under the carpet and I never found out exactly what happened. I would soon.

"Have you hurt your son?" I asked him, and right away, he shook his head.

"No, don't be crazy," he said, sounding genuinely shocked. "He's a boy."

He's a boy.

The only reason he had for not doing it.

He's a fucking boy.

"Your daughter then?" I asked him. "Have you fucked your daughter?"

He stared at me vehemently, and he smiled. "I know how to handle my family."

I decided he had to die.

Calmly, I sat down in a chair. I passed him some paper and a pen.

"What's this?" he smirked at me.

"You're writing your goodbye letter," I told him. "You're telling your daughter, and your wife, and your son, how very sorry you are for being such an unbelievable fuck-up and ruining all their lives. I want them to have some closure after you're gone."

"You're going to kill me?" he asked incredulously, laughing out loud.

"No," I explained. "You're going to kill yourself."

He didn't believe me at first. He didn't believe a word I said until I showed him proof.

I'd done some digging alright, and on top of the child abuse, I found something he thought nobody knew about.

There was a girl gone missing in the town he lived in as a kid. I went down there a couple of weekends ago.

I spoke to the bereft mother, who even after all those years passed, still only blamed one person – her daughter Amie's first boyfriend.

Aaron James.

She said he was older, bad news around town. She said everyone knew he was the one who'd fucked and strangled her daughter. And then fucked her again when her body wasn't even cold. She cried so much when she told me.

I talked to the local sheriff.

He told me they'd found some new evidence with the help of improved DNA tests becoming available. And finally, they were coming for him.

It was all true, and as Aaron James started to realize the manhunt was going to begin, his face paled.

"So, you have a choice, Aaron," I told him. "Either die now, as dignified as you can for a man like you… Or wait for them to come for you, ruin your family, and put your ass in prison or in the chair. Up to you."

He stared at me with so much hatred, and I reveled in it.

"You think I'm going to off myself on the word of a madman?" he snarled at me.

Instead of responding, I reached in my pocket with my gloved hands and brought out his own gun. His eyes widened. I'd taken it from his cabinet earlier.

"I'm going to enjoy seeing your brains splatter the walls," I told him, and he laughed out loud.

"I'm not going to kill myself," he told me. "You're fucking crazy if you think I will."

"I thought you might say that," I said pleasantly. "So, here's something that might persuade you."

I got my phone out and showed him several screenshots.

They were from his work emails. He was getting sued by a former student of his, and no one knew yet.

"Oh yes, I know all about her," I told him with a grin. "And I know you've been trying to keep it under wraps. But I know something you don't."

"Like what?" he laughed in my face.

"Your student, Priscilla?" I grinned at him. "She's eight months pregnant with your child."

He looked like he was going to be sick.

"Oh, I'm sorry," I said. "Did I say child? I meant children. She's carrying your twins, you fucking jackass."

He struggled against his ropes one last time.

"I'm going to untie you now," I told him. "And you're going to die."

He stared at me as I undid his ropes. The moment he was free, he jumped me, but I saw it coming.

He headbutted me fucking hard, but I blinked away the blood, pinning him against the wall.

"Time to die, Aaron James," I told him. "You don't even have to do it if you're still a pussy. I'll be happy to do it for you."

"I'd like to see you try," he snarled, and I walked him back to his chair with the gun jammed into his back.

I sat him down and looked him in the eyes, both of us knowing how his story ended. The only choice he had was whether he wanted to hold the gun.

"Be a man," I told him. "Be a man and blow your fucking brains out."

He reached for the gun. His fingers were shaking. I really thought he'd point it at me, and I didn't let go. We both held it as he pointed it at me first, but I made him move it until the barrel was under his throat.

And he was the one who pulled the trigger, with my voice in his ear telling him it would all be over soon.

His blood splattered everything. The walls, my clothes, the floor. It was everywhere. I tasted the metallic tang of it in my fucking mouth.

I left as fast as I fucking could. I didn't even have time to clean up properly.

I drove home blasting a song I'd long forgotten, because it was the only way I knew how to stay sane. He was gone. He was dead.

And it was because of me. I should've hated myself. I'd assisted him in killing himself. I had blood on my hands. Literally and figuratively. He was gone, gone, gone.

I parked and went upstairs, feeling like a monster.

I opened my front door and saw Pet on the couch. Her eyes widened.

"What on earth?" she asked me.

I'd cleaned off most of it. My nose was still bleeding from his headbutt though.

I wiped the blood away again, and it was only then that I saw him on the couch with her. Stranger.

I wanted to fucking kill him, too.

"Hey," he said awkwardly. "I was in the neighborhood, I thought you'd be home..."

"I'm home now," I barked at him. "You don't come here unless you're invited."

"I'm sorry," he muttered, getting up while Pet stared at us both. "I'll be going. I'm sorry, I shouldn't have come by like that. I won't do it again."

I stepped aside so he could leave. The look that passed between us made me think he knew what I'd done.

I locked the door behind him and ignored Pet as I went into the bathroom. She came after me, her soft voice scared and begging for an explanation. I looked into her pretty blue eyes and slammed the bathroom door shut. She didn't need to know.

Staring at myself in the mirror, I remembered I did it to protect her. To avenge her, to make sure that chapter of her life was over, and to make sure that bastard never hurt another girl, another child.

I threw up into the toilet a second later. Not for his sorry head blasted open like that, but for all the girls he'd hurt. For his daughter, for the pregnant girl who was barely a woman, but he'd forced motherhood on her because the sick fuck didn't even give a shit about protection. He was gone now. Gone forever.

I left the bathroom what seemed like hours later, and I felt like a very, very bad man.

So bad I couldn't even look Pet in the eyes when she bombarded me with questions. I didn't let her sleep in my bed that night, and I saw how it broke her. I watched her go to her room, closing the door painfully slowly, her eyes on me until there was barely a crack between the door and the frame. She was hoping I'd explain, call out to her, ask her to come to me anyway. But I couldn't. She could never fucking know.

I went to bed only after wiring the money I had set aside to the pregnant student, and James' family. I wanted them both taken care of. I made sure to make it anonymous through a glitch in their system, and only left a single message.

*For what he did to you. To get better.*

# CHAPTER 33
## *Stranger*

*knew it was a bad* day to go see them. But as soon as I realized she was up there alone, there was no going back.

I hadn't been alone with Pet since the day I met her. I'd seen them both several times since, fucked her with her guy there, both our cocks buried inside her. But not like this, never like this. Never just sitting down next to her, talking like we actually hung out outside of fucking each other senseless.

It felt too fucking good to admit. The girl was special, from her pretty pastel purple hair to the words that came out of her pouty mouth. She was so well-read it felt like she was much older than the eighteen years she'd turned a few months back before meeting King, as she told me.

I wanted to fuck her while we were alone. Wanted to bury my cock inside her while she begged for me and only me, begged for orgasm after orgasm. But

I didn't dare talk to her about it. I knew I'd already be in trouble if her guy found out I'd paid her a visit like this.

To be fair, Maria had been a huge help in my new stalking obsession. She'd started telling me all about her habits. I'd gone to a bar the girls had met up at twice, not that Pet ever saw me. I downed drink after drink, sometimes catching Maria's eye, but most of the time, just fucking staring at Pet like a damn creep. She was getting under my skin, making a place for herself right inside my head and getting fucking comfortable too.

After King kicked me out, I got real fucking worried though. Something was up with him. Something fucked up happened that night, judging by the blood on his hands, but he wouldn't talk about it. Not to me, not the next time I saw them both. He didn't say a word, just came all the way down Pet's throat right along with me as she sucked us both.

That night, Maria told me she'd be meeting up with Pet again, and like always, I went to the back of the bar to watch them. I had a few chicks come up to me, wet and hopeful as they twirled their hair and sucked their drinks through straws. I turned them all down, too focused on my girl who wasn't quite mine yet. I watched her come in, wearing some silly excuse for a dress that looked more like a scrap of fabric. It pissed me right off, the way people looked at her. Those hungry looks devouring my girl, thinking they could fuck her if they wanted to. I would kill someone if they went up to her.

Pet looked at her phone and furrowed her brows just as my own phone dinged with a text. I looked down to read it, taking my eyes off her for a moment.

*Looks like it's your lucky night, stud*, the text from Maria read. *I've had to cancel. If you're there, have a drink with her? Make sure you don't get caught. xx*

I looked back up, and there was a guy next to her. My blood boiled when he chatted her up and she smiled shyly. Still such an innocent little girl... What would that guy say if he knew she had two cocks buried inside her mouth only a few days prior?

I got up from my table and walked over to hers with my drink in my hand. No fucking way was I letting some damn jackass hit on my property.

"Missed me, Pet?" I asked her, and her eyes left the guy's and connected with mine.

She was surprised, her cheeks blushing as she smiled at me.

"Hi," she said, a little awkwardly.

"Move along," I barked at the guy. I set my drink down on the table and he glared at me. He wasn't bigger than me, though he was broader. But I towered over him, and I guess he realized he was at a disadvantage and finally backed the fuck off. "That's right, get lost."

I sat down next to her and she giggled.

"You know you don't need to get so violent every time," she told me, and I grinned at her.

"You kinda like it though," I said, and she didn't disagree.

"So," she went on, taking a sip of her Coke. Not even old enough to drink. Fuck. "You stalking me or something?"

"You could say that," I replied. "That gets you wet, doesn't it, little Pet?"

She looked away and I downed my drink in one go. I hadn't needed any liquid courage in a long time, but that night, I sure as hell wanted a kick.

"Are you glad I'm here?" I asked her, and she nodded slowly. "We haven't really talked outside of me telling you where to put my cock."

She nearly choked on her drink. "Shut up! Someone's gonna hear."

"Since when do you give a shit?" I asked.

"Since..." Her words trailed off and she glared at me. "Since I follow orders, and last time I heard, you weren't supposed to be giving them."

"Then why do you want me to?" I leaned over and tucked a hair that had escaped from her braid behind her ear. She looked away, shutting her eyes tightly. "Your skin is so soft."

"Don't do that," she said, and I grinned wider.

"But you like it."

"But I shouldn't."

"I say do what you want," I shrugged. "But hey, that's just me. Come sit a little closer, Pet."

She shook her head no, and I took it as an invitation. I got off my chair and sat down next to her on the bench. She looked at her lap when I put my arm around her shoulders. I leaned over to whisper in her ear.

"How long since you've come in public?" I asked gently.

"Don't," she replied. "We're not supposed to see each other like this."

"Then leave," I told her.

She swiped up her bag in a hurry and got to her feet. But I pulled on her wrist, gently enough not to leave a mark.

"Stay," I said, and she stared at me for a long time before sitting her perky little ass back down.

"Good girl," I murmured against her ear, and her breath hitched when I said it. "Do you want to play with me, Pet?"

"O-okay," she whispered. We both knew this was bad news, but neither of us could stop.

"I want you to come for me," I told her, and her breath caught again. "But not until I let you, pretty Pet. Not until I say the words."

I leaned in closer, settling a palm comfortably on her naked thigh. It looked enormous against her, so big it practically covered her whole leg.

"What would you do if your man walked in right now?" I asked her softly, and she jerked away from me, but I wouldn't let her move. "Would you apologize? Would you let him drag you to the bathroom?"

"Please stop," she begged, but I squeezed my hand tightly around her leg.

"Would you let him fuck you in the ladies' room?" I growled in her ear, and she put a hand over mine and squeezed my fingers. "Would you let him come in your ass in there, and plug it up? Would you let him walk you back out here with no panties on, hoping your ass doesn't leak around the plug and trickle down your long legs?"

"Please," she wheezed. She was already so close. Such a good girl.

"Would you let him make you come to me, and ask me back to your apartment, fuck you like a little cumtoy?" I went on. "Would you say it in front of anyone here with cum in your ass and your pussy dripping down your legs?"

Her fingernails dug into my skin and I gently took her by the neck and turned her towards me.

"Come for me, Pet," I told her, and I shut her moan up when I kissed her, swallowing her scream of frustration.

She'd never tasted sweeter than she did in that bar, the taste of Coke and lemon still lingering on her lips. I wanted to fucking devour her. I wanted her to come inside my mouth over and over again.

I didn't pull away until she was a shaky mess, and I could feel how sticky the insides of her thighs were.

The whole bar was probably looking at us but I didn't give a shit.

She looked at me before averting her gaze, staring at the table. Tears welled in her eyes.

"What's wrong?" My voice was so gentle it surprised me.

"He'll be mad," she admitted. "He'll be so mad if he finds out about this."

"I thought this was all his idea," I told her. "I thought he wanted you to fuck me."

"I know, but…" She swallowed hard. "I don't know, it's been weird… Since you came over."

"I'm sorry about that," I admitted. "I shouldn't have done that. I should've known better."

"You're doing it again now, though," she reminded me with a weak smile.

"I know," I grinned. "I can't help it. It's you–" I stopped myself from talking. "Anyway. Weird how?"

"He's been distant," she admitted. "Snapping a lot."

"He hasn't hit you, has he?" I asked roughly. I'd kill the bastard.

"No…" she shook her head vehemently. "Just the… you know, the usual stuff."

I nodded. She parted her legs a little, fingering the spot where I knew her brand was. I put my fingers over hers and she gasped.

"Does it still hurt?" I asked.

"No," she said. "Never, just feels a bit weird still."

"Do you like it?" I wanted to know. "Don't lie."

"Yeah." She gave me a big smile, with only a hint of sadness in it. "I love it, I like that it's there. A lot. Reminds me of who I belong to. My master."

My ego deflated. I wanted her to only belong to me.

"Do you want to get out of here?" I asked her, and she gave me a long stare.

"I have to go home," she said. "I'm sorry, I really can't go anywhere with you. I'm scared…"

Scared of that fucking jackass. I could've killed him. Should've, when I had the chance.

"That's alright," I told her. "I'll walk you home, come on."

She got up and I followed close behind. She didn't say a word when some guys wolf-whistled at her, and I gave them death stares so evil they eventually shut the fuck up. I took her hand on instinct, and it was tiny inside mine. She felt like a little doll, breakable, pretty and so fucking beautiful.

We walked in silence. I didn't want to push her, and she seemed to be deep in thought. Unfortunately, the bar was close to her apartment, and I regretted the fact as soon as we turned up at the building.

"I'm sorry I can't invite you upstairs," she said, and I shrugged it off. "I think we might see you in a week or so, though."

"Okay," I nodded.

She leaned over and gave me a hug. She felt good in my arms, and she fucking smelled amazing.

I pulled her back when she moved away, and let my lips linger over her ear.

"You could leave him," I told her. "You could be mine."

She moved away. Her eyes were far away when she waved goodbye.

I stood there like a fucking fool for long minutes after she'd disappeared into the elevator.

## CHAPTER 34
### *Pet*

F orbidden fruit had never tasted sweeter.

I hadn't seen Stranger since he'd walked me home, but I wanted to so very badly. I'd also decided I was done seeing him behind King's back. I would always tell him if I wanted something, so why should this be any different?

He told me Stranger would be coming over that night, and I didn't bother hiding my excitement. I think it was the happiest I'd been in weeks, jumping up and down for him as he looked at me thoughtfully. I still wasn't sure what his thoughts were on Stranger. He seemed so torn about the whole thing, yet he was the one who kept calling him to come back. And it excited me.

By now we'd settled into a routine. I'd wear an outfit King picked for me, and I'd wait for them in the playroom. Sometimes they took their time, others they just took me. I wondered what the night would bring as I lay down on the bed, my eyes fixed on the ceiling. This time, King had left a champagne bottle in an ice bucket in the corner. I was never allowed to drink, and it excited me to find it there.

The door opened and my heartbeat picked up just like it always did. But there was the sound of only one pair of footsteps this time before the door shut, and I looked up.

Stranger stood in the room with his cock bulging through his jeans and his hand hovering over it.

"He went to get something," he told me in a husky voice, and I swung my legs over the side of the bed.

I was wearing a black and purple set to match my hair. A pretty bra that was so sheer you could see my nipples right through the lace, and panties that covered more of my ass than the usual thong I wore. My stockings were black and so were my heels were, but the garter I wore around my thigh was purple. King bought me a new perfume, and the heady scent of it wrapped me in a cloud as I walked over to Stranger.

"He told you to come in by yourself?" I asked, and he nodded. "Are you gonna play with me?"

He nodded again.

His fingers tangled in my hair in moments, and he tugged hard. But his mouth felt sweet against mine, like a kiss between two clumsy teenagers. He fucked like a monster but he seemed to be less experienced when he kissed me. His tongue tried to devour me and I giggled against his mouth as he forced me closer.

"He didn't say I couldn't," he growled against my lips, his palm spanking my ass, hard. "You're such a good little girl, Pet. I want you…"

"You can have her," King's voice interrupted, and I looked up without breaking the embrace.

He came closer, and once again, my heart pounded when I saw him. I'd never get sick of the man, so perfect and farther away than ever, or so it felt.

"Come to me, Pet," he told me, and I broke away from Stranger, dropping to my knees. I crawled up to his legs and on instinct, I kissed the leather of his shoes. It made me drip, and it made him smile.

"What an overachiever," he told me. "I like that, Pet. Lie down on the bench."

I did as he told me, and Stranger helped me lie on my back with my feet firmly on the ground.

They joined me, and King held a candle in his hand.

"I want to play with fire," he said with a grin, and I gave Stranger a panicked look. But he merely smiled, like he was in on it too.

"Don't hurt me," I begged, and they both laughed.

"Those words might work better if we didn't know how much you love it," Stranger said. And then he pulled his shirt off, and I stared at the trail of hair leading from his sculpted abdomen down into his jeans.

"Hold her down," King told him, and Stranger stood behind my head, pinning my arms above me. I struggled, but it was really for show. I couldn't move an inch with him holding me like that.

King shackled my ankles and lit the candle. He held it over the floor first, and I watched the wax start to drip ever so slowly. The candle was purple, just like my lingerie and my hair.

"Ask for it, Pet," King told me roughly, and I glared at him. "Ask. For. It. Now."

"Please," I whispered. "I don't know what I'm asking for."

Stranger's hand smoothed some hair off my face, and he gently whispered in my ear, "Ask him to hurt you, Pet."

"Hurt me," I begged. "Please, hurt me."

"Tell me you want it," King insisted. "Tell me what you want, pretty Pet."

"I want that wax on me," I said. "I want it dripping over me, please."

"Good girl," Stranger murmured in my ear. His beard was tickling my neck and I wanted to giggle, but I was too fucking scared to make a sound.

We stared at the candle as the wax poured down. And then King put it over my belly, and the first drop hit my skin so fast I could barely react.

I hissed, but it only hurt for a second, and then it hardened on my skin. I stared at it in wonder.

"Get her tits out," King barked at Stranger, and he did.

I gasped as the candle went above them, and when the wax hit my rosy nipples, I screamed. But it turned into moans soon enough.

They played with me like that for some time. I could feel how horny it was making them. King was bulging in his pants, and Stranger was breathing so heavily I wondered how he didn't just come in his boxers.

"You have to fuck me," I begged. "You have to, I have to feel you inside me."

"We will," King promised me. "Just hold the fucking candle for me. Please Pet, do you promise?"

"Yes," I said, so hazy with lust I could barely see. "I promise, anything you want."

Stranger stepped away and I mewled when the bench suddenly started moving. It didn't stop until I was stood upright, with my legs spread and my arms now stretched up in the air. Stranger fixed them with rope, tying me down, and I cried out helplessly. My skin was covered in hardened purple wax.

"Play with her," King told Stranger, and he stripped down to his underwear before he came up to me.

His fingers spread my pussy open while King watched us, and I shivered when I came for the first time, creaming all over his fingers. I should've been embarrassed, but they'd teased me for so long I would've done anything to get off.

Stranger raised his fingers to my lips.

"Lick, pretty Pet," he told me, and I licked them, with my eyes on his and my pussy dripping.

I cleaned them off and begged for more, but he took a step back.

"You said you'd hold the candle," King reminded me. "So, open your mouth, wide."

I did, and before I could react, he stuck the candle inside my mouth. I cried out, and when I did, the wax dribbled down my chest and I struggled against the pain.

"Be a good girl, Pet," King told me. "It's not that hard, I promise. You will love it."

I felt tears running down my cheeks.

The candle wasn't thick, it fit easily inside my mouth as my teeth dug into the wax. It was long enough to extended several inches over my body, just the right length to drip down as I held it between my teeth. I couldn't make a sound. I was too scared of dropping it while it was still burning.

My eyes found Stranger, and he looked horny as fuck. It got me off.

King's fingers touched the wax on my tits, and he flicked my nipples until they got hard for him. I could barely move, feeling helpless as fuck as they both started playing with me. Fingers on my cunt, fingers on my nipples. One of them fucked my ass with his thumb, and I tried to ride it, even though it made the candle drip all down my front. I wanted them more than ever. Not just one or the other, both of them.

King moved away and I followed him across the room as he brought the ice bucket and champagne closer.

Stranger picked up an ice cube and ran it across my stomach. The wax was hot, but the ice was cold, and I suffered through it, my teeth digging into the candle in my mouth. They drove me crazy for so long like that, until King finally popped the bottle open.

I watched them drink from it, the candle burning more and more. I'd dribbled not only wax but spit all over my tits. I couldn't stop it. My pussy hurt from coming from their fingers, and my body ached from the position they forced me into. And I was pissed I wasn't gonna get any champagne if they kept chugging it down like that.

They drained the bottle, and then it was between my legs.

I tried to clamp them shut but they wouldn't let me.

"Be careful," Stranger told me, as they pushed it inside me together.

It was cold inside me, cold and huge, stretching my pussy so wide it hurt.

I started crying, and King came up to me, blowing out the candle and gently taking it out of my mouth.

"You don't get cock tonight," he told me, and I cried out. "I know all about your little meeting with him the other night."

Stranger looked at him with so much surprise, I realized he wasn't the one who told him.

"I still want to–" he started to say, but King cut him off.

"No cock for our little Pet tonight. You can fuck the bottle all you want."

And he pushed it deeper inside me.

I was so wet I could feel myself dripping inside it, and it made me blush.

"Please," I begged. "Get me off, help me come."

They did. Stranger played with my clit while King pushed the bottle in and out, over and over again, until my pussy was running all over my legs and my head lolled to the side from too many orgasms.

"I don't think she can take anymore," Stranger murmured to King, and I could barely make out the words in my state.

"I'll decide that," King growled at him.

The bottle went back in, more savagely this time. He wrapped his fingers around the neck and fucked me so tightly I cried.

And then I felt it shatter.

And I howled.

"Fucking shit, what did you do?" Stranger screamed at King, and I cried so pathetically I felt like a little girl again, because I couldn't say a single word.

"Fuck," King cursed. "Fuck, fuck, fuck, what have I done?"

I could feel it inside me. Feel the shards cutting into me, and my pussy clenched because that's what it did when it had something inside it, and they cut me so deep. My cries felt like they'd break the windows.

King pulled his fingers out of me along with the rest of the bottle. His hand was bloody.

"Is there anything left?" Stranger barked at him. "Check if there's pieces left."

But he couldn't. King just stared at his bloody arm, and then back at me as I cried, softly now.

He got up and walked away from me.

And he ignored Stranger shouting obscenities after him.

# CHAPTER 35
*King*

**I** *knew it was over the* moment I left her in there, with glass shards in her pussy and my heart at her feet.

Leaving the room was the move of a coward, but it was the right thing to do. I had to let them sort it out, I couldn't be there for it.

It wasn't supposed to happen, breaking the bottle in her pussy, and I would hate myself for it for the rest of my life. I knew I'd never be able to forgive myself.

I waited in the bathroom like a fucking coward, staring at my reflection in the mirror and wondering who the man looking back at me was. I barely recognized him anymore.

It felt like hours passed, but it must've been only thirty minutes. Someone banged on the bathroom door, and I forced myself to pull it together, to pretend like I did it all on purpose.

I opened the door with my eyes hazy, and my mouth set in a thin line, glaring at Stranger in front of me.

"You motherfucking sonofabitch," he growled at me, and then he was on me.

It could've been the fight of a lifetime, if I'd let him make it into one.

But I didn't.

I just let him hit me, over and over again, because I fucking deserved that and so much worse. My wound on my nose reopened, and I let the blood wash over my face as he hit my guts, my sides, everything he could. I took all of it and I welcomed the pain, because at least I felt something other than despair.

"You just fucking left her," he spat at me once he was done, and I lay on the floor wheezing and trying to catch my breath. "You fucking jackass, she could have bled out."

"Is she okay?" I asked, the only question that really mattered.

"Yeah," he laughed bitterly. "No fucking thanks to you. She has cuts inside her. I barely got all the damn glass out, you fucking sadistic piece of shit."

I could have explained it wasn't on purpose, but it wouldn't have done any good. I'd already lost her, anyway. I lost Pet the day I met her.

I got up from the floor on shaky feet, and I stared at Stranger, and he looked at me like he barely knew who I was. I guess he didn't really know much more than Pet. And he wasn't about to find out, either.

"I'm taking her with me," he told me in a flat voice. "I'm not fucking letting her stay here with you."

"Fine," I bit out. I think he was surprised by my reaction, opening his mouth to fight back before he realized I'd agreed. "Take her."

He stared at me for a while longer, then left the bathroom. I wasted several precious minutes by washing my face from the blood he'd drawn, and pulling on a dirty shirt from the hamper in the bathroom, because I didn't want to fucking walk around shirtless for this. My last moments with Pet...

It couldn't really be it. This couldn't be the end. I needed her. She was the air I wanted to breathe, hers was the only mouth I wanted to taste, the only pussy I wanted to be inside, for the rest of my life, whatever it fucking took...

But really, none of it mattered. I'd fucked up, and I'd hurt her, and now it was time to finally, finally say goodbye.

Things had to happen like this. It was no use fighting it. I just had to face it and say goodbye.

It still took me a while to get out of there, but when I did, I walked out with my head held high. That is, until I saw her sprawled on the sofa, wearing an oversized shirt. Not hers. His.

He was still shirtless. I wondered if he was just going to leave the building like that, with her in his crappy old band tee. She'd be cold. I couldn't stand the thought of her being cold.

"Take her stuff," I told him as he ran around the room, picking up shit. "Take her clothes, she'll be cold."

"She doesn't want anything from you," he spat at me. "I'm just getting my own stuff."

I stood there uselessly, and I watched her on the couch, facing away from me. She was holding her middle and crying so softly I could barely make out the sobs.

I wished he'd gone harder on me when he beat me. I wished he would've killed me right then and there.

But that wasn't part of the plan, just like the broken bottle wasn't. Maybe it was how it was supposed to happen.

"We're leaving," Stranger told me roughly, and I just gave him a blank stare. "Say your goodbyes. Fucking hurry though, and I'm watching you, remember."

I nodded, and walked over to her. She didn't look at me as I kneeled down next to the couch.

"Pet," I whispered, and she raised her beautiful head to look at me. Her eyes were red and puffy, her gorgeous baby blues merely a small light in her face. "I'm sorry for what I did to you. I'm so sorry."

"I don't want to go," she whispered back, and it fucking broke me.

I didn't want to let go.

I didn't want her to leave me.

I wanted to keep her for purely selfish reasons, and I knew I couldn't.

I finally had to sever our ties, so she could move on with her life.

"You have to," I told her gently. "It's time for you to go, my pretty Pet. It's time for you to move on."

"I don't wanna," she sobbed, and my hand touched the top of her head, barely, so scared I would break her.

"You have to go with him," I said. "I can't have you anymore, Pet. I'm not good for you. This isn't good… You have to leave, you have to be healthy with someone else. This isn't good for you. This won't end well."

"I don't care," she said, her eyes on mine. "I just want you. Don't you see that? I only ever wanted you…"

I glanced at Stranger, who'd turned his back on us. I could see how tense his shoulders were, how hard he had to fight the urge to throw me against the wall.

And then I kissed her, for the very last time.

And she tasted sweeter than ever before.

I knew that kiss would be on my mind the day I died. I would never be able to forget it.

I moved away from the couch, and let Stranger take my place.

He picked her up in his arms as if she weighed nothing, just like I used to.

He looked at me one last time, and I hated every second of this goodbye that I didn't want to happen.

"Take care of her," I told him, and he nodded. A silent agreement passed between us. "Make sure she's safe. Make sure no one hurts her."

Not like I just did.

"If you need to take her to the doctor," I added. "I can help… I have all the information, everything. Just let me know what you need. I want to help…"

"I have money," he spat at me, and I gave his outfit a doubtful look.

Work boots, those torn jeans, and he was still fucking shirtless like some damned savage. I could practically see Pet's pussy in that shirt of his, and I hated seeing it on her.

"I'll take your word for it," I told him, and I let him walk out of the room.

When they reached the door, Pet held out her hands and cried out for me, like she was still my little girl and I was still her master.

That was the last sight I had of her until they disappeared out of the apartment, out of the building.

The last sight I'd ever get of my perfect, pretty little Pet.

*The rest of the night* was a blur, and so was the week, the long days after that.

I fell asleep on the floor with her blood still marking the wood.

I drank myself awake at the counter, on the couch. I just kept drinking, drinking as much as I possibly fucking could.

It numbed the pain, but it didn't do much for the memories. Those were still fresh as a newly opened wound inside my head, ready to fuck with me any chance they got.

I missed her, she was like a fucking phantom limb. I missed her on the couch, her legs on my lap, tickling her while she picked a movie.

I missed her in the bedroom, curled up next to me, needily reaching for my body while she slept, needing me so much fucking closer than I could physically get.

I missed her in the playroom, missed her tied down and helpless, missed her greedy little pussy, missed her hungry mouth.

I missed her in the bathroom, the memory of shaving her pussy until she was perfectly smooth for me too fresh in my mind.

I missed her, always.

Calling Maria didn't help solve shit. I did find out Pet stayed in touch, and she gave me as much information as she wanted to after finding out what I'd done to her best friend. She was cold on the phone now, sweet Maria who would've crawled up to me given any chance she could get at one time. She hated my guts, and she had every right to do so.

I called Stranger, but he never picked up. I didn't bother tracking him down, knowing I'd only get kicked out if I found where he was staying.

I never called Pet once.

I deleted her number off my phone and off my records so I wouldn't tempt myself. I regretted it every fucking minute.

The place beside me where she slept remained empty, and I wanted her back. Wanted to feel the warmth of her body against mine, feel her body stir as she woke up slowly in the mornings. I couldn't take life without her, because life with no Pet in it was no life at all.

So, I just drank it away, drop by drop, glass by glass, and then, finally, bottle by bottle. I tried to leave my problems at the bottom of it, but it never quite seemed to work out that way.

And then I was there a week later, painfully sober, and even more painfully, alone.

I missed her with every fiber of my being, missed every bit of her, every cell that made her Pet, every thought that made her my girl.

And that night, in my study, I drank to her.

I raised a glass to the city, looking down at the lights, and I drank a single glass for my perfect pretty little Pet, knowing it was the last time I'd get to call her that in my mind.

She wasn't my Pet anymore, and she'd be happier for it. Eventually.

Goodbye, my Pet.

Thank you for playing with me.

Thank you for making me love you, even though I swore I wouldn't.

Goodbye.

# CHAPTER 36
## *Stranger*

I*'d never had a girl* in my apartment before her.

It felt weird to take her there after the ride in the cab. I kept her on my lap the whole time, barking orders at the taxi driver who seemed too freaked out by a shirtless tall as fuck dude to say a word back to me.

Finally, we pulled up in front of my building, and I gently lifted her out of the car and carried her inside.

The building sure as fuck wasn't as fancy as King's penthouse, but it was still nice; a townhouse in a row of houses that all looked the same. Possibly a strange choice for someone like me, but I liked living there. It was a tall building with too much space for just one person, especially given the time I spent in there, but I wouldn't give it up for the world.

I carried Pet up the steps and opened the door, locking it behind us. She held on to me so tightly it almost felt like I'd have to peel her off me. But I didn't want to. I wanted to keep holding her.

It was impossible to believe what that bastard had done to her, and I knew I'd regret not doing more damage to him when I'd kicked his ass. I didn't understand why he didn't fight back, because I wanted him to.

I wanted to kick him and punch him and hurt him while she watched. But he wouldn't fight back. And the thing that hurt more than any of his hits, was the way Pet still looked at him.

I knew if he'd asked her to stay, I'd be leaving without her.

There was something between them, a connection I couldn't understand. She couldn't let him go until he made her do it.

She looked small and vulnerable in my arms as I carried her up to the bedroom.

It was the mostly sparsely furnished room in the house, with only a bed and a lamp in there. I set her down and she pulled me on the bed with her.

"Do you want to go see a doctor?" I asked her as she squirmed against me, making me hard despite my best efforts to think about something else. "We can go to the ER, or I can call someone for you, it will be discreet, I promise."

"No," she said weakly, and gripped on to me.

My shirt looked better on her than it ever had on me. She was naked underneath, and when I tentatively reached between her legs, I could feel several bleeding cuts from the bottle. I cursed out loud.

"You need to," I told her. "Fuck, Pet. I'm going to call someone now."

"No," she begged, gripping me. "Don't, please. Not today. I can see someone tomorrow. I just want to stay with you tonight. Please."

I stared at her, her bottom lip quivering as her eyes filled with tears. This fucking girl... Only eighteen and she'd been through so fucking much already.

"Okay," I told her. "Tomorrow though, first thing in the morning, I'll have someone come over."

She nodded and held on to me so tightly. She felt so good in my arms, like it was the only place in the world she belonged. I didn't want to let her go.

I wondered what would happen if she wanted to go back to him the next day, because I knew by then I would never be able to let her leave me.

Holding her close, I buried my nose in her purple hair. It was a nasty reminder of him, because I knew it couldn't have been her idea. I wanted it gone. I wanted every trace of that bastard wiped off her, from her memory, too. I wondered how I could possibly make that happen, and if she'd even let me.

It only took moments for her breathing to get heavy, and I realized she'd fallen asleep in my arms. But I couldn't let her.

I felt anxious myself, nervous as fuck and needy for her.

I pressed my lips against hers, and they parted in her sleep, welcoming me in.

Kissing her as she slept, like she was my Sleeping Beauty, felt so fucking right. She barely moved in response, just moaned inside my mouth. I kissed her softly. Sweetly. In a way I'd never kissed anyone before, like my kiss could heal her of the shit she'd been through .

Her eyelids fluttered open when I moved back to look at her. She stared at me sleepily, and there was a hint of a smile on her lips.

"Am I yours now?" she asked, the words so soft I thought I'd misheard her at first.

"Do you want to be?" My voice was gentle, and my heart thumped awaiting her answer.

"No," she whispered, and snuggled against me.

I held her and wished I'd killed King. Maybe then she'd finally be mine completely.

*Putting Sapphire back together took weeks.*

A day before she could walk.

The doctor came in and took care of her cuts, no questions asked. Thankfully, most of the damage was outside on her thighs, and the doc told us she'd be fine in a week or two.

Three days before she stopped flinching when I called her by her name, not the nickname he'd given her.

A week before she started responding to it.

Eight days for her to come out of the bedroom and sit with me in the living room, watching mindless shitty TV for a few hours.

She didn't speak for the first few days either. And on day nine, she finally came up to me herself to ask for something.

I half-expected her to ask for him.

King had called me several times, but he hadn't called her. I never answered, but I didn't block his number either, and confused myself by not doing it.

It felt like it wasn't my decision to make. Like I wasn't supposed to intervene with her life in that way.

"I want to talk to Maria," she told me, and I nodded right away.

The first nine days of her being with me were spent in the apartment. She barely left the bed. I had food delivered because I couldn't bear to leave her alone, and I tried to use my shitty cooking skills to make her something edible. She never asked a question. Never asked for anything. We barely talked, and I needed her words so badly, but didn't want to force her.

I gave her my phone to call Maria, and she didn't question why I had her number saved already.

They talked for two hours, and I waited outside the bedroom like a moron.

At least she still slept in my arms every night. And every night, like clockwork, I'd kiss her when she fell asleep. She'd wake up for a moment and just stare at me before her eyes closed again.

The purple was starting to fade from her hair. She took long showers in the mornings and before bed, and the shower leaked purple down the drain once she was done. It was my favorite sight, and I felt like she was washing away her awful past along with that color.

The white-blond shone through her hair, only some streaks of lavender remaining. It looked pretty. I thought it made her look like a fairy princess or some shit.

She finally came out of the bedroom and handed me back my phone. There was a slight smile on her face.

"I'm sorry I've been so... weird," she said, and I shook my head like it didn't matter. "I'd like to pay you back... For everything you've done for me. Maria says I can stay with her now."

It felt like she'd stabbed me in the heart, and I could only stare at her.

"She'll pick me up tomorrow," she said.

"I don't want you to leave," I told her. "I want you to stay with me."

She let out a small laugh, saying, "But what's the point? We have nothing in common. We can't be together. You're..."

"I'm what?" I closed in on her, and she flinched. I felt like a fucking jackass. "I'm sorry, Sapphire. You should be able to do what you want."

"Okay," she whispered. "What do *you* want?"

"I want you," I groaned. "Isn't it fucking obvious? I've only ever wanted you."

"But I'm not..." She looked away for a second, then took a step towards me.

"I'm not the right girl for you."

"You don't know that." I wanted to touch her. I wanted more than just that nighttime kiss. I wanted back inside her. I wanted to own her body. I wanted to claim her mind. "Please, give me a chance. And I don't fucking say please often."

"Feels weird?" she asked with a giggle, and I grinned at her.

"Very weird, Sapphire."

She didn't flinch.

"I like sleeping next to you," she admitted, and looked down.

I wanted her eyes on mine, and I couldn't resist making her look up, my fingers holding her chin.

"I don't know anything about you," she said.

"I want you to know," I told her. "I want to tell you everything, pretty girl."

"Will you?" Her lashes were so long, and lighter without mascara. She looked so young without makeup.

"Yeah," I promised. "Everything. Right now."

I took her hand and led her to the bedroom.

The window was open, and it let in fresh air as we got on the bed and stared at each other.

I lay on my side, and she pulled her knees up and leaned against the headboard.

"I want to know…" she started. "Who you are. Everything."

"Ask a question," I grinned. "Anything. Ask away."

"How old are you?"

"Thirty-two."

"What do you do?"

I smiled. Already, a hard one.

"Mostly computer stuff," I explained. "From home."

"Like programming?"

"That too," I nodded. "I freelance. So, whatever project I get, I pick up."

"But that couldn't have bought you this house," she told me, smiling cheekily.

"You're right," I admitted. "It didn't. The house was my grandpa's."

"Where is he?" Her voice was softer now.

"Six feet under." My voice wasn't as jokey as I wanted it to sound. It was sad, and a little bitter.

"I'm sorry," she murmured. Her hand brushed mine, and I wished I'd made more shitty comments, had a worse life, just so she'd touch me again. "Do you have other family?"

I thought about them all. Sisters, parents, all of them. The family I'd been running away from for years.

"I do," I confessed. "I have a big family. But I don't see them, ever."

"Why? Do they live far away?" She looked curious.

"No," I laughed. "Same city. Just… differences."

"You should see them," she said. "Not that I don't get it. But you should. I'll see my parents soon too. I need to tell them about…"

She looked away, and just like that, the spell was broken.

I saw the tears slip down her cheeks, and they were, surprisingly, the first tears I'd seen her cry since it all went down.

"Oh, pretty girl," I groaned, and pulled her against me.

I felt her straining against my chest. Like she wanted to pull away, but couldn't bring herself to. She didn't say a word about him, but she didn't need to, either. I didn't want to hear their story. I didn't want to know she'd choose him over me.

And then her body started shaking, trembling and quaking in my arms. She hiccupped as she tried to catch her breath and I held her even closer.

"Sapphire, please," I asked her. "Try to breathe, please."

She still didn't say a word, but the sobs started to really wrack her body. She cried loudly, she cried like a little girl, with sadness so all-encompassing I had no fucking idea how to handle her.

Her hot little mouth reached for mine, and I couldn't resist her. I kissed her through the sobs, I kissed her through it all, and she tasted like love and tears.

"Please, Sapphire," I begged. "Please calm down, I need you to…"

She wouldn't let me speak. Just kissed me and let me drink her tears, and she kept crying so hard I thought she'd come apart in my arms.

I held her back and watched her, her face blotchy and her chest heaving.

"Please," I said again. "Just deep breaths, Sapphire. Deep breaths for me. Okay? Can you do that?"

She shook her head no, now having a full-on panic attack. It felt like the only thing holding the pieces of her together were my arms.

"Sapphire," I said gently. "Listen to me, listen to me, pretty girl. It's going to be okay. I'm not going anywhere. I'm going to stay right here, and we'll make it through, and you'll be perfectly okay. You just have to let it pass. Look at me, pretty girl, look into my eyes. Let me make it better, Sapph, please."

She looked up and we stared at each other. I felt like I was going to fucking cry too, and I blinked away the tears angrily.

"There you go, there's a good girl," I muttered, and she sighed.

It was those two words, and they worked like magic. She loved being a *good girl*.

She was still breathing heavily, but slowly calming down; slowly coming down from it.

"You're such a good girl," I told her sweetly. "Look at me, Sapphire. Do you want to know a secret?"

She looked up and her chest rose and fell as she nodded, whimpering those delicious sounds that made me want to fuck her, even if she thought she was a mess.

"Sapphire," I breathed. "My name is Felix."

She let out a sob and clung to me and I kept repeating it, stripping away the only shred of anonymity I had left.

"My name is Felix…"

ONE WEEK LATER

# CHAPTER 37
*Pet*

It *felt weird, sitting in* a bar with him and Maria. It felt like a new chapter when I hadn't even closed the last book yet.

I tried to come to terms with it and pretend it didn't feel weird, but I think all three of us knew it was awkward, though none of us said it out loud.

"Let's get another round," Maria said, jumping up and heading to the bar without asking what we wanted. Not like I could get what I wanted, anyway. The only reason I'd gotten into the bar was she'd begged the bouncer until he grudgingly let us drink, and told me I'd be flat out on my butt if he saw me with an alcoholic drink. So, Coke it was, while the two of them chugged down their drinks.

She left me sitting there with him… I couldn't get used to calling him by his name. Yes, I'd used it a couple of times, but it felt so strange, really like we were completely different, new people.

And I wasn't sure I wanted to be a new person just yet. I liked being Pet… a lot.

Neither of them had called me by that nickname in a week, and I figured it meant they were trying to make me move on. But it felt scary.

I hadn't been feeling great. It had been two weeks since I'd left that apartment, since King had decided he wanted nothing else to do with me.

The memory of what happened was still fresh in my mind, even though I tried to remember the good things, not the bad things. But I couldn't forget completely, and I couldn't bring myself to forgive him, either. What he'd done was terrible. The doctor told me I was lucky as hell Felix was there as I could've gotten hurt much worse. I didn't want to think about it. I didn't want to admit how badly I'd let King hurt me.

Truth be told, he'd been pushing me from the start. I just didn't realize how far he was willing to take the whole thing.

"Hey, Earth to Sapphire."

I looked up into his eyes.

I wasn't the only one staring.

He was one of those guys that just made girls stare. I knew several of them had noticed him when we walked in, and I felt a prick of jealousy when it happened. But he only had eyes for me, and it almost made me feel a little guilty. Almost.

"I'm here," I smiled, and he grinned at me as he downed his drink.

"Doesn't feel like it," he said. "Come on, try and have some fun with us. It's good that you're finally out of the apartment, isn't it?"

"Yeah," I shrugged. "I guess. It's nice seeing Maria."

"She's happy to see you," he nodded. "Try to enjoy tonight. There's another day tomorrow when you can feel as fucking miserable as you want."

I laughed out loud just as Maria returned with our drinks.

"She lives!" she grinned. "A laugh! What did you do, drug her?"

I giggled as she set down my Coke, spilling some over the edge. She was definitely a little tipsy, and for some reason, it put me in a better mood. I liked Maria a lot, and I was so happy it looked like she wasn't about to sever our friendship because I'd broken up with King.

I guess that's what it really was… A breakup. As non-traditional as our relationship had been, it was now firmly over.

He hadn't called once, and I didn't dare ask Felix if he'd contacted him. I saw the way he reacted every time I brought King up. He hated talking about him.

"Okay, fine," I said. "Let's have some fun tonight. I'm sick of sitting at home and worrying."

A look of disbelief passed between Felix and Maria and I glared at them.

"How about a little confidence in what I say?" I asked them in mock embarrassment, and they both laughed. "You know I can still have some fun, right? It's not like somebody died."

Well. Only almost.

"You got it," Maria winked at me, setting down her empty glass. God, she was really downing them. I figured she was pretty drunk already, and if she kept going at that rate, we'd have to practically carry her back home.

"Let's go dance," I begged her, and she was on her feet in a second.

Felix stared at me, saying, "I didn't think you were a dancer."

"I'm not," I said. "But I am whatever I want to be tonight."

I felt his eyes on me as Maria dragged me to the dancefloor. The bar served as a club once it got a little later, but right now, there were only a couple of people moving to the music. Maria didn't seem to care though, and she twirled me around the floor as if the loudest club music was playing. She made me laugh out loud, and I felt everyone looking at us.

I was definitely underdressed, wearing a silly pink dress with a skater skirt and a lace top. I probably looked even younger than usual, especially now that the purple had completely faded from my hair and I was back to my natural white blonde. But it felt good, and I loved dancing with her. She had a way of making all my worries disappear, and it felt so damn good. I let it all out on the dancefloor, and I let my fears drop down to the ground where I stomped all over them in my peep toe Mary-Janes.

I looked up to find Felix watching us, and I motioned for him to come join us. The music had gotten louder and the floor was filling up, but he still shook his head no, and I stuck my tongue out at him and kept dancing.

We ruled that dancefloor. Maria's laugh rang through the music, and I loved dancing with her. Her hands were hot against my skin when we touched, and I remembered that kiss in King's living room, remembered how fucking hot it felt even though I didn't want to do it at first. It made my panties a little wet, but I ignored it as I kept dancing, kept trying to forget.

I felt another pair of hands on me, big and strong, and I turned around expecting to see Felix.

But it was someone else, another stranger. He was handsome, but I didn't want him touching me. It scared me.

And then Felix was next to us, and he glared at the guy so much he took his hands off in an instant. And then he just stood there, glaring at me this time.

"What?" I asked self-consciously, raising my voice over the music.

"Don't fucking let them touch you," he barked at me, and I rolled my eyes.

"I didn't exactly give him a written invitation," I said. "And who are you anyway? My dad?"

"Fuck off, Sapphire," he bit out, grabbing my forearm. "We're fucking leaving."

"Hey!" Maria butted in, her eyes angry. "Let her have some fun, you moron. This is the first time she's had any in weeks."

"And you know what's good for her better than me?" he scoffed. "Sure thing, Maria."

"I'm her best friend," she argued, taking my other arm forcibly. "Come on, Pet, let's go."

She slipped, and we all froze.

My heart pounded for a second before I ripped my arms out of their hands, and they let me.

And then I ran outside, leaving my purse and my drink on the table.

I heard them coming after me, calling out for me to stop, but I wouldn't, couldn't, until I was in an empty alley. No one there but me, and the sound of their approaching footsteps.

I leaned against the brick wall and tried to catch my breath, realizing I wasn't really out of shape, just trying desperately not to cry or have another panic attack out there.

"I'm so sorry," Maria breathed, coming to a stop next to me. How she'd managed to get to me before Felix, and in those five inch heels, was beyond me. "I totally slipped, Sapph, I'm so fucking sorry, I feel terrible."

"It's okay," I whispered, looking at her with a small smile. "I know I'm overreacting…"

"Are you okay?" Felix finally caught up with us, his eyes on mine, demanding answers. "Please, Sapphire. Are you okay?"

"Yeah." My voice was shaking, and I felt embarrassed. "I just needed to get out of there, I'm really sorry…"

"It's fine," Maria said hastily. "It's totally fine. Do you want me to stay with you?"

I looked at her, feeling the blush creeping up my neck.

"I want to go home," I whispered.

"Oh, honey." She hugged me close. "You want to go to my place?"

I shook my head no. "I want to go with him."

We both looked at Felix, and he shifted his weight from one foot to the other awkwardly.

"We can go anytime you like," he told me. "Really, Sapphire."

"Okay, let's go now," I said, and he nodded.

"You want me to come with you?" Maria asked, and I shook my head.

"No, have fun tonight. I know you know some people in there," I nodded back in the direction of the bar. "I'm really okay. It's just too much, too soon."

"Okay." She kissed me on the cheek. "Call me tomorrow, babygirl."

"I will." I hugged her close, and then she was gone in a cloud of Dior's Poison and her clacky heels on the pavement.

I stared at Felix and he gave me a nervous smile.

"You ready to go, pretty girl?" he asked me, and I nodded.

We walked through the city, lit up in night lights, and my hand sneaked into his. He didn't look at me when I did it, just held on to me tightly, and I liked it.

When we were almost at his house, I tugged on his arm and stopped for a second.

"You okay?" he asked, turning to face me. "Come on, we're almost home."

"Why do you live here?" I asked. "Why this house?"

"I told you," he grinned. "My grandpa's."

"What does your family do?" I asked.

He didn't know, but Maria had told me what she'd found out.

He was a trust-fund kid, the weirdest one I'd ever met. Judging by his clothes, he looked like a twenty-year-old who belonged in the mosh pit. His parents owned a hotel empire.

"You know?" he raised his brows at me. "I think you do."

"I do," I giggled. "Maria told me."

"Of course she did," he sighed. "You two together… it's a mess waiting to happen."

"What do you mean?"

"She told me you kissed," he growled, and it was my turn to look away and be embarrassed. "Don't be shy now, Sapphire, cause I hear you weren't then, either."

"Shut up!" I giggled and hit him with my purse he'd brought for me from the bar earlier. "You don't know anything."

He took my wrists in his hands and pinned me against a shop window.

"I know enough," he growled in my ear, and my breath quickened when he let go of one wrist and gently slapped my legs apart.

"Felix," I breathed, but he didn't stop.

His fingers were touching them, and I could feel them shaking against the brand on my thigh. I could feel how wet I'd gotten, it dripping down my legs.

"Wait," I begged him, and he listened, his fingers lingering an inch away from my pussy. "I… I can't."

"But you want to," he said, his fingers making me squirm. "Tell me you want to."

"I do," I cried out. "Please…"

He touched my pussy once, long, strong fingers running along my soaked panties and making me mewl. And then they were gone, and he took my hand, and led me back home.

I scowled as he let us in, but he didn't say a word. We went into the living room and he turned on the TV. He had this strange habit of always leaving it on, saying he couldn't concentrate in silence. He was the weirdest, most chaotic person I knew.

The TV blared with the evening news, and I plopped down on the couch, still offended.

I watched the news, a local station reporting on a suicide in the community that was being investigated further as new evidence came out.

I only watched it cause it was the town where my parents lived, where I grew up.

But when I saw who they were talking about, my mouth ran dry and I could only stare at the screen.

Aaron James.

Dead.

Suicide.

I stared as the report ended as fast as it had started, and I felt dizzy and scared. For some reason I couldn't believe it. Couldn't understand it was really over, and he'd never be able to come after me again. I felt like I was going to pass out.

He was dead…

# CHAPTER 38
## *Felix*

I turned off the TV, *suddenly* distracted by the loud noises blaring from it. It was unlike me. Usually I always had it on, but it was interfering with my thoughts. I wanted them clear for her.

"You okay?" I asked her, and she tore her eyes away from the now black screen. "Is there something wrong?"

"Just... Someone I used to know." She shook her head in what looked like disbelief. "Just weird hearing that."

"The suicide guy?" I asked, sitting down next to her. I pulled my shirt off and dropped it on the floor. The AC was just starting up and it felt hot in the house.

Sapphire's eyes danced over my body and she crawled closer to me on the couch. Suddenly, she was in my arms, her ass firmly in my lap. I felt my cock stirring and wished I could calm the fuck down. I didn't want to push her, ever, especially after she'd already had a meltdown that day.

"Talk to me," I said, my hands touching to her thighs and resting dangerously close to the hem of her pretty pink dress. "Tell me about that guy."

She looked right at me, her pretty eyes focused on mine.

"I knew him for a long time," she admitted.

"You're only eighteen," I reminded her, tugging on a long strand of hair. I loved that it was back to blonde, had hated the purple with a passion.

"Since I was a kid," she whispered. "A baby, really. My parents were friends with him, and then he was a teacher at my school when I was older."

"Bad memories?" She seemed tense when I talked about him.

She kept looking at me as she nodded. "He... he raped me. When I was a kid. He tried when I was older, too."

I nearly jumped off the couch, and her words left my head pounding. I tried to understand what she was saying, at the same time convincing myself the guy was dead now, there was nothing I could do. But still, knowing all the shit this poor girl had been through drove me crazy. I wanted to help her. I wanted to make her whole again.

"And now he's dead," she said softly when I didn't respond. "I guess that's it, then."

"He killed himself," I repeated what we'd heard on TV, and she nodded.

"He had a family," she whispered. "Last time I saw him. He had kids."

"Would you like to get in touch?" I asked awkwardly, and she shook her head over and over again. "Did you ever press charges? Tell anyone?"

"I only told..." She swallowed, her pretty throat stretching. "I only told King."

I wanted to tell her if she'd told me, I would've fucking done something about it, unlike her jackass of a boyfriend.

"Are you okay?" I asked.

She nodded tentatively, and I held my legs up, making her slide lower on my lap. She giggled with her mouth inches away from mine.

"I want to kiss you now, Sapphire Rose," I told her roughly. "Is that okay?"

"Yeah," she replied breathlessly. "I think that would be okay. I want you to…"

So I did.

She tasted like Coke again, sweet and young. It was so hot in the room suddenly, it felt like our kiss was melting me.

She left her hands in her lap, a demure, pretty little sight when I looked down.

"Are you scared of me?" I asked her softly, and she shook her head, her forehead on mine.

"No," she said. "I'm not, I promise."

"You've barely touched me," I told her. "I thought… Sorry, I thought we fucking, I don't know, had something. Earlier. Before you left him."

"Yeah," she whispered. "I thought so too."

My heart fucking pounded. I wanted to lift her off her feet and fuck her against the wall, because we both knew she'd love it.

"If you want to go, it's fine," I said instead, like a damn jackass. My voice was rough again. "I can help you out."

"No." She pulled away, gave me an annoyed look. "I thought it was okay if I stayed."

"It is," I growled. "But you're driving me fucking crazy, Sapph."

"Why?" Her voice was soft and she ground her pussy against my lap. I moaned for her, feeling my cock straining against my jeans.

"Don't," I warned her. "Don't do that, pretty girl, or I'll do something we'll both regret."

"Maybe you should," she said into my ear, and my grip on her legs tightened. "Maybe you should at least try."

"I don't want to push you," I said back, her lips leaving a fleeting kiss against mine.

So young, but she was such a fucking temptress. He'd taught her well, or maybe it had simply been inside her all along. And I wanted her. God, I fucking wanted her so bad. I needed her tight little body, needed her sweet cunt, needed her ass. I especially needed her mouth, breathing my name against mine as I made her come over and over again.

"Be a good girl for me," I told her, and it was her turn to whimper. I'd have to remember what those two words did to my pretty girl.

She took her hair in one hand and raised it off the nape of her neck, fanning herself.

"It's hot," she complained. "Blow on me."

I grinned and blew on her skin. Her hair was sticking to her collarbones, and I saw sweat beading in the hollow of her neck. She made me go fucking primal. It was all instinct when I was with her, raw, primal instinct telling me to make her fucking mine, fuck her raw until she was fucking pregnant.

I closed my eyes tightly, trying to ignore the thought. I'd never had that before, never with Sapphire or any other girl. But now it was so fucking obvious what I wanted. I wanted to claim her, all of her. I wanted to fuck her full, and then keep trying until her belly swelled and her womb was full of me. I felt like a nasty pervert thinking about it like that.

"Felix," she said softly, and I turned my eyes to hers. "You stopped blowing."

I grabbed her, hands under her ass. Her legs wrapped around mine as I took her in the bathroom, stripped her of that fucking dress and her panties. She wasn't wearing a bra.

She pulled my jeans down in such a hurry she whimpered, because they wouldn't come off faster. And then I was pushing her in the shower, turning the water to ice cold, and pinning her against the wall, the water beating down my back as my mouth went to work on hers.

She was amazing. She was better than ever before, and my mouth couldn't get enough of her. I kept thrusting against her, my hips pushing against her crotch, so fucking desperate to be inside her. But she was too short.

I raised her up and she laughed out loud. My cock was probing at her pussy, and the water was the only thing I could hear besides her soft little moans. I wanted to be inside her. I wanted to fuck her so badly.

"Open yourself for me," I growled at her, and her shaky fingers left my hair and opened those pretty pussy lips for my cock.

I was inside her in seconds and she mewled as I fucked her against the tiles. She mewled, and then begged, and then whispered sweet dirty little things as I fucked her pussy, completely forgetting about her injury, because she kept begging me to go on.

Blinded by the water, I couldn't see shit. But I could feel it all.

The hot droplets of sweat sliding down my front, cold water beating down my back.

Sweet little Sapph breathing into my mouth, begging, begging, always begging for me. For my cum.

She felt insanely tight, and I couldn't let go.

"Please," she whispered. "I want you, I want you inside me, Felix, keep fucking me, I want you so much, only you can make it better."

I groaned and fucked her with no mercy, but with all the feelings I had for her instead.

I didn't fucking know how to describe them, but I knew I'd never fucked a girl like that. Like she was everything to me…

"Felix," she cried out. "Please, I want you to come, please, you have to."

She'd begged like that before, when I was playing with her and her man. But never with my name. And hearing it on her lips drove me fucking crazy. I wanted her. I wanted my cum inside her.

"Pretty girl," I breathed down her neck. "Little bit longer baby, please. I want to feel you some more, I want to stretch you."

She cried, soft little sounds as I pounded her, yet she wouldn't let me stop.

Every time I tried, too scared I was hurting her, bruising that sweet snatch, she scratched my back and urged me to go on. So I fucking did, until she was shuddering and jerking and coming all over my cock.

I felt the wetness despite the water, felt her leaking all over my cock.

"Did you squirt, pretty baby?" I asked her, my needy mouth latching onto her neck. "Did you fucking squirt for me?"

She could only cry in response, and her body went slack in my arms, but I had to keep fucking her. It was impossible to stop.

I remembered the little pills she took every night, the birth control she was on, for some strange fucking reason. And I really fucking wished she wasn't on them, because I wanted to fill her the fuck up, and have it grow in her womb. Our baby. Because she was my fucking woman, and I would've done anything in the world to prove it.

I wanted her so much it hurt. I wanted her even more when she was in my arms, knowing she was mine. I wanted to own every piece of that beautifully broken mind of hers. And I wanted to know it all, all her stories. Everything about her. I wanted her to be just mine, owned completely. Owned forever.

"Beg for it," I told her. "Beg for my cum inside you, baby."

"Please," she choked on a sob. "Please, Felix, fill me up, make it feel better, keep coming inside me, that's all I want, all I want is you, please…"

I came with her name on my lips, and I fucked her so deep she let out a little squeal. I kept my cock there, inside her pussy, as deep as it fucking went. And I creamed her pussy like that, all over her, coming so much I had to lean my forehead against the shower tiles and breathe slowly, while my cock was still exploding inside her.

She was shaking so much in my arms, and only after several long minutes I realized how cold the shower really was.

I held her in my arms as I turned the water off, and I carried her out into the bathroom. She felt sweet and tender as I put her down, and my cum spilled down her legs.

She looked down, and then back at me. And she smiled.

I was fucking in love with the girl, and the worst part was, I wanted her to know.

I wiped her down with a clean towel, and before she could object, I picked her up again. She giggled as I carried her back into the bedroom, setting her down on the bed like she was a doll, carefully, oh so carefully.

"Pretty girl," I whispered as I lay down next to her, covering her shivering body with mine. "Sapphire…"

"Thank you," she said against my lips, and I bit her bottom lip gently. She giggled.

"I'm in fucking love with you, Sapphire Rose," I growled against her mouth, and her pretty body froze.

She wiggled after a few moments, but I pinned her down.

"No," I told her roughly. "No getting away from that, Sapph. It is what it fucking is."

"Okay," she whispered. "You… like me?"

"No," I grunted. "I love you, you spoiled little brat. Just had to hear me say it, didn't you?"

She giggled and kissed me. Soft, sweet. And then she stuck her tongue inside my mouth and I bit her.

She nearly fell off the bed laughing.

"So what do you think about that?" I finally asked her. "What I just told you?"

She looked at me with those pretty baby blues.

"I think it's good," she said solemnly. "I think it's very, very good, that you love me."

# CHAPTER 39
*Pet*

"Do I look okay?"

I twisted and turned in front of the mirror nervously.

"For the hundredth time, you look amazing," Felix told me, wrapping his arms around my waist. "Seriously, can you fucking stop now? You're making me nervous."

"I just want to look good," I whined. "It's my first time meeting your parents. I want them to think I'm pretty, and smart, and good for you."

"If they don't, they're more stupid than I remember them," he told me with a grin, and I smacked him playfully.

He pulled me against him, his grip vice-like and impossible to get out of.

"Pretty girl," he murmured against my lips, and I smiled when he kissed me. We were going to a gallery opening that night, and I tried to ignore all the memories that whispered King's name in my ear. I had met him at one of those, but this time, I was going to be playing a very different role. No more stand-in waitress, tonight I was going to be a guest with a posh invitation on expensive paper, and I was going to meet my boyfriend's parents, and make an amazing impression.

I was nervous as hell, but I did my best to hide it and pretend it was all okay.

I wore a black dress this time around, a simple one with long sleeves that showed off my legs, but was covered up on top. I asked Felix if he thought I looked like girlfriend material, and he told me I looked like sex-toy material, to which I just rolled my eyes.

I leaned down to put my shoes on, my fingers shaking so much I couldn't get the little ankle strap to work.

He leaned down next to me, his fingers helping me attach the straps and gliding up my legs once he was done.

"Definitely girlfriend material," he told me seriously, and I smiled. I hoped his parents would think the same thing.

He'd recently confessed he hadn't seen them in a whole year. While he didn't seem to be too fussed when it came to his parents, I could tell he wanted to see his younger sister, Poppy. He spoke about her fondly, and I could tell he really cared about her. I'd asked if she'd be at the opening, and he told me she would. We were going through the mail, and the invitation was from his parents, for some kind of new artist they were trying to support, a woman named Daphne with no surname. I thought that was weird.

I managed to convince Felix to go to the opening with me. He wasn't crazy about the idea, but I could tell he wanted to see his sister, and I pushed those buttons until I finally got a nod from him.

It didn't make me any less nervous though, and the thought of meeting his family had me shaking.

We got into a cab in the evening, and Felix looked uncomfortable as hell in his suit. I couldn't help but giggle as he shrugged his shoulders, as if the blazer would magically disappear if he wiggled enough in it.

"By the way," he said on the way there, once I'd finally stopped teasing him about his outfit. "Maria's going to be there."

"What?" I gave him an excited look. "How do you know? Are you sure?"

"I thought you might be a little nervous," he replied with a grin. "So I got her on the guest list. She texted me this morning, said she was coming for sure."

"Oh, thank you," I breathed, kissing his cheek, because anything else in that cab felt weird, given my history with cars. "I'm so excited. I can't wait to see her and your family!"

He looked brooding as he nodded, looking out the car window, and I left him alone with his thoughts. It was obvious he needed some time to think, and I wasn't going to bother him. I could tell this was a big deal for him, and I already felt bad enough, thinking I was forcing him to do something he didn't want to.

From what I could understand, there hadn't really been a dividing fight in his family. He just didn't want to inherit his father's hotel empire, and after spending years in school, he rebelled and left. It didn't seem to me like his parents held a grudge, more like they were just worried about him. I'd tried to talk to him about it, but he seemed very closed off about the subject.

But I'd be lying if I said I wasn't excited to find out more about him, meet his family and especially his little sister. He spoke of her fondly, and she was just about my age as well.

We pulled up in front of the venue minutes later, and Felix helped me out of the car. My eyes widened.

It was on the same street as the last gallery opening I went to, but it was a famous art quarter in the city, so I tried not to think about it.

We walked inside, my arm hooked through his, and my steps shaky as he led me into the beautifully lit-up building.

There were lights in the ceiling, tiny little pinpricks of light that made the whole room look beautiful and almost fairytale-like. The art was similar and unusual for a place this modern. It seemed like Daphne favored woodland scenes, and I'd heard she put a fairy in all of her paintings if you looked close enough. They were huge canvases, too, not really abstract but different for sure. They were the first thing I noticed when I walked in, and I had to tear myself away from those scenes so I could join Felix again.

"I can see them now," he grunted in my ear. "Jesus fuck, why did I think this was a good fucking idea?"

"Felix!"

I looked up to see a girl running towards us. She was a brunette, pretty and slight, and she looked beautiful in a navy dress.

And then she was wrapping her arms around Felix's neck, and if they didn't look so very much alike, I would've been jealous of her obviously intimate motion.

"And you must be Sapphire," she told me with a big grin once she pulled away.

I smiled awkwardly. She must've been a few years older than me, maybe twenty-one, and I thought it would make things so uncomfortable, but she didn't even mention it. Just hugged me tightly and I let her, because it felt nice.

"So happy to finally meet you," she gushed. "I can't believe he's been keeping you all to himself."

She glared at her brother and I giggled.

"Nice to meet you too, I'm so happy to be here," I said with a big smile. "I can't wait to meet your parents as well."

"I think you'll like them," she winked at me, then turned her attention back to Felix. "I'm not letting you ignore us like that ever again."

"Yeah, yeah," he muttered, and she smacked him playfully.

"Whatever you had to deal with after Grandpa died has taken long enough," she went on, surprising me with her honesty and directness. "I think you should be back with your family. That's what he would have wanted."

He never got a chance to reply, as a couple in their late fifties approached us, smiling wide.

His mother was a beautiful woman, who aged gracefully and naturally, wearing a simple coral dress. His father wore a suit, and looked like the jolly old uncle everyone loved. I'd seen him on TV and in magazines before, and always thought he looked like a nice man. As we started talking, that proved to be true, and I liked his mom as well. She'd pulled me aside and mentioned she was a former beauty queen, and I could definitely win some pageants if I wanted to, so I should let her know if I was interested. It made me giggle.

Maria showed up a little while later, and joined our little group. It felt so good to have her there, during one of the most important moments in our relationship, and I whispered as much in her ear. She rewarded me by kissing my cheek and we both giggled when we remembered a different kiss a little while ago.

We were the chattiest group in the gallery for sure. And for once in my life, I felt happiness so strong I didn't even have time to think of anything else.

I did realize the same catering company was serving this event as the last time, and it made me grin thinking about that guy... Elliott I think his name was, shouting at everyone in the back. I kept my eyes trained in case I saw Veronica. I wanted one last laugh.

Then, someone got a microphone and announced the artist had just pulled up in front of the gallery. The whole place stirred, and we welcomed her with a round of applause. Except for Felix, who took the chance to wrap a hand around my waist and bite my neck, to which I giggled and tried to hide it as best as I could. I caught his sister watching, and she winked at me.

I couldn't see Daphne when they announced her arriving, and a throng of people lined up to speak to her. I only caught glimpses of her, red hair, curvy, sexy body in a black leather dress. She was beautiful from what I could see.

And then the crowd finally parted, and it was our turn to say our congratulations. But instead of the amazing artist herself, all I could see was the man with her.

My man, my King.

I thought my legs were going to give out on the spot, but I forced myself to stand still. I forced myself not to react the way I wanted to, not that I even knew what that was. Would I have ran, or would I have begged him to take me back?

It was so obvious they were together. The way he looked at her with affection, the way his hand lingered on the small of her back.

I hated her, I hated her so much I thought I'd just start crying on the spot.

I felt Felix tense when he noticed him as well, but it was a moment too late. We were already in line to congratulate the artist next.

"Hi, so lovely to meet you," she purred. She had a hint of a foreign accent, and I took her hand and gave her a robotic smile as she shook it.

I felt King's eyes on me, and I felt Felix's hand on my back, his fingers digging into my skin. I wanted to scream.

"You too," I murmured back.

"This is my partner, Mr. King," she went on, and my gut twisted when those words left her mouth. I knew I was going to be sick, but I made myself look at him, just one time, one last time.

He was still too handsome for words, still just as painfully dominant as he was in the beginning. And he stared at me like he knew exactly what was going through my head.

"Nice to meet you," I whispered, and he took my hand in his, and kissed it. His lips lingered on my skin, but I pulled my arm away when I knew we were being stared at. I felt the rage coming off Felix, I knew he was about to make a scene, and it scared me.

"Hello," King told me in his velvet, deep voice, and I took a step back.

The look in his eyes, the look that spoke of everything that had happened between us, and held a promise of so much more. He wanted me, he still wanted me, I was sure of that now.

I pulled away from him, from them both. I pulled back into the crowd, my eyes still on his.

"I'm sorry, if you'll excuse me," I whispered, and then I turned on my heel and walked away as quickly as I could before I did something monumentally stupid.

Once I got to the ladies' room, I was practically running.

I got into the cubicle and threw up in the toilet. Twice.

I gripped my stomach as I went outside and washed my mouth. I felt sick. So fucking sick.

Poppy was waiting for me in the room, and she looked concerned.

"I'm so sorry about that," she told me, and I could tell she was clueless about what happened. "It was so stuffy in there. Felix is waiting for you–"

Before she could finish, he burst through the doors of the bathroom.

"We're leaving," he said in a cold voice, and for once, I didn't argue.

# CHAPTER 40
## *Felix*

I had to practically *drag her* out of there.

Holding her up, it almost felt like she was passing out as I got her to the cab waiting in front of the gallery. My blood was boiling. I wanted to go back in there and beat him the fuck up for daring to show his face in public after what he'd done to my girl, and with another fucking woman, no less.

I got her into the cab, and was about to walk around to the other side of the car when I saw him coming out, his jaw set in a firm line as he made a beeline for us.

I slammed the door with her inside the cab, and glared at him.

"Take one step fucking closer and I'll kill you," I told him. I would have. I could have ripped his heart out and left it at her feet for what the bastard had done. "I'm fucking serious. Stop fucking moving!"

He raised his hands in front of him, as if to tell me he didn't mean any harm. But everything he fucking did was harmful. Everything he did hurt her. I wanted him gone for-fucking-ever.

"I just want to say goodbye," he told me, his voice dark. "I won't bother you again, I swear. I'll never come back. Just let me say goodbye to her. Wish her luck."

The cab driver honked his horn and I nearly jumped him at the sign of danger.

"Why the fuck would I let you do that?" I asked him, practically growling. "She's barely over what happened. Didn't you see what seeing you did to her? You pathetic fucking moron."

"Please." He came up to me, and I saw new lines in his face that weren't there a few weeks ago. "Please, just let me say goodbye. I won't touch her, I swear."

My hands shook with held-back punches as I opened Pet's door. I knew she could see outside, but the windows were tinted, so he couldn't see her.

I blocked the view inside the car and looked at her. Her face was so pale it looked white, and she stared at me with her eyes blank.

"Do you want to say goodbye?" I asked. "Tell me if you don't, I'll tell him to fucking go."

She shook her head, then nodded. She swallowed, hard. She looked scared as fuck. I wanted to kill him for that already.

"I'll say goodbye," she whispered, and I moved aside, my arm draped over the car door so I could fucking hurt him if he made me.

I watched him watch her. As soon as he saw her, his eyes got misty. It fucking hurt, seeing another man stare at my girl like that, and I wanted to hurt him even more.

He didn't come much closer, just a step or two, and then he kneeled down next to the car. Fucking dramatic as always, pretentious sonofabitch.

"Sapphire," he said, and just with using her real name, he earned my fist loosening up a little. "Sapph. I just want to say goodbye."

I could hear her sobbing already, soft little cries with his name dying on her lips. This was really the end. I could tell.

"Okay," she whispered. "Say goodbye."

I watched them stare at each other for the longest time, trying to read their expressions and failing miserably.

"I'm sorry," he told her, and she nodded, over and over again. "I'm so fucking sorry for what happened, I'm sorry for all the awful shit I've done to you."

"Okay," she repeated. "Okay, that's okay."

It hurt to watch them. It hurt to see her this way, this invested, this fucking in love with another man. I wanted him gone. But for once, I knew better than to interrupt. This was her final goodbye to what she had with him, and she needed this moment. I guess they both did.

"Goodbye," he said, his voice heavy. "Goodbye, my pretty Pet."

I pulled him up by his lapels as she cried out, and shoved him backwards.

"Fucking don't," I growled at him, and he raised his hands again.

A small crowd had gathered on the steps of the gallery, including my parents and his date. I wanted them all to see, but as we glared at each other, I heard my mom whisper my name in a shocked way. All my fault again, then. Fuck that. Fuck all of it.

I slammed Sapph's door shut and went to the other side of the car, getting in next to her. I ignored her sobs that usually turned me on like nothing else, gave the shocked driver our address, and stared out of the window the whole ride home. I didn't dare touch her, and she didn't reach for me, either.

*I felt like she would* never be fully mine.

I held her that night, tightly in my arms. I held her hair back when she was sick again the next morning, just remembering what happened in the gallery. I always held her, every step of the way. And it still didn't seem to be enough. I just wanted her to be alright. I wanted to fix her, but it felt like I never could.

"You know I'm not going to break when you're not looking," she told me the next evening, and I just pulled her closer instead of giving her a reply. "Come on, F. I'm going to be fine."

She'd started calling me F after teasing me for ages that my name reminded her of a cat she had as a kid. I kind of liked it. No one had called me that before, and it felt nice, felt intimate.

"I'm still not taking my eyes off you," I told her roughly, and she giggled and buried her face in the crook of my arm.

"I do kind of like it," she admitted. "I like you taking care of me. Even though I could do it myself."

For once, I didn't object. She'd showed more resilience and strength in these past weeks than I'd ever seen before, and I felt proud of her.

We watched TV in comfortable silence as it got dark outside, and I only got up an hour later when it was time to start thinking about dinner.

"Do you want takeout?" I asked her, and she nodded.

"Pizza," she told me, and I grinned at her.

"The usual?" I loved asking her that. I fucking loved knowing what her favorite was.

She nodded without taking her eyes off the TV, and I called and ordered three pizzas.

"We having company?" she asked, and I joined her back on the couch.

"Yeah, I invited Maria," I told her, feeling the slightest tension in her body. "I hope that's okay. I thought you might need some girl time after what happened… yesterday."

She turned to face me, turning off the crime drama we'd been watching.

"I just want you," she told me gently, and I looked away, rubbing the bridge of my nose.

"I don't believe you, Sapph," I told her, my voice rough. I hated myself for it, but I wanted to be fucking honest. "I don't think you only want me."

"But I do!" She pushed me away, and then pulled me back the next second. How fucking fitting for what was going on with us. "Why won't you believe me? You really think I don't need you, F?"

"You might need someone," I said, running a hand through my too-long hair. "I know you need someone. But I don't fucking think it's me, Sapph. I think you'd be just fine without me."

She climbed on my lap, and just like that, I was fucking smitten again. Her arms around my neck, her lips lingering over mine. She was everything. And for her, I was just a piece in the puzzle, a chapter in her book, and it fucking hurt.

"You don't think I care?" she asked me softly, and I looked away. "Look at me, baby."

That word. Baby. How it just started sneaking into our conversation. We'd just casually end our sentences with it. I'd never used it with anyone else, and I'd never heard her use it with King.

Baby. She was my baby. I loved my baby.

But would she ever be mine? Only mine?

"You're far away," she said sadly when I finally looked at her. "Why can't you be here, with me, F?"

"I could ask you the same question," I growled, and wanted to hit myself after. "I'm sorry, baby, I shouldn't have said that. It's just… it's fucking hard."

She ground her ass on my lap, but I stopped her. She always did it to get out of a conversation she didn't like, but I wanted to have an honest conversation for fucking once.

"Sapph," I said. "I need to know right now. I need to know if you'll ever be okay. If you'll ever feel about me the way I do about you. You know I'm not fucking playing."

"I know," she said. "I want to promise you everything, F. I want to promise you the world…"

She let her words trail off and I stared at her hopeful eyes.

But she didn't promise. I don't think she could have, not that day.

"Okay," I said, and I hated how defeated my voice sounded.

"Okay," she repeated, and hers was as deflated as I imagined mine was. "I don't want Maria to come over today. I just want to be with you."

"Alright," I said. "I'll give her a call and let her know. I hope you can eat your weight in pizza, though."

She giggled, and I kissed her, right on those pretty, pouty lips I wanted to be mine forever. And she smiled against my mouth. We both pretended not to notice the tears falling down her cheeks.

We sat there, two broken, fucked-up people, and we held each other together.

To be honest, it was the most we could have done in that moment.

And that was going to have to be enough.

For now.

ONE WEEK LATER

# CHAPTER 42
## *Pet*

**M**aria held my hand the whole ride home. I couldn't have gone to the doctor with anyone but her. And now, knowing the truth, I felt sick to my stomach because I knew I'd have to tell Felix.

We took the cab home together, and she insisted on staying in the car until he dropped me off, even though her place was on the way.

Once we arrived, I opened the car door with a heavy heart, and she squeezed my wrist tightly.

"You gonna be okay?" she asked me gently, and I gave her a weak smile.

"I'll be fine," I promised her. "I have to be."

She blew me a kiss as I walked up the steps to Felix's house.

He wasn't home, that much I knew. Since seeing his parents at that damn gallery opening, he'd been talking to them much more. At least one good thing came out of that stupid fucking day, and he was now working a part-time job in his dad's local hotel. It was management stuff that seemed boring to me at first, but then he told me all about the position, and I got excited as well. Not only because it seemed really interesting, but also because his dad had given him so much responsibility from the get go, showing how much he'd trusted his son all along.

And I knew Felix noticed as well. The way he smiled these days was much different than a little while ago.

I walked into the house and picked up the post absentmindedly, filing through bills and catalogues.

It felt natural now, living here with him.

We were talking about me going back to school, maybe. He was really supportive of the idea although I felt nervous when I thought about it.

I wondered how he'd take the news, especially knowing what happened in the playroom when both of them were still with me. I still felt those shards of glass inside me, and the thought made me sick.

I wondered if he'd be disappointed. That was my main concern. Would he even care though?

I felt a little sick with worry as I sat down on the couch with the mail. I went through a catalogue and put it aside before picking up a letter.

It was addressed to me.

I'd had some stuff sent to Felix's house, but not much, and I was only just getting ready to tell my parents about my new living situation. I doubted they'd warm up to Felix much more than they had to... King.

The letter looked official, and I opened it curiously. There was another envelope inside, but I read the enclosed letter first.

My eyes skimmed the words, but I had to read them several times to understand what they really meant.

*...we regret to inform you...*

*...due to the recent developments...*

*...charges will not be pressed.*

I couldn't understand, and my brows furrowed as I tried to make sense of the words.

Finally, King's name jumped out at me, and I started to piece the puzzle together.

Robotically, I realized what had happened, and my hand over my mouth was the only reaction I could muster.

I opened the other envelope, and I started reading. I swallowed the words whole. It was the only thing I had left.

*My pretty Pet,*

*I wanted to tell you how very sorry I am for everything that happened. But I also wanted to tell you a little bit more about the story, our story. Because that's what it's been all along, hasn't it, Pet? The love story of two people who were never going to end up together. But unlike you, I'm going to leave without having anyone else. And you'll be happy the way you are.*

*You have to understand, Pet, I'm a very selfish man.*

*When I saw you in that gallery, with the tray in your hands, I already knew I was dying.*

*I'd gotten the diagnosis a week or so earlier, and I was still pretty fucking angry about it.*

*I thought I could get it out of my system by fucking a pretty little thing like you.*

*That soon proved to be a wrong assumption. In moments, you were inside my mind, and you took permanent residence in my heart, something no other pet had ever managed before, but you did it at the click of your dainty fingers, as if it was the easiest thing in the world.*

*A few days after I met you, I refused treatment. I also decided never to tell you about my illness.*

*I knew it wouldn't do much to help our relationship. You'd be scared for me the whole time, refusing to do things I needed you for, worried about my wellbeing. And once I was gone, it would fucking break you. I couldn't let that happen, Pet.*

*You're a beautiful young girl with your whole life ahead of you. I knew you'd find someone else. And I knew who I wanted it to be.*

*I came up with the plan on that day. Find the perfect stranger and introduce him into your life without either of you knowing what he was doing there. He'd be my substitute at first, but in the end, he'd become what I could never be for you, because I didn't have the time.*

*I knew when he'd be in our neighborhood, I did the research. He had money, but he rebelled against it. Anything he made went to charity, he barely bought himself anything. I actually fucking liked the guy, until I saw him with you. I made sure you'd run into him, and I think I knew you well enough by then to make sure you'd choose him.*

*And you did, and it fucking killed me, because it was the beginning of the end.*

*I didn't want to watch you fucking him. I didn't want to fuck you while he was inside you at the same time. I knew I had to do it, Pet. I knew I had to make you fall for him and choose him over me.*

*I wanted to feel alone. I wanted you to leave me for him, because it was the only option for you to get out safe, and get out in time. It was getting worse then, Pet, and I felt sick a lot of the time, which is why I didn't spend much time alone. The doctors said I had a month, maybe two, but my condition would get progressively worse in those final few weeks. Leukemia, Pet, is a fucking awful cancer. It eats you from the inside.*

*There is absolutely no fucking excuse for what happened the last time you were in my apartment, and we both know that. I'll never forgive myself.*

*But I was having doubts. I wanted to keep you. I wanted you with me.*

*The bottle thing happened by accident. And the moment it did, I knew I had to walk away, because otherwise you'd never leave me. And it seemed like life had made the choice for me.*

*While I was in that bathroom waiting for him to take care of you, I wanted to fucking die. I deserved it. And the days that followed, the weeks that came after, were a fucking nightmare. I'm a nightmare without you, Pet. Living without you is like a bad fucking dream.*

*I knew you'd be at the gallery. I wanted to see you. I picked that girl just for you, to make you jealous. See, Pet? I was a selfish fucking bastard my whole life, until I said goodbye, and a while after. I called Stranger and Maria so many times, even after that. I told them to keep it from you, I just wanted to know what you were doing, and every time, I hoped they'd tell you anyway. I don't think they did.*

*It's getting really bad now, Pet. I can tell it's close, I'm really fucking dying. I thought nothing could defeat me, but you proved me wrong. You and your tight little body, your fucking twisted mind, your utter submission for me, Pet. I hope you can give yourself to him the way you gave it all to me.*

*I wonder if you still call him Stranger. I don't want to know.*

*There's one last thing to tell you, Pet.*

*The man who abused you. I wanted to hurt him ever since you told me. I knew you wouldn't have let me, so I kept it from you. I guess dying proved to be good in one aspect of the word, because despite my best tries, I seem to have left behind some evidence that led the police back to me. They think I'm involved in his death now, Pet, and I am. I didn't pull the trigger, but I sure as fuck helped him do it. It's good that I'm almost gone, so I don't have to rot in jail for what I did to* that man. But I want you to know, Pet, I would do it all over again, even if I was healthy, so I could see him die for what he did to you.

You're going to receive some things in my will, pretty Pet. Mostly money. That atrocious painting I bought you. I left Maria the apartment. I think she should have it. The majority is yours, and the rest is for James' family, to take care of the mess he left. I also donated some money to a charity for abused children.

I know I've said goodbye a few times now, Pet. But this one is going to be the hardest, because I'll be gone when you're reading this.

And I want you to know, Pet, you've been the only one. The only one who touched me in this way, the only one that left a mark. Not like the one on your thigh, pretty baby. One that no one could see on my skin, but they could see it in my eyes until the day I died. And I fucking feel you, Pet, I still feel you in my heart with every breath I take, in my lungs, in my head, everywhere, you're everywhere.

I'm sorry for everything, Pet. I should have never touched you in that gallery. I'm sorry for that, but I'm really not. Because I'll always be a selfish prick.

I hope you're happy. I hope you still think of me, because you'll be the only one to do that.

I love you, my Pet.

Yours,

HSK

I didn't remember when the sobbing started, but it got worse and worse as I tore through the rest of the envelope, looking for something, anything about where he was now. He couldn't be gone, he wasn't, there was no way. I would have felt it, I would have known in my heart, in my mind, in my belly, that he was gone.

There was nothing, just the letter, the one that came with it, a page filled with his beautiful words. Nothing until I ripped the envelope open and a small card fell out.

A somber black card with white ink, classy and beautiful in a way, letting me know the funeral had happened on June 6th. Just two days ago. I'd missed it. He was gone. He was fucking gone. It must've happened so soon after the gallery opening.

I started screaming. I started cursing. I ran around the room, I broke a vase, I smashed a glass against the tiles. I was so angry. So very angry, so badly hurt.

I didn't take my jacket, just slammed the front door shut and ran into the street.

A car honked at me when I ran in front of it, and the driver cursed out loud at me, screaming his head off, but the only thing I could do was run, run, run away.

# CHAPTER 42
## *Felix*

The news reached me that day at work. He moved in the same circles my father did, and he was the one to tell me about King passing away. I was sitting in my office, just looking at some footage and trying to determine if someone really was stealing the silverware, when he came up to me.

"I missed a funeral a few days ago," he muttered to himself as he went through some mail. "Dammit, should've gone to that one, too. Can you check my schedule, son? Is that meeting with the Robinsons still on tomorrow? I'd like to pay my respects, take some flowers to the grave."

I nodded and checked his itinerary, and my father left the card on my desk when I confirmed he was free the next afternoon.

It wasn't until later that I finally checked it, the black and white catching my eye.

I knew once I saw his initials engraved at the top of the card, I knew he was gone.

And I thought of Sapphire right away. I knew I needed to leave, and I knew if she'd found out, she wouldn't be home either.

I called Maria, who was sobbing profusely and I could barely make out her words. She finally told me she knew, and she suspected Sapph did as well, since she just got a letter about the will.

I knew she'd be at his old apartment, and it was the first place I raced to.

The doorman wasn't hostile this time around. Even he looked like he knew exactly what had happened, and he gave me a solemn nod as I took the elevator up to the penthouse suite.

She was sitting in a little heap at the door, crying so hard her eyes looked black and blue, not even red anymore. Her makeup was smeared, her pretty dress spotted with tears.

I sat down next to her, I didn't dare touch her. She just sobbed, sitting on the floor in front of his front door. She sobbed for what felt like hours, and I tried to ignore the tears welling in my own eyes.

Finally, she leaned against me, and she let me hold her.

"Help," she whispered, and my fucking heart broke for her. "I don't know how to make it better. I don't know, baby."

"I don't know," I said back. "I only know one way, baby."

"What is it?" Her sweet voice was so hopeful it broke me all over again.

"Come on, let's go home, and I'll show you. I promise I will." I stroked her arms.

"Just a little bit longer?" she asked through the tears, and I nodded.

"Just a little bit longer," I agreed.

*We got home an hour* later. She felt weak in my arms, but she wouldn't talk about it.

"You said you knew how to make it better," she told me, her bottom lip shaking as she looked at me, those pretty eyes so very desperate. "You said you knew how."

"Baby," I said softly. "I'm not sure. I can only fix it by breaking you and putting you back together, piece by piece."

She gasped when I kissed her, submitting to my lips completely.

I ran a hand up her thigh and she mewled needily, but she shoved me away, just a little, just enough to make me know she didn't want it.

"I don't want to today."

My hands trailed down her arms, but she wouldn't look at me. She seemed so upset, so fragile, so broken. I had no fucking clue what I was supposed to do with her, so I just stroked her pretty hair off her face, and decided to give her a moment to herself. I didn't want her to feel trapped with me, she probably needed time to think.

"Okay, baby," I told her with a small smile, drawing my hand back. "That's okay. Do you want to relax today?"

She nodded, but she wouldn't quite look at me. Her fingers were knotted nervously, her skirt so short it was exposing her inner thighs. I looked at the mark on her skin and melancholy washed over me. I wanted to be inside her.

"Go take a bath," I told her. "We can talk once you're done. It will make you feel better."

She nodded again and disappeared down the hallway. I heard the sounds of running water and did my fucking best to focus on something else, if only for a few moments. But it didn't take long for me to get really distracted.

I kept thinking about her. How pretty she looked in the outfit I picked out for her that morning, before we knew any of this was going to happen. She liked it so much when I did that, decided what she should wear. I thought about how hard she had been trying to please me. But today, she got to be as bratty as she wanted. I groaned and got up from my desk, walking towards the bathroom.

I tried not to fucking look at her. I felt so upset, so broken up about everything that had happened. But I still did it. Risked a single look through the door she'd left ajar, just like I always told her to. Still following rules even when she was so fucking broken. Seeing her in there, I had to suppress a groan. My fucking pretty girl.

The bubbles had dissipated and I could see her naked body in the clear, hot water. Her legs on either side of the tub, her head thrown back and her long hair spilling down into the water. One hand on her tits, the other busy playing with her pussy, when she told me moments ago she didn't want me to fuck her.

I gritted my teeth. Any other day I would've wanted to choke her for doing that.

I watched her for a while longer, the little gasps that leave her lips, the soft mewls that make me grow so hard I want to leak cum all over my jeans. Her fingers were dipping into her pussy under the water, and she teased her clit until she came with a stifled cry, my name a whisper on her lips.

It shocked me.

"Fuck, Felix... please."

No more of this shit.

I threw the door open and she jumped up in the tub, splashing water everywhere.

"Felix?" she asked tentatively, stuttering over the word. "I-Is everything okay?"

I didn't say a damn word. I reached her in two steps and dragged her out of the tub by her hair. She kicked and screamed and tried to resist but I wouldn't let her. I bent her over the side of the bathtub and my palm hit her ass so hard she cried out, tears welling in her eyes.

"What the hell is going on?" I asked her roughly. "You're making yourself come in the bath but you won't let me fucking touch you, little slut?"

My heart pounded. I was being a dick. I wasn't supposed to treat her this way, not after everything she'd been through. But I couldn't fucking help myself.

She cried so hard she nearly choked and it only made me angrier. I'd been so good to her. Really fucking good. But goddamn it if I didn't want to punish her hard for this.

I should be the one making her feel better, not those pretty little fingers.

I gathered her hair in my fist and pulled, making her look at me. She was sobbing, and I didn't want to know why.

"What kind of game are you playing, pretty girl?" I asked her.

She didn't answer.

With a single push, I sank her head into the water in the tub. She struggled, struggled like she was fighting for her life, but I held her under the water firmly while she screamed into the tub.

I pulled her out and she screamed like fucking crazy, trying to hit me, trying to bite me. She slapped my face and I let her, because I wanted her to get it out of her system. The anger. The rage. The unfairness of it all.

"You silly little girl," I told her softly. "Horny little girl. You don't want me touching you? Fine, let's see how you do without it."

I pulled her out of the water and kissed her so roughly, so savagely, she bit my lip in response, drawing blood. I wanted to hate her, wanted to hate the whole fucking situation but I couldn't. It was the only way. Being rough with her was the only way, and her lips begged for more in soft whispers as I claimed her mouth.

"Good girls come when I hurt them," I said into her ear. "Are you gonna come for me?"

"Yes," she cried out. "Please, I will, just let me, fucking please!"

Back in the water she went. Softer than last time. So soft she could've surfaced any time. I didn't want to hurt her, ever.

She struggled, but less than last time. My fingers wandered from her arms between her legs and she went fucking crazy when I touched her there. I laughed at her and pulled her out, leaning down to whisper in her ear.

"You're fucking soaked," I told her in a growl. "Is this what you fucking wanted, baby? Is this what you needed the whole fucking time? You wanted me to rough you up like I used to?"

"Yes," she begged. "Yes, please, I want that."

She looked up at me with big, wide eyes. Her makeup was running all over her face and her bottom lip was trembling, her chest heaving. I'd never been more turned on. I was going to burst if I didn't put my dick inside her right then and there.

I unzipped and pulled out my cock, and she started giggling like crazy. I twisted her arms and pulled her hair roughly while I thrust my cock inside her ass, dry. She started crying really bad, and it felt like music to my ears when she begged for more.

"Good little girl," I told her, holding her face an inch above the water. "Come for me and it'll stop hurting. Come for me and it'll make you whole again, pretty girl."

I knew she couldn't. I knew how badly it must have hurt. But she was gasping in moments, long, heaving breaths and little sobs as I fucked her ass, her hair dipping into the water below her.

"Felix, please," she begged.

"Please what?" I asked. I thrust a little harder just to hurt her, but it had the opposite effect. She was about to fucking come from having my cock inside her, raw and dry as fuck. "Don't you dare fucking come."

She moaned and laughed at the same time, a vicious little bitch.

"Stop fucking me then," she gasped, and I pushed her into the water again. Her hips bucked against mine and her pussy dripped all over my fucking balls. I pulled her out in time to hear her scream my name.

"Stop fucking coming," I groaned, my cock throbbing so much I felt like I'd blow my load twice. "Stop it or I'll stop fucking you."

"You won't," she giggled. Her hands went behind her back and she spread her ass wide for me. "You fucking won't, Felix, you can't."

I groaned and held her still, pulled out of her ass and jacked off into the hole she was holding open for me. It made her cry and beg for more.

I watched my jizz disappear into her asshole and felt like I was about to pass the fuck out. She was trying to catch her breath, her whole body shivering, when she started to giggle.

I pulled her into my arms and held her the fuck still.

"You're fucking crazy," I whispered in her ear and she cuddled closer. Her ass leaked cum all over my lap. "You know that, Sapph? You're fucking insane."

"You like it," she whispered against my mouth, and bit my bottom lip. "You fucking love it, Felix."

"Why didn't you want me to touch you?" I wanted to know. I fully expected it to be because of him. Because of King.

She smiled and kissed my mouth, then leaned down to whisper in my ear.

"Cause the doctor said you aren't supposed to fuck my pussy Felix, and I knew you would."

"Why not?" I stroked her wet hair and she leant against my touch, sucking my thumb into her mouth. I watched her do it, groaning when she let it out with a pop.

"It's not good for the baby," she smiled. "Surprise, my sweet F."

FIVE YEARS LATER

# EPILOGUE
## *Sapphire*

He tugged on my hand, trying to make me walk with him. I smiled at my little boy, loving that he knew the way by heart.

We'd visited the grave every week for his entire life, and he was used to spending Sundays this way. Visit the grave first, then lunch in a local place with our extended family.

"Reagan, wait up," I told him, trying to catch up. He was racing along, his little legs carrying him so fast I could barely keep up.

I finally reached him and he laughed when I pulled him into my arms. He was such a sweet little kid, bright eyes and a flop of dark hair that was getting much too long, falling into his eyes and reminding me of his daddy.

When I found out I was pregnant, I didn't want to know whose the child was. I knew there was a possibility it was Felix's, but I had a feeling, from the very start, that it was King's. And the moment I gave birth and saw my child's face, I knew who the father was.

We'd been open about it with Reagan all along. We explained the origin of his name just a few weeks ago.

"Someone said it was a girl's name," he said once, when he came home from the kindergarten.

Some kids had been picking on him, and I almost giggled when I saw how upset Felix was getting. I'd had to tell him he couldn't just beat up a five-year-old for his son.

"Then that kid was pretty stupid," he told his son through gritted teeth, picking him up and holding him in his arms. "You don't know what your name means, do you, kid?"

Reagan shook his head and Felix and I smiled at each other as I walked up to them.

"It means *little king*," I told him. "So the next time the kids tease you, just tell them that."

He'd smiled at that, just like he was then at the graveyard.

It was a beautiful Sunday, with summer just starting in the city. I held his hand and he led me to the grave.

I took some time to remove the burnt-out candles, and Reagan was my happy little helper. We lit some new candles, and just like always, I let King's son set them down on his father's grave.

He had a daddy, but he'd never get to know his father, and the knowledge of that pained me every day. But seeing Reagan grow up made it easier day by day, his beautiful smile, those bright eyes, all the ways in which he reminded me of his father.

"Do you want to say something?" I asked him, noticing his stern expression as he stared at the headstone.

"Yeah," he said, with an important look on his face. "I would like to tell him I stood up to the bullies today."

"Go on," I urged him, excited to hear what happened.

He puffed out his chest as he went on, talking to the headstone. The sight broke my heart, but I welcomed the pain. More often than not it felt better that way.

"I told them what my name really meant," he said. "And I told them my father was a real king, just like I'm going to be."

Tears welled in my eyes when my son looked at me with a wicked glint, one I knew all too well.

"And then I told them my daddy would kick their butts if they picked on me," he finished proudly, and I laughed out loud and hugged him.

"You did a good job, kid," Felix's voice interrupted from behind us, and Reagan took his outstretched hand. Felix nodded at me, and they walked to the bench a little way off, giving me a moment.

Reagan was the best gift I could've asked for, but what I was thankful for even more was the way Felix was around him.

He never, for one second, let me feel guilty. He took care of Reagan like he was his own, taking time off work to spend it with him, always worrying and fussing over our child. And that was really what he was, despite everything that happened before us. We were his parents, and we were the ones taking care of him and bringing him up.

I missed King. It felt like the light had gone out of my life when I learned of his passing. But now, with his son with me, I felt a little pinprick of light was in my life, and I lived for it, seeing it get bigger and bigger as the years passed and Reagan grew up into a healthy, happy little boy.

I stood at the grave, with my hand on my belly.

There was a new life growing inside me, and I wanted to ask for King's blessing.

I knew he couldn't say yes or no, of course. But I wanted this moment, just between us. I wanted to look up at the sky and let the wind dry the tears on my cheeks, and I wanted to feel like he'd approve of my new life. He said it was what he wanted for me, and I wanted to make him proud with everything I did.

I looked up at the sky and let the tears fall, my hand firmly placed on my growing belly. I was well into my second trimester, and I was definitely starting to show.

As I stared up at the sky, I felt a single kick in my belly, and I gasped so loud I heard approaching footsteps the next second.

"Baby, are you okay?"

I looked into Felix's eyes, and smiled at him.

"What's wrong, Mom?"

Reagan took my hand and I ruffled his hair.

"I just felt a kick," I told him with a big, silly grin. "The baby kicked!"

"Well," Reagan puffed. "That's good, right?"

"It's good," I giggled in reply. "It means she's okay and doing well."

Felix took me into his arms. He held me so fucking close I could feel his heart beating against mine. He held me so close I felt like we were one.

I pressed my lips against his, needily, quickly. He kissed me back with all the love he'd had for me all along.

"Thank you, baby," he whispered in my ear, and I grinned against his lips. "Thank you, my love."

Reagan asked if he could light another candle, *for the baby*, he said. I told him it was a lovely thing to do.

Maria was waiting for us by the car. Usually she came to the grave with us, but she seemed overwhelmed by the anniversary this time around, and didn't want to go.

We hugged tightly and she sniffled against me.

"Come on," I told her gently. "We have to pick up your date before we go to lunch."

"Ugh," she rolled her eyes, wiping her nose. "I am so not in the mood for a blind date tonight."

"I think you'll like this guy," I grinned at her. "Felix has been going on and on about him."

"Let's hope so," she groaned. "I'm ravenous. We leaving?"

"Yes!" Reagan pumped his fist in the air, making us all laugh. "I can't wait to see Grandma and Nanna."

I liked the way life had brought our families together. We were close with Felix's family, and what shocked me most of all, he managed to make an amazing impression on my own family, and they were regulars during the Sunday lunches we all had in the nearby town.

I took one last look at the cemetery over my shoulder. I could see his grave from there, illuminated in beautiful daylight. A single leaf, much too early for fall, fell down against the stone, and I smiled to myself as I got into the car.

"Goodbye," I whispered, and Felix put the car into drive. My engagement ring reflected the light and it looked like a wink.

I looked back at the cemetery, and I whispered the last words I always said when we left.

"Thank you, my King."

*The End*

# ACKNOWLEDGMENTS

Dear reader,

I don't know what to say. I should probably apologize.

I'm sorry this book was different.

I'm sorry if you're disappointed.

I'm sorry if you didn't love it.

I'm sorry if I broke your heart.

I broke my own, too.

I don't really do acknowledgments, but I guess there's a first time for everything, right?

This book was personal. This book was important. Not because it's based on me, not because I've seen this happen. Because it was the first story in years that I've *had* to tell. The story that was begging to be written, even though I wanted to push it aside. It wouldn't let me. Pet wouldn't let me.

First of all, I owe a big, big thank you to my editor John Hudspith. I remember reading my friend Jade's book years ago, and knowing, being absolutely certain, that her editor was the one I wanted to work with. I didn't have the money, or the balls, or the talent, to tell this story at the time. But the moment I felt ready, I knew I would ask you, John, to help me with this book. You've polished it to perfection and made me stop questioning myself and this story. You've made me love Pet again, and I will never forget that. Thank you.

To my writing partners in crime – Demi Donovan and Jade West. You make me better every day. Thank you for everything.

And a big thank you to my PA Tracy Smith Comerford. You believed in me from the start. I can't even handle myself, God knows how or why you do it!

A big thank you to my own King. You know you're the one. You know I choose you. Over and over again. Thank you. I love you.

To the Strangers, every single one of you. I like your crazy.

And finally, to my readers. You, reading this. Every single one of you. I see every comment, every like, every Tweet, every email. And sometimes, they're the only thing that get me through the day. Your amazing reviews, your beautiful words, the friendships I've made (looking at you, Emma), it all means the world to me. I am nothing without you.

Thank you.
xx, Isa

Printed in Poland
by Amazon Fulfillment
Poland Sp. z o.o., Wrocław